FALL

DOCTOR WHO – THE NEW ADVENTURES

Also available:

THE NEW

DOCTOR WHO

ADVENTURES

FALLS THE SHADOW

Daniel O'Mahony

First published in Great Britain in 1994 by
Doctor Who Books
an imprint of Virgin Publishing Ltd
332 Ladbroke Grove
London W10 5AH

Cover illustration by Kevin Jenkins

ISBN 0 426 20427 1

Phototypeset by Intype, London

Printed and bound in Great Britain by Cox & Wyman Ltd,
Reading, Berks

Prologue

Apocalypse Now

Qxeleq would have screamed, had she a mouth.

She had woken with a new sense of freedom, feeling the empty days ahead of her between terms at the hival university. Her exams were finished, passed, passed easily. In three weeks she would be celebrating the third anniversary of her gendering in the company of her friends, and their drones. And her drone, of course.

Her body was numb as she woke, responding sluggishly to her thoughts. It had been her first night sleeping in the open hive – she hadn't expected it to be this cold. After all it was summer and her body was covered by three light cloaks and a layer of sensitive nervous fur. Something was wrong. Even with her eyes covered she could feel darkness around her, reaching into her deepest soulcells, the reserves of ancient fears. Darkness.

The first Darkness was known to the entire Mind, forgotten between birth and death. There were childhood darknesses, crafted tales of fear before bedtime. But Qxeleq had seen actual, physical darkness. Deep in the hive – under the university where the older records were kept – there were no airholes or luminous wall linings, just the dark. Qxeleq had found a pocket of death trapped in the tunnels and she had panicked. To her everlasting shame, and the equally everlasting amusement of her cellmates, she had fled, half-flying, back to the hives of residence.

Once she had stood on the threshold of darkness. Now it was inescapable, surrounding her. She was surprised by

1

her calmness. The darkness didn't seem matter. She wasn't alone. She gave thanks to the Atheist Martyrs of Kaleidoscope Theory that she was lying beside the person she trusted most in the world. Xhallaq, her first dronemate, was with her.

Two seconds later she discovered that Xhallaq was missing. Her antennae began to twitch through the darkness, searching for the shape of Xhallaq's body. Useless – he had left her. Or he had been taken.

Qxeleq wasn't panicking. Not yet.

She panicked when she couldn't find the confined walls of the drone pit. She tried listening. Silence. There were no sounds echoing down from the mouth of the pit, from the hive. Desperately she tried to make contact with the hive Mind. An agonizing process – she dreaded the university ceremonies when it became necessary. This time she barely noticed how easily, painlessly she slipped into the state of union.

The Mind was barren. The chaotic chatter of six million people was gone. It had been extinguished, erased from existence.

Qxeleq ignored the shock of withdrawing from the Mindscape. More confused than she had ever been, she let her consciousness spread out, stretching to reach the countless embryonic auras that radiated comfortably in her womb.

These too were gone. Taken from her. Like the light, the sound, the Mind – burned away into nothing with the rest of her world. Her children were dead.

Everything she knew and loved, everything she had ever heard of had been shorn away, quietly and simply as she slept. One muffled apocalypse – then nothing but the sleeping body and mind of Qxeleq. Everyone was dead. From the lowest, most ancient and despised societology lecturer to the queen of the hive herself. Drones, workers, young queens, children, university and hive were gone. Possibly even the entire Earth was destroyed.

The voice of the darkness echoed around her, vicious, filled with malignance and sadistic amusement. A voice with two themes – no, two voices, speaking in stereo. The language the voices used was unfamiliar, but Qxeleq understood perfectly.

This is the way the world ends.

Qxeleq tried to scream. She discovered that she no longer had a mouth. No mouth, no eyes, no antennae, no wings. No body.

It occurred to her that she hadn't survived after all.

1

The Man with the Child in His Eyes

Autumn brought mists to the woodlands and the village, and the mists brought the grey man. He arrived early on a crisp November morning, stalking along a rough forest track. He came from the direction of the house – the 'Shadowfell' as it was known by some of the older villagers – making straight for the village. Once there, he asked questions. Questions about the house and the land around it.

The villagers were happy dealing with superstition and rumour. They had honed gossip to a fine art. The man seemed very interested in anything they had to say, so they gave him the answers they thought he was looking for.

They began with the premise that the house was inherently evil, then embroidered the theme until it became a catalogue of rural myths. The house was the scene of gruesome rituals and sacrifice, the evil atmosphere soaked into the foundations. Babies and women had been bricked up alive behind the walls – walls that had been known to bleed. The architect had scratched the designs into the wall of his cell in Bedlam. The earliest owner had been an aristocrat who sold his soul to the devil and had combusted as a result. The derelict house had been home to gangs of grave-robbers, cannibals, vampires or possibly all three simultaneously. The unimaginative majority simply said that the house was haunted, and set about producing inventive variations on murder, revenge, sex and epic genealogies.

4

The grey man sat and listened to each story with barely a flicker of interest. He didn't spend anything. He sat alone and dry in the pub, frightening the regulars. He spent five minutes dispassionately reading the names on the war memorial, but the villagers didn't charge for that. Realizing that there was no profit here, they closed ranks and the flow of information dried up.

The man left the village, heading back through the woodlands towards the house. It had passed noon, and the mists were beginning to clear. The man trudged along the track to the house, following a route that was a good three-quarters of a mile longer than any other. The grey of his clothes was perfect woodland camouflage, blending in with the bark of the naked trees.

The track brought him to a ridge on the fringe of the woods, overlooking the rear of the house. He squatted down on a cold tree stump, and began to watch. A breeze blew up, growing into a harsh and violent wind. Dark clouds conspired on the horizon. Drops of water fell through the shifting air, a herald of storms in waiting. The grey man ignored them.

He *was* grey. Grey coat over a grey shirt and trousers. Grey shoes with loosely tied grey laces that never came undone. His hat: casual, wide-brimmed, grey. Even his skin: paper-thin, cold and bloodless, tinged grey by the cold daylight. His hair, though, was white, but streaked with lines of pure black. Almost grey. His eyes . . .

His eyes were hidden, covered by dark glass lenses in a wire frame perched on his thin nose and sharp cheek-bones, beneath a forehead worn with an eternity of frowning. His eyes were invisible. They might have been grey.

Sitting on the stump, watching the house, something ancient and eternally patient was brooding.

Something was wrong about the house.

The man in grey had learned nothing from the villagers. He knew more about the occupants of the house than they ever would, but he lacked psychology – insight into the workings of the alien and impenetrable minds in the house. In the villagers he found a wealth of information, none of it helpful, a patchwork quilt of superstitions and gossip, escalating in outrageous claims. The village seemed populated by superstitious rumour-mongers and frustrated novelists. It was almost as if they had gravitated to the area in order to exchange the products of their lurid imaginations. Something in the air? Or the water? More likely it was the result of complicated interbreeding.

Some of the stories, the man considered, might be true. There might be people bricked up in the walls, or the foundations, though he doubted that the walls had ever bled, except perhaps with dry rot. The architect might have been insane. Judging by the sprawling, styleless shape of the building that was probably true. The house boasted one gargoyle too many to be the work of a sane man. It was a monstrosity, rising out of the bleak landscape like a jagged, rotten tooth. It was horrible, but it was still standing, and in a twisted way it was beautiful.

The house was isolated. Communication was limited; a weekly delivery of groceries, stationery and the odd luxury from the village; an irregular flow of mail in both directions. The householders rarely showed their faces outdoors, never in the village. It was a mile from the nearest proper road. It seemed unusual that a house should be built so far from the rest of the human race.

He realized what was wrong. The house was out of balance. It had too much weight, concentrated around a single point on the architecture. Lines of universal force radiated round it, swirling in a whirlpool pattern to tighten into that singularity, like a knot in the grain of wood.

The corners of the grey man's mouth twitched slightly.

'There,' he said, satisfied.

He rose from the stump and climbed down a muddy slope to the back of the house. A low barbed-wire fence cut the house off from the woodlands. The grey man scaled it, leaving a small fragment of his coat on one of the barbs. Beyond the fence a sprawling hedge rose out of the landscape to bar his way. The grey man didn't count gardening skills among his better qualities, but he couldn't

6

fail to notice that the hedge was overgrown. It probably hadn't been checked for years. It was riddled with holes. One was comfortably sized and the man was able to push through it quickly. He emerged on the other side, brushing away loose leaves which had settled on his shoulders. He stopped, turning slowly to draw in his surroundings; his first clear view of the house's garden. It was a small, thin strip of stone, lined with flowers and bushes that had been left to fend for themselves. The plants were either dying or weeds. The air was a hazy green and thick with the sickly smell of decay – where the plants weren't green they were grey or brown. November rot.

It was impressively overgrown. The slabs on the ground were almost invisible beneath the dirt of ages. Weeds thrived, rising tentatively from cracks between the worn stone. Brickwork hollows surrounded the area in which the grey man found himself. These too were submerged by bushes, by the green. Vegetation ran riot over brick, chaotically clawing back that which had originally been its own. Dying flowers wound together with weeds, crushing the remnants of the human building.

Perfect.

The walls of the house were visible nearby, beyond another hedge. They rose sheer out of the ground, broken irregularly by wooden frames and glass, or gargoyles, or (the grey man clicked his tongue with distaste) plastic pipes. The walls soared upwards, elongated out of normal proportion. The line of the roof was distant against the grey sky. It was unsettlingly high, a house that liked to play at castles.

It seemed a melting pot of styles. Bare patches of red brick moulded smoothly into plain walls of cathedral grey. Glass and aluminium fitted snugly into an indented corner where a conservatory had been added.

More interesting than the house was the statue which stood in the grounds, close to the grey man. If the brick remains had once been a building, the statue would have stood at the entrance, impressive in its day. Now it was shrouded in weeds and almost defeated by the weather, but it had survived well enough to catch the eye of the grey man.

It wasn't particularly good. Competent but uninspired, a simple scene of religious vengeance. A bronze-skinned, bare-chested angel, holding a lowered spear, staring into the sky. Its face had been obliterated, eroded by persistent rain. A second angel knelt beside him, his wings torn and ragged. His head was held low and had been protected. The carved expressions were still intact on the angel's face – fear, hate, shattered pride, pain, guilt. Mostly fear. The angel was staring down an infinite abyss, terrified. And the abyss was staring into him.

The grey man found an almost obscured plaque on the base of the statue. It read, simply, *Fall*.

Of course – the man realized – the angels Michael and Lucifer. The triumph of righteousness and purity over ambition, false pride and evil intent. The man in grey smiled, understanding what he found so fascinating. It seemed that Michael was stabbing Lucifer in the back.

'Most appropriate,' he decided.

He turned sharply and ambled over to a sprawling bush on the periphery of the garden. It was a skeletal excuse for a plant, a thick rib-cage of twisted branches. The grey man plunged an arm into its heart. The bush squealed and the man withdrew.

Shortly afterwards a girl crawled out from behind the bush. She smiled without hope at the grey man, blushing deeply. The man's eyes narrowed, drawing in her features.

Girl – that was wrong for a start. She was about seventeen, possibly eighteen, an age still given to clogged pores and greasy hair. Despite this she was probably attractive. Long, dark hair framing a thin face given to presentable misery. The impractical – and badly lacerated – walking clothes, anorak and recently unwashed hair said *tourist*.

Her eyes, he noticed, were worried, verging on fear. Too real to be put down to the simple embarrassment of being caught spying. The dark rings under her eyes told him she'd been crying.

8

'How d'you know I was there?' the woman asked. The accent was familiar but not a local one.

'I pay attention.'

The woman shrugged, trying to seem nonchalant but only succeeding in looking worse. 'I'm trespassing, aren't I?'

'Yes, but I can't condemn that. Don't worry.' A baffled, edgy look slunk across the girl's face. 'You're on holiday aren't you?'

'How d'you know that?' The girl rounded on him, genuinely angry, genuinely afraid.

'Your clothes, your accent. The anorak gives you away.'

'Oh.' The girl slid from anger to embarrassment. She glanced round the garden, avoiding eye contact. 'Sorry, it's my brother. He's only ten, you know what they're like.'

'Yes,' the grey man lied. He was fighting back the demons of awkwardness. This woman was clearly distressed, and he wasn't entirely sure how best to handle the situation.

'I'm supposed to be looking after him. Only I've, uh, misplaced him.'

'And you think he's here?'

The girl nodded, fixing the grey man with a hollow-eyed stare. She suddenly appeared gaunt and worn with frustration.

'He was going on about this place all morning. Wanted to come down here to,' she paused to add a contemptuous depth to her tone, 'to play. Thought no one lived here.'

'It does look like that, doesn't it?' The grey man hoped he was sounding reassuring. 'How long ago did you, um, mislay him?'

The girl shot a glance at her wrist.

'Over two hours ago,' she replied. She giggled, with no humour, just embryonic hysteria. 'We should've been back by now. Cheese sandwiches for lunch.'

'I haven't seen anyone for a while, certainly no boys. Ten years old or otherwise.'

The girl's face registered disappointment. The grey man wasn't fooled. He could see her nonchalant calm was a barely credible front. Her reserves were being worn down gradually by fruitless searching. He counted himself fortunate that she wasn't hysterical yet – he *knew* he wouldn't be able to deal with that. He was uncomfortable dealing with humans. Especially emotional ones.

There is nothing you can do to help her. Reassure her. Get rid of her. With luck her brother will have beaten her back to wherever she's staying, and helped himself to her sandwiches.

'I'll keep an eye out for him,' he suggested. 'It might be best if you told your parents . . . you are here with your parents?'

The girl nodded.

'They'll kill me for this,' she said.

'I'm sure everything will be all right,' the grey man told her, faking conviction.

The girl nodded unhappily. She edged towards the hole in the hedge. He wheeled round to watch, but didn't try to follow her.

'If you do see him, tell him his family's waiting for him. Tell him that Rose told you.'

'If I see him,' the grey man called back. She was already gone, slipped through the hole into the outside world. The man turned away. He was feeling hollow and useless, as if someone had just kicked him and he didn't know why. Or how to react.

'O Rose,' he said, faking bitterness for his own benefit, 'thou art sick.'

The grey man spent no more time in the grounds. He wanted to leave the bitter taste he associated with them behind him. Telling himself that he had wasted too much time, he strode uneasily round to the house wall, searching for a suitable entrance. Nothing too conspicuous. This was something that had to be done as quickly and quietly as possible.

The door he found was perfect. It was set in a hollow,

cut into the ground, half-hidden by bushes. Steps sank into the hollow to the door, blocked by piles of abandoned cardboard boxes. Insects constructed intricate societies in the damp patches, eating away at corporate logos.

The grey man had studied the writhing, shifting lines of the cosmos as they twisted around the point of the irregularity. They swirled into an eye which the man had located underneath the house. In the foundations, perhaps, or a cellar. He was delighted to discover a doorway that led to the very place he wanted to go. The boxes weren't a formidable barrier.

It was an unmarked door. The man guessed that it was a tradesman's entrance with access to the cellar, from a time when tradesmen came here. Possibly it hadn't been used for years. Centuries even. He shoved at it.

The door crashed open. It hadn't been locked. It hadn't even been properly closed. The lock – a basic mechanism – had been forced.

The opening was dark and silent. The smell of ancient things abandoned to rot drifted from within. And something else – the sickly smell of decay, like the garden but different. The stench was stronger, more bitter. It wasn't the smell of rotting vegetables but rotting meat.

The grey man crossed the threshold into the dark. Wood slammed against wood behind him. The man wheeled round to find the rectangular shape of daylight blocked out. He turned slowly, thinking that he heard something. A quiet, childish giggling, but with an edge, with malice, with an ugly depth. Barely audible. Perhaps.

He began to search. Before the door closed light was a minimal luxury. Now that was gone. Darkness wrapped him, drowning him. This didn't bother him unduly; he could feel the shapes of the rooms and their contents spread out around him.

Shuffling forward, the grey man tripped over a wooden beam and pitched forward. Grey cheeks flushed pink, and he cursed his stupidity. Broken nose, some bruising. Stupid, stupid. He righted himself, feeling his bone struc-

11

ture slip back into place, and his skin healing. His pride was irrevocably damaged.

Again! Giggling. The sound of malicious amusement, louder and longer this time. He knew, definitely, that he wasn't alone.

'Who's there?' he called out softly.

The pause was broken by the sound of a voice, nearby but distant. A voice full of pain and fear. Horrified, the man realized it was the voice of a child.

'No more . . . please, it hurts . . .'

Further understanding crept within the grey man, accompanied by a deeper thrill of horror. He stumbled blindly through the darkness towards the voice, succeeding in tangling himself in the cobwebs which sprouted exactly where he wanted to go.

'No!' he called. 'Rose sent me! You know Rose?'

'Rose? Yes, she . . .'

The voice broke suddenly, clinging onto the sound of the word like a jammed tape recorder. Then it changed, turning the word into a scream. A scream of fear and pain, and worse than pain. The sound escalated, shrieking upwards into higher pitches, higher volumes.

The grey man listened, paralysed with his own fear, horror and revulsion. Someone, he thought, must hear this. Someone . . . There are people living on the floor above, they must . . . He should do . . . He should do *something*. He *should*.

The scream stopped, prematurely and permanently.

The man in grey buried his face in his hands.

He lowered his hands.

He saw the lights.

There were two crackling balls of electricity, spitting random psychedelic sparks, alive, sentient, studying their quarry warily. The force-lines of the cosmos plunged round into the hearts of the electrical flames. The man saw their raw power. He never imagined they would be like this, even in his most pessimistic forecasts. Immense power combined with immense intelligence, cunning enough to distract him for so long. Physically they were beautiful. Their minds were huge and full. They could have been giggling.

The light they cast was intense but did nothing to relieve the blackness. It made the dark deeper by contrast.

The grey man watched them patiently, waiting for the inevitable and no longer caring. Then he turned his head away, unable to bear the sight.

'Well?' he demanded, without hope of an answer.

The attack came swiftly. The lights swept forward and began to burn him. A reservoir of energy concentrated into the exact physical space he occupied. The lights spun round him, pumping more energy, channelling it through his body until it swelled, bloated with the unbearable pressure, and burst. His molecules splintered, stripped away until they were meaningless particles drifting around in the darkness. More dust.

The grey man's body was destroyed less than a second after the attack. Whether the lights were surprised that his energy-index remained intact, he couldn't tell, but he doubted it. They knew their enemy. They concentrated their attack on his soul.

The new attack was gradual, subtle, eating at the structure of his mind, crashing mental blocs together into a confusing sculpture of chaos. The man's mental helix shrieked. The pain was ... distracting ... but tolerable. Even in torture he could recognize a skilful strategy. His mind was consuming itself. The worm Ouroborous, feeding on its own tail ...

No more than he deserved. He allowed the pain to wash over him, and tear what remained of his mind to shreds.

Rationalizing while still coherent. Events seriously out of hand. Priority engage specialist operators. Destabilize scenario! Danger, but ...

His last coherent thought: This has happened before. Last time, I died.

The lights hissed and withdrew to contemplate their other victim while the grey man's mental helix imploded

13

silently. The entire process had taken something less than five seconds.

Outside the clouds burst and it began to rain.

2

Ace of Wands

A woman dreamed in the darkness.

Her name was Jane Page, Sally Carpenter, Elisabeth Pinner, Christine Dennison, Penny Holmes, Stephanie Lister and many others. She could be whoever she wanted to be, or whoever she was required to be. She never used her real name any more. There was a serial number buried somewhere in a computer file – that was all that remained of her 'real' self. She loved the freedom of not being tied to a single identity.

Sally Carpenter was a housewife. Elisabeth Pinner made dresses. Christine Dennison was a student. Penny Holmes, a secretary. Stephanie Lister ran a painting business. Jane Page was 'something in computers'. No matter which job she claimed, her work was the same.

She dreamt that she was required to be Jane Page.

She fell through the darkness, lost in the patterns of her bodyless mind. The dark was warm and infinite. She dreamed patterns of total order, a private world of angles and straight lines, sanity and uniformity.

There was someone singing in the back of her dream. She couldn't ignore it, but she couldn't concentrate on perfection while the song distracted her.

There was a hissing, guttural voice crackling in the high notes of the song. Whispering to her, whispering her name.

'Crazy Jane. Crazy, crazy . . .'

She dropped through the darkness, dreaming. Dreaming the darkness.

* * *

'Question. Why is it so bloody dark in here?'

Ace had a headache. A vicious, slow throbbing of muscles beating against the inside of her skull. Movement was agony. There was no justice in the universe – she hadn't been drinking.

She lay still on her bed in her room in the TARDIS, staring at the darkened square of ceiling, trying not to move even when the shape of the pillow became uncomfortable beneath her head. She couldn't sleep, couldn't think straight, couldn't do anything, and there was someone slicing chunks out of her brain with a blunt knife. Hell must be something like this, with time off for good behaviour.

She whiled the night away working her way through a complex train of interconnected, trivial thoughts. One thought led to another and another in a meandering line through her memories. Killing time, trying to sleep. After a couple of hours, she gave up and took a couple of aspirin. It left her with a dead taste in her mouth, which didn't make her feel any better, so she crawled, half-dead, back to bed.

She touched her hair nervously, seizing clumps between her fingers and tugging. It was comfortably long now, but she repeated the ritual endlessly, just to reassure herself. The hairs bristled tediously against her hand. Five minutes later, she had drifted into a light sleep, which gave way to a deep sleep and dreams.

She dreamed about the Doctor, flying through time and space in a gleaming structure the size of a city. Only, when he opened it up, there was only a cupboard inside. No, that was putting things the wrong way round.

Bigger inside than out. The city, the living machine was inside the police box. No doubt about it. The Doctor was explaining it to her. Not the usual, probably untrue, spiel about dimensional transcendentalism or forced perspectives. Something different. Something weirder.

'Have you ever considered,' he was intoning, monotone lightened only by a slight Scots accent, 'that you might have things the wrong way round? That the world is on

16

the inside, and the TARDIS is the outside? There are an infinite number of doors and each and every one leads into a different part of time and space.'

He leant forward, his dark, hard features swimming unevenly in and out of focus. He tapped her nose with his finger. Patronizing. He didn't try it when he was real. Scared of losing the finger.

The Doctor had moved on. He was gliding through the darkened passages of the TARDIS. He passed through corridors – gleaming white plastic walls with their indented roundels. He passed through cloisters – dark passageways of stone clad in ivy. He passed deeper into the heart of the TARDIS. All the lights were dim, the distant mind of the TARDIS was accommodating its passengers, maybe even imitating them. It was asleep.

The Doctor was moving through the corridors like a haunted man. A fiery but dark purpose burned in his sharp, grey eyes. Stalking the passageways of his home, seeking out the dirty walls and slapping on thick layers of white emulsion before anyone else could see them . . .

And then Ace woke up.

Her headache was gone, worn away by pills and sleep. Generally, she felt fresher, relaxed, calmer than the last miserable evening. She woke happier, in the dark. The fascinating ceiling was invisible. The walls were invisible. She sat up in bed and looked around, recognizing the vague shapes of familiar furniture. That was unusual. Not actually disturbing, just unsettling. Normally, when she woke, the TARDIS would perceptibly brighten, flooding the room with a comfortably low level of light. Not this time. The TARDIS wasn't responding. The bedroom remained obstinately dark.

'Question,' Ace said. 'Why is it so bloody dark in here?'

No response. No sudden hum of power. No flare from the brightening triangular lights set high on the walls and the ceiling. No light.

Ace toyed with the idea that the Doctor had been messing around with the TARDIS environment circuits. Or maybe she wanted darkness – a subconscious demand that the TARDIS was reacting to. It was more than just a time machine, or her home – it was a living thing, infinitely more complex than herself. Even the Doctor, for all his Time Lord insight, didn't understand it. Only the TARDIS really knew. Maybe this was all planned . . .

There was no sound.

The sound of the TARDIS was a constant thing, a never-ending low drone. Never distracting, always there, just on the edge of her hearing. It was reassuring sound, it meant that the TARDIS was working properly. It was the life of the TARDIS. It never stopped.

The TARDIS was silent.

Ace got out of bed and stumbled through darkness to her wardrobe. She dressed quickly, pulling on her combat suit, leaving off the gloves and the optional extras to save time. First things first. Wake the Doctor. Possibly he'll know what's going on (*that* was optimistic). Wake Bernice, then . . . well, then the Doctor can sort it out.

You're scared. You're scared the TARDIS might be dead.

'Ace?' the voice came from the far side of the door, muffled but still unique. 'Ace, are you awake?'

'Doctor,' Ace called back, fighting the urge to whisper. 'What have you done to the lights?'

'Nothing,' the voice replied with urgent honesty. 'Ace, please come out here. Emergency situation. Battle stations.'

You're not alone, she told herself, *he's scared too*. Something in his voice gave it away. He was speaking faster, sounding lighter than normal. Ace wasn't fooled.

She unlocked the door, pulled it open clumsily. The Doctor stared back at her on the other side.

Ace saw that she'd been right. He was scared. It was on his face. His marvellously flexible features were softened into a picture of unhurried determination. Ace saw a mask. The Doctor's face was a fluid mix of features that never seemed the same twice, a face of infinite facets balancing dark wisdom and authority with childish wonder. It was the face he had been born to wear. Even

18

in deepest contemplation, there was always something magical and lively there, persuading Ace that life might be worth living after all. She couldn't see it now. He was truly afraid.

A masochistic voice piped up at the back of Ace's mind. *There must*, it said, *be something seriously wrong.*

'Take this,' the face said, as something was shoved into her hands. Looking down she saw a plain plastic cylinder, a battery torch, identical to one she used to have as a kid. She'd had hours of fun with that. Minutes at least. The Doctor also wielded a torch, the dull beam aimed straight at the floor.

'Don't use it till mine goes out,' the Doctor told her, in a gentle Scots lilt. For a second, it seemed that the Doctor, the real Doctor, was back. Then his face flattened again.

In the shadows behind the Doctor was Bernice Summerfield. The aggressive sharpness of her thin face was softened and blurred by drowsiness. Someone else, Ace noticed, caught unawares by this *emergency situation*. She seemed pale and gaunt, though that was probably the dim light more than anything else. Her dark hair was a mess, reminding Ace that her own was probably in a worse condition. Bernice's clothes were a hastily assembled collection, probably the first things that fell out of her wardrobe. Very practical.

The Doctor was immaculately presented, by the Doctor's standards at least. His hair was, if anything, tidier than usual, displaying generous amounts of his high forehead. His clothes were, amazingly, cleaner than normal. The usual suit, its smooth cream seeming drab in the omnipresent darkness. His shirt was darker than normal, but still managed to contrast with the coarsely textured black tie he sported. Ace had long ago formulated the theory that he had twenty or thirty identical sets of clothing in his wardrobe, and wasn't greatly surprised.

'Doctor, what the hell's going on?' she appealed to him, cramming every heartfelt inch of exasperation into the question.

'Haven't a clue,' the Doctor replied, seeming better for

19

saying it. 'I think a trip to the console room's in order, answers for the rooting out of. Shall we go?'

'Don't have much of a choice, do we?' she said, trying to smile. The Doctor tried to smile back, then he swept away. Ace fell into step behind him, following the dark shape of his shoulders and the beam of light in front of him. She found herself walking shoulder-to-shoulder with Bernice. At first there was an awkward silence. Ace was too frustrated by the lack of any obvious options to talk, while Bernice seemed drowsy. Probably recovering from being woken in the middle of a hangover. Ace turned to her. She had to talk to someone, if only to exorcise the frustration. And she wasn't too keen on holding a conversation with the Doctor's back, was she?

'He hasn't told you anything, has he?'

'What? And break the habit of a lifetime?' Bernice managed a tired smile.

'He looks bloody terrified.' Ace let her voice sink to a low whisper.

'You should have seen him when the lights went out. I told him he hadn't fed the meter in a while and we'd been cut off.'

'And?'

'He didn't laugh. Do you think we have a crisis?' Benny sounded tense and cheerful. Ace found she didn't want to answer.

'What do you think?'

Bernice hummed softly, before replying.

'I think we should panic.'

'Don't panic now.' Ace shook her head. 'Save it for later.'

The console room was dead, crypt-dark and sepulchre-silent. The console was lifeless, its central column motionless. Even the tiny lights built into the internal structure of the column had been extinguished. These were the pulse of the TARDIS. If they were dead, so was the ship.

Without the activity of the console, the room seemed empty. It was a massive room anyway, but now it seemed cavernous. It was the burial ground for something ancient and incomprehensible. Ace felt like she was disturbing hallowed ground. Their footsteps echoed off the walls.

The Doctor didn't seem to feel the heavy atmosphere. Either that or he was doing a good job of ignoring it. He made for the console. Ace and Bernice edged uneasily along the periphery of the room, watching the Doctor work. Ace enjoyed getting involved in the mechanics of the TARDIS, but this was one time that the Doctor could have the centre to himself. Bernice was watching the Doctor with clinical detachment, one professional in one field observing another. When she moved, it was stiffly, carefully measured. Ace could see that she was one step from panic. Grudgingly, Ace admitted that she was too.

It depends, she thought, on what the Doctor does.

He was a small man, but as he leant over the console to study the dead instruments, his silhouette contracted. His head shrunk into his shoulders as he leant further forward. A ghostly torchlit reflection of his face appeared in the central column, twisting in the curve of the glass. There was something about the inhuman silhouette that Ace found eerily familiar. It was just like normal. The Doctor working in a well-lit console room, bent over the console, his face set in concentration, head lowered to display a receding hairline. He might have been setting co-ordinates or reading from a rare first edition perched on the console top, taking readings from delicate instrumentation, thumping the delicate instrumentation whenever he didn't like the readings. It was one of the regular features of Ace's life. The difference now was the darkness and the desperate atmosphere.

He worked faster than usual. Normally he was careful. Now, he circled the console, fruitlessly trying to find something – anything! – that worked. Ace watched his frustration grow. After a few minutes, he straightened up to stare stone-faced at his companions.

Almost in unison, they moved to join him at the console. 'Everything's dead,' he said softly. He leaned forward

21

again and tapped on the console top. He straightened up and Ace was surprised to see his smile.

'Phenomenal power . . .' he said, slowly and softly.

Ace felt herself smile too, involuntarily. The real Doctor was back, magical and lively as ever. Nothing had been explained – but that was further proof that the Doctor *was* back.

'Pardon?' she heard Benny distantly.

'Sorry, no . . .' the Doctor mumbled. 'This reminded me of a sticky situation I've been in before. Daleks perhaps. No, this is different.'

Please, Ace wanted to scream, *don't say that we're perfectly safe*.

'We're perfectly safe,' the Doctor continued. Ace scowled.

'That's very encouraging,' Benny chimed softly. 'Please don't spoil the effect by adding "until the air runs out and we asphyxiate" or something similar.'

The Doctor shook his head without looking up.

'Not all the systems have been shut down. The TARDIS is dormant, not dead,' he stated, with uncharacteristic simplicity. 'All the essential systems are working perfectly. Oxygen.' He shot a wry glance at Benny.

'The lights are down,' Ace pointed out. She shivered. 'And the heating.'

'Yes, but the internal gravity's on. We can live without light. We can't live without the shell that keeps the vortex out. Or the failsafe that stops the TARDIS from erasing itself. And the heart, the basic life and mind of the TARDIS is being sustained.'

'Okay, it's a black-out, but we're alive. Why?'

'I don't think,' Bernice began slowly, glancing between Ace and the Doctor, 'there's anything wrong with the TARDIS. This is external. We've been nobbled.'

'Right,' the Doctor continued. 'We're still in flight. There's an external force that's moving us under its own steam, to its own destination.'

'Doctor,' Benny murmured.

'You're saying it's moving us?' Ace queried, ignoring

Benny who was trying to catch her eye. 'It must've bloody massive energy reserves, right?'

The Doctor shook his head vigorously. Manic light gleamed in his pupils.

'Massive is an understatement. It would have to be the equal to the Eye of Harmony, at least. Which means,' he fixed Ace with a steely glare, 'when we land, I want you to be polite to *everyone* you meet.'

'What? You think I wouldn't?' Ace retorted, feeling reassured enough to try some honest sarcasm.

'Fascinating though this all is,' Benny purred, 'I think the time rotor's trying to attract our attention.'

Ace looked.

There was a small light burning in the heart of the column, flickering weakly like a dying candle. Ace automatically glanced upwards, at the lights set on the walls. These remained dead. She looked back at the console. The light there had grown noticeably larger and brighter. Too bright to be the normal column lights.

'We've been reconnected?' suggested Benny.

'No,' the Doctor whispered, almost hypnotized by the light that tore deeper into the TARDIS core. 'No,' he repeated, lending more weight to the syllable.

Then he went mad.

His fists slammed on the console top. Fingers smashed against all the buttons in reach. Levers were pulled, switches flicked, dials sent reeling, empty spaces thumped until they were dented. Fury was carved onto his face. Pure, near-bestial rage, caught in the now blazing light from the time rotor.

'This is my ship!' he screamed, staring into the glare. 'My ship!'

The light screamed too. The delicate rods and instruments inside were drowned out by its brilliance. As the light grew more intense it sang. A simple, high-pitched harmonic, radiating out of the column, across the room. Ace found it almost soothing; Benny turned away, lost to the turbulence around her. The Doctor it drove into deeper fury. He still mouthed the same anger, but it came

23

out silent, washed away by the music of the light. His face was caught in the golden-white light; he might have been weeping. Ace called to him, but even she couldn't hear.

The light seeped from the console and burned into the room. Ace flung her arms in front of her face and turned away, the image of the Doctor still staring into the core of the agonizing light caught inside her eyelids.

The music reached a crescendo. The console room bleached out in a holocaust of white.

The shape punctured the universe, flooding into the gaps between atoms. The cosmos retaliated, forcing back the intruder. The shape shimmered in and out of existence, fighting to maintain its grip on the universe. Gradually it solidified.

The lights were drawn by the sound more than anything else. The sound of ancient engines forcing themselves to make one more jump into reality, the shrieking pressure, the violent crescendo.

The lights contemplated the shape. A tall blue box. A hundred intricate angles that gave it a unique shape. A light flashing feebly on the roof. The words over the doorway: POLICE PUBLIC CALL BOX.

Not fooled by appearance, the lights saw it as it really was.

Time machine.
Gallifreyan.
TARDIS.
Time Lord.
Renegade.
Doctor!

Satisfied, the lights vanished, spitting and shrieking, into the dark.

3

Edge of Darkness

Harry Truman stared into the bathroom mirror, hating his reflection. The face that stared back was a patchwork mass of scar tissue and deformity. The face that he had been born with had burned away a long time ago. Truman spent hours searching his reflection for an echo of his lost features. He found none.

He hated the thing in the mirror. He wasn't alone – most others who had seen it found it repugnant – but Truman's hate was deepest. He couldn't have lived with one deformity – here was an army of them! Scabbed, swollen remnants of the original flesh hung loose on the bone. Weals lacerated it, torn out of the face like a freshly ploughed landscape. Occasional flashes of smooth bone jutted through the skin. His eyes bulged out from their hollow, fleshless sockets. Everything he'd feared, every deformity, every nightmare, had been visited on his face. His new features taunted him by adopting the inflections of his once handsome visage. Truman hated it, because it was him.

The deformities were broken by jigsaw patches of smooth, blotchy skin grafts. Plastic surgery had been a mistake. An expensive mistake. At the time it seemed to make sense. Truman was no longer able to concentrate, his new face distracted him – he would spend hours tracing the lines of his features in preference to work. He missed the old familiarity. None of his colleagues or his friends had been comfortable around someone who had to hide behind a mask. Surgery seemed a promising option, but Truman already had an abundance of flesh, and adding more only made things worse. The surgeons were deranged chefs, slapping on more layers onto an already rickety and overworked cake. It hadn't improved his appearance, it made him poor and disillusioned. Truman stopped caring then. He walked out of his life, giving up everything.

His old life was gone. He had spent a year shedding memories and friends. A half-remembered year of homeless wandering, when the scope of his ambition contracted to bare existence. A year of hiding in hostels. A year that wiped away his past. The name of his company was gone. Memories of friends, enemies, neighbours and lovers were reduced to a gallery of meaningless faces and idiosyncrasies. His life became a blur of empty remembrance. Even the circumstances of his accident were forgotten. Only his name and a handful of memories survived.

And his face. Always his face.

It had taken a year before he found anything new. He came to the house out of desperation, drawn by a vague hope of manual work. He found himself with a permanent position in a home that offered stability and isolation. He found himself employed by people whose loyalty, respect and friendship were quickly forthcoming. He wore a mask in their company, but they had a fair idea of what it hid, and they didn't mind. Truman found a niche and a purpose.

He still hated his face, but it didn't seem to matter any more.

'Monster,' he told his reflection. It smiled bitterly at him.

Reluctantly he replaced his mask. It always took longer than he expected. He had to make sure that it was placed correctly and tight. He had nightmares of it coming off at an awkward moment.

The mask was a simple, wooden plate smoothed into expressionlessness. It covered Truman's face from his hair to below his chin, incorporating an elaborate mouthpiece which could be removed so that he could eat in public.

Tear-shaped holes were cut half-way up the wood, while a slot was dug over his mouth; enough to see and talk. It was a well-ventilated item, cushioned, comfortable. It had been made for him after the accident; one of the few things he had never thrown away. He hated it.

The mask made him faceless. It had no features, beyond the slight curve in the mouth-slot forming an inane smile. It was a grotesquely bland thing, like the theatrical masks of comedy and tragedy. Truman's mask grinned. It stole his self-expression, a blessing sometimes. Mostly he found it isolating. No one saw deeper than the vacant grin, the real Harry Truman. The mask made him more of a freak than the twisted mess it hid.

Truman scowled at his reflection. It grinned at him.

'Bastard,' he said. The mask, its mouth fixed, said nothing.

The bathroom door opened behind him, dry hinges groaned with the effort of movement. Truman didn't bother turning. He already saw the newcomer, framed in the doorway in the mirror.

A woman's features swam on the surface of the glass. A soft face surrounded by a stream of loose hair. Her eyes were inquisitive and dull simultaneously. Her name was Sandra. She had been a part of Truman's life for two years.

She stared at Truman's back, smiling uneasily.

'Harry,' she said slowly, almost as if she were framing a question. Truman nodded then added a soft 'yes.'

He turned, nervously straightening his tie. Instinctively, one hand leapt to check that his mask-straps were still tight. He smiled widely at her, blissfully aware that she couldn't see it.

Sandra was one of his employers, his friend. With little age difference between them – and no one else in the house of a remotely similar age capable of holding a sensible conversation – they had been drawn, naturally, together. They respected and liked each other, shared loyalties and confidences. Truman had come to realize that he wanted more. Something more special, deeper,

27

more intimate. Something – and he admitted this grudgingly – more physical. He had admitted none of this to Sandra, certain though he was that she suspected. He was sure that she wouldn't agree. That even the slightest inference might spoil the friendship they shared.

Truman's eyes didn't stray from her. There was little else in the bathroom worth watching. It was a soulless place, its sterility sharpened by the pervasive smell of disinfectant and the persistently crooked mirror. There was nothing in the room that was not purely functional. Sandra's presence breathed life into the room.

The lights came on. They were an old system of fluorescent tubes, which took several attempts to kick into life. They would flicker wildly (on special occasions they strobed). This time the light was harsh and steady. It flooded the room and Truman got a clear glimpse of his closest friend.

She was smiling dreamily and looking straight at him. Her eyes weren't properly focused. They never seemed to settle for more than a few seconds – one of her most attractive, irritating mannerisms. She was simply dressed, a bland contrast to the features which Truman adored. Jeans and a sweater: an unexciting combination rendered interesting only by the shape of the body around which they moulded.

'Shower?' he asked. Sandra mouthed *yes*. Instantly, unbidden, a picture of the showering Sandra leapt before Truman's eyes. The beautiful, perfect image smiled coyly, then vanished. Truman shuddered, blinked and forgot.

'Ah. I'm just leaving.'

'Don't let me hurry you if you're not done.' Sandra's mouth formed a sympathetic smile. She stepped to one side, blocking Truman's exit. 'I've got all the time in the world.'

Truman stopped sharply, wondering if she registered his unease. She probably couldn't avoid it, it was written all over his . . .

Stupid.

Truman relaxed, his confidence returning to him, his eyes locking onto Sandra's warm features.

'Have you talked to Justin?' Sandra asked, eyebrows arching. Truman shook his head.

'He won't let me near him,' he said, picking his words carefully. 'He sits in the corner and waves fruit at me.' Sandra looked away suddenly. Truman trailed off. 'He's not getting better, is he?'

'Not much, no.' She was dismissive. Her back was turned to Truman. Whether she was deliberately avoiding his gaze he couldn't tell. 'He doesn't talk any more, he rambles. He's as coherent as a three-year-old, and as predictable. He talks about you a lot. He's very possessive.'

'I'm sorry,' said Truman. She didn't seem to hear.

'The rest of the time he's worse.' Her voice sank into a dull whisper. 'It is him. It's the real him, I know it is. But it's only the worst parts of him. He hates everyone. Hates Dad, this house, himself, you, me . . .'

'He doesn't hate you.' Secretly Truman hoped otherwise.

'He does. A part of him does. He still wants me, for all the wrong reasons. He's quite gentle at times. But that's all. He's regressed to the state he was in six months ago. One part of him just wants to . . . use me, and the other's a toddler who'll go to pieces without me. Six months' work. Bang! Gone in five minutes.' She slumped on a chair in the corner, shooting Truman a glance packed with pain and suppressed resentment. Her shoulders sank forward and her fringe fell over her face, obscuring her eyes. Truman felt she was crying; he wanted to try and comfort her, but he knew Sandra well enough to check himself. This was anger. Some frustration, mostly anger.

'I'm sorry,' he said again.

'It's not your fault,' Sandra growled through clenched teeth. 'It could have been you in there. It's his fault for wanting to go alone in the first place . . .' She broke off suddenly. Angry eyes concentrated on Truman. 'You want him to go in again!' Her voice was hushed and powerful.

'You're scared of going in alone, and you want him to go with you. You want to know if he's up to it!'

'No!' Truman snapped truthfully, preparing to go on the defensive. But Sandra was already shaking her head.

'I'm sorry, it's just so . . . bloody frustrating. Everything I've built in the last six months has just turned into shit. It's going to take years to get him back to normal. Just when I thought I could let him go . . . *this*.' She slumped, not speaking for almost a minute. 'When do you take the plunge?'

'In about five minutes,' Truman said without confidence, though he was heartened by Sandra's look of apologetic shock. 'I want to get something on tape for your father. He's desperate to try it himself. It was all I could do to talk him out of it.'

Sandra nodded.

'It'd probably kill him,' she agreed. 'Look at Justin.' She checked herself, adding, 'I'm not building your confidence, am I?'

Truman tapped the side of his mask and smiled ruefully.

'It can't do anything to me that hasn't been done already.'

Sandra smiled and rose from her chair. Her lips pressed briefly against his mouth-slot. Beneath the mask, Truman flushed.

'Good luck.'

'Thank you,' Truman replied stiltedly, before scuttling out of the door. It closed behind him. He stood waiting on the landing, his eyes closed. The image he'd seen before flickered under his eyelids. The hateful, enthralling picture of Sandra – smooth, soaking and perfectly naked – slowly, in monochrome, liked a jammed projector playing an endless loop of old film. It was a thrilling image, ultimately unreal. But so *vivid*, like a fragment of an old memory plucked from his subconscious. That was impossible. The woman in the shower was Sandra a good five years younger than she was now. It could only be a confused memory, mixing his past reality with his present fantasy.

It wasn't until he was disturbed by the sound of a key turning in a lock that he turned away.

He did have a job to do.

When leaving the TARDIS Ace always had the feeling of stepping from one world to another; the disconcerting realization that the enormous, complex machine she had left shrank to the shape of a police box on the outside, a police box in the weirdest surroundings.

The TARDIS had materialized with unusual smoothness. The light at the heart of the console waned and snuffed itself out. The room filled with darkness again and the console remained dormant. The doors had hummed with life, swinging open of their own accord.

Faced with little choice, they had left.

Outside the TARDIS it was dark. The air was heavy, thick with the stuffiness of an undisturbed room. Brick rose in the darkness in all directions, picked out by the beam of Ace's torch. Instinctively she felt they were underground. She associated the claustrophobic sense of pressure with depths. She'd once spent three weeks in a disused mine on a nameless alien world, alone with a small, tense squad of corporate mercenaries. She'd felt the same sense of confinement there. She hadn't forgotten it.

They were, apparently, alone. Ace was sceptical. She emerged from the TARDIS tensed for a fight. There could be anything waiting to meet them and, though their surroundings seemed deserted, she pressed up against the side of the police box before taking a look round.

Her torch picked out crumbling brickwork or loose wooden partition structures where walls should be. Shining the beam at the ceiling, she saw that it was supported by an undisguised network of wooden beams. The whole thing looked fragile. Thick, ancient cobwebs were strung between the beams, probably all that was holding the ceiling together. Ace lowered the torch slowly, catching a snatch of Benny's back on its way down. Less cautious than Ace, she was already over by one of the walls, studying the brickwork. Ace ignored her and swung the light to the floor.

The floor was a minefield of strewn wooden beams and crumbling blocks, piled on plain boards. All were covered by a carpet of dust. Ace cast the beam further round the room, picking out more interesting hazards – chunks of plaster, large shards of broken glass, abandoned ornaments. The light brushed over the shattered features of a human face, and Ace tensed before discovering that it was a plaster bust, one side smashed in. Just more rubbish. The room was a store for anything that someone at one time had decided to dispose of. Ace relaxed; there was no sign of anything immediately threatening.

A dark shape moved clumsily round the side of the TARDIS, but this was only the Doctor, locking the TARDIS door. He moved slowly and unsteadily, like a troubled man.

'There's no point doing that,' Ace pointed out. 'If they can control the TARDIS, they can get the door open.'

'True,' the Doctor mumbled, shoving the door to ensure it was locked, 'but it should make it a little more difficult. Besides, we don't know who else is out there.'

Typically, he seemed entirely unaffected by the events of the last half-hour. He looked healthier than ever, almost refreshed.

'Anyway,' he announced, 'until we find whatever's brought us here, the TARDIS is out of bounds.'

'What?' Ace exploded, 'All my bloody gear's in there.'

'Gear?' The Doctor looked at her suspiciously.

'Weapons, explosives, heavy technology,' Ace rattled off the list of her prized possessions, all the things which the Doctor disapproved of. Long-standing experience suggested that he wasn't going to be swayed. She stopped talking and swore inwardly.

'My diary,' Benny said. 'I left it in my room.' She stared imploringly at the Doctor but he adopted a grainy expression and shook his head. Benny sighed slowly, gesturing around the room.

'Do you have any idea where we are?' she asked. 'Somewhere unpleasant, am I right?'

'Earth,' the Doctor replied, without elaboration.

'Couldn't you be more specific?' asked Ace, beating Benny to the question by a second.

'Not really. We're probably somewhere in the northern hemisphere. We're underground.' Ace smiled to herself as he spoke. 'In the cellar of some sort of structure. A large house, a hotel, possibly a warehouse.'

Ace hugged herself. Derelict houses formed part of a vivid childhood nightmare. She'd grown much since then, but there was still a kernel of disquiet buried in her subconscious. There was something here, an echo of that experience. She shivered, then scowled, hating her obvious weakness.

'What about the date?' she asked.

'I couldn't tell you.'

'Twentieth century?' Ace prompted. It was an informed guess. The TARDIS had a knack of gravitating to that period. She'd asked the Doctor about it once and he'd summed it up as familiarity.

'Possibly.'

'Somewhere unpleasant,' Benny added cheerily.

'I can't tell you,' the Doctor shrugged. 'Something's interfering with the TARDIS computer systems.' He paused briefly. 'First there is a mountain. Then there is no mountain. Then there is.'

'The easy ones first, eh?' Benny responded. 'I should've guessed.'

'I'm going to see if there's a way out,' he said distractedly. 'Five minutes. Don't go wandering off on your own. Or together for that matter.'

Without waiting for an answer, he slipped into the darkness.

Benny rubbed her temples in a weary, soothing motion. Ace grinned and leaned back against the nearest wall. The brickwork felt alarmingly soft against her shoulderblades. Bernice joined her by the wall, running a finger down its length. Ace could almost hear the dust accumu-

33

lating on her fingertip, the layers of centuries being bull-
dozed aside.

'Fascinating dust,' Benny said, voice not dissimilar to
the Doctor's. She blew the dust from the end of her finger.
Disturbed flecks sparkled in the beam of Ace's torch as
they drifted to the floor.

'Just dust.' Ace shrugged.

'How many times have I told you, Ace? There's no
such thing as "just dust".' Benny adopted a light accent,
startling the other woman with her uncanny vocal impersonation of the Time Lord. 'Dust is fascinating, vibrant
and sexy. If you really want to find out how a civilization
works, look in its dustbins. History is made in pigsties, not
palaces. Why do you think we spend so much time in the
seediest dumps in the universe?'

'Tell me about the dust, Professor.' Ace decided to play
along.

'Well,' Bernice slurred, slipping out of Gallifreyan
accent and into the familiar tones of a bored and boring
school lecture, 'dust is interesting because it, er . . . it tells
you a lot about the places in which it gathers. The dust
here tells us that, uh . . .'

'That this place hasn't been cleaned for a few decades?'
Ace prompted.

'Centuries.' Benny smiled. She moved closer to the wall,
pressing her hands against the brickwork. Intrigued, Ace
crouched beside her, shining the beam of the torch onto
the patch of wall Benny was examining. Bernice's palms
ran over the surface of the wall, pressing fingertips against
the textured brickwork, and tapping at the crumbling
mortar.

'Seriously,' Bernice said, after an oppressive minute's
silence, 'the architecture's a mess, chronologically speaking. This isn't really my field.'

'What d'you mean?' Ace asked, with cautious interest.

'Some of this is prehistoric. Sixteenth century.' The
patch of wall she pointed to was, as far as Ace was concerned, undistinguished. 'But there've obviously been a
lot of alterations in, uh, the eighteenth century. And

they've been changing it almost continuously since then. This wall's unstable. It looks like they've been ripping out bits of it on a regular basis. Replacing them with identical bits, of course.'

'Right.' Ace nodded. 'Why bother?'

'Probably because if this wall comes down, it'll bring the rest of the house with it,' Bernice said, carefully lifting her hands from the surface. 'Mind you, I'm not an expert. You don't like this place, do you?' Her voice became lower, huskier. 'I can tell.' Ace ignored the urge to shiver again, and nodded.

'Not this place,' she said, 'just old houses in general. Empty rooms and passages. You think you can hear voices on the edge of your hearing. Ghost voices, scratching in the darkness, behind the walls.'

She blinked, turned to made eye contact with her companion.

'Just something from when I was a kid,' she said. 'A stupid thing. Did you ever have anything that scared you?'

'I used to have nightmares about a six-foot green spider wanting to eat my face while I was asleep,' Benny replied lightly. 'Then I discovered what "sterile environment" meant.' She stopped, her face withering into a picture of embarrassment under Ace's steel glare. Ace smiled and Bernice's guilty expression broke up.

'I've found a way out.' The Doctor stepped out of the darkness. Ace had shifted her body into a defensive posture before realizing who it was. Her composure recovered, she breathed heavily with relief.

'Sorry, did I startle you?' he asked, radiating innocence. 'Sorry,' he repeated himself, with greater conviction.

'Turned up anything?' Bernice asked, finding her breath.

'A door. It's partially blocked, but we should be able to get through.'

'The question is, do we venture forth like brave-hearted heroes, or lock ourselves in the TARDIS like honest cowards?'

'We go.' Ace was determined. Be constructive. There

35

was no point lurking in the TARDIS. Take the fight to the enemy. Benny nodded, saying nothing. The Doctor glanced between them, studying their faces. Finally he nodded.

'Once more unto the breach,' he said, forcing a smile. 'Follow me.'

The door was closer than Ace expected. It was little more than a rotting wooden frame set into a shallow cutting in the brickwork. There were some planks half-heartedly nailed across the doorway, but they were rickety and loose. The wood itself was brittle; the boards came away with minimal effort. Beyond the door was another uninspiring stretch of cellar. One plain brick passageway led off into the dark and a smaller side-passage – also brick – also terminated in darkness.

It was cleaner here, less cluttered. The floor was bare, clear of abandoned furniture and dust. There was an atmosphere of care and attention to this place which the other rooms lacked. The brickwork here seemed sturdier, less likely to crumble at the slightest touch. Glancing down the side-passage, Ace saw that there had even been an attempt to disguise the nature of the walls behind a smooth plaster finish. The other rooms had been derelict, obviously undisturbed for years. Not here. Ace could believe that people actually worked here.

The Doctor agreed. He pointed his torch upwards, so that the beam danced on the ceiling. Picked out in the light, was a web of dangling wires connected to an exposed light-bulb. The Doctor cast the beam further down the passage, finding further bulbs set at regular intervals along its length.

'The lights suggest that someone uses this place,' he said. 'Lives here. Possibly.'

'Possibly?' Ace asked.

'It looks industrial. Very heavy and intricate, without the need to disguise its functional nature. Hardly the norm in a domestic situation? Besides, how old is it? It's not proof of anything.'

'This is the bit where one of us suggests we split up and look around,' Bernice said chirpily. There was something gleefully sadistic in her psychology that thrived in adversity. 'And the monster picks us off and eats us one by one. Since you two are looking so grim, I think it's going to have to be me. I'll go this way,' she said, pointing down the length of the main passage. 'You two try down the other way. Meet back here in five – ten minutes. Scream if there's any trouble, yes?'

There were nods, a brief exchange of torches. Then Bernice slipped into the darkness and the Doctor and Ace pulled into the side-corridor, walking side-by-side and in silence.

The passage ended sharply in a plain metal slab of a door. The beam of the Doctor's torch flattened against its smooth surface, revealing that it had been painted an unappetizing shade of cabbage-green. The paint was beginning to flake. The door was indented with a hand grip, but was otherwise unfriendly and impregnable.

Ace stopped by the door, and stared at it single-mindedly.

'Ace, I'm sorry if I've seemed a bit brusque,' the Doctor said softly, close to her ear. 'It's just I'm very worried about the TARDIS.'

Ace hummed an acknowledgment but didn't look at him. She was preoccupied with the door. She dug her hand into the indentation and tugged.

'Ace, you've shown me you can survive in a totally alien environment without the TARDIS to fall back on,' the Doctor continued, apparently oblivious to her efforts with the door. 'In that respect, you're a better person than I am. I need the ship. I don't want to see it hurt . . . damaged.'

The door hadn't budged. Not an inch. It couldn't just be the weight. It had to be locked.

'There's something in this place powerful enough to tear the TARDIS from the vortex. If that thing is malevolent then imagine what it could do to you, or to Benny? We're playing in the dark, gambling for our lives, with a hand we don't understand, against a dealer who's cheating. If I seem on edge, it's because I'm worried. Terrified,' he added.

'You're not alone, Doctor. Perhaps I'm just naturally antagonistic . . .' Ace muttered, tugging sharply at the door several times, failing even to make it rattle. 'Why won't you open, you bastard?' she yelled, her frustration finally getting the better of her.

'It opens inwards,' the Doctor hummed. Ace landed a vicious thump on the side of the door and it opened silently. A vexed smile settled on her lips, a light blush on her cheeks.

The room was as functional and bare as the rest of the building. Its walls were an insipid shade of grey-brown, occasionally enlivened by colourless scraps of wallpaper overlooked when the rest had been scraped away. The other rooms had been cold, but the chill was pronounced here. Briefly, Ace felt the sharp, icy brush against her skin, before her combat suit reacted and grew warm. Though colder than the rest of the cellar, the room seemed lighter. It was dark, but not the enveloping blackness of the other rooms. It was half-dark, the shadows robbed of their deeper levels.

Ace glanced upwards, and saw a light fitting dangling from the ceiling by a bare flex. There was no bulb.

The room was unfurnished. Almost.

It was large, grey and ugly. It squatted in the corner of the room daring anyone to come near it. It was, simply, a wardrobe. It brushed the ceiling. It was almost as wide as it was high, its bulk magnified by the metal out of which it had been built. The doors were wooden, but these were only panels slotted into heavy metal frames. The box sat against the wall and brooded. *Wardrobe* was too weak a term for the sombre artifact. It was a sarcophagus.

It had captured the Doctor's interest.

'Ace,' he called eagerly, 'what do you make of this?'

It was impressive, but Ace was unmoved by the Doctor's enthusiasm.

'Look at it,' he said, the excitement in his voice suddenly

replaced with a deep and resonant note of authority. Ace looked.

'What for?' she asked.

'Watch,' the Doctor commanded, seizing the handle on one of the doors. It came ajar gently after a slow tug, and as it opened it gained a halo.

The light grew suddenly. It blazed from the newly formed crack between the doors, suffusing the gap, streaming into the room. It was sterile and powerful – Ace raised an arm to protect her face from the glare – but not artificial. It was a natural light, like a snatched glimpse of a sun at its zenith.

The Doctor slammed the door, hiding the light. Ace blinked frantically; her eyes felt as if they were on fire, and a staple-shaped image lingered on her retina for more than a minute. She kept blinking, grateful for the coolness of the air.

The Doctor was talking.

'It's light,' he was saying. 'Intense light. First in the TARDIS. Now . . . Well, that couldn't have been artificial, there's no connection.'

'And what does that tell us?' Ace challenged him.

'Nothing. I have suspicions.' The Doctor mused momentarily before adding, 'No proof.' He shrugged wearily and shook his head.

Ace moved to the sarcophagus, slowly reaching out to touch the door. The Doctor intercepted her quickly, seizing her by the wrist and shooting her a sharp glance.

'No,' he insisted. 'Leave it.'

'Why?'

'I want to know what it is before I go charging in,' he told her. 'And I want to find Benny first. We need to stick together.'

'Dear diary, I'm not writing this down – if I could I'd be Mr Tickle – so I'm going to have to memorize this, or paint it on the walls.'

Soon after she had left the Doctor and Ace, Bernice found her surroundings changing. The brickwork and plaster of earlier sections gave way to walls lined with wooden panels. The barely concealed wiring of the lights system disappeared into the ceiling. The dry dust taste at the start of the passage was replaced by the fragrance of old varnish blending with wood, echoes of a natural, forest freshness. Only the atmosphere was unchanged, as trapped and oppressive as before.

'I've been going for almost ten minutes now,' Bernice told herself with a soft whisper, 'and, tell the truth, Bernice Summerfield is lost. Not *lost* lost,' she corrected herself, 'just disorientated. This house is like a maze without any options. No turn-offs, no junctions, no forked passages, no doors. A very easy maze in fact. All I have to do is turn round and keep walking. But you wouldn't believe the number of twists and turns there'll be on the way back. The architecture's too complex for its own good. This is *not* the work of a sane man, trust me.

'I'm turning back now, the Doctor and Ace are bound to have found something more substantial than corridors. Something more substantial will have found them. *He'll* be surrounded by a death-squad led by a fascist whose pet hate is confident, charismatic fast-talkers. *She'll* be locked in a dungeon about to be married off to and-stroke-or ritually sacrificed by a drug-crazed alien mastermind who doesn't know what he's letting himself in for . . .'

She closed her mental diary and turned, shining her torch down the corridor. She stared briefly, swore and dropped the torch. The light went out to the sound of cracking plastic. She scrabbled round for it in the darkness, finding it quickly, not surprised to find the lens smashed and the bulb badly damaged. The light was a dim spot glowing in the dark, the torch sizzling as it shone. She swore again, louder this time.

'Hello again diary,' she said bitterly. 'Have just vandalized the torch. It's giving off less light than something very dark indeed, and I get the feeling it's going to explode in my hand . . . I'm not bothered, I can get back though it'll take a bit longer and I'll be making nose-contact with more than one wall on the way. It's just . . .'

She paused, trying to remember what she had seen – the brief glimpse down the passageway.

She saw the passage behind her, spreading away in a straight line back to the door where she had left the Doctor. She hadn't exaggerated the rambling nature of the corridor, the fiddly confused turnings. So if they suddenly weren't there any more . . .

'What a terrible blow, the archaeological world has been robbed of the mind of its finest student,' she said finally. 'No, it's nothing, a trick of the dark.' She was talking louder now, trying to reassure herself. 'I'll find out soon enough.'

She edged forward through the darkness and collided with an oak-panelled wall. Her confidence flooded back. Her sanity was no longer in question.

Casting round for the right direction, she saw the light.

It was a thin strip of brilliance, running along the ground where the floor met the wall. It didn't illuminate the passage, but it was there. It had to be a crack; a slight gap between the wall and the floor. And if there was light coming from it, Bernice reasoned, then there had to be something more than bricks, mortar and plaster finish behind it. Since she hadn't noticed a single door here before, there must be a hidden entrance, concealed by the panels.

She edged along the wall to the light, hands brushing across the panels in the vain hope of finding some sort of handle. A hidden door would have a concealed opening mechanism, and that would be hard to spot *with* a torch. She was on the verge of turning away when it occurred to her that there had been no light when she'd gone past; she couldn't have failed to notice it. Therefore, it had been turned on recently, after she had passed this section.

Which meant that there was someone in there.

She considered heading back to find the Doctor, but the light might be turned off in the meantime and she would have no chance of finding it again. Besides, she'd never been reliant on the Doctor to take the initiative.

She rapped her knuckles against one of the panels.

The wall swung open to an accompaniment of squealing hinges. Light filled the corridor from the open doorway. It framed a tall and handsome man, stooping slightly. Benny estimated that he was in his mid-twenties, though something worn in his face suggested he was much older. The youthful spark in his eyes and the innocent smile wouldn't have looked out of place on a three-year-old. His appearance careered towards the unkempt, enhanced by the uncombed mess of dark hair and about two days' worth of unchecked stubble. He was dressed plainly in fading grey trousers and a baggy, off-white shirt which, Benny noticed neutrally, was wrongly buttoned.

He stared at her until she felt uncomfortable, then lost interest and began gazing distractedly round the passage.

'Oh,' he said eventually. 'I've been expecting you, haven't I? Come in.'

It was an ordinary mug – decorated in blue and white stripes – cold and quite empty. Bernice could see a vague reflection of her face swimming on the smooth white surface at the bottom. Wondering what to do with it, she looked up, leant back in her wickerwork chair, and smiled questioningly at her host.

The man raised an identical mug to his lips and smiled back at her.

'Drink up, Laura,' he said. 'It'll get cold.'

He smiled again, dangerously toothy this time. Bernice raised the hollow vessel to her mouth and pretended to sip. She glanced around, drinking in the simplicity of what was – for want of a better expression – her host's cell.

It was a plain room, though not an uncomfortable one, decorated in a tasteful shade of pale pink. Most of the available floor space was consumed by furniture; a couple of chairs, a desk covered in writing materials and reams of much scrawled-upon paper, a small bookcase sitting innocuously in one corner, straining under the weight of hundreds of books. There was even a wash-basin built into one wall. The bed devoured most space, squashed into a corner. There was also, her host assured her blithely, a wardrobe hidden behind a couple of doors set flush in the wall. The other door was the one through which she had entered, equally well hidden on this side of the wall. Her host had been very secretive about its opening mechanism and so, Benny realized, there was little chance of making a quick get-away. Though her host seemed charming and harmless, there was something about him which made her teeth itch.

She couldn't pin down exactly what it was that disturbed her. Perhaps something in the way he moved. His body language was too loose, too smooth, lacking the stiff, jerky movements most people affected in social situations. He was too easily distracted – his eyes never focused even in the middle of conversation. He had been expecting her, but knew nothing about her. There had been little things but nothing tangible that she could latch onto, until he had started pouring non-existent tea from an imaginary pot.

That was it. The man was a fruitloop.

Benny grinned, pretending to enjoy the tea, finding it best to humour him until the Doctor and Ace arrived and she had numbers on her side.

'My name isn't Laura,' she pointed out. 'It's Bernice.'

'Cranleigh,' the man responded, grinning happily. 'My name,' he added, like a child trying to impress its parents with a newly learned scrap of knowledge. Benny nodded and made exaggerated gulping motions. Cranleigh was leaning forward towards her – not paying her much attention, but looking as if he was poised to spring if she made the wrong move. She resolved to be careful and moved lazily across the room to the bookcase, where she made a show of studying the titles on the spines.

Eliot, *Wuthering Heights*, *The Man In The Iron Mask*, Coleridge. Any moment now the Doctor and Ace would come down the passage looking for her, see the light, investigate. *Northanger Abbey*, *The Prisoner Of Zenda*, *To Kill A Mockingbird*, *The Condition Of Muzak*. She seemed to remember leaving the remains of the torch outside too; they couldn't ignore that. Lewis Carroll, *The*

Magician's Nephew, Blake, *Melmoth The Wanderer*. She glanced at Cranleigh, and a chill coursed through her body when she saw that he was absently toying with her torch. She returned her gaze to the books. *The Man Who Was Thursday, Foucault's Pendulum, The Dice Man*.

'They're left over from my days at university,' Cranleigh pointed out proudly. 'I did a couple for the degree.'

'Which university?' Bernice asked, running through the names on the spines. There was something reassuring about Cranleigh when he was talking, something unnerving about his silences.

'Cambridge, Laura,' he replied. 'Where we met!'

Suddenly Bernice preferred the silences.

'My name is *Bernice*,' she snapped. She fell silent – realizing that she could hear other voices. Distant and muffled but still distinct, the Doctor and Ace were calling her. Obviously they'd tired of waiting and had come searching. Their cries were hardly circumspect or inconspicuous. Benny found that oddly reassuring.

'You have friends,' Cranleigh said, cutting off Bernice's attempt to call back to them. He'd lost the cheerfulness and innocence. It was still a pleasant, even tone but suddenly dangerous. His mouth twitched into a humourless smile. He rose and crossed to the light switch.

The lights went out, plunging the room into gloom.

'Perhaps they won't find you. Just because you can see a door doesn't mean ... doesn't mean that anyone else will. Do you think?'

His loose movements were gone, swept away by a different set of dangerous, tense mannerisms. The new deep shadows of the room emphasized them. The stooped, almost hunched figure before her didn't seem entirely human any more.

'You're mad,' she said simply. There was no point in adding anything else. Mad said it all.

'I'm as sane as a hatter,' Cranleigh protested.

'You must be mad,' Bernice pointed out, trying to sound relaxed, aware that it wasn't working, 'if you think I'm not going to shout back.'

44

'Yes,' Cranleigh said, more a gesture of the lips than a sound. Then, suddenly, he moved. He threw himself forward, far quicker than Bernice had expected. He lunged at her, throwing her back against the bookcase. Caught off-balance in a shower of tumbling paperbacks, Bernice found herself pinned against the wall by Cranleigh's light bulk. He was a wiry man and Bernice realized that a well-timed shove could send him sprawling. She almost managed it.

Then he pressed the kitchen knife against her throat and she decided to keep very still indeed.

She had no idea where he had got the knife from, or when he had picked it up but frankly she didn't care. The fact of the knife was enough for her. There was no pressure – it barely touched her skin – and that was reassuring. He wasn't really trying to kill her, he just wanted her to be quiet. He was a loony with a knife, but maybe he wasn't really a violent loony. Maybe he was a good loony. Maybe he could be humoured.

No. The knife was there. It was brushing her skin, but it was enough. The thin sharpness of the blade against her neck was so light it tickled, but it might dig tighter at the slightest provocation. Cranleigh could kill her on the spot, given reason. He might not want to, but he could. And would.

Bernice froze. Discretion was the better part of valour, and if she was really discreet, she might get out of it alive. She hoped.

'There is a method by which the vocal cords of the subject may be severed without causing undue damage to the subject's person,' Cranleigh continued, voice as bland as the presenter of an archaeological documentary. Bernice had fallen asleep to voices like that, though none of the commentators had Cranleigh's advantage. 'This method is specialized. I'm not a medical man, and if I attempt it the result will probably be fatally messy. I don't want to make you dead; there are simpler methods of keeping you quiet. Understand?'

Bernice understood. The Doctor and Ace's shouts grew

louder. Benny closed her eyes and kept quiet, even when Ace yelled right outside the door. The volume of the cries gradually dropped away. Finally there was silence.

Dear diary, I'm up shit creek.

'Well now everything's hunky-dory,' Cranleigh said, smiling like a toddler. The knife remained bristling at Benny's throat.

4

Stairway to Heaven

'Up,' the Doctor decided. 'She must have gone up.'

Bernice had disappeared. The Doctor and Ace had expected to find her at the meeting point before them, her face a parody of impatience, ready with a joke about the failure of certain Time Lords to live up to their title.

She hadn't been there. After five minutes of waiting they decided to search for her. They'd agreed, jointly, that she wouldn't have gone back to the TARDIS while her curiosity was aroused, so it seemed probable that she'd forgotten her self-imposed time limit and was wandering round the passages somewhere, wrapped in her own thoughts. It was the sort of thing Benny would do.

Ace suspected that she'd walked straight into trouble. That was also the sort of thing Benny would do.

They'd followed the entire length of the main corridor – a plain, straight and unbroken passage. It was wrapped in cryptic darkness but was still unmistakably empty, devoid of human life in general and Benny in particular.

Ace started the shouting. The silence in the cellar was setting her teeth on edge. It was a death-silence, a well of noiselessness, as if the life had been sucked away, leaving only the shadows.

. . . *sucked out by that thing in the wardrobe* . . .

She tried telling herself that she wasn't scared, but she wasn't being honest. She could lie to other people but not to Ace. Why bother, she already knew the truth. At the moment the truth was that Ace was terrified. There were voices at the back of her head. Voices like the sound of finger-nails scraping down a blackboard. They weren't a comfort in the darkness; they tempered the silence with new inflexions. This house had a deeper power than any haunted venue from her childhood.

She had yelled suddenly. It made her feel better, and – who could tell? – maybe Benny would hear it. The Doctor hadn't liked it, suggesting that it might also attract the attention of any passing maniac. But he joined in eventually.

The oak panels of the passage gave way to exposed wooden beams, to the framework of a room – the bottom of a shaft that extended to the top of the building. It was a stairwell, tapering with perspective towards the distant roof. Countless wooden steps wound along the walls, escalating towards the heights of the attic. Even the dusky gloom that filled the shaft couldn't dispel the awesome sense of distance. It provoked an impressed whistle from Ace.

'Four storeys at least.' The Doctor craned upwards then turned to Ace, looking like a man with uncomfortable news to divulge. 'We've not passed Benny. She's not answered our hardly inconspicuous calls. And this is the only way she could have come. So . . .

'Up.' He aimed a finger roofwards. 'She must have gone up.'

Ace had already worked that one out.

'I think we should go after her,' she said after a moment's consideration. 'Go through the house one floor at a time. Keep a low profile. Could be risky, but it's better than abandoning Benny.' The Doctor was nodding his agreement.

'Whatever's going on here, Bernice has probably walked right into the heart of it by now. That curiosity's going to kill her.'

'Like the cat?' Ace asked, unable to help herself. Shit! Cliché!

'True, but that doesn't mean that curiosity isn't worth it,' the Doctor replied. 'Besides, I like cats. Shall we begin?'

48

'I'll take the first, you take the second, okay?' Ace suggested, and was taken off guard by the Doctor's scowl.

'No!' he snapped. 'Benny's an archaeologist – a scientist – she'd do this methodically. She'd start from the bottom and work up, or . . .'

'Start from the top and work down,' Ace interrupted impatiently. 'Right, one of us takes the top floor and works down. The other heads up from the ground. We'll meet in the middle.'

'It sounds simple, doesn't it?' The Doctor shrugged. 'I'll work up from the ground.'

'Hey,' Ace protested, 'it's going to take bloody years to get up top!'

'It was your idea,' the Doctor reminded her. 'Think of your reputation! You're not going to let a few flights of stairs daunt you? Besides, your legs are younger than mine.'

Ace shrugged and gave up. The Doctor smiled roguishly at her and bounded up the stairs, three steps at a time, to the first half-landing. There he stopped and turned round, eyebrows arched with curiosity. Ace followed him, preferring to stroll up a sturdy wooden ramp that took up half the width of the steps. She'd been like that as a kid – climbing the inclines rather than the stairs. It had always seemed more fun. Still did.

'What do you make of it?' the Doctor asked.

'Easy on the feet.'

'As a functional feature of the house?'

'Comes in handy if you're moving heavy gear up and down stairs?' she suggested, glancing at her feet. Judging by the criss-cross patterns of wheel tracks impressed on the wood, it was being used frequently, 'Maintenance work, a lot of it. Be a bastard getting a barrow up the stairs without it.'

Further up the steps sprouted a threadbare and tasteless carpet, its colours and patterns worn down into near-greyness by years of use.

'My mum had a carpet like that in her room,' Ace said. Strange how details like that stuck in her mind.

'Well, it accounts for your disturbed childhood,' the Doctor mused. Ace smiled strainedly, and began up the next flight of stairs. Might as well get a lead on the Doctor while she could.

'See you in the middle.'

'Ace,' the Doctor called, a sober inflection to his voice. 'This house is a dead place. I'd never forgive myself if any of us were to join it.'

Cranleigh's cell was buried in silence, punctuated only by the harsh, desperate sound of his breathing. To Bernice it seemed that he was more terrified than she was. She was a captive audience to his distraught, exaggerated mannerisms. Every twitch, every nervous shake of his head, his haggard stare – it was almost a performance. The knuckles of his knife-hand were white and trembling, and Benny was certain that he might start hacking away at her throat out of sheer panic. She remained calm and did nothing which might provoke him. One of her legs was going numb, but she didn't dare move it.

'It's okay,' Cranleigh said. 'They've given up on you.'

'They weren't good friends,' Benny risked a lie. If Cranleigh thought that the Doctor and Ace weren't going to put much effort into their search, it might calm him.

'You should get better ones.' Cranleigh stepped back. Benny relaxed.

But only slightly.

'Would you like me to kill you?'

'No.'

'Okay,' he nodded. He was still close and tense enough to launch himself at her at a moment's notice, but Benny took the opportunity to move around, shaking the blood back into her dulled leg. Cranleigh watched her warily, but he held the knife as though he wasn't entirely certain what it was for.

'Laura,' Cranleigh began. 'You don't mind if I call you Laura?'

'By all means.' Humour him, Benny. *Laura* it is. Why not?

'You can call me Justin. Justin Cranleigh – good name, good initials. Justin time. Justin case. Justin this. Justin that. Justin sane.' He giggled at a private joke. 'Me. A good name. If I was a girl, I'd have been called Kate. Kathryn with a "K". Like "Laura" but spelled differently.'

'My name is Laura,' Benny replied cautiously. 'So who am I?'

'Just a name on a list,' Cranleigh answered, a wistful quality in his voice. 'The girl in the room next to me, the same seminar as me. The attractive girl. A good friend. The girl going out with me tonight. My first serious girlfriend. An angel. A memory. Gone.'

'What happened to me?' 'Laura' continued with a sense of trepidation.

'You died,' Cranleigh said, his monotone unsullied by emotion. 'Suddenly but without pain, in your sleep.'

'I'm sorry.' Bernice dropped the imitation. It was too sad and personal, like wearing the clothes someone had died in. 'I'm not Laura. You just want me to be.'

Cranleigh nodded slowly, whispering as if he wasn't strong enough to manage anything louder.

'After she died, I think I went mad. I'm told I'm mad now. Everyone tells me now.' He was rambling but Benny clung on to every word. 'Different colours of madness. Now I'm living in a kaleidoscope. I see everything as red and green and purple. I can see things you can't see. I couldn't then; everything was a grey shade of madness. I hurt people, women, girls who thought I was looking for permanence, when all I wanted was a couple of nights. I couldn't hold onto them, could I?'

Benny shook her head noiselessly, unwilling to interrupt.

'After you there was only the one. The serious one. Lots of others, but only one serious.' He glared at Benny, daring her to challenge him. 'I wanted to let her go, but she almost died too. Well, I couldn't let her go, could I?! She was screwed up. So like you – pure, innocent, stupid and lovely. In every way like Laura. You understand?'

Bernice didn't, but she nodded anyway. It was the answer he expected.

'Okay,' Cranleigh said, sounding more rational than many others Benny had known. 'I confess my madness. The doctors tell me, but they lie. All doctors are liars. I'm not really insane at all,' he continued, leaving Benny to struggle with the contradiction. He leant forward and spoke in the voice of one revealing a terrible secret of the cosmos: 'I have been *spiritually ransacked*!'

'I don't believe it,' Benny replied, echoing her thoughts.

'It's true. True. True man. Tru-man. Truman. Truman. It's Truman,' he insisted, flexing his jaw earnestly. 'Watch out for him, for his face. Don't let him fool you.'

'Truman?' Bernice asked, even more lost than before.

'Truman's taken everything of mine and twisted it into his own. He's taken my life, my reason, my voice. He wants *her* too. I can see what he thinks. He wants to take her and use her in the same way I did, because she's mine. He'll have everything and I'll be a mindless husk of a body, howling for my lost marbles.'

Benny couldn't think of anything sensible to say.

'Mind you, he's going to have to die one day.' Cranleigh waved the knife meaningfully. 'Maybe I'll repossess him. Maybe it'll kill me. I don't know what happens. It's his face. That's the only part of him that isn't mine, you see. It's everything that he *is*. Not that you'll see it.' He gradually faded into total incoherence, words degenerating, becoming shapeless. Benny kept listening. She could almost hear the meanings – thoughts and imaginings spilling from his mouth as gibberish.

'Justin?' A new voice cut through his mutterings. The gentle but precise tones of a young woman.

'Oh my God!' Cranleigh jerked back to coherence, if not sanity. His eyes darted around, panicked, before settling on Bernice. 'It's her! Hide! She'll go mad if she catches us together.'

Not so much because we're together, Benny thought, more because I'm here at all.

'Hide!' Cranleigh hissed again, chewing at his knuckles.

Benny agreed – there was no point in giving herself, and the Doctor and Ace, away to any sane people. Where to hide though? The room was devoid of cover – unless she scrambled under the bed.

'Where?' she asked, urgently.

'Wardrobe.' Cranleigh pointed frantically at the doors he'd indicated earlier. Benny nodded. 'Take this.' Cranleigh pressed something into her hands. Benny nodded again and ran to the doors. They opened smoothly.

'Justin, let me in.' The voice was outside.

Benny pulled the doors closed after her, carefully leaving a gap small enough for light, air and eavesdropping. Once inside the cramped safety of the wardrobe, she relaxed. From outside came the sounds of the cell door opening and indistinct greetings. It sounded normal.

She glanced down and saw her fingers wound around Cranleigh's knife.

The knife he'd been holding to her throat.

She suddenly felt incredibly self-conscious and had to fight the urge to laugh uncontrollably. She thought of her childhood games of hide-and-seek when she would give herself away with a burst of stupid laughter. She'd grown into a teenager, the hiding became more serious and the giggling less sensible. She'd controlled the urge then. She managed to control it again, smothering it in the back of her throat.

The wardrobe became a shrine. A cubby-hole of desperate, holy hush broken only by the gentle beating of Benny's heart beneath her ribs. For a paranoid moment she felt certain that they could hear this outside.

She emptied her mind and tried to listen. This proved to be hopeless. Cranleigh and his girlfriend were having a heated and probably interesting conversation out there, but it was too low to hear. Cranleigh was a born mumbler and the woman's voice was soft, treating him as gently as possible.

The next thing she heard was a lengthy and passionate sound, filled with an obvious pleasure. Cranleigh and the newcomer *kissing* and taking a great deal of time about

53

it. Benny suddenly felt a stab of guilt. She was listening to something private and intimate and she felt dirty. She leaned back against a wall and waited for it to end.

It occurred to her that it might not end. Hadn't Cranleigh said something about this woman being his only 'serious' girlfriend? How serious, she wondered? What if they were meeting for something a little more intimate than a snog? If this woman was Cranleigh's lover they could be there all night. That was fine, she was happy for them, but it meant that she would have to spend the whole night hidden in the wardrobe. She was trapped by something more subtle than a maniac with a knife.

This was stupid. She got the urge to break down and laugh again. Good thing she hadn't hidden under the bed. No, it was serious.

She allowed her eyes and mind to wander. Both gravitated to the opposite wall, drawn by a dark irregularity in the texture of the wood. She leant forward, pulling away the piles of clothes which obscured the shapes, and uncovered a hole.

It was a hole into a lightless nowhere. Benny judged that she would be able to squeeze through with minimal difficulty. An escape route. A coincidence perhaps, but a wonderful one. Better than that – judging from the preponderance of yellowing brick visible through the hole beyond the wardrobe wood, it led into an area of the cellar similar to the place where she had left the TARDIS. Maybe even the same place. This wasn't mere coincidence. This was synchronicity!

She realized that the sounds outside had returned to mundane conversation. Conversation that was now just about audible.

'Wedderburn said he heard screams from the cellar today,' the woman was saying, her tones bordering on the maternal. 'Did you hurt yourself?'

'No.' Cranleigh's voice was less distinct. 'I heard them as well. It wasn't me. It was something else.'

'It couldn't be . . .' The maternal voice stopped. When the woman continued, she no longer addressed Cranleigh as a child but as an exasperated equal: 'Sometimes I find it very difficult to tell whether you're telling the truth, Justin. There is no one else down here.'

'There is!' Cranleigh blurted. 'There's a girl.'

Benny froze, shocked by the sudden betrayal. Five minutes ago, he'd been terrified that this woman would find her, but now . . . She realized that it was pointless to place trust in someone as confused as Cranleigh.

'There was a girl,' Cranleigh repeated.

'Yes,' the woman continued, as if stating an obvious truth, 'there's a girl now, but there wasn't before.' Benny's resigned pessimism stumbled. It seemed that she might go undetected after all.

'Not you. A real girl. In this room,' Cranleigh insisted. 'In the wardrobe.'

'In the wardrobe. Of course. Tell you what, I'll look in the wardrobe, and we'll see who's right shall we?'

Perhaps, Benny thought, I haven't got away with it after all.

Seconds later the wardrobe door was flung open and Benny caught her first glimpse of Cranleigh's girlfriend. A pretty woman, if not a beautiful one, with a light complexion and slightly chubby features that were both good-humoured and attractive. There was also a darker quality in those features that suggested deep, upsetting experience. If that had come about through a long period of contact with Cranleigh, Bernice could understand it. The woman's hair was long, dark brown and worn loose. It was also slightly damp and carried with it the faint smell of shampoo. There was something soft about her eyes, which Benny put down to the natural bemusement of finding a total stranger lurking, knife in hand, in your boyfriend's wardrobe.

Bernice smiled uncomfortably. The woman didn't smile back.

'You see,' the woman turned to address Cranleigh, 'There's no one here.'

Benny froze. The woman turned to take one last glance back into the wardrobe, her eyes met with Benny's for an instant. In that instant the woman seemed to see Benny for the first time, a flicker of realization crossing her face. Then the eyes parted and the recognition faded.

'You know,' the woman murmured, voice a little shakier, a little less certain, 'for a moment I thought . . .' She stopped herself and shook her head. 'There's no one there. Trust me.'

The door was closed and the wardrobe filled with darkness.

Okay Benny, two – no, three – possible explanations. She might be more of a headcase than he is: not implausible under the circumstances. This might be something devious – maybe this girl knows something.

Or maybe she hadn't noticed. That instant when their eyes met – *that* had been genuine. She had seen Bernice for that instant, then dismissed her as a figment of her imagination.

Whatever it was, she wanted to get out before the woman changed her mind and came back for another look. She tucked the knife carefully into her boot, then slipped into the hole. Even if it turned out to be a dead end, she could always turn back and risk a night of eavesdropping. The darkness was ominous but it offered escape.

She pushed forward into the gloom, imagining that she could hear voices ahead. No, not voices. Someone laughing. Giggling like a manic child.

The kitchen was little more than a scullery. It was a drab workspace tucked away behind a featureless door at the back of the house as if it was an embarrassment to the architect. From the look of things it was used as no more than a cupboard, a passage through to the back garden, a place to do the washing up.

But it *was* used.

The Doctor had spent some time wandering around the passages of the ground floor, following his nose. Close to the stairwell the passages had been draughty and functional, lacking carpets or even wallpaper. The further from the staircase he got, the better decorated the passages became. Furniture, pictures, ornaments adorned the warm corridors. Oak panels replaced bare plaster. The plain doors of the earlier section, cardboard-thin and covered in layers of flaking grey paint, gave way to heavy, elaborately decorated entrances of varnished oak.

The scullery was empty, but confirmed his feelings. The house was occupied. It was a home. Tins, cartons and boxes were stacked neatly in the cupboards; a pile of freshly washed plates was still dripping soapy water onto the draining board by the sink; fresh footprints stained the check-pattern lino; a half-empty mug of lukewarm coffee sat on the kitchen worktop beside a crumpled magazine: *Green Finger Tips Monthly* open to a well-thumbed page on cultivating exotic plants in a temperate climate.

The Doctor picked up the magazine and flicked through it. It was proof that this was someone's house and that he, and Benny and Ace, would be in trouble if they were caught.

How much trouble, he wondered? Perhaps it would be trouble with an ordinary householder, accompanied by a threat of petty but complicated legal action. Perhaps it would be trouble with the sort of people who could reach into the time vortex and snatch the TARDIS like a fairground game. Deciding that he'd rather avoid either, he dropped the magazine back onto the table and made for the door. Time to round up his accomplices. Ace first, since he had a vague idea of where she might be. Try to find Benny with a minimum amount of fuss. Get out of the house then return with some plausible story which might get them in legitimately.

Ace first.

Leaving the scullery he almost collided with one of the occupants. A man, dressed in a tweed suit and standing at the end of the passageway by a door. His back was turned to the Doctor, and the Time Lord was able to slip back into the scullery doorway and watch the man from a less conspicuous angle. The Doctor estimated that the man was in his mid-fifties, his white hair still flecked with grey and occasional flashes of black. Initially, the Doctor had thought that he was a short man, but he suddenly realized that the man was tall and stooping under the low ceiling. The man carried a parcel under one arm – brown paper, tied with string – and with his free hand he was trying to slot a key into the door's lock. His hand shook and it took several attempts for him to unlock the door. Casually, the Doctor noticed that the skin on the man's hand had a rich tan. His problems with the key over, the old man hastily pushed his way into the room, slamming the door shut after him. The key turned in the lock on the far side of the door.

Certain it was safe to emerge, the Doctor slipped down the passage to the door and stared at the inscription stencilled on it.

CONSERVATORY.

Someone was talking on the far side of the door – a strong voice, wavering slightly. It was just the one voice, never interrupted, never answered. Of course – he was talking to the plants! The Doctor moved away, slipping back to the staircase. He glanced upwards, his hearts falling at the sight of countless stairs rising towards the top floor. Unless Ace was anything less than meticulous in her search for Benny, that's where she'd be. And Ace had grown into a very meticulous young lady in the time he'd known her. He moved forward.

The stairwell above him unfolded. The roof of the building receded, accelerating into the distance until it became infinitely high, a shaft ascending into celestial heights. Steps still ran along the inside of the shaft, winding their way towards the infinitely distant roof. The Doctor could see no further than the thirtieth or fortieth storey. Real or illusory, it was a terrifying sight. The Doctor was reminded of the optical illusion staircase, winding to join its own tail; Ouroborous, the alchemical worm, incarnate as architecture; the Möbius staircase. The illusion, the visual deception fascinated him. But weren't there people pictured on that staircase? Miserable, ragged wretches condemned to tramp up those steps forever. It occurred to him that they would see something like this – infinite steps climbing towards an invisible vertex.

Light flared at the top of the infinite staircase, flickering like sheet lightning. A haze of glowing light hovered in the shaft, gradually expanding, gradually descending, slowly winding down towards the ground floor. The Doctor recognized a highly unstable spatial anomaly collapsing in his direction and decided that down was a safer bet. He belted down the single flight of steps to the cellar.

Bernice's mind was screaming a chorus of derision and delirium. Something sick and evil had got inside her head. It shrieked and howled, delving into her mind, picking out old memories, tearing open old wounds and fears. There were voices in her head and they burned. Her stomach was churning with nausea and her chest felt tight and trapped. She choked and retched, desperate to breathe.

She couldn't remember how it started. She'd been wandering lost in the darkness of the cellar. She'd found, she'd seen . . . no, she'd smelt it first – a sickly sweet scent of decay tainting the musty air. *Then* she'd stumbled right into . . . what? She couldn't remember, except for half-formed glimpses flashing between more pleasant thoughts.

Before she'd realized what it was, she'd stepped into it. She looked down and saw the mess on her legs, and . . . What? She'd freaked out. Had she been sick? It felt like it. And then, then . . . Something else found her. Lights at first, then voices, presences, slipping into her undefended mind.

Suddenly she was a teenager again, back at the school she'd hated, among people she'd hated. They all talked about it. Because they shouldn't send those sort of people into battle, the sort of people who'll turn and run at the sight of the bloody mutant dustbin bastards? But they've got the whole command structure in their pocket. Even cowards and traitors get their kids into military schools. Right? One person. One person in particular talked about it a little too loud. One person caught Benny's attention.

One person she'd almost murdered there and then. Her class-mate was lying comatose on the floor in front of her now, as she had done over half her lifetime earlier. She'd held back then, not entirely sure why. Compassion? Guilt? Given time to think, she might have carried on. Killed someone.

Now you have all the time in the world, Benny.

There was something sharp and hefty in her hands. A broken-off chair leg, one end a mass of shattered wood and splinters. She knelt down and drove the splintered end into her class-mate's face. Shattered skull. Brain damage. Death. A living human being turned, instantly, into an empty shell. The teenage Benny Summerfield – *do you realize what you've done* – stared into the dead, mangled face, and screamed.

Don't be so wet Benny, the voices told her. *You're pandering to your cultural programming.*

It wouldn't have taken much. A little more time, a little more pressure, and that could have been you. Bernice Summerfield – murderer. They would have executed you or sent you into war as Dalek fodder. Doesn't matter. Your guilt would have been the worst of it. Do you realize what you've done?

Who are you?

You, as you might have been. Your past is a kaleidoscope of wasted chances and missed paths. Watch.

They'd shown her a life of Bernice Summerfield as it might have been. If she'd not gone to Heaven; if she'd not met the Doctor; if her one and only serious love affair had worked out; if she'd had a family; if someone had found out about her 'professorship'; if she'd stuck out school and gone to war against the Daleks, or the Draconians; if her father had come home.

Then they showed her lies. Isaac Summerfield's face blanched with terror as the Dalek warship decloaks ahead of him, his voice screaming the orders to pull back into hyperspace, abandon his convoy; Claire Summerfield making love to the corps officer sent to inform her of Isaac's disappearance – Benny watching secretly, not understanding; the Doctor laughing as he destroys worlds, ignoring the pathetic pleading voice begging him to stop; Benny as a teenager sitting on a pile of corpses, swinging a bloodied chair leg.

Then they showed her an inalterable truth. A tiny, fragmented memory highlighted and repeated over and over again. Her mother screaming in the heart of an explosion, igniting like a slow-motion firework. Clothes and skin burning, sending a cloud of black smoke tapering into the atmosphere. Screams becoming howls becoming a terrible, pitiful moaning drowned out by the roar of the flames.

Bernice panicked. She plunged into the darkness of the cellar away from the hateful voices and the images they conjured up. She closed her eyes tight, trying to blank everything out. There was just the taste of blood in her mouth, the groaning, churning nausea in the pit of her stomach . . . But she could still *see* . . .

The door loomed out of the darkness in front of her, opening and closing in the draught. She crashed through, pushing herself up the steps beyond. Then she was outside, leaving the cellar, the voices and the images, the thing she had seen. The evening air, the clear drizzle was cool. Benny slumped against a wall of the house. She wanted to cry with relief. Cry or giggle, maybe both. She was free, outside and – thank God – it was over.

Someone touched her hand, lightly. She tensed and growled, throwing her arms in front of her face. It wasn't over. Not over at all. Plunging back down into despair . . .

Her arms were prised away from her face with a surprising gentleness. Benny blinked in the evening light, staring at the man in front of her. He was a man of average height and build, maybe in his mid-fifties, not particularly athletic. There was something ambiguous in his appearance that made it impossible to pin down details. He was wearing a shabby raincoat, a broad-brimmed hat perched on his head, his eyes were hidden behind an incongruous pair of dark glasses. There was nothing striking about his appearance. He was grey. Grey clothes, grey skin and a grey, gentle smile.

He extended a grey hand towards her. Benny took it gratefully then pitched forward into a delirious, psychedelic darkness.

5

The Atrocity Exhibition

'How are you feeling?' Sandra was asking. 'Any better?'

Justin Cranleigh was feeling better now than he had done for weeks. The pain of his madness had gone. The agonizing, endless headaches; the disjointed thoughts; the voices whispering on the edge of his consciousness. All gone, replaced by a clear head, sharp senses and peace. When he replied his voice was full of energy and confidence.

'Much better,' he said, pulling Sandra tighter into a hug and kissing her neck. 'It's your influence. You have healing hands. And lips. And thighs. Now we know what to do if I have a relapse.'

He froze, keeping Sandra's body locked in the embrace, content to feel the shape of her body through her dressing-gown. They hadn't done anything as close as this for almost two years, and Cranleigh wanted to savour every second. He moved to kiss her again but was disturbed by a nagging doubt at the back of his mind.

'How about you?' he asked. 'How are your eyes?'

'They're getting better,' Sandra said, her hand movements slowing to a limp halt. 'They've been fogged up really badly, but they're clearing again.'

'Can you see me?'

'Well enough,' she replied, placing a hand on the side of his face.

'I've been thinking.' Cranleigh tried to sound nonchalant. 'Neither of us are suffering from anything genetic, nothing hereditary, so why don't we try for a baby?'

The answer came from her hands.

They said *Yes*.

She smiled at him, lips curling, eyes hollow and dormant. Slowly, she began to shuck off her dressing-gown, baring her shoulders.

She hadn't changed in two years. Cranleigh could remember every inch of her body from the last time they'd made love, just before he'd begun the downward spiral into madness. The shape of her body, the texture of her skin, the things they'd said together – alone, in the dark. Everything was the same. She was still beautiful.

There was a small, metal crucifix hanging round her neck by a chain. The shape of the cross lay flat on her chest. An icon – Christ dying for his sins. It was *looking* at him.

What are you smiling for?

'Ignore me,' said the icon. 'I'm just hanging around.'

'Would you like me to take it off?' Sandra's voice seemed distant in contrast to the icon's clarity. Her hands reached for the chain.

Cranleigh's nerve went. He stepped away in alarm.

'I'm just going out for a breath of fresh air,' he said evenly. 'I may be some time. Don't start without me.' Sandra nodded dreamily and whispered something sensual. Cranleigh flashed a manic grin at her before darting to the door.

It's a crazy thing, he was telling himself, just a pre-coital glitch. It's been a long time, you're panicking. Spend five minutes wandering around, getting a grip on yourself. Then back here and get a grip on herself. Okay?

It wasn't okay. He was going mad again. Irrational desire to rush out of the room when you could be writhing on the bed with the girl of your dreams and some of your nightmares! *That* was mad.

Once outside, out of Sandra's view, he slumped against the wall and began to shake. He was sweating, breathing heavily. Needed to relax, calm down. Five minutes in the corridor and he'd be feeling better than ever.

The stranger appeared out of the darkness. A short,

dark-haired man with a lined, intense face. Devious eyes sparkled in deep sockets beneath a pair of bushy, black eyebrows. Dressed in a cream-coloured suit that almost shone. Careering down the passageway, without any care for silence or caution, he was the most conspicuous house-breaker Cranleigh had ever seen.

Feeling strength and sanity rushing back to him, he stepped into the path of the intruder. The man ground to a halt, shooting him an unnerving smile.

'Hello.' He had a distinct Scots accent. 'Delighted to meet you at last, you must be . . .?'

'Who are you?' Cranleigh snapped. 'What are you doing here?'

'Don't you know?' the Scottish voice continued smoothly, rattling off sentences at incredible speed. A consummate bluffer, this one. 'I arrived this evening, I'm a guest here and . . .' he trailed off, confronted by the scepticism in Cranleigh's eyes. 'I'm the Doctor. Don't ask for an explanation. You wouldn't believe it.'

'Cranleigh?' Another voice – smooth and familiar – came from the passageway behind him. 'What's going on? Who is this?'

Cranleigh turned slightly, keeping a wary eye on the intruder.

Harry Truman stood further down the passage, wearing an immaculate dinner-jacket – the closest thing he had to a uniform. He was laden with expensive video equipment and Cranleigh immediately guessed what he'd been doing. Trust *him* to come out unscathed and sane as a house brick! Not that he could show much with his features hidden by that ugly, leering mask.

'Harry, I've just . . .' Cranleigh began, before his sanity collapsed.

The relapse came without warning. Suddenly his head was screaming at him. An insect buzzing filled his ears and his vision broke up, fracturing into a thousand – no, infinite – pieces. The mask leered at him, laughing. Giggling and shrieking and howling like a thing possessed. Laughing at him. At his madness. The mask. Truman.

Cranleigh screamed. He launched himself at the man in the dinner-jacket, determined to wrench the mask from Truman's face. Put it on the floor and stamp on it. Crush it the same way that Truman had crushed him. Truman was everything. Truman's mask was everything. His enemy, at the centre of his world. The Doctor slipped from his memory.

In the long run there was only Truman.

Cranleigh smashed against Truman, sending both reeling. Truman was a larger, stronger man and Cranleigh simply hadn't the strength to knock him over entirely. But he was tottering, cradling his video camera like a baby. Seeing his enemy defenceless and off-balance, Cranleigh leapt again, lunging at Truman's mask, trying to dig his fingers into the eye sockets, wrench it away, see the real face of the real enemy.

Behind them, the Doctor slipped away, back towards the stairs. Cranleigh neither knew nor cared.

Ace had seen a small part of the house but she could tell that it was bloody weird. She'd been scouring the passageways for Bernice, mapping out a floor plan in her head. It would come in useful when she explored some of the lower levels. The problem was . . .

The problem was that, though she knew she was branching out and exploring new ground, it looked as if she was going round in circles. She'd head off down a corridor which she knew led to a blank in her mental map, only to find herself in a part of the building which she had explored before. She'd wander into a room already searched, which should be on the other side of the house. Finding herself back at the stairwell, she decided to walk in an unbroken straight line until she reached the house wall. She ended up back at the stairs.

Well weird. No wonder Benny was lost.

Most of the rooms she'd seen were decorated. Bedrooms, a living room, a study, a cramped bathroom. Proof that this was someone's home. Ace didn't worry about it.

So long as she was careful she wouldn't get caught. And she was careful.

This latest room was new to her. It was a nursery. A tiny room crushed into a corner of the house. The room was darkening – evening gloom filtering through a stained-glass window that was set high in one wall. The window was covered in a screen of cobwebs, but was still beautiful, its colours undiminished by time. Evidently the room hadn't been used for years; the furniture was buried under a fine layer of dust; the air was musty and still; complex cobweb patterns accumulated in the corners. There probably hadn't been any children in this house for a long time. Despite this, the room was preserved – furniture, toys, books, a cot and everything – probably the same as it had been for decades. A mobile hung from the ceiling, its movement clogged by web. A pile of threadbare dolls and teddy bears sat in the cot, glaring at Ace with glass eyeballs. An elegant rocking-horse gathered dust in a corner, beside a derelict doll's house. A chart was nailed to the wall – A for apple, B for baby. Kid's stuff. Someone trying to hang onto their past.

Ace had hated being a kid, but felt a sudden pang of nostalgia for a less complicated time, for something she'd lost. Then she felt a shiver of apprehension, as if something terrible and tragic had once happened in this room. Something that couldn't bear being disturbed.

The silence was broken by a light giggle. The sound of a young girl playing. It was too perfect, too stilted to be natural. It was like an old, worn tape-recording. Disembodied laughter. Ace wheeled slowly, casting around for the sound.

The window. It was coming from the window, which was now looking much cleaner than it had done before. The cobwebs were gone, melted away, and the glass was . . . moving.

The colours of the glass were swirling in a lazy, whirlpool motion, bleeding into each other, forming shapes. Figures, landscapes, profiles. The giggling grew louder as the colours began to swirl faster. The effect was hypnotic,

67

Ace watched warily. Suddenly the colour drained out of the window entirely. The glass darkened, deepened, emptied. The window became black. Ace's features reflected starkly on the dark surface.

Ace watched it closely before realizing that nothing more was going to happen. Not yet. Not while she was there. She slipped back into the passage, making a note of the nursery's position on her mental map. She'd be back.

There were sculptures in the cellar. Two vaguely man-shaped figures standing upright in the darkness. Both statues were half-finished, their shells broken with cavities or missing limbs or parts of the head.

The lights buzzed around the sculptures, refining their creations. They were making good progress. Bernice had proved an amusing diversion, but it hadn't slowed the sculpting. The structures would be finished within an hour.

As they worked, they communed. The occupants of the house, the time travellers, all offered ample variety – but there was a need for flavouring. A disruptive element. A random particle. *Yes.*

Suddenly Jane Page was lying face down on the ground, her hair filthy with mud and her head groaning with pain. For a moment she didn't want to move. She wanted to lie still and die. Not an auspicious place to go, but better than in bed.

Eventually the pain subsided and she staggered to her feet. She was surprised by how stiff she felt – as if she hadn't moved for years – and though the headache had gone, there was now an incomprehensible song playing in her head.

Maybe when she fell over she'd hit her head and tuned herself in to a pirate radio station. She did her best to ignore it, wiping the mud from her hair and wondering how the hell she had managed to fall over in the first place.

She couldn't remember. It was all blank, which was not

good. She'd got into a fight in Liechtenstein six weeks earlier, been beaten up pretty badly. She'd passed the medical afterwards, but what if this was something long-term? What if she had memory loss for the rest of her life? Her career was screwed!

That reminded her. From the look of things, this was the woods around the enemy's house. This path she was on, she remembered, eventually joined up with a lane leading to his front door.

She pulled open her trench-coat and reached inside, fingers brushing against the reassuring square shape tucked under her shoulder. Good. Should be an easy one. Guy was a cripple, wasn't he? She pulled the shape from its holster in readiness. It was the right weight in her hand. She tightened her coat against the rain and set off, humming an accompaniment to the song in her head. It had begun to repeat itself.

The man in grey was shambling up the hill to the woods. From a distance, he would have seemed almost invisible in the deepening darkness. If they were concentrating, watchers might pick out a patch of artificial grey moving against the hillside, but little more than that.

In a darkened room at the back of the house someone was watching the grey man. They stared through cold binocular lenses. Their vision wasn't perfect, but they could see far closer, in greater detail, than would be apparent to the naked eye.

The watcher's vigil was interrupted by a voice from the doorway, the creamy tones of Harry Truman. He'd burst into the room without knocking, something he only did rarely. The watcher turned slowly.

'What was it like?' his voice was soft.

'Boring. Lots of empty white spaces,' Truman replied. He tapped at the camera he was cuddling. 'I doubt the tape's going to be very exciting, sir.'

'I'll watch it anyway.' The watcher absorbed the brief account. 'Leave it on the table.

'He's back,' Truman's employer continued evenly. 'The

man in grey. I've just seen him up on the hill. I wonder what he wants?'

Truman looked up sharply, as sharp as his mask could convey.

'I should have told you earlier,' he said, voice fluctuating and full of unease, 'Cranleigh caught a burglar. Then let him go again,' he added lamely.

'When and where?' the watcher asked calmly.

'The cellar, five minutes ago. He could be out of the house by now.'

'But he might still be inside,' the watcher responded, gliding forward to examine the video equipment. 'Did he seem violent?'

'He looked as if he'd fall over in a breeze. He's very conspicuous too. Cranleigh and I'll go after him.'

'Cranleigh?' the watcher frowned. 'Okay, but be on your guard. He might not look dangerous, but ... you know. And keep an eye on Cranleigh.'

Truman withdrew. The watcher scrabbled at the video, punching impatiently at the eject button. The cassette hatch swung open smoothly, revealing a melted mess of plastic where the tape should have been. The watcher placed a tentative finger on the shapeless lump, then pulled it back hastily. The remains of the tape were cool but fluid, and a perfect fingerprint was now impressed onto its side.

The grey man had reached into the woman's mind and closed off those areas of her memory causing her distress. When she woke, she would forget. The memories would return slowly. They would disturb but not panic her. He decided against taking her into the house, preferring to leave her, sheltered from the rain, by the conservatory door. Certain she was safe, he withdrew to his vantage point on the hill.

The last time he had approached the house, he had blundered badly. He had allowed his instincts to draw him into the conflict too early. He had wandered in without preparation, without thinking, without any real knowledge of the beings inside. He had gained nothing.

This time he would be cautious. He would wait and watch. Something would happen eventually, he had introduced instabilities into the situation which might force a reaction.

He frowned and turned away from the house. Something was happening, but it was coming from the woods rather than the house. A *shape* was moving through the trees. Its path was erratic, but nevertheless it was clearly moving towards the house.

The shape was *wrong*. It didn't belong. It didn't fit into the architecture of the cosmos as it should be. As it moved the universe jarred around it, like the creatures in the cellar, except that it had physical presence. And where the lights had been negative, this was positive.

No. Not positive. Neutral, perhaps?

The grey man stepped forward to meet it.

It looked human. No, it *was* human. A woman in her mid-twenties. Dark-haired, wearing a tight, black trench-coat. Where the man was invisible in the evening gloom, this woman looked like a tear in the fabric of the night.

The man raised a hand and called to her:

'Stop. You should not . . .'

He got no further. The woman shot him through the head, killing him outright.

When his two captors launched into their inexplicable fight, the Doctor's initial instinct was to run. Not a clever move, he realized as he hurtled down the cellar passage. He might have bluffed his way through it – as it was, the house would be on the look-out for him within minutes.

The anomaly had gone. The stairs were normal again. The Doctor paused for breath, but a glance back down the corridor persuaded him to keep moving. The two men had stopped fighting and were careering after him. They weren't moving very fast admittedly – the young man was shambling as if he'd forgotten how his legs worked, while the masked man was laden with video equipment – but they'd catch him if he tarried.

He bounded up the stairs back onto the ground floor.

His immediate plan was simple. Get out of the house, out of the grounds. Then he could stop and take stock of the situation. There was a door in the scullery, if he could reach there.

He turned a corner and almost crashed into a man, the old man he'd seen earlier. He was, as the Doctor suspected, a tall man stooping in the low passageway. His features were worn with the passing of time, but his body was still lean and athletic. The ageing process had been kind to him. His skin was tanned, contrasting with his neat shock of white hair. He stared at the Doctor, eyes reflecting confusion and wariness.

'Hello,' the Doctor rattled before the man had a chance to speak, 'I'm the Doctor.'

'Doctor?' The man's face lightened, almost with recognition. He smiled and extended a hand. The Doctor took it, guardedly. The man had a strong grip.

'Wedderburn,' he said simply, in a vague London accent. The Doctor raised an eyebrow questioningly. 'Charles Moore Wedderburn. Ah, of course, it isn't me you're interested in.'

'It isn't,' the Doctor replied, voice neutral.

'You *are* one of Keightley's mob?' Wedderburn went off at a conversational tangent. 'Up from Cambridge to see how the whizz-kid's doing? Not much of a kid nowadays. Not so much whizz either!' Wedderburn laughed. The Doctor felt obliged to join in.

'I'm afraid I wandered off,' the Doctor said, avoiding a total lie. 'I seem to have lost myself.'

'Ah,' Wedderburn nodded knowingly. 'That's to be expected. One of the side-effects. But you'll know about that.' He drew the Doctor aside and pointed to the door of what the Doctor recognized to be the scullery. 'There's a kitchen down there. I'm just locking up, so why don't you pop along and put the kettle on. I won't be a minute.'

The Doctor strolled towards the scullery. A snatched

glance over his shoulder proved that Wedderburn really was locking up. He had been accepted as genuine.

A genuine *what*, he wondered.

The old man had changed since the Doctor saw him last. His movements were easier. When he'd opened the door, he'd been fumbling, his hands shaking. The Doctor put it down to age or a muscular complaint. Arthritis, maybe? Wedderburn's smooth movements belied that impression.

The kettle was warming up as Wedderburn returned, apparently still convinced of the Doctor's integrity. He seemed harmless enough, offering tea and conversation. He could turn out to be a mine of information, and maybe an ally.

The kettle began to scream. Wedderburn took it off the boil.

'Well,' he said. 'Let's talk about Winterdawn.'

The song wasn't budging, but Page was learning to live with it. She'd indulged in target practice on her way down – some old tramp nobody would miss – and found that she was still accurate. She'd slipped the gun away as she entered the grounds of the house.

There was no point to subtlety. Go through the front door.

It loomed before her. A great slab of oak masquerading as a door, decorated in brass. She stabbed the doorbell and was pleased to hear the sound of a simple bell. Nothing tasteless. No tinny attempts to mimic the national anthem.

She huddled in the porch, singing to drown out the bloody awful song.

'The bells of Hell go ting-a-ling-ling for you but not for me.'

The door was opened by a woman. Mid-twenties, Page estimated. She stared at the newcomer with big, round baby eyes. She was wearing nothing more than a plain dressing-gown, showing slightly more cleavage than Page would have been comfortable with, clearly been thrown

73

on hastily; Page felt a tingle of satisfaction as she realized that she might have interrupted a moment of special intimacy.

'Hello?'

'Avon calling.' Page punched her smartly across the jaw. The woman crumpled. Page stepped through the door, across the body.

That was the easy part. Now. Winterdawn.

Ace was sticking close to the nursery. She wanted to be where the weird stuff was happening. Since she was also supposed to be searching for Benny she couldn't waste time hanging round for the next bout, or for the Doctor to put in an appearance, so she decided to look round the rooms nearby. Fingers crossed the architecture wasn't about to do another double-take.

The first she searched turned out to be a store-room. No sign of Benny, perhaps, but still interesting.

The room was large and undecorated, its walls painted an ugly shade of military grey. Dust was everywhere. The atmosphere wasn't as tight or as heavy here as it had been in the children's room. There were no imposing stained-glass windows, just a normal skylight. This *was* turning black, but only with the onset of night. Furniture, ornaments and decorations were all hidden under white dust-sheets, the exception being a cabinet in the heart of the room. It was an ordinary mahogany box, decorated in a vaguely oriental style – stylized dragons were etched into the metalwork. It sat smugly, whispering two simple words; *valuable antique.*

Ace threw open the valuable antique, half-expecting a blaze of light to emerge and consume her. It failed to materialize. The cabinet was empty. It was just a box, smaller inside than out. Ace lost interest in it and began to inspect the rest of the items on offer. Sheets were pulled away with a flourish, revealing other antiques. Furniture, statuettes, ornaments, stacks of paintings; Ace thought they were nothing special. But hidden amongst the ordinary junk, there were more interesting things.

74

The first was a plant. It didn't seem unusual at first, but gradually it clicked with Ace that it wasn't ordinary. It wasn't a Perivale household plant, it was tropical, buried under a sheet in an unheated room, and it was *thriving*. It was exotic even by tropical standards. Its blooms were a riot of colour – purple, yellow, blue, orange – erupting from all angles of the stalk. Its patterns were chaotic and zig-zagging rather than elegant or intricately repetitive. The stalk was thick and twisted, growing upwards in a spiral. There were other plants, but none were identical. Each was unique.

There were insects – dead where the plants were alive. They were buried under glass, graves marked by index-card epitaphs. The handwriting on the cards was near illegible but seemed to consist of names, dates and lists of unique characteristics. No two insects were the same; they were deformed. Nature had been over-generous to most, bestowing extra wings, limbs or heads. Others were less fortunate: wingless, legless or – Ace's skin crawled – headless. Ace almost dropped the display case out of nauseous disgust.

There was something worse; a stuffed animal, a rodent. When she first saw it, Ace thought there were two, both mounted on the same stand, but there was just one. It had two bodies, one growing out of the stomach of the other.

Ace wanted to get out. An irrational desire – the animal and the insects were dead; in life they would have been harmless. But still she felt sickened. Benny wasn't here obviously, and the Doctor would be fascinated by this stuff. Ace couldn't see any connections yet, but she'd lay odds that the Doctor would. She turned towards the door.

The antique cabinet burst open without warning. Something emerged, seven feet tall, alien. Something that was simply too big to fit, that hadn't been there when Ace had looked. Something thrusting between Ace and the exit. It was a bloody great insect. The fine hairs that covered its body were twitching, its complex mesh of wings folding and unfolding on its back, antennae flailing.

It was *agitated*. Ace's face was reflected a thousand times in its compound eyes. Ace watched it unfold before her, scrutinizing it with a mixture of revulsion and caution.

The creature reared up and lurched towards her.

Benny woke to find holes in her memory. She remembered leaving Cranleigh and his girlfriend to their own devices, crawling into the cellar, then . . . blank. In the cellar there had been . . . something evil, something that should have been etched into her memory.

It wasn't. The thoughts had been stolen.

She remembered a man. A man in grey, she'd met outside the house. She'd collapsed, drifting in and out of consciousness. Snatches of the man's intonations echoed in her skull, meanings eluding her. Now she was safe and well with half her mind missing and a headache the size of the Draconian empire in its place.

She was sandwiched into a corner where the wall of the house met a wall of glass – an extension beyond the boundaries of the house. Inside was gloomy, but she made out overgrown vegetation shapes silhouetted against the glass. It was a conservatory, with a door not two feet from her. She could get in without going through the cellar. She couldn't face the cellar alone again. She'd find the Doctor and Ace. This required a team effort.

She got up, opened the glass door and plunged into the undergrowth.

Winterdawn. The Doctor found a name that went with the house. Professor Jeremy Winterdawn. Wedderburn implied that he was as famous in scientific circles as C. Moore Wedderburn was in botanical circles. The Doctor nodded patiently, sipping his tea.

Wedderburn imagined the Doctor was a colleague of Winterdawn's, come to check his progress. The Doctor waited patiently for further elaboration that never came. Wedderburn assumed that he knew everything already.

'How long have you known Professor Winterdawn?'

the Doctor asked politely, contemplating the unfortunately low level of tea left in his mug.

'Since childhood. We were at school together,' Wedderburn explained, helping himself to biscuits. 'We both ended up in science. Physics for him, botany for me. We stayed in touch. It was Winterdawn who persuaded his college – your college of course – to fund my American jaunts.'

'Botanical expeditions?' the Doctor questioned. The tea level approached the dregs.

'The one true faith. I was an environmental crusader. Partly, I wanted to see the rainforests while they were there. The research element was a part . . .'

'And publicity?' the Doctor asked smoothly.

'Was the main reason.' Wedderburn's face lit with enthusiasm. 'It worked too. We made an impact. Not great, but still a hit. That was the serious part of the expeditions. The research was good, it turned up some fascinating uncatalogued species and mutant strains. But the important work was getting people to understand what was happening. It still is now.'

'You're not angling for a grant, are you?' the Doctor asked, getting into the feel of his role.

'No.' Wedderburn smiled ruefully. He was a compulsive smiler. 'I'm too old. I'll be dead when the last tree goes. Hypocrite that I am, I've lost the will to fight.'

'There are others,' the Doctor said, encouragingly. Wedderburn nodded, but didn't reply.

'I've never actually met Professor Winterdawn. I know him by reputation,' the Doctor ventured, lying easily. 'I've only recently joined Professor Keightley's team. And I don't quite understand why he isn't working at Cambridge.'

'Well, after the accident . . .'

'Accident?'

'Keightley didn't tell you?' Wedderburn clicked his tongue in mock irritation. 'There was an accident five years ago. A domestic – a car crash. Jeremy and Jenny were driven off the road by some maniac. *She* went through the windscreen. *He* survived, just about. The moment he came out of hospital he handed over all his research to Keightley and took off. Resigned his seat, came back here. It was Jenny's family's house, but she'd left it to him.'

'But he's still working for them, for us . . .'

'Keightley – stubborn female that she is – talked him round,' Wedderburn explained. 'Besides, his private research into the Thascales theorem uncovered a few things that set his mind racing. He's a freelance. All unofficial, that's why the mailing company was set up.'

'Mailing company?' the Doctor echoed.

'Don't you know?' Wedderburn's eyes narrowed, the first signs of suspicion nurturing. 'You should.'

'I'm easily confused.'

'You're a quantum physicist. It's an occupational hazard.'

The Doctor changed the subject before Wedderburn's doubts could grow.

'Tell me about some of the others here,' he asked. 'I saw a man earlier – I didn't have time to catch up with him. Tall, wears a mask, carries a lot of electronic equipment around with him?'

'That's Harry Truman. More tea?' Wedderburn asked, receiving a nod. 'He's a sort of all-purpose, resident . . .'

Wedderburn's sentence was cut short by a shrill yell from the corridor. A choked expletive turning rapidly into a scream, not of fear but of pain. The Doctor recognized the voice.

Bernice Summerfield.

6

The Man in the High Castle

The darkness *changed*. Where the first darkness had been
a vast emptiness, the new dark was crushing, claustrophobic. Qxeleq could feel the walls. She could feel her body.
She could *feel*! All her built-up fears and frustrations
resolved themselves into one massive physical effort – a
thrust of wings and antennae, hammering against the
edges of her prison.

She exploded into the light. Light – stark and artificial
– but light all the same and pleasant to her eyes. It illumin-
ated a bizarre room, unlike anything from the world
Qxeleq had known. It was too angular, lacking the graceful, soaring curves of the hive-structure buildings. The low
ceiling left barely enough room to hover. The floor was
covered in objects of a wholly incomprehensible nature.
Portable murals on stretched frames; grotesque models;
boxes filled with a hundred esoteric items. Many defied
description.

Qxeleq saw that she wasn't alone. A creature prowled
on the edge of her senses – not one that had ever belonged
to the Mind. It was mammal. Qxeleq didn't share the
squeamish antipathy to these animals felt by so many in
the Hive, but this one here made her stomachs turn.

It was one of the kind that stood upright on its hind
'legs' – Qxeleq's friend Xzhara kept a couple as pets, but
this was twice the size and hairless – except for a clump
of strands sprouting from its head. Qxeleq had never
learned how to differentiate genders, but she instinctively

felt that this one was a female. Its body was covered by interwoven, rigid cloaks.

In contrast to Qxeleq's own cloaklessness, this mammal was *clothed*.

Qxeleq had been abandoned alone in a terrible, unfamiliar environment. She understood nothing, everything terrified her. In the heart of this insanity, she was presented with this sick caricature of normalcy. A mammal cloaked, mocking her. Disgusted, she hurled her full weight at the diminutive figure.

Until now the mammal had watched Qxeleq with repressed hostility. Under attack, she moved. Moved *fast*. She was smaller, more agile, better constructed for fighting than Qxeleq. She had the advantage of speed, but Qxeleq was stronger and obviously the more intelligent of the two.

The mammal took the initiative, slamming her body against Qxeleq's brittle shell. Dull pain echoed through her body – an irritant rather than a real blow. The mammal thrashed wildly against Qxeleq's hide. Pointless. Naked she was, but her body was naturally armoured. She took the offensive, digging her antennae into the mammal's skin and clothes, seizing its head between her jaws. Crush the skull, twist the head off. Squeeze.

The mammal, sensing imminent death, began to beat at Qxeleq wildly. Flailing punches, stupid blows. Qxeleq didn't care. Squeeze and squeeze and squeeze and . . .

Suddenly there were a hundred limbs descending towards her head. A hundred fists merged into one blow striking her left eye. A million optic nerves shrieked. Pain coursed through her head. She howled in agony, released her grip on the mammal's head, hurling the creature across the room like a toy. The mammal's body smashed into a pile of boxes on the far side of the room. Then she lay still.

The pain seared the left-limb side of her face. Her vision had become blurred, chaotic fragments. Instinctively she began to stretch her wings – to fly away, escape into the hiveroof – before realizing how useless it would be in this *cupboard*. She wanted to leave. Run away somewhere where the pain would die.

The darkness was before her. Qxeleq embraced it.

Then there was no pain.

Ace scrambled back to her feet and her senses. Her ribs were tender and bruised, there was a blood taste on her lips, but there was nothing broken. That was luck, she realized with a hint of self-loathing. The insect might have been slow – and Ace was the one packing the brains and human ingenuity – but it had been a big bastard, armoured like a tank, vicious with it. Given enough time it could have taken her apart. She'd been lucky hitting the eye, wounding it. It was crawling back into the cabinet – retreating to its hole. Satisfied it was completely inside, Ace leapt forward, slamming herself against the doors, trapping it.

There was no pressure on the doors, no resistance from inside. Not now, but that didn't mean it wouldn't get hungry again. She wanted to avoid another fight if she could help it – no point in getting her head torn off for nothing – so she cast round the room for something to jam the cabinet shut. Questions formed in her mind, irritating questions without simple answers. Where had the insect come from? It was too bloody big to fit inside comfortably, maybe the cabinet was at the wrong end of a transmat gate? Maybe it was dimensionally transcendental? Where did it fit with the other weird shit? There had to be a link. Somewhere.

A voice broke into her train of thought. Smooth, resonant, disdainful.

'Perhaps it's the burglar season, Cranleigh. We seem to be suffering from a plague of them. Maybe we should set traps?'

It came from the doorway. Careful to keep her back pressed against the cabinet, Ace craned forward to see the newcomer. A tall man in a dinner-jacket with a grotesque blank for a face. It was grinning perversely, but the eyes behind the mask were glaring with contempt.

Behind him, a second man – casually dressed, casually attractive. He too stared at Ace, without the obvious disgust of his masked colleague, without any emotion whatsoever. His body was hunched and twisting, as if he was forcing himself to seem small.

'Come away from the wardrobe. Keep your arms by your sides,' the masked man ordered, not bothering to look at her. As if she wasn't at all important. She disliked his manner immediately, and shook her head in defiance.

'I'm warning you,' he continued, bored, 'my friend is a dangerous psychotic who could rend you limb from limb at the slightest provocation.' Ace's eyes flicked automatically to the second man, who smiled meekly, avoiding eye contact.

'What planet're you from?' she growled at the mask.

'Move away,' the mask repeated, 'slowly.'

'You're in charge here,' Ace continued in a low, dangerous voice. 'You're behind all this. You know exactly what's going on, don't you?'

The mask said nothing.

'People who wear masks,' Ace continued, her temper slipping into her voice, 'have something to hide.'

Still nothing.

'I know what's in this box,' she yelled. 'We know everything you're up to. Me and the Doctor, we're going to sort you out!'

'The Doctor?' the voice asked lightly, mask cocked to an angle, so that he was looking directly at her. Ace bit her lip, realizing what she'd given away.

'That was the man in the corridor.' Mumblings from the dangerous psycho. 'That was his name. His name that was his. Name his that was. What his name that? Wame nat hos.'

'So what's in the box?' The mask's tones were smooth and goading. Calling her bluff. She could deal with that.

'Insect.' Ace tried to sound nonchalant. 'Don't think I haven't seen it. Freak. Monster. Bit like you.'

The mask said nothing for a while.

'Original, but hardly plausible,' he said, finally, moving

towards her. Ace slipped into a defensive posture, glaring aggressively.

'Don't,' she warned, 'come,' (he wasn't listening), 'any,' (still coming), 'closer!' She smashed a fist into his stomach. The mask reeled – not as much as Ace hoped. She'd misjudged the . . .

An arm smashed across her face. A knee embedded itself in her stomach. She bent double, collapsing to the floor in agony, nose bleeding. It hurt. The masked man was quick. He'd lashed out with a force that came hand-in-hand with pleasure. Under normal circumstances Ace would leap up and castrate him with her bare hands. Normal circumstances didn't involve giant insects trying to unscrew her head – she didn't want another fight now. She'd lose, for one thing. So she lay still, waiting for the pain to subside.

'Let's see the monster, shall we?' The mask flung open the cabinet doors with a flourish.

The cabinet was empty.

'What a shocking waste of space.' The doors slammed. The blank non-features of the mask swam into view, leering down at Ace. 'Get up.'

Ace made an act of standing up, glaring at her attacker. It was the only resistance she felt able to put up. That and a contemptuous dismissal, spat through clenched teeth.

'I was wrong – you're not in charge. You're a hired thug.'

'Ladies first,' the mask said wearily, indicating the door.

Cranleigh lingered after Truman had taken the burglar away. There was something about the woman's story that struck a chord. Monsters living in cabinets, like a dream he'd once had, or a story he'd heard. He stole over to the cabinet, placing shaking hands on the handles.

The woman had been lying. The box was empty. He'd seen it. But there was a part of him that wanted another look, desperately wishing the story to be true. He pulled at the doors, certain of disappointment.

He stared into the cabinet, into two vastly complex

compound eyes. The eyes of a monster. Grey and pink and massive, wings and tendrils, mandibles, antennae, exoskeleton like leather. A monster to end all monsters, living in his attic. The stories were true. Thank God.

Cranleigh gazed at the monster dreamily. A part of him was so happy it wanted to kiss the creature below that beautiful, infinite eye. The rest screamed, slammed the doors and fled from the room.

By the time the Doctor reached the conservatory door the yells had stopped. It didn't matter. This was where the sound had come from. This was where Bernice Summerfield was.

The door was locked.

Wedderburn was heading towards him, not walking as such, but without the urgency that he felt the situation entailed.

'Open the door!' he snapped.

'I . . .'

'Are you going to open the door, or am I going to force it?' he roared, bristling with impatience. Despite his bluster, he was still carefully observant. Wedderburn was stalling, deliberately trying to slow him down. Not out of malice, perhaps.

'I . . .' Wedderburn stalled again. The Doctor dismissed him from his thoughts and turned to the door. More haste was needed, less subtlety. A sharp application of pressure just . . . there. He kicked the door to one side of the lock. Wood cracked, splintered and gave way. The door swung open with a modest creak and the Doctor flung himself into the room.

The air of the conservatory was heavy with the scent of chlorophyll, the light suffused green. The floor was covered in steaming hot vegetation, growing from deep earth trays. The walls were hidden behind moist tendrils. The conservatory was sweltering – Wedderburn wasn't sparing his heating bill. He had recreated the Amazon in miniature. His own tiny piece of paradise.

The comatose body of Bernice Summerfield lay

slumped on the edge of Eden, half-obscured by ankle-deep greenery. The plants around her were writhing. They were orchids – larger than average and coloured white, brown and grey – and *moving*, thrashing about on thick but flexible stalks. A few bell-shaped heads bobbed up as the Doctor approached, guilty children watching a teacher bear down on them. Others ignored him, craning forward to get closer to the body.

Limp tendrils extended from the heads of the plants, attaching themselves to Benny's exposed flesh, clustering around her neck and wrists, jostling for positions like suckling animals. Each tendril twisted and throbbed as something pink and liquid coursed through them. Benny's skin was chalky white. The Doctor abandoned caution and smashed his way across the room towards his companion.

'Break the feeding lines,' Wedderburn called. 'Try not to damage any of the flowers.' The Doctor barely heard. He reached Benny, seized a clump of tendrils in his fist, wrenched at them. The lines remained firmly attached to Benny's skin. A cluster of orchids surged forward, spitting more tendrils at him. They lashed at his face, nuzzling round his neck. There was a sharp pain as one managed to break the skin. He ignored the discomfort and concentrated on Benny, tearing at a single tendril until it snapped. Blood fountained from the severed end, spilling down his shirt, leaving a pink, sticky stain. It was far too much to be healthy.

'Leeches!' he yelled, redoubling his efforts. More tendrils were broken, more blood spilled. The broken lines plugged straight back into Benny's bloodstream.

'Doctor!' Wedderburn yelled. 'Pull her clear, *now*!'

Something heavy and wet landed in the next flower bed, others followed, slapping down in the midst of the orchids themselves. The plants stopped suddenly, as if considering. The Doctor seized the opportunity, scooping up Benny's uncomfortably light body, dragging her out of the orchids' reach. The tendrils fell away, latching instead on the red mounds closer to hand. There was a raw, bloody stench in the air. An easier target.

'That should keep them distracted,' Wedderburn said wearily, throwing another chunk of meat. The Doctor didn't thank him. His attention was focused on Benny and the wet stains that welled up around her neck and wrists.

' "Mutant varieties"?' he shouted, incredulous anger directed at the botanist. 'They're not mutants, they're . . . *alien*!'

'They're strange, I admit. I found quite a few mutants in the Amazon – plants and animals. But these are the weirdest.' There was a measure of pride in Wedderburn's reply. Too much to avoid the Doctor's anger.

'Don't you realize how irresponsible you've been? You're talking about them like prize-winners at a village fête. They could have killed her!'

'Yes, they *are* prize-winners! Vampire blooms. Until recently it was our big myth.' Wedderburn scowled, his pride stung. 'It's hardly my fault if someone decides to stroll in the middle of them, is it? Why d'you think I lock the door?'

The Doctor looked away, into the cold face of Benny Summerfield. She could be bleeding to death. She could be dying in his arms. Another dies, *always* another! Suddenly weary, he let his face sink into his cupped hands.

'I'm sorry,' he mumbled. 'I didn't mean . . . It's just . . .'

He felt a hand press against his shoulder. Reassuring.

'I think we should leave the argument, Doctor. I mean, the blood loss could be . . . we should do something, get medical help.'

'Then we'd better get started. What do you suggest?'

'What's your name?'

'Truman.'

'Hi. I'm Ace.'

Beat.

'I said, "hi". You deaf or stupid or what?'

Beat.

'Is there anyone in there? Am I getting through to anyone? Helloooo . . .?'

Beat.

86

'You don't say much, do you?'

Beat.

'Why do you wear that mask?'

Beat.

'Acne, is it? I used to suffer myself, until a friend introduced me to Spot-Away ...'

'Shut up.'

'It talks! It sings, it dances, it plays the bagpipes. You're a thug. Hired muscle. I've seen hundreds like you, mate.'

Beat.

'Where are you taking me?'

'To Winterdawn.'

Beat.

Ace and Truman marched on in silence.

On the second-floor landing, the silence was shattered.

'You don't seem to understand.' A woman's voice, not one Ace recognized. The tone was reasonable going on hysterical, trying to sound calm and collected when they really wanted to scream their head off. Ace knew this, she'd sounded like it herself on many occasions. If you can keep your head when all about, and all that shit.

The woman's diatribe was cut off by a low, muffled voice. That *was* calm and collected. Ace couldn't quite get the gist of it, she guessed that it was something reassuring.

Truman seized her by the shoulders, squeezing so it felt like his fingers were digging into the bone. Ace put up a token struggle – she had a right to, he was bloody hurting her.

'Journey's end,' Truman whispered in her ear. 'Now, you're going to be very good for me, keeping quiet and still while I introduce you. Got that?'

'Get ... aaah!' There was a wrenching pain as the masked man twisted her arms behind her back.

'I'd enjoy hurting you,' he whispered. 'Don't give me an excuse.'

Ace scowled. Pointless – it wasn't as if he could see her face. She wanted to scream something loud and abusive at him, but he might try something permanently painful.

Not that she couldn't take it, but at the moment, it would be useless.

She'd seen hundreds like him before.

The woman was shouting again.

'I'm telling you, there's this mad bitch wandering round the house! She's already attacked me! And you're just sitting there . . .!'

'Do you expect me to do anything else?' low and reassuring rumbled, briefly audible. Deep. Male.

'You know what I mean. Someone's got to go for the police.'

'In we go,' Truman whispered. He shoved Ace through the door, keeping a firm grip on her arms.

'We *can't* call the police. Not . . .'

'Look what I've found,' Truman announced.

Ace glanced around the room, drawing in first impressions of her captors and their environment. The room was plainly decorated, starkly furnished – a few scattered chairs and a table. Ace's eye was caught by a pile of video equipment on the table, but she swiftly re-focused on the others in the room.

At first she only saw the woman. Dark-haired, mid-twenties, rather attractive. She watched Ace with an unnerving and creepy stare. One of her cheeks was slightly bruised, dull purple showing brightly under the electric light.

Truman's grip loosened. Slightly.

Ace didn't see the man for a moment, concealed as he was in an awkward position behind the door. Truman jerked her round and she was able to see him glide from the shadows, watching her with a cocktail expression of suspicion, fear, disgust and curiosity.

He had probably been a tall man. Ace guessed that he was no more than sixty, but he seemed much older. There was a weight, a weariness, on his face that reminded her that one day she could look and feel just the same. His features were fine and sharp, arched eyebrows and hollow eyes giving him a dark, satanic look. His hair was combed into a flow of grey and white, his eyes hid behind a pair of wire-rimmed glasses, but he peered constantly over them, as if they were for effect only. Despite the sense of age that surrounded him, there was also something young and fiery. The resemblance between this man and the young woman was unmistakable.

The old man was dressed in a dark, crumpled suit. His legs dangled, useless and painfully thin, at the front of his wheelchair.

'Who are you?' he hissed. 'What are you doing in this house?'

'She claims her name is Ace,' Truman said, leisurely sceptical. 'I found her in the attic store-room. She spun me some yarn about a monster hiding in the wardrobe.'

A smile flickered on the old man's icy features.

'The creative imagination is alive and well. What's she doing here? A burglar, or something else?'

'Look, I'm intruding,' Ace decided to risk Truman's wrath and try a reasonable approach, 'But it's an accident. We didn't mean to . . . to come here.' She stopped, realizing how pathetic it sounded.

'Try and stay in the realms of the everyday.' The old man was incredulous. Ace didn't blame him. 'Who's "we"?'

'Her accomplice is the man I've already seen,' Truman interceded. 'A medical man apparently.'

'I can speak for myself,' Ace hissed.

'So you can,' the man in the wheelchair agreed. 'Well, Ace – if that's your real name, something I doubt very much – welcome to my home. I am Professor Jeremy Winterdawn and this is my daughter, Cassandra . . . But you've already met.'

Ace glanced at the silent woman, a stranger. Winterdawn was trying to get her off-guard.

'Sandra, is this the woman who attacked you?'

Ace froze, forcing herself to do a double take. Winterdawn wasn't being obscure, this was mistaken identity. Both she and the Professor were staring at Cassandra now, waiting for the answer.

'Well, come on. How many burglars can we possibly

89

have? It must have been her,' Winterdawn snapped impatiently.

No, it couldn't, Ace thought. It must have been Benny. Wouldn't hurt a fly normally, but capable of great violence.

'I can't tell.' The woman shook her head, still staring at Ace with a force that should have made her eyes bleed. She looked as if she was on the verge of tears. 'I couldn't see properly. I *can't* tell!'

There was a short, awkward silence. Ace kept quiet.

'Truman,' Winterdawn said at last. 'Go and find her accomplice.'

There was a *swish* of air behind her, and Truman's vice-like grip vanished. Only when he was out of the room, the door closed behind him, did Ace relax.

'I'm sorry about him,' Winterdawn said evenly, hiding any hint of emotion. 'He enjoys his work too much. What am I going to do with you?'

'Call the police,' Cassandra said, so quietly that Ace barely heard her.

'My daughter has a problem with her sight,' Winterdawn continued, in the same even tones as before. They were too reasonable, Ace realized, too deliberate. 'Five years ago, pieces of a car managed to lodge themselves in her optic nerves. She's had surgery of course, but the results are patchy. Her sight comes and goes. What sort of human being *are* you?' Winterdawn dropped the blandness and exploded, his anger directed solely at Ace, 'How could you attack a *blind* woman!'

'I didn't . . .' Ace began, but she was cut short by Winterdawn.

'What am I going to do with you?' he growled again, calmer, but more threatening than before. There was hate in his eyes, and something else, something potentially dangerous. They scared her.

Wedderburn was beginning to doubt the authenticity of this 'Doctor' character. His sudden appearance, the questions he asked, his ignorance of details he should have known inside-out . . . he hadn't even mentioned his proper name. He was, Wedderburn considered, a little too good to be true.

Wedderburn had suppressed his doubts at first, too consumed by guilt to pay them much attention – he had, after all, almost been responsible for this woman's death. Once things calmed down, the doubts resurfaced. Who was this woman? How did the Doctor know her? What was she doing in the conservatory?

He'd helped the Doctor carry her to Sandra's bedroom. It was close and convenient and there was a medical kit stowed away under Sandra's bed – the first place Wedderburn thought of. The Doctor immediately began to rummage through the white tin box, rooting out bandages, cotton wool, plasters, clotting pads – anything to staunch the bleeding. His concern for the woman was obvious and genuine, Wedderburn realized, but in all other things he was a liar. He'd incriminated himself, asked who Sandra was. A black mark against him – everyone on Keightley's team had heard of Sandra. Jeremy loved talking about her. It was inconceivable that the Doctor could be genuine and not know the name.

'Another one of the team?' Wedderburn asked as they gathered round the unconscious woman, working on her wounds with the plasters. He adopted a simple, honest smile, and the Doctor had nodded automatically, 'Getting younger, aren't they? Mind you, Keightley was only twenty-three when she started brow-beating people with that paper on temporal logic . . .'

'Moore,' the Doctor looked up sharply, 'be quiet. Please.' From then they worked in silence.

Laid out on Sandra's bed, Bernice Summerfield resembled a cold stone effigy. Fake or not, Wedderburn didn't want her death on his conscience and he threw himself into the task of helping the Doctor stem the bleeding. It wasn't, he discovered, as bad as they had first feared. Thank God. The moment this was done, he'd get away. Find Winterdawn. Get the truth.

'It all depends now,' the Doctor said, squatting wearily

on the end of the bed, not caring to meet Wedderburn's gaze, 'on how much blood she lost in the first place.'

'She'll live,' Wedderburn told him, with conviction. 'The plants are used by the local tribes in ritual blood-letting. Most survive. According to their legends, the valley is blessed by the gods. Blessed or cursed.'

'It's entered their culture?' The Doctor considered this information carefully. 'Yes, that makes sense. For the mutation to be so widespread suggests that this valley has been subject to it for generations.'

'Yes, that's what I thought, so we . . .' Wedderburn cut himself off as the door to the bedroom was flung open. It wasn't, as he'd hoped, Jeremy or Sandra. Just the familiar, shambling shape of Justin Cranleigh.

'Is Sandra . . .?' Justin began, glancing anxiously around the room. 'Laura,' he said, as his eyes lighted on Bernice, but he lost interest and began to stare at his feet, hugging himself compulsively. He seemed even more distracted than usual – something had clearly upset him.

'She's not here, Justin,' Wedderburn told him. 'She won't be long.'

Justin sagged with disappointment.

'I'll sit in the corner,' he said, ambling across to the corner of the room and sinking into an awkward cross-legged shape, saying nothing more. He had captured the Doctor's attention for the moment, and Wedderburn took advantage of this distraction to slip from the room. Checking that he wasn't being followed, he slipped along the passageway towards the stairs. Jeremy would probably be in his study or Jenny's old room . . .

A blank, white face grinned at him suddenly. Wedderburn almost had a heart attack on the spot.

'Sorry,' Truman said. 'I didn't hear you coming.'

Wedderburn pressed a hand to his chest. Truman *grinned*. 'You haven't seen a man – short, dark hair, white suit?' he asked. 'Professor Winterdawn's getting anxious about him.'

'Oh, the Doctor,' Wedderburn replied, smiling expansively. 'He's in Sandra's room.'

* * *

'Are you going to call the police?' Ace asked drably, without any hint of aggression. There was no point in aggravating the situation. Still, she was hoping to provoke some reaction. Winterdawn was upset by the attack on his daughter; it seemed at odds with his earlier refusal to contact the authorities.

'No.'

Maybe he had something to hide?

'Not tonight.'

Something tonight? Something that could be cleared away by the morning?

'I didn't attack your daughter.' Ace underlined her words with conviction. 'Believe me.'

'How can I believe you?' Winterdawn snapped. 'Give me one good reason.'

That was the problem. There wasn't a good reason. There was only her word and, since she'd already been collared as a burglar, that would carry no weight. She switched her stare to Cassandra, offering a silent appeal for help to the woman. She didn't acknowledge it.

'I can't,' Ace said, pained.

'I say we lock her in one of the cellar rooms,' Cassandra said. 'We can keep her there until you see fit to call the police.'

'You could let me go,' Ace suggested. That was a stupid mistake – she realized that the moment she'd opened her mouth. Winterdawn wasn't laughing.

'When Harry gets back, he can take her.'

'I could . . .' Sandra began. Winterdawn interrupted with a curt 'No.'

'I'm not incapable.'

'She might kill you this time.' Ace had killed more than a few people in her time but only people who deserved it, or non-people like Daleks. Being described as a potential murderer was something she almost found offensive.

'I'm prepared this time,' Sandra continued coolly.

The stalemate was broken by the arrival of another man whom Ace didn't recognize. Tall, sun-burnt, the same age as Winterdawn but athletic compared to the hunched shape in the wheelchair. Twenty years ago, Ace might have found him attractive.

'Jeremy, I need . . .' The newcomer checked himself, noticing Ace.

'Moore, this is Ace. She's a mugger,' Winterdawn introduced her without enthusiasm.

'Ace.' The old man smiled at her. 'One-fourth part of the Hand of Fate, right?' Ace managed a Truman-like grin.

'Moore, I'm busy at the moment,' Winterdawn fidgeted, but his protests were blocked by Sandra who stepped forward and seized Ace by the shoulders, taking over where Truman had left off.

'It's all right,' she said. 'Ace is just leaving.' With less force but more grace than Truman displayed, Sandra manoeuvred her captive from the room. Outside, her grip loosened.

'Thanks,' Ace said, rubbing her shoulders.

'You can get to the cellar under your own steam. Don't try anything.'

'I won't, believe me.'

'I do.'

'You know I didn't attack you,' Ace asked, hoping for a positive answer.

'I've no proof you didn't, but I don't think you did,' Sandra told her. Positive enough.

It would be easy to give her the slip, but it wouldn't be right. It'd be proof of her guilt, wouldn't it? Not that she was keen on the prospect of being cooped up in a cell for the best part of the night. Not enough action.

'I hope Truman didn't hurt you too much,' Sandra made small talk. 'He gets a bit carried away. Most of the time he's gentle, sweet.'

'Are we talking about the same Truman?' Ace asked, slipping into sarcasm overdrive. 'Tall bloke, wears a mask, smiles a lot, psychotic tendencies? Very sweet, very gentle.'

'Well, I'm looking at it from my perspective. He'd chew his arms off to get into bed with me.'

94

'And has he?'

'Not yet, but it's only a matter of time.'

'Why does he wear that mask?'

'He's scarred. He had an accident about three years ago, screwed up his face, his life, everything. I don't know the details.'

'Maybe I've been a bit...' Sandra tugged on her shoulder, pulling her into the darkness of the stairwell. She had a silencing finger raised to her lips, another pointing down the stairs to the landing below.

A dark shape was moving there. It looked like a woman. It moved like a hunter, like so many killers Ace had known. She knew, instinctively, that this woman was bad news.

The hunter slid open a door on the landing and slipped inside. The door closed and Ace felt safe to breathe again.

'That's her,' Sandra whispered, with certainty and conviction. 'She's the one who attacked me, I recognize her. D'you think we should go after her?'

'Not a good idea,' Ace said simply, out of a sense of self-preservation. 'It was definitely her?'

'Definitely, positively, absolutely not you,' Sandra whispered. 'So who the hell are you anyway?'

'You wouldn't believe me,' Ace said, wondering why everyone she met managed to gravitate to that question eventually. It had ruined several good relationships in the past.

'I'm broad minded. Try me.'

'You'd have to see it to believe it.'

'Show me.' Sandra hissed insistently, clinging to the question more tenaciously than anyone Ace had known. Leech-like.

Ace looked at her and made a decision.

'Okay.' She dug her hands deep into her jacket pocket and produced a small metal item which she held out for Sandra's inspection. The other woman looked at it without comprehension.

'We'll need this.' Ace told her. 'I, uh, stole it from a friend. Lifted it from his pockets.'

'What is it?'

'TARDIS key.'

'What?'

'You'll see.' Ace pocketed the key and smiled with sadistic expectation.

The corpse of the grey man grew cold on the path. The rain lashed harsher, droplets of water mingling with congealing blood. Tears of rain ran down the dead cheeks.

The air stirred by the pathway.

Quantum particles buzzed with expectancy. A pulse disturbed the surface of reality. The quanta interacted, weaving patterns, changing the shape of the world. The pulse grew. It reached the atomic level, shifting electrons off their orbits, sending atoms colliding against each other, molecules knitting together.

As the pulse took physical shape, so it took on a mental shape. It began to form a cohesive unity, a whole that meshed with its past experience. The pulse *remembered* its self, its shape, its identity.

Atoms bonded together, forming minute architecture, growing ever more ambitious. More matter was drawn together by the pulse, imploding round a single core. The process was agonizingly slow.

In slightly less than two seconds, the pulse had built a body for itself. The body was full-grown, clothed, self-aware, physically identical to the being it had once been.

The grey man stared down at the corpse that had once been his body. Respectfully, he stripped it of its hat, coat and dark glasses.

The old body dissolved. Nothing was left but a few fragments of metal. The grey man did not care to inspect them. He knew what they were.

He pulled on the coat and hat over his new but identical clothes, head, hair. He slipped the glasses over a pair of hollow, ancient eyes – they were always unique. Feeling whole again, he set off for the house.

He had miscalculated again. He'd not expected any

further external disruption, and consequently he'd lost another body.

A sudden thrill shot down his spine. They were gone. The malignance had shrivelled up and died. The house was free. He hadn't been needed after all.

Maybe the Time Lord . . .

No. That was too easy. The forces had moved on. They must have gained some mobility, maybe even physicality. This was disturbingly predictable. Each time he approached the house, he carried a set of assumptions that were immediately cut away from beneath him.

If they weren't in the house, where were they? The grey man cast round, locating the distortions. Shapes moved through the grounds in the twilight. *Human* shapes, with the aura he had already encountered. Hoping they hadn't seen him, he crouched down behind a bush and listened for their approach.

There were two, speaking in human voices, human language. English. They sounded young but adult. One male, one female. Cultured tones.

'They're going to have to go.' Female.

'Possibly.' Male. 'You really think they're a threat?'

'On their own, perhaps. Together . . .' the female left the threat hanging. 'They're devious sods, and scientists – men of reason – for all that means.'

'Nice garden.'

'Possibly? Greenfly?'

'In November?'

'The women are a bit dangerous.'

'Individually. Not as a cohesive group. Lovely shrubbery. Pink.'

'Two borderline psychotics, a cripple and an irresponsible freeloader who claims to be an archaeology professor.'

'Our sort of people.'

'Uh huh. Lovely statue. Let's vandalize it.'

There was a static buzz. The air filled with the stench of molten metal.

'I think we should kill some plants.'

'I wouldn't. You might disturb the god hiding behind that bush.'

'Perhaps you're right. I say we go sit on the hill, soak up some atmosphere and wait for the end of the world. What say you?'

'As you will so mote it be!'

'That's what I like to hear.'

'I love this language. So many consonants, so many syllables!'

There was a rustling as the creatures forced their way through the hedge. Then nothing. Certain they were gone, the grey man emerged from hiding. He had registered everything the couple said, but understood little. Nor did he know how much of it could be taken on face value. They had known he was listening. Perhaps that was inevitable. He'd have to wait and watch events unfold. Perhaps *that* was inevitable.

He felt impotent.

The statue stood before him, changed. It was melting. Michael's arms were moulding into Lucifer's back. Michael's wings dripped onto the ground. Lucifer's face stretched, welling tear-like towards the ground. The rain sizzled against it, turning instantly to steam.

The grey man stared at the mess, wondering why he felt sad. He wondered what had happened to Rose's brother. On the hill creatures were waiting for Armageddon.

He was afraid their wait might not be long.

'A scientist?' Winterdawn was saying. His eyes narrowed with concentration, his brow furrowed. 'Is that what he said?'

'Yes. I don't know if it's true,' Wedderburn replied, anxious to return to the point. 'Look, is he genuine or isn't he?'

'No,' Winterdawn replied, sinking back in his chair and humming thoughtfully between words. 'No, I know the present research team and besides, Claire would tell me if she was sending someone up.'

'Maybe it slipped her mind.'

'Nothing slips her mind.' Winterdawn tried to suppress a smile. 'No, you've been taken for a ride.'

'I say we go and find him before he gets away.'

'No point, Truman's already gone for him.'

'Then what? The police?' Wedderburn asked hopefully. He knew what Winterdawn's reply would be. There was a fanatical light in Jeremy's eyes. That light had once shone in his own eyes.

'I don't know,' Winterdawn mused. 'A scientist? Is that what he said?'

The Doctor kept a lone, silent vigil over Bernice, distracted by nothing, not even the burblings of the deranged individual in the corner. He was certain that Benny would be all right – she hadn't lost that much blood – but if something happened and he wasn't there . . .

Benny murmured something, shifting uneasily on the bed. Her eyelids flickered. The Doctor felt something akin to relief.

'Cellar,' she muttered and tried to roll onto her front. She groaned, letting her eyelids float open. The Doctor leaned forward.

'Don't try to move yet,' he advised – no point keeping her in the dark. 'You've lost a lot of blood. One, maybe two pints.'

'A couple of pints?' Benny's strained voice conveyed good-natured horror. 'That's very nearly a couple of armfuls. Good thing it wasn't any more, because I've run out of arms. Doctor?'

'Yes?'

'Do you ever have one of those days when you feel it was a real waste of time getting out of bed?' She managed a weak grin.

'Frequently.' The Doctor managed a stronger grin. It faded as he heard the door handle turn behind him. He leaned forward and whispered in Benny's nearest ear:

'Act dead.'

'Who needs to act?' she whispered back, but let her eyelids drift shut.

The Doctor turned, recognizing the figure in the opening doorway. The man in the mask, minus his video equipment, but still instantly recognizable. The mask smiled at the Doctor with an air of self-satisfaction. The man behind the mask seemed unsurprised by the Doctor's presence – without expression it was difficult to tell. The Doctor distrusted people who wore masks. He couldn't see what they were thinking. He wanted to know what they had to hide.

There was something unnervingly familiar about the newcomer, something about the way he moved.

'Doctor,' the mask addressed him.

'I'm afraid I don't have the pleasure.'

'Harry Truman.' The chill in his voice was belied by his smile.

'Oh yes, I think we've met. We had a lively debate about a place called Manhattan. Something about the ethics of using fission weaponry on civilian populations?' He smiled at Truman, receiving a grin in return. He doubted it was sincere.

'You will come with me please,' Truman continued. 'And your friend.' The Doctor dropped his bluff, became defensive.

'Benny stays here. She's lost a lot of blood, as Wedderburn will attest if you want to ask him. I don't think she should be moved.' He waved in the general direction of the corner where Justin sat, his arms crossed guardedly. 'Your friend can keep an eye on her.'

'Very well,' Truman conceded, with a speed the Doctor wasn't expecting.

'Let me check on her before I go,' the Doctor asked.

'By all means. Be quick.'

The Doctor turned away, deeply irritated. Truman's concessions were less altruistic than they appeared. If he'd been argumentative, the Doctor could have stalled him for half an hour.

'I'll be back,' he hissed into Benny's ear.

'Doctor,' Bernice murmured. 'His body language. Wrong. Not natural.'

'Thanks. Try not to move,' the Doctor whispered, straightening up and quietly digesting the implications of Benny's advice.

'Are you ready?' The Doctor nodded, making for the door.

The door was blocked.

Specifically, the door was blocked by a woman. A woman in her mid-twenties, wrapped in a trench-coat-shaped section of night. Her angular features were topped by a high expanse of forehead and a mess of dark hair, slightly muddy. Her hair had been artificially darkened; her blonde roots were showing. A pair of deep blue pupils stared from beneath a pair of moon-shaped Lennon-glasses.

The detail which stood out more than most was the stubby gun clenched tight in her fist, one finger itching on the trigger. The wrong end of the gun was pushed directly into the Doctor's face.

'Now that I have your attention,' the woman said, 'which one of you is Professor Jeremy Winterdawn?'

7

The English Assassin

Jane Page loved guns. She loved the feel of hard metal crushed into her small hands. She loved the reactions of her targets – counting the seconds of life they had left to them. She loved the shock that passed through her as the bullets exploded from the barrel. She loved the mess – the chunks torn from the victims' bodies, chipping away at flesh and bone like a sculptor working on marble. She loved that.

She loved the power, the kick, the gun.

Her eyes clicked between the three men before her. The thin-faced man squatting in the corner didn't seem to be bothered. He had noticed the gun and simply didn't care. Disappointing.

The masked man was more predictable. He hovered in the background, unprepared to attack. She could read his eyes. He didn't have the nerve.

The third man stood on the receiving end. If he tried anything, he'd lose most of his face. But there was nothing in his eyes that suggested fear. There was *reserve. Patience.* His eyes – inscrutable pools in hollow sockets – were defiant. He wasn't moving. He wasn't even shaking. Page felt fazed.

Make some distance.

'Move back slowly, until you're standing against the wall,' she said – a request, not an order. They moved anyway. She couldn't see the small man's eyes so clearly now, and felt better for it. Relaxing, she noticed a fourth target, a woman lying flat on the bed apparently asleep –

no threat. The woman's clothes were blood-stained. Page noticed the large stain dried into the small man's shirt. Curiouser and curiouser.

She returned her gaze to the men. Any one of them could have been Winterdawn. She didn't have a description – she didn't need one normally.

'This,' she said confidently, holding up her gun, 'is the Siddley "Churchill" Automatic. It fires an explosive bullet that can perforate steel plate. The effect on the human body is *unfortunate*. I am prepared to use this weapon on each and every one of you, if it means I get Winterdawn in the process. Do I make myself clear?'

'Pull the trigger,' the small man said suddenly; his voice had the texture of gravel and was full of persuasive charm. 'Take our lives.'

'Don't give her ideas, you stupid bastard,' the mask hissed. Page's lips twitched into a smile shape.

'Pull the trigger. Now.'

'I'm tempted,' Page said, without humour. She dropped the smile. 'I'm not a thug from a cheap movie. I don't gloat. I don't weaken. I will, if necessary, leave this house cold, dark and empty. Believe me.'

The silence that followed was intense and frustrating. Page ached to tighten her hand. Just slightly. The small man stared at her, his eyes buried by shadow. Between the shadows, Page could see a cross-hair target.

Tighten. Now.

The man blinked and turned his head slightly. Page's smile mixed relief and anticlimax. She brushed a casual hand through her hair, training her gun on the silent, mask-less man. He stared back with a baby-eyed expression. 'You! Are you Winterdawn?'

'His name is Justin Cranleigh,' the masked man droned with withering disapproval but little resistance. 'He's not a well man. You can't . . .'

'I can,' Page whispered. No one could have heard her, but the small man suddenly turned and caught her gaze again.

'He's right. My name is Justin,' her target confirmed,

103

voice meandering. 'On the right occasions, when the moon is high and I feel fine. I'm the lord of creation, but don't spread it around – they don't *like* me up there.'

Page scowled. There was always some joker who thought he'd be clever.

'I'm not impressed,' she said. 'Really.'

Cranleigh stepped forward, pressing his palms together in prayer. He raised his head to the ceiling, his eyes rolling with manic light.

'I had a gun once, but Nancy broke it. Should have stuck to her dolls. I never forgave her that. And then she died. Amen.'

He drifted aimlessly round the room before collapsing onto the carpet by the bed. The woman on the bed moaned something incomprehensible in response.

Had her hands been free, Page would have clapped. Slowly.

'How about you?' she asked, bringing the gun round to bear on the short man. 'No games. The truth.'

'Truth?' The man's thick eyebrows quivered and he spoke smoothly: 'You wouldn't believe me if I told you anything like the truth.'

Page smiled generously, ignoring the urge to squeeze.

'Try me.'

The short man nodded, breaking eye contact. He had found something fascinating about his feet.

'Call me the Doctor. I am a wanderer. I was born on the planet Gallifrey in the constellation of Kasterborus. I travel in time and space in a machine called the TARDIS. I arrived here by accident, drawn by an alien force. I've never met Winterdawn; there are a lot of questions I want to ask him.'

'Three out of ten. Not as convincing as Cranleigh,' Page told him, stifling an ersatz yawn. She jerked the gun round so it aimed between the eyeholes of the masked man. 'How about you?'

'My name is Harry Truman . . .'

'Mister President, this is a surprise.'

'*Really*.'

'Go on.'

'I'm twenty-seven. I was born in Bromley. My twin sister Nancy . . . died three days after she was born. I was academically excellent. When I was eighteen, I started a degree in English at Cambridge. My girlfriend, Laura, was also studying English. We were going to get married . . .'

'Stop it.' Cranleigh was climbing to his feet, staring malevolently at Truman. Warily, Page shifted her gaze to the fruitcake.

'. . . She died unexpectedly. I left Cambridge and joined a firm of . . .' Truman continued oblivious.

'Stop it!' Cranleigh roared, his hands pressed to his temples. Truman's voice wavered.

'That's me,' Cranleigh whispered, tears streaming down his face.

He hurled himself at Truman, hands locking round his throat. Their combined bulks smashed against the wall, a mass of thrashing limbs and violent blows. Cranleigh was single-minded in his attack, Truman in his defence.

This was genuine. It was spontaneous. Page felt her grip on the situation slipping away. The threat of the gun was useless. No one cared about the weapon clasped limply in her hands. She felt useless.

'Excuse me!' The woman on the bed was sitting upright and beaming at her happily. Page spun, pushing the gun at her. 'Don't point that thing at me, I don't know where it's been.'

Then there were hands against her shoulder, tearing at her gun-arm, jerking it upwards.

'Benny!' a gravel voice was yelling by her ear. 'Help Truman!'

Adrenalin surged. Page's fingers clenched.

There were explosions. Gunfire blowing chunks out of the ceiling. Page's body thrilled as the shots pulsed through her. A hand was wrenching the gun from her fingers. Another hand pressed against her neck, fingertips pushing nerves – a light touch, but significant.

Page took a deep breath and fell into unconsciousness.

* * *

The Doctor coaxed the gun from the woman's limp fingers. He let the arm drop softly.

The gun in his hand was harsh. Physically it was warm, but it had a cold lining that stabbed at the Doctor's soul. It was not an object he cared to hold. It was *tainted*. He buried the loathsome item under a pile of T-shirts in the wardrobe. Then he did his best to expel it from his mind.

Truman was unconscious, half-slumped against the wall. The Doctor's immediate fears – that Cranleigh might have killed him in his frenzy – were assuaged by the regular movements of his chest. Cranleigh himself was paralysed, staring at the man he'd been throttling not a minute ago. Either Benny was more persuasive than the Doctor had thought, or Cranleigh had shifted back onto a diffident gear.

Benny also crouched beside Truman; unlike Cranleigh she was active, her hands fumbling at the back of Truman's head. She was unfastening his mask – the archaeologist's curiosity was active. The Doctor felt that she was disturbing something that should be left hidden. He moved forward, perhaps to stop her – too late. The mask came loose.

The Doctor paused, realizing that he, too, was curious about the face behind the mask. Besides if Benny's enquiring spirit was on the prowl once more, it meant she really had recovered.

Bernice flashed a brief thumbs-up sign at him and pulled the mask away completely.

Beneath the mask was an unexpected, horrific face.

Bernice Summerfield stared. The mask was forgotten, clasped between her hands.

Justin Cranleigh reacted violently. He shrieked, hurling himself across the room, hiding behind the bed and moaning pitifully.

The Doctor recovered quickly. He plucked the mask from Benny's hands, lowering it back over Truman's face.

Then everyone felt a lot better.

Ace led Sandra into the TARDIS console room – still and

impressive despite the shroud of darkness – and waited for the inevitable display of weak-jawed, wordless wonder.

Probably something sadistic about that, but why not? She'd gone through it just like Mel and Benny and everyone else. She had never forgotten her first sight of the TARDIS. It was something that was going with her, inexorably, to the grave.

Sandra stood in the doorway and stared. Ace failed to suppress a smile.

Wide-eyed, Sandra wheeled round and began to enthuse in Ace's direction.

'It's big,' she exclaimed breathlessly. 'Jesus, why didn't you tell Dad?'

'You want a serious answer?'

Ace was smiling, disturbed. There was something wrong about this reaction. Okay, there was the surprise, the shock, the astonishment, the mind-dulling incomprehension – all this and more. No, there was something that rang false. It was the *enthusiasm*.

'You should have told us. He'll love this. He's never done anything on this scale.' Ace's smile lost its sadistic sheen, giving way to an uncomfortable grin.

'I mean,' Sandra warbled, 'I don't get the theory, but Dad's always going on about size. Anything larger than a tea chest and we get "dimensional regression feedback". Sounds crap, but I assume I know what he's on about.' She turned back to Ace. 'Why'd you put it in the cellar?'

Ace's jaw made up-down motions, but she had nothing to say.

'I mean, you brought this to show Dad?' Sandra continued, acquiring a confused slowness. 'I assume this is stuff you've done parallel to his work. Dimensional transcendentalism? Yes?'

'Shit.' Ace forced her heavy tongue into the shape of words. 'You've seen stuff like this before?'

'Yeah!' Sandra nodded, frowning uneasily. 'Yes.'

Ace wandered out of the TARDIS pondering on her feelings of frustration. Not frustration, perhaps. Unease. If Sandra was right – if Winterdawn had devised something on the same principles as the TARDIS – it followed that he could have brought the TARDIS to the house.

Couldn't he?

She felt like a little kid, going off to a birthday party in a new set of clothes, to find that everyone else dressed identically. She felt hollow, a sense of lost purpose.

Sandra followed her, hugging herself in the cold of the cellar. Like Ace, she seemed at a loose end.

'Run this by me one more time,' Ace said weakly. 'Your dad's done something like this. Bigger on the inside than the out, dimensionally transcendental shit.'

Sandra was nodding.

'Very small working models, as a sideline of his main work. I don't understand it – I've a BA in English, I'm not a quantum weirdo.'

Ace looked up at her, suddenly finding a new purpose.

'You don't have to understand it. Tell me about it.'

Sandra smiled awkwardly, a lop-sided sort of smile. A smile loaded with the same sadism which Ace had felt herself, quite recently.

'I can show you,' she replied.

There was a man and a woman on a hill, sometimes talking, sometimes thinking, sometimes watching the house below them.

'I think,' the man said, 'that everything should be perfect for our arrival. We don't want rogue elements running around confusing everything.'

'Not at first,' his companion responded. 'You mean the woman.'

'Don't state the obvious – of course I mean the woman. What do you suggest?'

'Temporal dislocation. She's not doing anything now and we can always stick her back in if things get boring.'

'It's done.'

Their laughter drifted down the hill to the grey man who was crouched in a nearby hollow. He wondered what they were talking about.

Dear Diary.

Benny scribbled hurriedly, scratching her words onto a scrap of paper with a blunt pencil.

Just a quick update – the Doctor's threatening to do something esoteric and I want to be watching when he does. A lot's happened since I last wrote. Here goes: threatened by a psycho with a knife; enjoyed five moments in a wardrobe listening to a couple snogging; had weird experience in a cellar; drained by vampire orchids; held at gunpoint by mad woman. I lead a strange life, but you know that, diary dear.

Never apologize, never explain.

According to the mad woman's business card, she was one 'Jane Page – computer systems analyst'. Must be a more dangerous profession than I'd previously imagined. I say 'was' because she's gone now. We all thought she was out of it for a couple of hours, but no – she crawled away from under our very noses (we being the Doctor and yours truly, plus the psycho who's turned out to be quite nice – you can never tell with the quiet ones). The Doctor was a bit worried but he managed to get her gun off her beforehand. That's still hidden away somewhere safe. It goes to show – he doesn't know everything.

He hasn't got a clue about what's going on. Apparently it's all down to some quantum physicist engaged in work that is definitely very secret and probably very illegal. If he's like any of the quantum physicists I know, he's lax when it comes to the laundry and other mundane mortal workings but that's hardly a crime (not yet anyway).

Doctor's worried about Ace. We haven't seen her for hours and she's . . .

'Benny!'

Speak to you soon if I don't get fried.

The Doctor and Cranleigh had moved Truman onto the bed where he now lay, cold and unconscious. Benny strolled over to them, watching them carefully. It was like a Victorian medical scene. Cranleigh was a grieving relative, hovering concernedly on the edge of the bed, staring with ill-matched eyes at the 'patient'. The Doctor was a grim physician, dressed in white rather than black, lurking on the fringes of the painting like something unholy, something fatal, something soul-crushingly good.

That, Bernice reflected as she moved into the frame, makes me the whore who gave the stupid sod syphilis in the first place.

Truman's dinner-jacket and shirt had been loosened, revealing large expanses of his chest. Benny wiggled her eyebrows suggestively.

'Is it true what they say about men with hairy chests?' she asked.

'Probably not,' the Doctor replied. 'Give me your knife.'

'What?'

'I noticed it as I was carrying you up here. Give give.'

Benny prised the knife from her boot, remembering that it was really Cranleigh's – unsuitable though he was to be in possession of such an item – and she wondered briefly whether he was going to claim his property. No, he wasn't interested.

'What are you going to do?' she asked, handing it to the Doctor.

'Nothing permanent,' he replied, pressing it against Truman's chest.

There should have been a scratch. There wasn't.

'Isn't this a bit dangerous?' Benny asked, uneasily. It would be novel if the physician took to stabbing the patient.

'Only for him,' the Doctor murmured, sinking the knife deep between Truman's ribs. Benny started.

'Jesus!' she shrieked. 'You bloody stupid . . .!'

'Look,' he suggested, regret absent from his face.

There should have been a mess. There wasn't. No blood. No gore. No mess. It wasn't the wound made by a knife. It was smooth, large enough for a cricket ball to squeeze through comfortably. Truman's skin rippled and whirled around the hole, as if alive.

Benny felt her own skin crawling. Truman's body had parted without injury to grant the knife passage. The Doctor withdrew and instantly the hole sealed itself. Flesh flowed into the wound until there was no sign that there had ever been a break. Truman was healed. Good as new.

'He'll wake up in about quarter of an hour,' the Doctor told Cranleigh, 'right as rain. I want you to be here when he does.' He turned back to Bernice.

'Something obscene is happening in this house. Something that destroys lives and minds. Something that revels in deception. I'm not sure what, but I'm ninety per cent certain of who's behind it.'

There was a gentle cough from the door. Benny didn't recognize the man standing there. A man in his late fifties, tall, tanned, perhaps attractive.

'Hello Doctor. Professor Winterdawn would like to see you.' His voice was gentle and mellow. 'Now.'

8

Anything Done for the First Time Unleashes a Demon

Why, everyone wanted to know, were there blood-stains on that photograph of John Pilger?

The room was a silent place, grown dusty through five undisturbed years, its cold air thick with memories. It was a place of heavy darkness and melancholy. Winterdawn could remember a time when it had not been dark. The light was long dimmed, but Winterdawn could still see patches of it. Intense flecks, starfire-bright, radiating warmth. Everything had been kept as he remembered.

The photographs, the furniture, the ornaments. The bed she slept in, the books she read, the odds and ends on her bedside table. All served as reminders. So much a part of her.

Daring to touch something, Winterdawn reached for the book on the bedside table. Pilger's *Distant Voices* – its cover discoloured by brown stains – blood snowflakes flattened across the author's features. Winterdawn skimmed through it without concentrating. Letters, words, sentences, paragraphs – all blurs of black on white, their meaning wrested from them. Winterdawn wasn't reading; his mind was wandering through pastures of bitter memories, through the earliest months of his loss.

The rain drummed a constant beat against the window, the book remained wedged in his cold, numbing fingers. Nothing broke his train of thought.

Winterdawn remembered.

The chair was unfamiliar then – an awkward shape

trapping him wherever he went. He writhed in constant frustration, straining to break free of this bulky prison. He was strapped into a chair like a condemned man.

The air round him was alive with the buzz of expectant voices. Young voices, student voices, offset by the more mature droning of underworked lecturers. Sitting in a draughty church hall waiting for a meeting to begin, waiting to watch a debate more heated in their imagination than it would be in life.

The discussion was a formality. It couldn't reverse the UN's decision.

There was a crowd of protesters in the hall. A far cry from Grosvenor, Winterdawn felt. He wasn't sure what they were protesting about. Some seemed opposed to UN adventurism in the Persian Gulf. Others were protesting – and Winterdawn found this particularly embarrassing – about discrimination against the 'limbically disenfranchised'. Winterdawn listened, wearing an expression of grim neutrality. Inside he was cackling.

There were about forty or fifty observers in the hall. Hardly a capacity crowd, but forty-nine more than Winterdawn expected. Winterdawn was there as representative of the Miracle Workers. Keightley was there too, sporting a Mona Lisa smile and a pair of distorting spectacles. The UN had sent a representative too – a pale man on the edge of his fifties who cracked his knuckles and chewed nicotine-replacement gum, an ex-soldier who wanted to be somewhere else.

There was a murmur of discontent from the anti-imperialists as the chairman announced the UN's terms for the return of Thascales' research.

There was a blanket of silence when Keightley replied that *everything* would be returned – all the original material, all the subsequent research – and all projects suspended. Keightley spoke in a dangerous voice that sounded as though she was enjoying the situation.

Winterdawn wheeled himself forward and watched the expectant faces – the more alert demonstrating the facial symptoms of perceived betrayal.

I despise you. I despise this sick world humanity has built. I am going to smash it. Everything you have ever believed in, everything you hold dear, he declaimed, but only in his imagination.

His genuine speech was more mundane:

I am resigning. To spend more time with ... with my daughter.

He'd thought he'd got away with it. Five years of covert research. He was so close to the breakthrough. He'd thought he'd won. Then this Doctor had come to the house. A coincidence perhaps? Winterdawn doubted it, but he was nonetheless pleased by the stranger's arrival. He could contain his excitement no longer. At last, there was someone who would understand, someone in whom he could confide, even though it meant the end of his work.

Winterdawn snapped the book shut and restored it to its place on the bedside table. When he looked up the Doctor was standing in the doorway.

Winterdawn studied the newcomer with an analytic eye, absorbing every detail into an educated first impression.

The Doctor was not a tall man. He was slightly built, though Winterdawn felt that this belied a powerful, physical strength. He was dressed in a cream-white suit that struck Winterdawn as incongruous but not exceptional. His appearance was unremarkable, saving his face.

The Doctor's features were vague, almost fluid. One second he seemed to be an old man, his face worn by centuries of careful studying. The next he had the smooth face of a child, radiating angelic innocence. His hair was a thicket of dark curls, receding to reveal a high, intellectual forehead. Then there were his eyes: whirls of black light like holes in space, doors into the infinite. Eyes that watched patiently.

'Doctor.' Winterdawn smiled generously, hoping to start off on the right foot. The Doctor said nothing. The silence was painful but Winterdawn continued: 'I'm Professor Jeremy Winterdawn. I welcome you as a fellow scientist.'

The Doctor strolled through the gloom, speaking in a

low, powerful voice as he moved, his head held at a slight angle.

'There is something sick happening in this house. There's an evil atmosphere here. Thick and dense. It's like a web that's ensnared me, drawing me to this house. Since then, one of my friends has almost been eaten alive by those obscenities in the conservatory, having first been threatened at knife-point by your pet lunatic!' The Doctor's voice rose in pitch, volume, anger. 'I've been held at gunpoint. I've no idea where my other friend is, nor why I'm here at all. But I know the sort of power that's responsible. As I said, there's something sick happening here, and *you* are at its heart!'

Winterdawn drummed his fingers on the side of the wheelchair, hesitating before breaking the silence.

'This was my wife's room,' he said, firmly, reasonably. 'You will not shout in here.'

The Doctor looked up slowly, then nodded.

'I'm sorry,' he said, quieter than before. 'But I demand an explanation.'

'You're hardly in a position to demand anything.' Winterdawn managed to muster a threatening tone. 'You've broken into my house. The best you can expect from me is a good word to the police. That's assuming you haven't taken or damaged anything.'

'You won't call the police. You'd have to explain what you're doing. Something illegal isn't it?'

Winterdawn remained calm and decided to bluff.

'Is it?'

'Benny was almost killed.'

'By her own negligence, if Moore's to be believed.'

'By his prize-winning plants!'

'Who were doing no harm until she blundered into the middle! Is it illegal to keep carnivorous plants? Is it immoral, even?'

The Doctor considered then shook his head. He wasn't giving up though.

'What about Cranleigh? What did you do to him?'

'I took him in! He's my daughter's fiancé, he hasn't got

115

a family prepared to look after him. What do you expect me to do? Let him live on the streets? Besides, he'd been here for years before he became unstable.'

'You let him play with a knife!' The Doctor's tone was accusatory.

'Not with my knowledge.'

'Irresponsible.'

'But hardly a crime! Unlike what you've done,' Winterdawn growled, tiring of this exchange – it was apparent that the Doctor had no idea what he was doing. 'Is there anything else you would like to accuse me of?'

The Doctor blinked slowly, then glanced around the room. He was still angry, but stripped of his accusations there was very little he could do. It was genuine anger though. He had actually believed – probably still believed – that Winterdawn was up to no good.

And he was a scientist . . .

'I'll tell you what I've been doing,' Winterdawn offered.

'Please,' the Doctor replied guardedly, 'as a fellow scientist.'

Winterdawn smiled slightly, and was pleased to receive a smile in response. The Doctor's anger was harnessed by his curiosity.

'Have you ever heard of Professor Carl Thascales?'

'The name rings a bell.'

'He's dead. He drove his car into a wall in the mid-seventies. His body was burned beyond recognition. Nasty.' Winterdawn squeezed the arms of his wheelchair, his knuckles whitening. It was a habit. 'Until then he'd been working at Cambridge on his own theories into "interstitial time", by which he meant . . .'

'An envelope of non-space, non-time,' the Doctor interrupted, 'underlying the "real" universe. It surrounds and separates every space-time event. A theoretical zone of nullity; "the gap between now and now". Literally, outside reality.' He smiled smugly.

'Oh.' Winterdawn was more irritated than anything else. 'You know.'

'I am a fellow scientist,' the Doctor replied, wearing his innocent child's face.

'Until about five years ago I worked with a team at Cambridge who sought ways of *applying* theoretical quantum physics. We wanted to manipulate space-time. We were miracle-workers, we wanted to walk on water.'

'And did you?'

'No. We ended up impersonating Saint Peter. Our theoretical knowledge was probably the most advanced in the West, but still limited. It'll be centuries before the technology exists for any practical use. Our task looked impossible.'

'But on the quantum level,' the Doctor wore a wry smile, 'nothing is impossible.' Winterdawn nodded happily.

'We made a couple of discoveries. Thascales' main body of research had been bought up entirely by the UN but it was made available to our college. There were probably funny handshakes involved ... It turned out to be – we thought – gibberish. Then we read closer and discovered that there was something to it after all. Complex themes running through it which were just enough to make it look credible. Thascales had come up with some amazing stuff that had been totally overlooked.

'The UN withdrew all the rights to the research. They were entitled to, of course, but it was disappointing for us. We'd come so far and we were being stifled by official cowardice. So we decided to continue in our work secretly. I'd ... had my accident,' Winterdawn tapped the arms of his chair, 'so I resigned my seat at the college and disappeared into the sunset with illicit copies of our work. I'm still paid out of the college funds. All my results are sent to Cambridge through mailing companies set up when I resigned. Clandestine and, I confess, utterly illegal.' He held up wrists to the Doctor. 'It's a fair cop. I'll come quietly.'

The Doctor turned away frowning, then glanced back sharply.

'There's more to it than that. What have you done?'

117

Winterdawn paused, eagerly anticipating the collapse of the Doctor's composure.

'It took me five years. I have found a way to physically enter the interstitial gap.'

The Doctor batted an eyelid.

Winterdawn savoured the silence.

'That's impossible,' the Doctor said, with superficial confidence.

' "But on the quantum level, nothing is impossible",' Winterdawn replied smugly. 'Cranleigh's been there,' (don't tell him what it did to his mind), 'Truman made recordings.' (Don't tell him what happened to *those* either.)

'You said yourself,' the Doctor was rationalizing, 'it will be centuries before the technology exists for any practical application. Thascales can only have given your work more theoretical depth, you couldn't have developed the technology, unless . . . You said something about a couple of discoveries . . .

'Technology bequeathed to you from somewhere?' He spoke under his breath, no longer addressing Winterdawn. 'Human technology – not in this period. Something extra-terrestrial then . . .' Nonsensical though it was, Winterdawn was intrigued by this speculation, but decided to chime in with a suitable prompt.

'Something Wedderburn found on his expeditions.'

'Expeditions? Yes, the Amazon,' the Doctor mused, without dropping his obsessive line of enquiry. 'And what else did Wedderburn find in the Amazon? Local wildlife exposed to a powerful mutagenic over a long period of time!'

He turned back to Winterdawn, a look of triumph in his eyes.

'Wedderburn found something in the Amazon. An alien artefact emitting high levels of radioactivity. He brought it home, and you were able to apply it in your work. Am I warm?'

'Warm-ish,' Winterdawn conceded, surprised at the accuracy of the Doctor's deduction. 'I'm not sure about an "alien artefact" – I'm not that credulous. I have no idea where the thing comes from nor why it does what it does. But I don't care. It's an instrument for the manipulation of reality, Doctor! It can warp space-time round my little finger.' Or it would, he added silently, if I understood all its functions. 'Do I sound obsessive?'

'It's the mark of a committed scientist,' the Doctor replied. 'You've been using it to mess about with your architecture?'

'You've noticed that? That's accidental, I'm not sure why it happens. Do you believe a word of what I've said?'

'Every syllable. Unless you're a better liar than I credit you for.'

Well, Winterdawn thought, *there's no answering that.*

For a moment he wanted to climb out of the chair. He wanted to stare the Doctor in the eye without getting a sore neck. He wanted to move properly. Just once.

'It's true, I've seen it.'

Sandra was standing in the doorway, the woman who called herself Ace beside her. Both wore smiles that were not so much smug as triumphant. Winterdawn started, suspicious of the sudden rapport between his daughter and her attacker. He had no idea of how to deal with this sudden alliance. Fortunately the Doctor took the lead.

'Ace? Have you been all right?'

'Shoved about a bit. Nothing damaged. Did you find Benny?'

'She's fine, a few pints short of a cardio-vascular system perhaps . . .'

Winterdawn's eye lighted on Ace's hands – on the object cupped in her palms. It was no larger than a tennis ball, transparent, glowing with a soothing blue light. And powerful. Fear tightened something in his chest.

He barely heard the conversation. His mind locked elsewhere.

'Yeah?' Ace might as well be speaking from the other side of the solar system. 'Doctor there's some weird shit happening in this house. You know . . .'

'I know.' The Doctor plucked the object from her hands.

He scrutinized it with the bearing of a professional. 'Pyramid power?'

'Tetrahedron power, Doctor.' Winterdawn became anxious to regain a hold on the conversation. 'You hold in your hand the final wonder of the world. God's own decoder key-ring.'

The Doctor was talking, not to Winterdawn but to Ace. Winterdawn felt rejected.

'Where was it?'

'In that big wardrobe we saw when we first turned up. The one with the built-in floodlights. Sandra showed me.'

Winterdawn took this news in his stride. Betrayed by his own daughter. So what? Did he care?

Did he?

'This woman attacked my daughter,' he said.

The Doctor turned sharply, a dark expression on his face.

'Ace?' The Doctor asked.

'No,' she replied.

'No,' Sandra reiterated. Winterdawn recognized the sincerity in both their voices. They weren't lying. In fact there didn't seem to be any tension between them at all. Sandra had shown Ace the tetrahedron voluntarily, and that was proof.

'I'm sorry,' he said, meaning it. 'I'm sorry.'

''Sokay, I forgive you.' Ace winked. Winterdawn bit his lip, digging his tooth deep. There was a vague taste of blood.

'You must be Sandra,' the Doctor was saying, apparently seeing the matter as cleared away and forgotten. He placed a friendly hand on Sandra's shoulder. 'I've heard so much about you. I had to borrow your room. There's blood on the covers and a bullet in the ceiling but it was all for the sake of a dear friend.'

'Doctor?' Sandra grinned nervously, shooting an awkward glance at Ace.

'That's him,' Ace muttered.

'Yes.' Sandra's manner became dark as she prised the

intruding hand from her shoulder. 'I've heard a lot about you too.'

'Doctor,' Winterdawn interrupted loudly, determined to regain the initiative. 'You know what's happening; you know what I'm doing and you know how. Does my work interest you?'

The Doctor fixed him with a sincere stare. 'Very much so.'

'I'm going into the interstitial gap tonight,' Winterdawn continued, ignoring the concerned expression flashing across his daughter's face. 'I was going to take Truman, but I'd prefer it if he stayed behind with the tetrahedron. And I don't want to go alone.'

'Yes . . .' the Doctor replied guardedly, clearly aware of what was coming.

'You're a scientist, Doctor. You seem intelligent, imaginative and open to new experiences. Would you like to see the cosmos from the outside?'

'Will you stop struggling?' Truman hissed. He had the third intruder of the night in an armlock and was debating whether to twist it into a more painful position. He'd found her in Sandra's room, conspiring with Cranleigh (of all people!). This one called herself Bernice, which was an improvement on 'Ace' at least. Unlike the sour and sullen Ace she was attractive, articulate and awkward, trying to fidget her way out of his grip.

Truman had hit on the idea that there was a paranoid conspiracy going on. Was it coincidence that four intruders were loose in the house on the same night? The Doctor and the woman with the gun were still running round free somewhere, there was that weirdo Winterdawn had claimed he'd seen watching the house . . . Something sinister was going on and Truman would lay odds that Winterdawn's experiments were at the heart of it.

Bernice tried to jerk her arms out of his hold, but he twisted viciously until she screamed.

'Shut up!' Truman recognized the quiet desperation in his voice. 'For God's sake shut up.'

'Have you ever thought,' Bernice said through tightly clenched teeth, 'of going into public relations? You'd go down a bomb.'

Truman pressed his free hand under her jaw, forcing it closed. His fingers brushed slowly against her face and hair, but he withdrew the hand hurriedly after the woman sunk her teeth into his index finger.

'Don't ever, ever touch me there!'

Truman twisted her arms viciously.

After considerable effort (he'd have to go back and check the furniture for finger-nail scratches) Truman finally got the unco-operative bitch into the presence of Professor Jeremy Winterdawn. He was coming down the stairs, wheeled down the ramp by his daughter. She was all right, thank God.

'Professor Winterdawn. May I present,' he announced with considerable difficulty, 'yet another of the Doctor's friends?'

'Let her go.'

Truman started, swinging his gaze upwards to see the Doctor hovering on the stairs behind Sandra, Ace at his side. She was wearing a vicious expression that did little for his life expectancy. The Doctor had placed a restraining hand on her shoulder and Truman was at least grateful to the little bastard for this. For the moment, his reaction was simple surprise. His triumphant smile cracked and fell open.

Bernice pulled herself free, but Truman didn't resist.

'Harry, there seems to have been a small misunderstanding. This is the Doctor and Ace, and you appear to have hurt one of their friends.' The voice was coming from another galaxy. Truman caught the gist. His eyes flicked between the Doctor and Winterdawn and for once he was grateful for the mask.

'The Doctor,' Winterdawn explained, not unkindly, 'is going into the gap with me tonight. Whenever you're ready, Harry.'

'Yes, of course,' Truman mumbled as Professor, daughter and wheelchair moved past him down the ramp. The

Doctor followed them, speaking softly, reciting a rhyme which Truman hadn't heard since childhood.

'As I was going up the stair,
I met a man who wasn't there,
He wasn't there again today,
I wish, I wish he'd stay away.'

'What's that supposed to mean?' he snapped, though suddenly fear – rather than hate – of the Doctor was dominant among his emotions.

'Don't you know?' the Doctor asked. Truman's aggressive stance dissolved into outright terror. The Doctor's eyes had been steel-grey and terrible and his voice was harsh with truth.

Ace allowed Benny to slip alongside her at the back of the procession.

'Hello,' her companion announced with a cheerfulness Ace felt was misplaced. 'Here we are three jolly souls all together again.'

'Two jolly souls and one bloody idiot,' Ace announced, jerking her head towards the Doctor's back. A weary frown crossed Benny's face.

'What's he done this time?'

Ace told her.

'That's the stupidest thing I've heard this century,' Benny proclaimed.

'That's why I'm doing it,' the Doctor mumbled.

'You're mad,' Ace lowered her voice to a quiet hiss. 'Winterdawn's a fruitloop. I wouldn't want to be alone in the same *room* as him and you're taking him on a round trip out of reality!'

'Trust me,' the Doctor whispered. 'I know what I'm doing.'

Ace doubted it.

There was a hush in the cellar room, of the kind Benny usually associated with religious ceremonies. Something sacred was about to take place and from what Ace had told her, it sounded like human sacrifice.

123

The wardrobe was a wardrobe among wardrobes, but nothing more than that. It didn't strike her as a potential entrance to other worlds. But then, neither would a police box. The doors had been thrown wide open, revealing bugger all. Three walls, a ceiling, a floor, solid. It was seriously unimpressive. Benny was cursed with a sceptical streak and by the feeling that the Doctor wouldn't be going anywhere.

Truman sat cross-legged on the floor, a bland masked monk in meditation. The tetrahedron sat before him, glowing deeper in response to whatever it was he was doing. Benny had seen more convincing light bulbs and still wasn't prepared to let the 'interstitial gap' have the benefit of the doubt.

Winterdawn was talking to his daughter. They were too distant to make out anything that was said, but Benny could sense a certain guardedness in their conversation. Winterdawn making back-up plans probably. In case of emergency pull here. The Doctor inspected the cabinet briefly before cutting across the room to join his companions.

'Ace, Benny,' he said. 'Are you sure you won't come? It'll be a fascinating experience.'

'Only to watch your back.'

'My back is fine. It doesn't need watching. Benny?'

'No thanks.' Benny smiled lightly. 'I don't believe in it.'

'Well, if I can't tempt you . . .'

' . . . As the bishop said to the actress.' Benny grinned salaciously.

'I *will* see you back here in a couple of hours,' the Doctor said, and it seemed to be an effort for him. 'That's a promise. Keep an eye on Truman.' And he turned away from them, moving towards Winterdawn.

'Good luck.' Ace sounded uncomfortable, stopping the Doctor in mid-stride. 'Professor,' she added, breaking into a pleasant smile. The Doctor half-turned back to them and flicked at his forelock.

'Thank you Dotty.' He trundled across to join Winterdawn.

'What's he mean about Truman?' Ace whispered.

'Have you seen his face?'

Ace shook her head.

'You haven't missed much.'

Benny let her concentration wander around the room. It lighted on the features of Professor Winterdawn, now talking eagerly to the Doctor. The old man's face was alive with a cheery enthusiasm which struck a chord somewhere in Benny's consciousness. There was something beautiful about his behaviour, a good-natured obsession which Benny recognized as part of herself.

... and there was something dark and sick and rotting and buried clawing at the back of Benny's mind scratching away the warmth and the cosiness ...

Benny felt nauseous. She almost doubled up, but controlled herself by biting her lip, chewing with vigorous concentration.

'Ace,' she said quietly, but with a heavy emphasis.

'Yeah,' Ace replied but she was watching the Doctor, and Benny felt insecure voicing her thoughts without proper eye contact. Sandra slipped across the room to join them, sparing Benny her embarrassment.

'They're going,' was all she said. Benny tried to let her fear slip away while she watched. It didn't work. There was cold pain in her chest.

The Doctor pushed Winterdawn and his chair into the sarcophagus, pulling the door closed behind him. Anticlimax.

A handful of uneventful seconds slipped by.

Light exploded from the sarcophagus. Searing light seeping from cracks and gaps in the wardrobe's shape.

Hiroshima light was followed by a long, deathly Hiroshima silence.

Benny's composure was cracking. She was certain that they would open the wardrobe and find a couple of incinerated bodies, one tangled up in a molten metal frame. The other ... the other she didn't want to think about.

'It's okay,' Truman said softly. 'They've gone.'

There was another long silence bereft of the tension

which characterized the first. It was broken by the distant doorbell being rung in short but rapid bursts. An impatient caller, apparently. Sandra smiled easily at the other women and slipped out of the room.

'Okay,' Ace said. 'What's wrong?'

Benny stared at her, unwilling to divulge her thoughts.

'I'm not stupid. I can tell when something's up,' Ace persisted. Benny nodded and drew her companion into a corner as distant from Truman as possible. A mixture of relief and trepidation built up inside her as she began to air her fears.

'Do you feel that there's more going on here than Winterdawn is saying?'

'More,' Ace replied coolly. 'I'm certain.'

'You are?'

'You'd be certain if you'd almost had your head torn off by Winterdawn's twenty-foot pet locust! And there's an attic window which changes colour.'

Benny blinked with practised calmness.

'What if I told you there's a woman loose trying to shoot people? Winterdawn a speciality.'

'She's got a sensible attitude towards him.'

'I'm trying to be serious!' Benny snapped, her composure caving in again. She'd promised herself that she wasn't going to cry.

'Have you ever had a nightmare which is so ... so bloody awful you're grateful to wake up? And after it you start to get the feeling that it wasn't a dream, it really happened and you're just trying to forget it?

'I had a dream after I'd been attacked in the conservatory. I dreamt I was in the cellar and there was something terrible there with me. I found something sick, a slice of genuine evil. And I ... I think I did.'

Briefly she felt awful. She'd been spouting rubbish and Ace was going to laugh in her face and make her feel like shit. She wasn't certain what she believed herself. She should have kept quiet. Ace said nothing – Benny took this as a bad sign and let her depression mature.

'Do you want to take a look in the cellar?' Ace asked,

breaking Benny's fears. 'If you were just dreaming it can't do any harm. If it's real we'd better see what it is. Right?'

'Right. Thanks,' Benny replied elatedly.

''Sokay. Afterwards we can go hunt my big insect, right?'

Benny was grinning as she nodded, but still she was afraid of the cellar. It couldn't have been a dream. Dreams don't inspire so much fear.

Sandra reached the front door, unlocked it and pulled it open. Her apology had begun before it was fully open.

'I'm sorry you've had to wait so long, but this is a big house and I was busy in the cellar.' The apology was abruptly curtailed when she saw the figures on the far side.

There were two people standing on the porch. Sandra knew neither. They were tall, sharp-featured, blue-eyed and blonde. Both wore the same patient expression. Sandra was startled by how attractive she found both.

Their clothes were formal; the man in a suit, the woman in a dress offset by her hair which hung around her shoulders. Hair and clothes that seemed perfectly dry, though they must have walked through the rain up a muddy track to have reached the house.

'Good evening,' the man announced in tones just slightly too rich for Sandra's liking. 'My name is Gabriel.'

'And I am Tanith,' the woman continued. 'We are not expected.'

Their faces cracked open into self-satisfied crescent-moon smiles.

9

Virtual Murder

Winterdawn falls.

... this being only a couple of days after the grosvenor march he is staring at the woman who will be his wife and it occurs to him what a startlingly beautiful woman she is and he doesn't know her name ...

... so who are they? funny people or five? they'll stop this work over my dead body did you get the number of that maniac he looked familiar ...

... perception of the immortal soul crosses his mind it is an egg ...

... he finds himself hanging upside-down for no immediately apparent reason the world is running in slow motion a bead of blood gradually seeping from his leg moulding itself into a perfect spheroid and gently descending to impact on the cover of the john pilger book jenny keeps on the dashboard the blood explodes flattening itself across the cover and he finds himself staring into the face of his wife again and again it occurs to him what a startlingly beautiful woman she is and it occurs to him that while his wife is strapped into the seat beside him her beautiful head is lying in a ditch by the roadside not three yards away ...

... winterdawn begins to scream ...

The Doctor falls.

... thirteen shafts of cold obsidian hollow and rotting that is my soul my soul my soul damn you my soul and it is not theirs to take ...

... there is only one thing only one and one alone ...

... i am the light and the resurrection i am the devil come to do the devil's work i am faust come from a race of fausts who sold our souls for thirteen long lives while others drop like mayflies and come friendly bombs and drop on gallifrey i hated that world i hated it all ...

... i swear to protect the ancient law of gallifrey with all my might and main and to the end of my days i will with justice and with honour temper my actions and my thoughts ...

... i am a kind man who never uses violence where it is not necessary i am never cruel or cowardly violence always rebounds on itself i love life ... it becomes necessary to seek out and entrap evil in order to destroy it before its twisted roots blossom if innocents suffer that is a sad consequence of my action the greatest good for the greatest number life is expendable my enemies will be exterminated ... do I contradict myself? very well then I contradict myself, (i am large, i contain multitudes) ...

... my companions you gave me my life and sometimes you gave me yours too i loved you all i never want you to leave because it is like death for me how many times have i died how many lives have i cut away from myself through pursuit of righteousness regardless of consequence and how many resurrections staged i am an old man who is about to die young ...

... raise my body to a burning cross i have fought evil and evil has made me and in the scheme of reality i am what i am i am not a time lord i reject the title i am myself i am a doctor and healer a good man i've got nothing to say but what a day how's your boy been good morning good morning good morning believe me believe me believe me ...

... we are but shadows and shadows of shadows ...

Winterdawn seizes the arms of his chair, finger-nails digging into the leather upholstery, a desperate effort to steady himself.

'Believe me,' the Doctor whispers, tears leaving long stains on his face.

Winterdawn found himself gasping for breath. The experience had left him exhausted and exhilarated. Pleasure and pain entwined together. He threw his head back and breathed heavily.

The experience had lasted for no time and forever – it couldn't be compared to such limited concepts. It just was.

'I think,' it was the Doctor's voice, but it seemed strange and new to Winterdawn, 'our ordeal is over.'

'Oh God, yes,' Winterdawn replied between breaths. 'What did you see ... no, don't tell me, I don't want to know. Where are we?'

'Nowhere and everywhere, Winterdawn,' the Doctor replied, his voice rich with confidence. 'In the heart of darkness.'

Winterdawn let his eyes slip open, and stared into the infinite.

And the infinite stared back at him.

Interstitial space unfolded. It was an incomprehensible sight. For a second Winterdawn's mind rejected everything around him and he was plunged into a shroud of darkness. Then the shroud slipped.

Winterdawn was reminded of a kaleidoscope – a banal analogy, but the best he could manage. The colours were clear and precise and sharp. They *sang*. Floating and merging and swirling into a whirlpool. Even the colourlessness was beautiful. Winterdawn had never realized that grey could contain so many tones and shades and mixtures.

He blinked and everything was obsidian. Shiny, brilliant blackness. Then white, then chessboard, then pale green like a rough sea journey.

Winterdawn threw back his head and howled.

'Yes!' he screamed at the sky. 'I have abstracted reality! I have unbound the quantum Prometheus! I did it!' He brought his hands together in a single motion. A thunderclap shook the scenery.

'Doctor, you don't know how this makes me feel. This is wonderful, I feel – Jesus, what a load of crap – I feel amazing! I want to sing and dance.' He slapped his hands against the back of his head, his enthusiasm waning. 'And dance. Anyway,' he continued, outlining his plans for the Doctor's benefit, 'this is the beginning. From here we can access any time-space event in history. We could travel to alien galaxies in a matter of seconds. There'll be matter transmission, inter-real travel, maybe even time travel. It begins here – a scientific, social and metaphysical revolution!'

'A journey of a thousand miles begins with but a single step.'

'I couldn't have put it better myself.' Winterdawn smiled. 'Shall we explore?' The Doctor smiled thoughtfully and Winterdawn, not expecting anything other than a positive response, took this as a 'yes'.

'There should be a gate around here somewhere,' he said. 'Our link back to reality.'

'Generated by the tetrahedron?'

'That's right.'

'In turn, operated by Harry Truman.'

Winterdawn nodded.

'I see,' the Doctor replied. 'Perhaps . . .? Yes.'

He stretched an arm into the psychedelia. His fingertips seemed to penetrate the skin of the interstix, sinking into invisibility. His knuckles, hand, wrist and arm were consumed by the envelope of interstitiality.

Pain flashed across his face, vanishing as suddenly as it appeared. Winterdawn had a brief glimpse of tremendous, momentary effort. Then nothing. The Doctor's arm returned. A shape sat on his hand. It was an oval cut into the side of reality, filled with glowing colours as bright and clear as anything else in the gap, yet fixed like a stained-glass window. The gate suggested immutability, stasis, order in the chaos that surrounded them.

Gradually it dawned on Winterdawn that the oval was not in the Doctor's palm but distant. His sense of perspective was eroding. A wonderful feeling.

131

'You see, it was there all the time.' The Doctor smiled irritatingly. 'We just had to look for it. This is our lifeline back to normality. I suggest we don't stray too far.'

Winterdawn smiled.

'It's Truman isn't it? Okay, maybe you've reason to dislike him, but he's basically a good man. Trust me!'

The Doctor was silent, his face shorn of features.

'Shall we go?' Winterdawn asked, after a moment's silence.

'After you,' the Doctor suggested.

'Come on. Give us a push.'

The darkness was unwholesome. The usual musty scent was tinged with something sick, a familiar but elusive scent which made Ace's flesh shudder. It scared her. Bernice's fears had something going for them after all. A couple of hours down here and even she'd be a gibbering wreck.

Her torch beam punctured the darkness. It shed little light on her surroundings, but enough. Benny was ahead, trying to find something familiar. Ace let her beam dance on Benny's back and followed her lead.

'This looks familiar,' Benny called. 'Very familiar. Try singing, it can only inspire me.'

'I've got a bloody good voice,' Ace protested.

'I'm sure it went down well with the deaf community of Perivale.'

'I'd like to hear you do bet . . .' Ace broke off suddenly. Her right foot had sunk into something soft, wet, cold, unpleasant. She shook her leg violently, but the offensive article refused to budge.

'Shit,' she muttered.

'What is it?'

'I've put my foot in something.'

'That's nothing new. Can it wait, I think I've found . . .'

'Just give us a light,' Ace snapped.

'Okay, okay,' Benny muttered. Her torch light swung round and struck Ace painfully between the eyes. 'And in the darkness God said . . . oh shit!'

The light snapped off. A Benny-shaped shadow disappeared into the dark.

'What is it now?' Ace called, feeling the hounds of anger straining on the ends of their leashes.

'Ace,' Benny's voice was a quivering cocktail of hysteria, revulsion and horror. 'It's someone's head!'

The tetrahedron's inner light pulsed smoothly and slowly. It never failed to relax or soothe Truman. He was even beginning to feel kinder towards the Doctor and his entourage. Maybe he was wrong. His problem, he felt, was a lack of *empathy*. He rarely considered other people's motivations. There were still some doubts whispering at the back of his mind, but he let these slip away, losing himself in the pulse of the pyramid.

Something soft lighted on his shoulder. A small, warm hand. He let his gaze swing upwards and welcomed the sight of Sandra Winterdawn. She was standing over him, smiling at him with a warmth that, Truman felt, he hadn't seen before. He tried to return that warmth from behind his mask.

'Hello Harry,' Sandra said gently, and her voice had a new smoothness, an exciting emphasis. 'Can we talk? I mean, you have to work this thing.'

Truman shook his head. 'It works itself. I watch in case it does something wrong. Sit down, please.'

Sandra lowered herself into a squat on the far side of the tetrahedron. Truman found his attention caught briefly by her bare legs – uncovered just below the hem of her dressing-gown. Checking himself before his obsession became obvious, he raised his gaze and was entranced by Sandra's face. If it wasn't one thing, it was something else – not that he minded.

'You know,' Sandra began, picking her words with undisguised awkwardness, 'how close I was to Justin before he began to . . . lose himself?'

Truman nodded, grateful for the mask which hid his expression and the guilt that came with it.

'I first met him seven years ago. I loved him then. He

133

was a wonderful lover, and I ignored his faults.' She paused to glance around the room. When she resumed, her voice was disjointed, stumbling wildly through her words: 'My affection dried up long before his madness developed. He hurt me. Not physically, but he was screwing up my mind. And I *stuck* with him! I should have thrown him out but I didn't. And I don't know why.'

'I don't think I should be listening to this,' Truman whispered, taking advantage of Sandra's pause to voice his fears. He felt like he was breaking a taboo, rummaging around in her soul.

'Please, it's important.' Sandra smiled. Truman nodded resignedly.

'He was an emotional wreck. He'd do anything to get me the way he wanted. I don't think I saw that then, but I knew something was going wrong, I knew I was losing something. Then, of course, his mind cracked – don't know why, don't care. You turned up soon after – you know the rest. I was devoted to him, I nursed him back to health even though I knew he'd be just as bad as before, and having restored some measure of his sanity I watched everything collapse after five bloody minutes in Dad's experiment. Five *minutes. Wonderful!* One and a half years of putting up with a harmless nut, six months working on his mind, five minutes . . . ! And for not *one* second of all that time did I love him! I'd lost that. It was gone and it's *never* coming back.'

'I see,' Truman replied softly. 'Why do you . . .?' Sandra pressed a finger to the mouth of his mask. Instantly he fell silent.

'Justin is my patient, not my lover. Not any more.' Light tears began to bloat under her eyelids. 'Harry, I know more about you, about how you feel, than you realize yourself. When I was eighteen I thought I'd found a bloody good bloke, and he was but he was also immature and spiteful. You're like him, as he could have been if he'd grown up. You're *better* than he was.'

Truman let his tongue roll around the inside of his open but invisible mouth. 'What are you trying to say exactly?'

'Oh for Christ's sake you stupid bastard, do I have to spell it out for you?' Sandra screeched, tears flowing freely now. 'Don't you know what you want? How you feel? I know . . . I know and . . . and I want it too.'

'You are being serious, aren't you?'

A face red with anger and frustration screamed at him, 'Yes! Yes! I'd screw you on the floor here and now if it wasn't for the absolute certainty that Dad and that weirdo Doctor would come rolling out of the wardrobe in the middle of it! I-love-you-you-gormless-git!' She jerked her head out of eye contact, breathing heavily. Truman waited, shocked, for her to recover her composure. Delighted too, and excited, but mostly shocked. There was a suddenness and a certainty to the proceedings which left him numb. Suddenly everything was right with the world, his desire was in reach. It was too much to take in one go.

Sandra turned back to him, her face a normal, beautiful pale white. She'd wiped the tear stains away.

'Do you understand now?' she asked, voice little more than a whisper.

'Yes,' Truman replied, 'but I can't believe it.'

'Yes you can. Touch me. Touch me somewhere you really want to.'

Truman thought briefly about all the parts of her he wanted to touch and nervously settled on that one place for which his desire overrode everything. There. Tentatively, as if he was about to handle something rare and delicate – and he was – he let his hands brush against her face. One light palm pressing against her cheek, the other cupping itself under her chin. Sandra leaned back, her eyes closed, her breathing deep. Truman began to move his hands, stroking her face as delicately as he could possibly manage.

Her skin was warm and slightly damp with sweat. It was a good thing, the best thing Truman had known in his life.

'Don't stop,' Sandra was whispering, repeating it like a holy chant. He had to in the end, withdrawing his hands

135

in slow motion. Sandra opened her eyes and stared at him. He stared back, wondering what to do now.

Sandra leaned closer, pushing her head towards his. Instinctively Truman let his head swing round to meet hers, their faces locking together in a perfect, passionate motion. Sandra's soft lips pressed forcefully against cold, dead wood, an inanimate grin, the lips of the false face.

Truman could feel the pressure of her beautiful mouth through the hole in the mask. It was a second before that pressure became unbearable.

He dragged himself away from her, pulling away from her grip, burying his face – his mask – behind writhing hands. He screamed, at the frustration, at the injustice, at the insides of his mask.

'Take it off!' It wasn't a suggestion, it was an order. He stared at Sandra through the sockets of the mask, watching her pull round to face him. 'Take it off.'

'I can't.' Truman mustered as much calm as he could manage. He stabbed a finger viciously to his temple. 'Here is a *mess*! You don't want to know, believe me.'

'No,' Sandra replied in the same steel voice, 'I do. Take it off. Now.'

'No!' Truman screamed, desperately shaking his head.

'Then I will.' Hands clamped themselves onto the side of the mask and wrenched with an unexpected strength. The mask flew away from his face.

Sandra flinched as she saw his face. But it was momentary and it disappeared with the speed of its arrival.

There was silence, encapsulated in a second.

'You're beautiful,' Sandra said.

'You're lying,' he accused. 'You can't see properly.'

'I wouldn't lie. And I can see perfectly.'

Truman found himself kissing her before he realized what he was doing. It was a wonderful feeling – to kiss again, to kiss properly for the first time – made more wonderful still by Sandra. She wasn't repulsed. She was enjoying it. *Enjoying!*

They broke off simultaneously, staring into each other's eyes with a new understanding.

136

'Stop shaking,' Sandra insisted, smiling with a vicious and exhilarating arrogance. She closed her eyes and in the single most sensual movement Truman had ever seen, peeled away the top of her gown to reveal beautiful, milk-white shoulders. Truman just stared. He never understood quite what happened next. There was a flurry of limbs and wild actions and suddenly Truman found himself lying on his side on the floor, half-pinned down by Sandra, her thighs wrapping around his hips. Her dressing-gown had mostly slipped away, revealing far more of her wonderful body than he had ever hoped to see.

Everything crystallized into a single moment stretching into forever.

. . . Truman leant forward, pushing a hand under one of Sandra's breasts, his lips against hers, everything was perfect and . . .

Eternity was blown away by a modest cough. A meaningful cough from the other side of the room. The moment unravelled. Truman looked up.

There were two figures. Two utterly normal and utterly unfamiliar figures. Truman stared at them in disbelief, feeling no guilt, no shame. He wondered why they seemed so ridiculous.

'And what will daddy say if he catches you?' the male figure asked.

Truman stared at the man's hand.

The man was holding up the tetrahedron for him to see.

The tetrahedron-light was dying, pulsing slow and dim.

In another facet of reality, Winterdawn *knew*. His head snapped up in alarm.

'The gate!' he yelled. 'The gate is closing!'

The Doctor was already spinning the wheelchair round, shoving it with vicious energy. The chair hurtled back at immeasurable speed. Kaleidoscopic unreality became fantasmagoric truth – colour blurring around them like a tunnel of blazing light. The gap became focused by their thoughts, their desire to reach the gate.

It was visible in the distance – a pin-point of fixed colour.

The light at the end of the tunnel, Winterdawn snatched wildly at his random, incoherent thoughts, *is the headlamp of an oncoming train.*

'How do we know?' the Doctor screamed, voice caught in the slipstream, absorbed into the sound and momentum of the tunnel.

'We don't *know*!' Winterdawn howled back, uncertain whether the Doctor could hear. 'We *feel*!' It sounded hollow – facile even. A burst of optimistic rationalism surged inside him. Maybe it was a false alarm, a panic reaction to some extra-real phenomena – *anything* so long as the gate was there.

It wasn't. Stained-glass colours flared at the end of the tunnel. The light streaked. And then, then there was no light, no colour, no tunnel, no sound, no urgency, no gate. The Doctor pulled the wheelchair to a halt, though it felt to Winterdawn that they were spinning unguided through the dark like a space capsule out of orbit. They hurtled past meaningless grey shapes that pierced the gloom.

One of the grey-shapes was the Doctor. He was larger and darker than Winterdawn remembered.

Winterdawn hugged himself as an icy hopelessness cut through him.

'I'm sorry,' the Doctor's voice was light. 'I was too slow.'

'No. We were too far. We couldn't have made it in time.'

The Doctor became a brooding shape on the edge of his vision. Winterdawn also fell silent, because there was nothing to say.

Then there was.

'You understood Truman better than I did.'

The Doctor shook his head slowly.

'No, *you* were right. I don't think this is deliberate. I don't know . . . Truman fascinates me.'

'He does? He's always seemed perfectly normal to me.'

'Normal?' The Doctor swung round so that Winterdawn

138

caught a sudden blast of sharp features. 'How long have you known that he isn't human?'

Truman extricated himself from Sandra's tangled limbs. The strangers didn't move, nor did Sandra – she lay on the floor, half-covered by her gown, watching the new-comers in meek abeyance.

Truman was reacting. The shock faded, replaced by anger and shame at the shattering of *his* private moment, of Sandra's moment. Their moment of intimacy. But even his anger was counterbalanced by his curiosity.

'How did you get into this house?' His voice shook, restrained.

'Through the front door. Ms Winterdawn let us in.'

'No. She wouldn't let strangers in.' Truman surprised himself with his reasonable tone.

'Oh she knows us,' the man replied. 'Not as well as you know us.'

'I don't know you,' Truman snapped, but he began to doubt what he was saying. There *was* something familiar about the pair.

They were immaculate. They were beautiful. Truman had never seen a more attractive woman than the blonde standing in front of him – not even Sandra – though her sexuality was lined with an icy, physical humour that Truman found repellent. There was something in their appearance that was sickening – flesh too pale, features too precise, too perfect to be genuinely attractive.

They were there, in his deepest, darkest memories.

'I know you?' Anger evaporated, replaced by fear.

'Forgive us,' the woman replied. 'Our manners are so very coarse. I am Tanith and this is my brother Gabriel.'

'Harry Truman,' Truman replied weakly, automatically.

'No,' Gabriel insisted. 'Harry Truman does not exist.'

'I exist.' It was a statement of fact. No argument.

'You exist. Harry Truman doesn't,' Tanith pointed out.

'Then who am I?' he laughed, bewildered and afraid.

Gabriel's reply was soulless and deadpan. And, Truman realized, true.

'You're Justin Cranleigh.'

Truman made tiny shakes of the head, but it was self-denial. Tanith was talking but he didn't take it in. Only the gist, the bare bones.

Justin Cranleigh was a vain and stupid man, a man whose mind worked on such a simple level that he was the perfect victim for Gabriel and Tanith's mental attack. It came quickly but viciously. They used his mind as a blueprint. Minor background details they changed, memories they blurred. They drove a block through his mind – a trauma, a terrible accident – a fiction to cover the memory gaps. In the process, Cranleigh was driven insane – a side effect. Gabriel and Tanith noted it, regretting nothing.

They took Cranleigh's revised mind and shaped it, built it a body from the stuff of chaos from interstitial space, the building blocks of reality. This proved a partial success. Their creature seemed perfect but his body structure was unstable; there were physical defects. But it lived.

Several weeks after Cranleigh went mad, Truman arrived in response to an advertisement. The two identical minds had a certain rapport, but no one saw the similarities. Cranleigh himself had only made stabs at the truth, in the darkest moments of his madness.

Tanith stopped talking. Truman let his body sink into itself.

'Why?'

'You were a prototype,' Gabriel announced. 'For a project we are about to launch in this house.'

Truman didn't care. He could no longer care.

'You are a great achievement.' Tanith told him. 'You're Justin Cranleigh as he might have been. Compared to him, you're a saint.'

'Look.' Gabriel pointed at Sandra. 'She loved you more than she ever loved him. We didn't make her feel anything – all we did was remove her inhibitions. She was a distraction, but not a hollow one.'

'I see,' Truman continued, pulling himself up in an

attempt to regain his dignity. 'You're going to kill me, aren't you?'

'How can we kill you? You were never alive to begin with.'

'We are going to dissolve your body,' Gabriel said, without a hint of emotion or relish. 'Your mind-set will be re-absorbed by Cranleigh.'

'And that will restore his sanity?'

'No.' Tanith's retort was dull but Truman had caught the hint of a smile twitching on the edge of her lips.

'Just one thing,' Truman said. 'You say my accident never happened. What about my face?'

'Look,' Gabriel said, and brought the tetrahedron up to Truman's face. In each surface he saw his face, reflected.

His face was no-face. From chin to hairline, ear to ear, there was nothing but blank flesh.

'I saw the scars,' he said. This wasn't enough to shock him, not now.

'You saw what you wanted to see,' Gabriel said. 'Your mind could shape your face briefly. That's how you manage to eat and talk and see and kiss.' He rolled to a halt, then checked himself. 'Sandra saw a blank, but she didn't care. It was your face; she thought it was beautiful.'

Truman nodded and smiled. Imagined a smile.

'Goodbye Truman,' Tanith said suddenly. 'I liked you.'

She raised her fist and pushed it into Truman's head.

Truman felt no pain, no fear, no anguish, just a gentle suggestion of decay. His mind crumbled away at the edges, the remains floating away into a vacuum. Memory, experience, sensation eroded. It was a good feeling.

My name is Harry Truman.

Harry Truman.

Truman.

T . . .

Tanith swept across the room to recover the abandoned mask. She clasped it in both hands, stared into its hollow eyes and smiled at the empty grin.

'How sad,' she pronounced.

*

Benny was a weight against Ace's side – propped upright only by Ace's strained efforts to hold her. Ace's experience of journeying from the cellar was one of exertion, of stumbling in the darkness, of grim silence broken by Benny's infrequent mumbling. Not that she minded.

There were bodies in the cellar, maybe twenty or thirty. Serious collateral damage. No, sod the euphemisms: *corpses*. Men and women, old and young. Ace couldn't blame Benny for freaking out.

They'd found the body of a little boy on the edge of one pile. Better preserved than the rest, he could only have been there for a few days. Benny crouched over his body, crying quietly, making no secret of it. She'd touched the kid's face.

Cold, dead, blue-white. Serene but lifeless. It crumbled and broke apart as she touched, sunk into the skull. If she could have ignored the churning in her stomach, Ace might have found it fascinating.

Benny had collapsed into a shrieking mess on the floor. Ace took it better. Her horror was more refined. Fear, revulsion, frustration – all compacted into a cold arrowhead in her mind – the desire to find out what could have done this to all these people and crush it. Maybe that was no better a reaction that Benny's.

She was no longer fazed by some of the things she'd seen in her travelling with the Doctor. When you're up to your neck in shit on some alien world while what started as an exercise in precise military planning is turning into an exercise in getting out with your major organs intact it wouldn't pay to freak. Ace had done it once and almost lost her legs and central nervous system as a result – never again. She'd become hardened to death and gore. She'd told the Doctor.

'You're lying,' he had said.

'No. This shit doesn't screw me *period*.' She was trying to sound cool.

'It should.' The Doctor pulled a sour face. Ace had withdrawn to her room for a few hours of self-examination. She'd ended up crying into her pillow for something delicate and gentle that she'd lost for ever.

She put an arm round Benny, half-leading, half-dragging her into the darkness. The bodies and the sickness they left behind them.

She was already thinking dispassionately. Why should the bodies corrupt so quickly? How did they die? Who had killed them? She found herself discounting Winterdawn. Obviously you couldn't get a wheelchair down there, but also it wasn't his *style*. Ace had him marked down as the sort of person who put non-traceable poisons into china cups at tea-parties, not a cold-blooded killer clutching the throats of anyone who came in reach. He was too sinister to be *that* banal.

They reached the central cellar passage. Ace had become tired through the exertions of propping up Benny, and pushed the older woman up against the wall where she had a more solid and enduring support. Ace slumped beside her, pressing her hands against her face and drawing in huge breaths of air.

'How are we Dorothy? Have we found the hidden treasure?'

Ace pulled her hands from her face and glared with a sharp intensity at the figures advancing towards her. They didn't seem to be walking. Their legs went through the motions but their feet weren't quite touching the ground. They were gliding. Two: a man and a woman. The bloke was sexy but there was something callous shining in his perfect blue irises.

She didn't know who they were, but she found herself accepting their presence automatically. They were just there. They were who they were.

'What do you know?' she spat.

'*Everything*,' the woman replied. Ace shivered, believing her.

'I'm afraid,' said the man, voice smooth as an eggshell, malignant as cancer, 'things have changed. The Doctor will not be rejoining you. He has quite literally shuffled off this mortal coil. He'll miss the fun and games.'

'Tomorrow,' the woman's mouth curled into a smile that bit into Ace's soul, 'we are going to have a great time. That's a promise. Be good.' With that the pair strolled away. Ace said nothing, watching their retreating backs as they slid into the darkness.

Well now Ace, there are two more names to add to the list of suspects.

Another figure detached from the shadows, hurtling down the tunnel towards her. A flustered and upset woman in a fluffy dressing-gown.

'Oh thank God.' Sandra collapsed against the wall beside Ace. 'Thank God,' she repeated, digging her fingers into the brickwork. 'Thank God.

'Harry is dead!' she howled, her face turning red and gushing tears. 'They killed him. They took him apart. He didn't have a face. We were in love. He didn't have a face, oh God, he didn't have a face . . .'

Ace pulled her arms around the woman, smothering her in a comradely embrace. Sandra buried her face in Ace's shoulder.

'What did they mean?' Ace whispered after a moment's silence. 'What have they done to the Doctor?'

'They killed Truman.' Sandra's voice was terrible. 'He was the gate, their link back to the real world. The Doctor, Dad, they're trapped.'

Ace released Sandra and slammed herself against the wall. A dull pain cracked along her spine but it only made her more determined.

'What do we do?' It was Benny's voice at her shoulder, a voice looking for a lead. Ace glanced at Sandra and realized that she too was waiting for someone to make a decision.

Well, it wasn't as if the Doctor was going to turn up, handing out advice to anyone stupid enough to listen.

'I'll tell you,' she told them. 'We get out of here, out of this house, out of the way of these – who d'you say . . .'

'Gabriel and Tanith,' Sandra confirmed.

'We get out of the way of Gabriel and Tanith. Then we think about what we're going to do. Then we come back

144

in force. And we blow them off the map. How does that sound?'

She glanced between Benny and Sandra. There was no dissent.

The rush for the door was a shambles, a mass of limbs and bodies all consumed with but a single thought. *Escape.* Ace didn't try to impose any order. She was more worried about what would happen if Gabriel and Tanith tried to get in their way. Ace became obsessed by them – there was something about them that demanded obsession. They were enigmas. Ace remembered the sight of the TARDIS central column bleaching white with an alien power, and wondered just how much power these enigmas might have. Not too much, she hoped.

They didn't appear. Ace was surprised. Maybe they weren't as all-knowing as they claimed. The front door loomed up before the women like a grey altar slab, and Gabriel and Tanith were yet to appear. Sandra fell against the door and scrabbled at the locks and bolts that held it in place. With a desperate flourish she threw the door wide open.

The three women stared through the door – not at the quiet night-time countryside but into the heart of a swirling, buzzing void – a wall of static on the far side of the door. The void dared the women to approach it, certain that they couldn't. It was a door to nowhere.

The Doctor had never realized how claustrophobic an infinity could feel. He travelled through the vast wildernesses of time and space dimly aware that there were limits to his world, too distant to lace his *wanderlust* with boredom. He would never see everything.

Here interstitial reality expanded into eternity in all conceivable directions. He and Winterdawn were nothing, less than beads of water in the ocean of reality. They were without depth or weight. But somehow infinity seemed to crush around them, tightening like the darkness in a prison. It was a cell of inconceivable magnitude perhaps – but still a cell.

He had seen Truman's face. He only had himself to blame. He should have told Winterdawn, then none of this would have happened. No, that was pointless. The old man would have thought he was mad. Besides, he was certain that Truman hadn't closed the gate deliberately.

'How many Zen Buddhists does it take to change a light bulb?'

Winterdawn was slumped in his chair, stunned – almost paralysed – by the simultaneous closing of the gate and the Doctor's deductions about Truman's real nature. Or unreal nature. The jokes kept his mind off their predicament.

'I don't know, how many?'

'Three. One to change the light bulb, one not to change the light bulb and one to neither change nor not change the light bulb.'

The Doctor smiled. It was all he could manage.

'What about the one to neither change nor not change nor neither neither change nor not change the light bulb?'

'I'd forgotten him. Sorry.' The Professor's voice was old, drained of vitality.

'You don't suppose someone else could re-open the gate?' the Doctor asked, not hopefully.

'I don't think so. Truman and myself are trained. If anyone else tries, it'll almost certainly wipe their minds,' Winterdawn spoke calmly. 'We are stuck here, my friend. And there's no one to rescue us.'

'That's an assumption.'

'A reasonable one,' Winterdawn insisted. The Doctor found his cheery pessimism unnerving. 'There's one way out of here. One way, and even that may be barred to us. Here where the mundane facts of reality are locked away, can we age? Can we starve? Can we die?'

'It makes no difference. This is death,' the Doctor replied, darkening the atmosphere. Winterdawn looked at him quizzically.

'Death being a concept-condition with no physical or geographical or meaningful existence. This being a concept-place with no physical or geographical or meaningful existence. A living death.'

'You must be the life and soul of the party,' Winterdawn replied sourly.

'That's what Oscar Wilde told me. I think he was being serious then. I knew I had to come here in the end. The ancient mariner beached at last, on the high tide in the coast of nowhere. How does it feel to be free?'

'Hollow,' Winterdawn replied. 'There's something I must tell you.'

'Yes?' The Doctor looked up, intrigued. He couldn't understand how anything could be considered important in a place as uniform and levelling and empty as this. He was seeing things from the perspective of a Time Lord, with the resignation of a Time Lord and the despair of a Time Lord and the – Rassilon help us! – blunted imagination of a Time Lord. Winterdawn couldn't cope with the enormity – he was too human, too subjective in his thinking.

How much simpler things must seem, through the eyes of a human being.

'This place isn't part of the real universe. I think it might adapt itself to us.'

'Death is sentient. There's a cheering thought.' The Doctor smiled lopsidedly. And he meant it.

'It may look calm,' Winterdawn continued, ignoring the Doctor's interruption, 'but I doubt it will last. I believe the interstix is preparing to challenge us. I, uh, should have told you. Cranleigh was the first to enter the gap – of his own volition. He was . . . insane, for two years prior to that, but he'd built up his mental reserves, made something of a recovery.'

'And five minutes in the gap demolished his mind?' the Doctor asked, not expecting any answer other than a sincere 'yes'. There didn't seem to be another option.

'He was in a confused state, and he was vulnerable. I imagine the interstitial forces latched onto that immediately. We're better prepared, but we're going to be here for much longer than Cranleigh. We may go mad.'

147

'Look on the bright side. It'll be something to do.' The Doctor tried to smile. Winterdawn's expression remained grim. He jerked his chair forward, closer to the Doctor.

'I told you that I'm not entirely unobservant,' he said, staring up into the Doctor's eyes. 'It's impossible for you to have duplicated and surpassed my work into transcendentalism without the aid of the tetrahedron. Even if you could, it seems unlikely that you would disguise the result as a phone box and hide it in my cellar. Your conclusions about Truman fit the facts but it's what I'd think of immediately. There are things you've said that strike me as odd.'

'What do you want to know?' the Doctor replied guardedly.

'Are you human?'

'No.'

Winterdawn leant back in his chair, and raised a finger to rub his lower lip thoughtfully. Apart from that, he seemed almost unimpressed.

'Extraterrestrial?'

'Yes.'

'And your two girlfriends?'

'Ace was born in North London in 1970, Benny on an Earth colony in 2422. We travel in time and space in my police box.'

Winterdawn glanced down at his feet, then back up at the Doctor. He was laughing, tears guttering down his face like an overloaded storm-drain.

'Doctor, we may be trapped here for eternity, but at least we'll have something to talk about!'

The laughter broke off, cutting into a sharp yell. A thin red weal was cut into Winterdawn's cheek. The Professor raised a hand to his cheek, tentatively pressing his fingertips against the blood.

There was a sharp pain on the back of the Doctor's hand. He looked down and saw that a similar gash had appeared across his knuckles – blood rushing in a trail from a small incision.

In the heart of the wound was a tiny fragment of glass.

148

There was a gentle, rushing sound and tears erupted on the sleeve of his jacket. Something cut into his neck.

'The attack,' Winterdawn whispered.

A cloud was hurtling towards them from the unreal horizon, propelled by forces undefined by physics. The cloud glistened and sparkled with light. It was a cloud of fragments, a cloud of glass.

Suddenly they were in the heart of the cloud, in the middle of a maelstrom of glass shards. Pinprick pains erupted on the Doctor's face and hands, his clothes shredded in the onslaught, glass buried itself into his flesh and his eyes, his sight misting red with congealing blood. Winterdawn was flailing in the storm, knocked from his chair and thrown aside, screaming in agony. The Doctor's sight dulled into blackness. His senses were drowned by a chorus of nerves. They deafened him with their song of pain.

The Doctor opened his mouth to howl, only to find glass lodging in his throat. His pain escalated until he ceased even to feel it. There was just an agonizing nothing, wailing in the eye of the storm.

10

Love among the Ruins

The chair was harsh against Ace's back and there was a disturbing lightness on her chest. Horrible things danced in the darkness on the insides of her eyelids. Gabriel and Tanith had shaken her up more than she had believed. Still sleeplessness was security. Anything could get at her while she was asleep. She didn't believe that anything was going to try. Everything would happen, Gabriel and Tanith had promised, in the morning. She believed them, Christ alone knew why.

They had taken refuge in Sandra's bedroom. Ace had assumed leadership of the group, insisting they go somewhere safe and stay there *together* – safety in numbers, right? After they'd settled in Ace had realized they'd missed someone out. Cranleigh was loose in the house – easy prey for Gabriel and Tanith – and Sandra had mentioned someone called Wedderburn. Despite protests, Ace refused to let anyone go and find them, and the guilt was beginning to gnaw at her.

Ace was sitting on a chair propped up firmly against the door. She was grimly determined to stay awake. Benny was still messed up after her experiences in the cellar and Sandra was a wimp anyway. No one else was going to look out for them. Not the Doctor.

She stared across the room at Sandra, tucked safely in bed, sound asleep. She had cried her way into oblivion. For the past couple of hours she'd entertained Ace with a decent impersonation of a human-shaped rock.

Bernice was restless. She'd slumped quietly on the floor,

slipping into a light and troubled sleep, constantly turning and twisting, kicking her blanket away from her. Ace was tempted to cover her up but found that she couldn't budge from the chair. Benny was probably freezing, but Ace was loath to move. Jealously perhaps. Benny looked so much better than she ever had. Better body, figure, build.

Life, who needs it, eh?

Her eyes left Benny and latched onto the bullet hole clumsily punched into the ceiling. How the hell had that got there, she wondered? Whoever did it was using some bloody heavy artillery.

Ace wished she had a gun. Sod the Doctor and his stupid 'guns are for the limp-brained' moralizing. She needed the reassuring squareness pressed against her chest right now. There was something about Gabriel and Tanith that shitted her up. Something worse than evil, worse than death. She didn't know what it was but she'd have felt better if she had the means to shoot it.

The next minute Benny was shaking her awake. She woke swearing.

'Good morning.' Benny sounded cheerful but hollow. 'It's wonderful to find you so keen and ready for action.'

'Shitshitshitshit,' Ace spat, wondering what had died in her mouth. Her eyes leapt from Benny's lively but pale features to Sandra, who was hovering behind Benny's shoulder. Everyone seemed okay.

'Gabriel and Tanith have been,' Sandra said coldly and things weren't okay any more. Ace glanced round and saw that she was still jammed tightly against the door. No one could have got in, unless they could walk through walls, which was a possibility she hadn't discounted. She had to force herself not to howl with laughter. No, this was hysteria. This was not good.

'When? How? What?' she snapped, focusing herself on the matter in hand.

'They pushed this under the door.' Benny was bland. 'Ten minutes ago.'

She held a piece of card between finger and thumb. Ace stared at it.

GABRIEL & TANITH
cordially invite you to a breakfast
IN YOUR OWN HOME
to *celebrate*
THE END OF THE WORLD AS WE KNOW IT
and the birth pains of a new reality

'It's rather stylish,' Benny chimed in suddenly. 'Warped but logical.' Ace stared at her in uncomprehending malice and she broke off. 'It was only a thought. *I'm* not going.'

Bernice stared awkwardly at her feet, both planted firmly on the dining-room lino. Foremost in her mind was a sense of confusion. She looked away from her feet and stared coldly at Ace and Sandra, who shared the same bewildered facial expression. Benny was in doubt that her face was set similarly.

Sandra had left first, shuffling wordlessly out of the room. Ace immediately sprang after her – not to get her back in, as Benny had supposed – but to follow her downstairs. Then Benny felt herself shamble after them. There was no coercion – she knew exactly what she was doing and exactly why she *needed* to do it. Now she had stopped those motives seemed obscure.

Maybe it was mental control. Maybe it was a need. Maybe they *had* to see Gabriel and Tanith. Maybe the Doctor was going to land the TARDIS somewhere peaceful. Pigs would sprout wings and defy the laws of aerodynamics.

Maybe she'd just got a touch tipsy and would wake soon in her room in the TARDIS. But everything that had happened since Gabriel and Tanith seemed dreamlike. It felt so unreal that it had to be true.

She let her eyes pan down the length of the room, contemplating the present contents of the non-real paradigm that Sandra called her 'dining-room'. The table, a hefty oak affair, was already laid neatly. Lace cloth buried beneath cruet, a jungle of flowers, cutlery tray, toast rack and butter dish. And plates. Five plates bearing piles of something greasy but appetizing. Benny decided that cholesterol poisoning was preferable to starvation. This particular strain of food didn't seem familiar but since the Doctor had a peculiar inability to master the culinary arts she'd probably tasted something similar, incognito, aboard the TARDIS. Benny wanted to swoop down and consume everything on the table, up to and including the begonias, but she held back. She glanced at Ace again, seeing equal uncertainty in her companion. Ace wasn't looking at the table but over it, her gaze fixed on their hosts.

Gabriel and Tanith stood with their backs to the window and the morning sun. Benny remembered little of last night and she hadn't known what to expect from this pair. Ace had told her that they were attractive with a loathsome edge, but Benny wasn't so certain. It was true, they were physical marvels. They were beautiful as angels, gods walking among their mortal followers. They were attractive and desirable and Gabriel was hunky enough to give her a hot and sticky thrill whenever she really thought about him, but – and this was a positively humungous 'but' . . .

They were repulsive. There was not one aspect of their oh-so-beautiful appearance that didn't make Benny want to retch with disgust. They were stunning corpses with rotting souls. When they smiled Benny felt her stomach trying to eat through her intestines.

They weren't dressed as she remembered. Gabriel had changed into a dark green velvet suit with a thick collar and a neck clasp. A patterned smoking jacket tightened around his stomach like a miniature corset, and a ruffled shirt made the space up to his neck. There was an elaborate ring on his finger, inset with a jewel the colour of blood. Tanith wore a heavy white felt suit, a check-patterned necktie clutching at her throat. A formless white cap balanced on the top of her head, forever on the verge of collapsing. Their appearance carried with it a brooding elegance, which seemed to enhance their wretchedness.

'You had to come in the end.' Gabriel smiled lopsidedly,

watching them through half-closed eyes. 'Welcome little ladies, little dolls.'

'Sit!' Tanith declaimed, throwing her arms wide open in a too-expansive gesture of welcome. 'Eat, drink and be merry!'

'For tomorrow we die?' Ace growled by Benny's ear.

'Oh, we have no intention of keeping you waiting.' Gabriel's voice was honey. 'Now, your places are allotted, your breakfasts full and English.'

Sandra moved jerkily to the nearest chair and lowered herself onto it slowly. Benny noticed that she was shaking, manipulating her cutlery crudely, fumbling as if they were unfamiliar utensils.

Benny was next. She found her plate accompanied by a label bearing her name in a Gothic hand, alongside a scratchy caricature of her features. This was exaggerated and spiteful and it left her feeling wounded, in a small way. She kept silent, took her place and began to eat tentatively, prodding at the food trying to work out what it was and whether or not it was still alive before slashing at it with her knife. It tasted okay. Whatever else they might be, Gabriel and Tanith were good cooks.

Ace hovered defiantly in the doorway, watching with deep suspicion as the domestic scene unfolded before her. Only Benny seemed to notice her stance. Faced with a choice of giving in to pressure or being both ignored and hungry Ace chose the former. She sat warily between Sandra and Benny, glaring across the table and occasionally deigning to eat something.

There was a glass by Benny's plate, filled almost the brim with milk.

'You don't have anything with a bit more body I suppose?'

'A couple of things,' Tanith replied. A faint smile crossed her face.

Silence ensued, punctuated by the sound of cutlery cracking, four jaws grinding, tension expanding across the table, minutes aching past.

'We are,' Gabriel broke the silence, 'in residence in the

now disused room of the late Jennifer Winterdawn. I hope no one has any objections.'

Silence.

'Dad wouldn't like that,' Sandra said softly.

'Your father has no objection,' Tanith giggled. 'He is beyond such mortal concerns.'

Benny's body contracted, a protection against the sudden cold.

'What have you done with them?' Ace said with a clarity and a politeness that she only used when she was being really hostile.

'They are gone, locked forever in limbo. It was simple, implanting suggestions in their minds, playing on their curiosity.'

'They have been written out of the book of life,' Tanith embellished the theme. 'They were cluttering up the plot.'

'You see,' Gabriel added, 'you three are superb, lovely human beings. The Doctor and the Professor are less so. We really wouldn't get on with them, so we shunted them out of reality.'

'My brother says that they are a couple of devious and untrustworthy types who, given time, could work out what makes us tick and then how to stop the pendulum. You three, on the other hand, are wonderful individuals but completely incapable of working together without the guidance of your patriarchs. A sad fact but true. The Doctor is a loner at heart. He believes that he can use friendship to build a shell against the cold and heartless world he is forced to confront. He doesn't need you, but you need him.'

'He'll get back,' Ace said, her hostility undiminished. 'Be sure.'

'He will not,' Gabriel snapped. It seemed to be the end of the matter.

'So what do you want with us?' Benny chimed in.

'Anything you can do,' Tanith replied, 'we want it.'

'And what are you doing?' Benny pressed her point home.

'Taking on the universe,' Gabriel replied. 'We've

already destroyed it, you understand. Things can never be the same again. There is a monumental battle between creator and creation which must inevitably lead to the destruction of one or the other. We're going to have fun finding out.'

The pause was shattered by a low, melodic song emanating from Tanith's lips. Benny didn't believe that something so disgusting could be responsible for something so beautiful.

'Spread a little happiness as you go by . . .'

Gabriel was on his feet, his arm a motion blurring across the table top. There was contact – a crunch of flesh against flesh. Benny whirled round to see Ace's head lolling backwards, blood rippling from the corner of her mouth. For a horrible moment Benny was afraid that Gabriel had broken her neck. Then she straightened up, wiping the blood away. A smear remained.

Both Gabriel and Tanith were standing now. Tanith was passive, hands tucked into her jacket pockets, a mischievous smile on her lips. Gabriel was a brooding, aggressive hulk, licking spots of Ace's blood from his fist.

'Happiness,' Ace snarled. 'Yeah.' She delivered an ocean of saliva into Gabriel's face.

Benny felt a desperate thing trying to claw its way out of her stomach. She'd never believed there was really such a thing as evil. She'd never believed that such an absolute concept could have a tangible existence. But here it was now, standing in front of her.

Absolute physical Evil. With a big 'E'. She said so.

'Evil?' Tanith's voice was a cool hush, a missile-launching-sequence hush. She didn't raise her voice and that made Benny feel worse. 'You *dare* compare us to that trivial nonentity? Evil is a fashion victim! We go beyond evil and its pallid opponent.'

'We are lovely, loathsome, wonderful, worthless, superlative and shit. The word made flesh!'

'The universe in microcosm. The cosmos incarnate. The totality of all things incognito. And more. And less.'

156

'We are mad love in an existential universe. We are nihilist messiahs.'

'Not born, aborted into the universe. We have the light. We have the knowledge. We have the power and the glory forever and ever amen.'

'We are freaked out. We are totally off our trolley. We are one coconut short of a fairground stall. In short . . .'

'We are deranged. We are psychopaths, sociopaths, up the garden path.'

'We are mad. And you are trapped with us.'

Delicious smiles played across their faces. Insane, ripe smiles.

'But,' Gabriel clapped his hands together, his voice gaining a strident, plummy quality, 'you don't want to hear about our problems.'

To one side of Benny, Sandra began to retch frantically.

'Which one do you like?' Gabriel asked his companion.

'Oh, Dorothy.' Tanith gazed lazily at Ace who squirmed aggressively. 'The way she moves is thrilling. Then Sandra, a bedtime confection.'

'You don't rank Bernice. My favourite: the fake. The completely unqualified archaeologist who got away with it because she was *good*. What a wonderful world she must have lived in, not knowing how much was real and how much wasn't. A beautiful twilight world.'

'You're talking about perception, my brother. I'm talking about sex.'

'The same thing surely?'

'Shut up!' Benny screamed, surprising herself with her force and her venom. 'I don't want to listen to any of this!'

A silence descended on the room. The noiselessness of a funeral.

'Come here Benny,' Gabriel said. Not a request.

'No,' Benny insisted.

'I said, come *here*!'

Suddenly there was a rod of agony driving through bone and muscle and tissue and sinew and nerves, piercing her spine. She felt herself go rigid, her body stiffening

157

soundlessly. Her eyes bulged, as electrical pain surged through her nerve system. There were needles through her hands and wrists and shoulders and head and knees and feet and thighs. Invisible wires tore into her body, now loose, now taut. Her wires wrenched, she leapt to her feet in a single jerky movement. The puppet masters tugged again and she was pulled across the room until she was face to face with Gabriel.

Ace was shouting at the back of her head. Benny tried to concentrate on what she was saying, but found it impossible. The limits of the world had shrunk to include herself, her pain, Gabriel, and the space between them.

Gabriel leant forward, his fingers locking round her neck. The pressure on her body loosened. She was free but there were other pressures now, Gabriel's thumbs nuzzling under her chin. She looked into his eyes and saw nothing. No pupils, no retina, no whites, no colour.

In that single, quiet moment Benny knew that she was going to die.

'Hello Benny Summerfield,' Gabriel said. 'Remember me?'

'I remember you.' Talking was an effort. 'I saw you in the cellar.'

'You saw the whole of me. These bodies are fragments of what we are.'

'You showed me things.'

'We showed you all things. We can see all things. We draw our sight and power from the structure of the universe itself. All space. Omnicognition.

'Do you know, Benny, how easy it is to kill someone?'

'Yes.' She didn't speak, but Gabriel seemed able to hear her thoughts.

'Oh, it is much easier than that. Much easier,' Gabriel continued. 'Life is fragile and death is final. All I have to do now is grind my thumbs, perhaps for a minute. Then you can let go.'

'You're not scaring her! You're not scaring anyone!' Ace was yelling out of Benny's vision. Briefly Benny found herself feeling friendlier, closer, to Gabriel than her travelling companion.

'Yes. Yes, he is.' Benny was shocked to feel tears brushing her skin.

'You think of hurting her and I'll kill you! Bastard!' Ace howled.

'Ace,' Benny's voice was loud and wavering, 'if you don't shut up now then I will come back and haunt you.'

Gabriel was nodding.

'You understand,' he seemed soothing and reassuring, 'the finality. When I press I will destroy a life. It is *that* simple. There are millions who don't know you and don't care about you. There is pressure and something lively and pleasant and valuable will leave the world for good. As I press you will understand what it is to die, what a terrible thing I am doing, the absolute certainty that the end of your life is here and now. Life is life and death is death. These are facts. They cannot be abrogated. Goodbye.'

Gabriel began to squeeze. It was a gentle sensation but Benny was panicking. Inside she was screaming in terror and anguish, filled with a dreadful fear of the unknown and an eternal nothing. Bedtime existential terror she'd felt before, never this close.

Oh God, I don't want to die!

'Stop it!' Ace shrieked, but the voice was distant. Benny's eyes were closing. The world was dark and airless. Ace's voice was her last link with life. She needed to cling to it. That voice which had sounded so disgusting less than two minutes ago. She loved it now. She loved Ace. She loved life. Ace was howling. Everything was going.

Then there was no pressure. The hands were still there, clenched round her throat, but no longer pressing. Benny breathed vigorously, not daring to make another move, too scared even to open her eyes.

'We understand.' Tanith's voice. 'We understand exactly what it is to kill, exactly what is lost at the moment of death. We understand how valuable each and every life is.

'We just don't care.'

159

Suddenly Benny's dark world was whirling and tumbling. A giddy sensation clutched her. She was falling through the darkness. She clutched herself protectively, bruising her back and shoulders as they smashed against something solid.

The pain was dull and natural. There was nothing at her neck. Her eyes fell open and she saw that she was on the floor, half-crouched, half-lying where Gabriel had shoved her. He stood over her, smiling graciously. Benny flinched, certain he was going to kick her.

'And what about the people in the cellar?' Ace said accusingly. 'Did you make them understand?'

'Ah, you've put two and two together,' Tanith replied. 'It wasn't a massive leap to that conclusion I trust?'

'We killed them.'

'Don't worry. They suffered. Each killing took hours, packed with intense torture.'

'They saw the other bodies. They understood that they were going to die. They had no illusions about that.'

'Why?' Ace was saying. Not shouting. Whispering terribly.

'Those killings had a purpose, though one I doubt you would appreciate.'

'We are not, as you may have noticed,' Tanith took over, 'human. We are incorporeal creatures, beings of pure energy drawing our strength from the cosmic structure itself. We could do anything in that form, but we prefer to address the human race in its own shape.'

'We lured people to the house, killed them and removed parts from their genetic structures. And we sculpted them into containers for our essences.'

'To all intents and purposes now, we are fully human. We have human bodies and human organs and human responses to external stimuli.'

Benny stared up at them, disgusted.

'You said you could do anything! Why was it so bloody necessary to kill those people? Couldn't you have grown those bodies on your own?'

Tanith nodded.

'It was more fun this way.'

'You're sick!' Ace was yelling.

'Delightfully so. *Elegantly* so.'

There was a crash and a thump above Benny's head. With another crash Ace leapt onto the floor by Benny's side, her body hunched and arching forward. There was an intense animalistic feel to her movements, a predator ready to strike. In one hand she held a knife – the same knife Cranleigh had once pressed to Benny's face. Ace must have found it in Sandra's room.

It was motionless in Ace's rigid hand.

'Time for the surgical cure, sickos,' Ace spat.

'Oh put it away, you don't know where it's been,' Tanith snapped.

'It's been in Benny's socks. *Not* pretty!'

Ace said nothing. She held the knife still.

'Melodrama,' Gabriel said. He reached forward, locked his fingers round the blade and pulled it from Ace's grip. He screamed and dropped the knife, his hand was curling into a fist. Benny saw the blood seeping between the cracks in the fingers onto his wrist. Impossibly white skin stained dark pink.

The pain was etched onto his face. So tangible and real, he couldn't be faking. It had hurt him.

Benny looked across to Tanith and saw the woman shaking her head. Smiling too. She reached the knife before Ace had a chance to dart for it.

Eventually Gabriel's scream dulled into heavy breathing. He released his injured hand and raised his head so that all in the room could see his haggard, satisfied expression. He opened his fist into a flat palm, displaying a deep red gash, still open and dribbling blood.

'Something with more body, Benny,' he said shakily.

Benny tried to resist. God knows she tried, but the minds of Gabriel and Tanith were too powerful for her. She sprang forward, raising her head to nuzzle against the outstretched palm. Sick with herself she began to bite at the wound, letting the blood flow into her mouth. Blood guttered into her mouth. She began to lick generously, spooning more and more between her lips. The blood was tasteless but it was the sensation that drove her on. It was electric, like a first kiss, like the first time she'd had sex.

'No!' She pulled her mouth from his hand, spitting bloody saliva flecks. Scowling, Benny let her body sink into a protective foetal shape. She felt dirty and degraded and violated and deprived and sickened.

'We are leaving now,' Tanith said. 'You can do what you like.'

Benny didn't see them leave.

Ace was crouching beside her, an arm hugging round her waist. Benny felt warm, as if it was her mother holding her. It was a good feeling.

'Those two are on a power kick.' Ace's voice was gentle as her body. 'Everything they do is aimed at degrading us. If they force us to do these things, if they force us to *enjoy* them – then that's their problem not ours. We're going to take everything they throw at us and throw it back at them. And we're going to win. They're never, ever, going to get away with this.'

'Ace,' Benny said, clutching at the collar of Ace's combat suit. 'They're going to kill me. I'm not going to leave this house, not under my own steam. When I'm dead I want you to remember: I loved travelling in the TARDIS. If you see the Doctor again, tell him that I loved him. He was a git, but I loved him. And I loved you. Remember.'

'You're not going to die.'

'I am,' Benny replied as if it was a certainty. And it was.

'No,' Ace insisted. 'I'm going to do something. Anything. You with me?'

Benny stared at her shaking hands. They didn't seem like parts of her body. They were distant things, parts of a distant creature.

'What are you going to do?'

'I don't . . .' Ace began.

'I'll tell what we're going to do.'

Benny stared mutely at Sandra. Her clothes – the

clothes she'd put on not half an hour earlier – were scuffed and dirty and stained grey with vomit. Sandra herself was in no better condition, but there was a new hardness in her eyes.

'I'll tell you. We'll go down to the cellar, get the pyramid going, and get Dad back – and your friend.'

'We can't!' Ace was scornful. 'Only Truman knows how to use the bloody thing. And he's dead.'

'No, he's not,' Sandra replied, her hardness becoming something cheerfully manic.

Moore Wedderburn held the broken orchid stem between finger and thumb, sighing as he inspected its wounds. The flower was weak. Wedderburn saw how close to death it was and felt something cold brush his soul.

He placed a finger in his mouth and tore repeatedly at the skin with his canine tooth until he drew blood. Gently he rubbed the blood into the broken stem. The plant writhed rhythmically. Wedderburn felt warmer as he imagined it singing. The chattering of the other orchids drew his attention. They had scented the blood and were hunting its source. Wedderburn pulled his finger away hastily.

'Did she scare you?' he whispered to his plants. 'Blundering in here like some mad elephant. Were you frightened?'

The plants danced to a wave pattern.

'Blood for you tonight,' Wedderburn whispered, thrilling himself with the extent of his morbid fantasy. 'A whole carcass. No, two! I promise.'

The orchids swam, tied to the flower beds. They indulged his imagination and Wedderburn was grateful. The real world intruded suddenly – a sharp knock on the door. Wedderburn shook his head wearily.

There were two at the door, neither known to him. Rather glossy and unattractive like characters from some unspeakable American soap opera. He glanced anxiously between the two.

'Good morning Mister Wedderburn,' the young man

said with restraint and politeness. 'Jeremy said we would find you here.'

'Forgive our appalling lack of manners,' the woman said, edging in before Wedderburn could speak. 'We both studied under Professor Winterdawn. He invited us to an evening here but until now we've been forced to decline.'

'My sister and I were impressed by your book.'

'A page-turner. I couldn't put it down.'

Wedderburn laughed at this and the young couple joined in.

'May we come in?'

'I'm afraid that might be awkward at the moment . . .'

'No, we understand. A scientist and his work should not be separated.'

'Goodbye Mister Wedderburn,' the woman smiled and suddenly she and her colleague were gone. Wedderburn closed the door after them, feeling slightly nonplussed. The list of people stalking the corridors of the house without his knowledge was becoming voluminous. The Doctor and his friends, the woman with the gun (*he found he couldn't quite visualize her properly . . . her image blurred in his head . . . had she ever been there at all . . .?*) and now this pair. Whatever their names were.

He shambled back to his work table, to his books, to his seeds, to his meticulously cleaned tools, to the neat brown packages of raw meat.

Cranleigh glanced from woman to woman with dull eyes. His sanity was focusing sharply, but the tiny packages of clarity were coming less frequently and disappeared with greater speed. The final descent was coming soon. The line of madness that, once crossed, could not be passed again. He half-welcomed the prospect of permanent insanity.

Sandra he regarded coldly and without affection. The understanding he had gained when Truman's mind had burst in upon his own was uncomfortable. The woman before him had openly scorned him. So many things she had said about him, so many of them true. Truman's mind was an uncomfortable growth, a tumour on his mind, screaming at him from the inside of his skull. He had his enemy's experience and knowledge. Sandra knew this. He knew that he could operate the tetrahedron for them. But he didn't see why he should have to.

Sandra was clutching the side of the sarcophagus, steadying herself against oncoming blindness. The woman called Ace stood beside her, silently clutching the tetrahedron to her chest, her fingertips running along its sharp edges. Then there was Bernice, sitting in the corner, casting suspiciously round the room – a shadow of the fierce spirit he'd met before.

'Will you do it?' Sandra was asking. She had asked this several times already and was beginning to sound like a jammed record.

'Why?' His voice had the texture of sandpaper.

'Dad and the Doctor are trapped. They can't get out unless you help.'

That was a good argument. The best, in fact. But Cranleigh's nature rebelled. It knew the consequences of such an action and it held him back.

'No,' he said softly.

'Will you do it for me?' Sandra's dying eyes were imploring.

'No,' Cranleigh insisted. 'We, I, will never do anything for you again.'

The woman in the corner. Bernice – *remember her name, Bernice* – was rising to her feet, eyes fixed on him. Existential terror seized Cranleigh by the lungs. He felt dwarfed in comparison to the vision before him.

'Would you do it for me?' asked Laura.

Cranleigh gazed at her for a moment, his lips parted.

'Give it here,' he said to Ace.

He took the pyramid from her unresisting hands.

Gabriel and Tanith lay together on the double bed in the room once occupied by Jeremy and Jennifer Winterdawn. They had chosen this place specifically. This room had been preserved by Winterdawn. This room had been transformed through grief into a shrine. It was a place of sanctity. Gabriel and Tanith enjoyed the sensation of violating this place. Breaking the taboos, tearing down the holy of holies.

They had been lying on the bed for so long that their bodies had left an imprint on the sheets. Their bodies were locked into an embrace, but not a passionate one. They had been lying still. Still and silent.

Gabriel put an end to it, whispering into his sister's ear. 'Do you see what they're doing?'

'I see,' Tanith replied. 'Pointless. They won't gain anything.'

'They won't, but it worries me.'

'Yes, they're beginning to rationalize.'

'I think we need to unbalance things again.'

'A wild card?'

'Quite so.'

'I know the very person.'

Cranleigh sat prone, eyes closed, legs crossed, the tetrahedron a glowing shape before him. He excluded all else from his consciousness. There was Cranleigh and there was the pyramid.

He felt that he should be humming something religious.

Then the world turned inside out and he was staring at his mind.

I am Justin Cranleigh (Harry Truman).

I am I.

The I in the Pyramid.

The universe warped around the inside of his mind.

He lay in bed beside Sandra, two weeks after they'd first met. He was deeply impressed by how young his lover looked. She lay on her side, a cigarette in her mouth, the bedclothes pulled up below her breasts.

Cranleigh fumbled at her crucifix. Apart from this she was naked, but Cranleigh found this last decoration clawing for his attention.

'Can't you take this off?' he asked. 'It's distracting me.'

166

'No.' Sandra snatched it from his grasp, pressing it to her chest. 'My dad likes me to wear it.'

'Bible-basher, eh?'

'No.' Sandra shifted in bed defensively, pulling the sheets up. 'He's a Christian Socialist.'

'Doesn't he know they're both dead?' Cranleigh quipped.

'He's also a quantum physicist so I assume he's got a fair grasp of how the universe works.'

'Ah.' Cranleigh leant back, trying to think of something witty.

'He was on the Grosvenor Square march, you know, the big one in the sixties. That's how he met my mum,' Sandra shrugged, pulling the sheets down again. 'He's always going on about bloody Vietnam.'

'I've slept with the daughter of a religious fundamentalist ageing hippy leftie? Shit! Any other skeletons?'

The world changed again.

The girl was not familiar. Not attractive, either. She was frumpy in a baggy shirt and jeans. Dark-haired and dark-eyed, wavering around Cranleigh's age. He didn't know her.

'Laura?' he asked, innocently. No that was wrong.

'I am as dead as she.' She edged into the light and Cranleigh saw that her eyes were hollow black sockets. 'My name is Nancy.'

'Oh, hello.' Cranleigh blinked again. 'You're my sister?'

'As I might have been. Don't worry, you didn't kill me. It was a simple case of negligence. One of *millions*!' Nancy spat. 'As it usually is. Three days eh, what a long run. One of us had to survive. Don't worry,' she added hurriedly. 'I'm not real.'

Cranleigh nodded sagely.

'Oh piss off!' Nancy screamed at him. 'You don't know what I'm talking about. You're disgusting and I hate you. So there.'

A figure, no more than a shadow, stood behind Nancy. He was tall and gaunt and grey, but Cranleigh caught a fleeting glimpse of him.

'This is really crap for a baring of your subconscious soul,' Nancy decided. 'Where are the weird camera angles and shifting psychedelic backdrops? Where is the strange muzak and the bizarre fantasies?'

Something changed in Nancy's face. The callous angles in her eyes softened. She held out a hand to her brother, wearing a mask of desperation.

'You know more about Gabriel and Tanith than you are aware. Truman was their creation and he is now lodged in your brain. Listen to me. I am a figment of your imagination. I am not part of what they're up to. There aren't that many potentials in which I survived. I am beyond their reach. Thank God. Oh thank you God.'

The figure of his dead sister shrivelled up into an embryo.

Cranleigh found himself kissing Laura, still a naïve teenager. He gazed on her face but her features eluded him. She did, he supposed, look something like Bernice Summerfield.

'Don't let me go!' Tears ran down his face. 'Please don't ever let me go!' He pressed his face into hers and let her warm dark hair bury him.

'Sorry Justin,' the pure, long-forgotten voice whispered, 'time to die.'

There was a burst of white pain in his mind and body simultaneously. Some detached part of his consciousness watched, casually noting the wave of pain sweeping away nervous gates, memory traces, synapses, cerebral paths, DNA and molecular structures, shattering them into incoherence.

Cranleigh clung ferociously to the last fragment of his sanity.

His name. His wonderful name.

'My name,' he told himself again and again, 'is Harry Truman.'

Then that was gone and he was a shapeless thing without mind or memory. Three women stood over him, their faces ablaze with terror and concern. The thing recognized none of them, nor did it care. Its world was empty save for a chorus whose gentle whisper bounced on the inside of its skull.

Slowly mastering the functions of his lips, he began to slur the words.

'We live! We live! We live!' Cranleigh was raving. Sandra was kneeling beside him in concern. She clasped one of his hands between her own, but he tugged it away from her, drawing it to his chest. He shook and giggled and chanted.

'He's having a fit,' Ace said, not coldly.

'No,' Benny said. 'We've destroyed his mind.'

Sandra's face was bland and empty. Too numb for hysteria, Benny felt. They'd done something really stupid this time hadn't they? And which bimbo had got down on her knees and pleaded with Cranleigh to stick his head in the blender in the first place? Benny bit her lip out of self-disgust. She glared at Ace, tears welling in the corners of her eyes.

'We did this,' she scowled. 'We've blown him away.'

Ace wasn't looking at her though. She stared past Cranleigh, past Sandra, past Benny. There was an abstract quality in her eyes and, given Cranleigh's condition, the effect was surreal. And not a little sick.

Sandra was rising, edging backwards slowly.

Irritated, Benny turned from the man she'd killed, jerking round to stare at the doorway.

Not three feet from her head was a vicious stump of metal; a thin, hollow tube erupted phallically from its end. A glove-covered finger stroked its trigger. It was a beautiful piece of weaponry, Benny was certain, capable of shattering the human skull like an egg – a fact that robbed it of its beauty. It was aimed, reassuringly, just above her left ear.

The gun was the possession of a singularly familiar woman in a black coat.

Jane Page was smiling, her mouth a humourless crescent.

'I should warn you that I am capable of killing everyone

in this room before you could reach me.' Her voice was monotonous, flat with contempt.

'Don't worry, we could guess,' Benny snapped as she raised her arms. She might have made a joke of it if there hadn't been a gibbering wreck of a man lying at her feet. The world had lost its sense of humour.

'Oh yes. You staged a remarkable recovery last time we met,' Page sneered. 'What happened to the little weirdo?'

'He's dead,' Benny said before anyone else got a chance to reply.

'Good, good.' Page smiled again. This time it was genuine, designed to make Benny feel worse. It worked.

'Your name is Jane Page, isn't it? Computer analyst,' Benny continued, innocently. 'Good pay? Nice hours?'

'You found my card.' Page continued, blandly and accurately. Something passed across her face, something akin to doubt. She clutched her gun closer to her. 'Why didn't you take . . .?'

Benny stared blankly. She hadn't found the gun when she'd searched Page. You wouldn't think you could hide something that bulky from even the briefest body search. She started to back away, but found a hand locked around her ankle. Cranleigh clutched at her, his other hand flailing wildly. Trying to sit up, Benny thought, and forgetting how.

'We live!' Cranleigh howled, as if it was the most important thing in the world. Benny glanced at the pistol and realized that it was. 'We live!'

'Not for much longer if you don't shut up,' Page laughed. Benny managed a weak grin. She stared at a woman who was totally sincere. She meant that as a joke. A sick mind, but not a mad one. There was something deeply rational about Page's behaviour which set Benny's teeth screaming.

'Who exactly,' Ace began – a polite sentence spoken pointedly, 'are you?'

Page freed a hand to scratch behind her ear.

'I don't think there'll be much harm in telling you,' she

announced. 'No one's going to believe you, even if I let you live.'

She was afflicted with an artificial cough, after which she continued.

'I work for the Cabinet Office, for a counter-espionage agency which takes orders directly from the Prime Minister. Republican Security Intelligence. Plebs call it DI5.'

'You're mad,' Ace said coldly. It wasn't an opinion.

'Not mad, simply a patriot. Britain must be defended from those who seek to despoil it. My colleagues and I provide that defence. You must understand the need for purity. The imperative to keep the island free.'

'Free from what?' Benny asked. 'The living?'

'Those who do not hold to the democratic principles of the Charter, those who despise their country, those who oppose Fundamental Humanism. Disturbed people, who would be considerably helped were they to be terminally re-educated . . . No,' she cut herself off. 'I hate euphemisms. I kill people. I kill the people who deserve it.'

'Like us?' Ace again, sailing too close to the wind for Benny's liking.

'Like Winterdawn. For the most terrible crimes,' Page rattled on, relishing the exposition. 'Sedition, subversion, sabotage, alliteration. A naughty boy. Very naughty. How's that?' She grinned expansively at Ace.

Her concentration on the most obviously aggressive woman was, Benny realized, a mistake. Page had let her guard waver, and Sandra took the opportunity of the lapse to jump on her. In that second, Winterdawn's daughter lost any semblance of human shape. She was a mass, an aggressive shapeless thing with a million blurred limbs. Claws tore at Page's face and hair and clothes. She clung to Page's body, burying the assassin under her own flailing mass. There was something sleek and deadly and uniquely violent about Sandra in a fury. She was working off her anger at a world that was doing its best to spite her.

It had to be that, Benny reflected, tentatively slipping forwards to help, you wouldn't get me leaping on a trained killer unless I was really pissed off.

171

Sandra was screaming. The only word Benny caught was 'father'. The rest seemed to be nothing more than a long, slurred mix of swearing and abuse.

The scream found an accompaniment – a chorus with one, harsh note. It cracked suddenly against the far wall. Further disharmonious bursts smashed into the ceiling. Ace had already hurled herself onto the floor and Benny followed. The chorus burst into full song – a dull rattle of gunfire, drowning Sandra's solo, driving metal across the room and into the fixtures. Gunfire exploded randomly across the room. The floor-boards a foot from Benny's face cracked and splintered as a number of bullets panned across them. Benny looked up wildly and saw Page trying to twist the pistol round to aim at Sandra, without much success. Sandra had a firm grip on the assassin's wrist and was shaking it wildly.

Page emitted an effort-filled howl and Sandra was no longer writhing on her back. She had been sent flying, hitting the ground with a dull thump. She sprawled on the floor, moaning in hysteria and pain.

The gunfire stopped. Page – less the cool and emotion-less killer, more dishevelled and primally violent – sprang forward. She planted her boots onto Sandra's face and chest and between her legs. Despite the crude, brute violence there wasn't much real power there. She wasn't trying to break anything. She was just trying to cause pain.

Judging from Sandra's shrieks, she was succeeding.

Benny forced herself to her feet, aware that her pain was dull and flat from hitting the floor too fast – not the sharp pain of a bullet. Ace was already up and springing at Page. Instantly she found the muzzle of Page's gun before her – a dark, hollow eye staring like death into her own. She stopped and backed away, hands raised point-edly. Benny shared the gesture.

'This must be Winterdawn's daughter.' Page retained her calm. There was blood on her face and she kept as cool as ever. The kicking must have sated her blood-lust. Her coat was stained with blood, making it seem blacker

172

than ever. It was like a funeral shroud, the robes of a dark angel.

The Angel of Death leant down and tore open Sandra's shirt. She clutched downward and wrenched. Sandra shrieked again.

Page held up Sandra's crucifix like a trophy. Blood seeped down her arm, smothering the icon.

'This,' Page continued, 'is exactly what I'm talking about. In order for individual freedom to flourish we must unchain the human mind from the dogma of the Group. The individual urge of the strong society is secular in character.' She flung the crucifix away.

She's quoting, Benny thought. That's far too meaningful to be original.

'Don't you believe in anything, Page?'

'I believe in the greatest good for the greatest number. Bentham said that, and he was right. I believe that the strong should be allowed to get on with it and if anyone can't stand up to that then tough. Society benefits.'

'That's fine. I enjoy discussing the nature of freedom with gun-toting psychos. If you're going to kill us do it now and be done with it. Better still, give us a three-year start.'

Page smiled. It was not unwholesome.

'Why should I kill you?' There was something delightful and innocent about that voice. 'You three are exactly what I've been looking for. I can *use* human resources. Hostages.'

'No,' Ace said, her mouth an aggressive 'o'-shape, teeth bared and clenched.

'You forget. I have the superior means of coercion.' She tapped the side of the gun meaningfully.

The silence that followed was tense and menacing and thankfully short. It ended with a slow murmur of pain. Cranleigh was still on the floor, howling plaintively. His left thigh was a mess of congealed blood and muscle. His face flexed with pain, but his screams were half-hearted, as if he was losing control of his vocal cords.

Benny moved towards him but a sharp rattling from

Page's gun had her drawing up short, slipping into motionlessness like a party game.

Some party.

'I'm going to *help* him,' she protested.

'Why bother?' Page asked casually and sincerely.

'You've crippled him!' Benny squawked her outrage. It wouldn't do much good. Page's mentality was sealed firmly against the calls of compassion. Page adopted a strange half-smile, half-sneer.

'As above, so below.'

Benny stared. There was nothing she could say.

'If you're so concerned, one of you can stay behind and clear up.' She prodded her boot into Sandra's stomach. 'Since you're lying about anyway, it might as well be you. Good luck with him.'

She turned back to the others. A triumphant, expectant smile twitched like a dying thing on her lips.

'Let's go, shall we?'

Benny's feet moved like lead. There was a dogged reluctance to her movements. Ace remained stiff and stationary. Her face was curled up into an expression of disgust. Fingers stabbed viciously in Page's direction and for a moment Benny was afraid that Page might take a shot at her. Her terrible fear of death, submerged by Page's appearance, suddenly resurfaced at the back of her mind. She shuddered expectantly.

Page didn't shoot. Ace spoke.

'You listen to me, bitch,' she said, cold and self-assured. 'You've got that gun now, but you drop your guard for a second while I'm around then I'll kill you. Understand?'

'Perfectly,' Page replied, her tones and smile sweet. 'I won't drop my guard. Shall we go?'

'Time travel, eh?'

Winterdawn sounded cheery. Winterdawn sounded weak. A weak man trying to sound cheery.

The Doctor had his eyes tight closed. The darkness inside his eyes seemed warm and reassuring. A cosy, stifling sensation that reminded him of a childhood when he

174

was smothered by the lethargy of Gallifrey. With his eyes closed he had his illusions. He couldn't see the corruption, the cynicism, the heartlessness of the adult world. Why should he have to open his eyes? Why couldn't he stay here like this forever?

He was scared to open his eyes. After the glass storm, he was afraid there might be little of them left. Bloody bundles and severed optical nerves. He shivered at the thought. He couldn't live without his eyes.

He let his lids slide open.

There was no pain. There was nothing wrong with his eyes.

The interstix flickered around him – meaningless patterns dancing on an infinitely distant, infinitely large cyclorama. He could see it perfectly. Something like a sigh passed his lips.

He looked at his hands, his clothes, his legs. They were undamaged.

'It's an illusion,' Winterdawn's voice cut through the stillness. He was lying on his back on the invisible floor of the gap. Beyond him lay his chair, tipped on its side. One of its wheels spun slowly under its own power – the other lay on the pseudo-ground several metres distant.

'It looked real from here,' the Doctor called.

'Our minds made it real,' Winterdawn replied thoughtfully. 'It was a purely mental attack. No wonder Justin went mad.'

The Doctor knelt by Winterdawn and spoke softly:

'There's another possibility.'

'Yes?'

'The attack *was* physical. We suffered terrible injuries but we don't realize it because this place is fooling with our perception. This is the mental attack. Can you move?'

'For a scientist you ask some incredibly stupid questions,' Winterdawn snapped, the discomfort of his position etched onto his face. The Doctor nodded grimly and lifted Winterdawn into a sitting position.

'Better?'

'Thank you.' Winterdawn smiled weakly. 'I wanted to

175

talk to you about time travel. It is possible then? Really real?'

'Really real.' The Doctor smiled.

'I knew it!' Winterdawn announced, glee and triumph shining in his eyes. 'I knew it! I wish I could have proved it! So Einstein was wrong!'

'No.' The Doctor shook his head. 'Einstein was right. His assumptions were wrong. I tried to put him right but he wouldn't listen.'

Winterdawn's thin lips bristled into a smile.

'Do you travel all the time? You're not tied to any time or place?'

The Doctor nodded.

'I rarely settle. Perhaps I should. I did once, but I was a different person then. It's always been just me, my TARDIS, my companions . . .'

He trailed off slowly on a wistful note. Winterdawn's face was curious and cautious, anxious to enquire further, uncertain of whether he was trespassing on private ground, breaking personal taboos.

'I'm sorry,' he was saying slowly. 'I didn't mean to . . .'

The Doctor tried to raise a hand to shield his face and his feelings, but he thought better of it.

'I'll tell you,' he said firmly. 'It doesn't matter now. My family is gone, long gone. My friends . . . I . . . I have my companions. I've had many fellow travellers in a long life. I'm much older than you can imagine. I've had so many friends. But they all go in the end. It's so easy to let them go, so difficult to find them again. Sometimes, you see, I miss the old stability, the warmth of belonging to a single place.

'But I think I'd be just as lonely there.'

Winterdawn nodded and looked away. The Doctor raised a hand to his forehead, a shadow blocking out his eyes. Silence ruled for a long instant.

'I wish I'd said goodbye properly,' the Doctor said softly. 'I don't like this. I can think of better places to die.'

His head swung upwards, new vigour burning in his

eyes and his soul. His hands clapped together, releasing a sound like a roll of thunder.

'Let's see if we can get this chair of yours fixed.'

11

The Masque of the Red Death

Sandra's world was close, a lightless shroud smothering her. Her sight had waned, given up on her. Five years ago this terrified her. Five years ago it was like being captive in a tiny epoch of death. She had grown used to it, learned to live with the paranoia and the loneliness. She could taste nothing but the bitterness left by Page. She could feel the cold air on her face and a dull ache on her chest where a crucifix should be.

Without sight, her world became a world of sound. The sound of her voice, confident and soothing as she tried to coax some spark of thought from Cranleigh. Her world became a monologue. How long had she been speaking? Time gave way in the darkness.

'Everything I told Harry was true,' she was saying. 'I'm sorry if that hurts. I went to Harry because I realized – had been forced to realize – how much more I felt for him than for you.

'But . . . God, this is going to sound like gibberish. But I loved him because he *was* you. All the things I liked about you, that drew me to you in the first place. I liked you at the time.

'You remember how we met? Mum and Dad met up that way. Mum told me, it was just after the Grosvenor Square thing. Afterwards my mum said, "Okay, what's your name then?" and he said, "Winterdawn," so Mum said, "I think we're on a first-name basis now." He was never quick on the uptake.'

She hugged herself against more than just the draught.

'I don't think I can help you. I can't even see you. I don't think you'll die. Does it matter? If you live or die . . .

'I think it does. I don't know, you're still in there somewhere. You can't erase the human spirit like that.' (fingers click) 'Part of you still hears me. It's just a question of drawing you out. I'll count to a hundred . . .

'One, two, three . . .'

She stopped, alerted more by instinct than anything else.

'Who's there?'

'Only us!' Gabriel and Tanith's voices sang.

'*Get out*!' Sandra roared, but in the darkness her voice seemed faint.

'Don't take on so.' Gabriel.

'We only want to talk.' Tanith.

'*We* made breakfast. *Page* had the gun.'

Sandra sniffed disdainfully and drew her legs up to her chest.

'What are you going to do?'

'We are going to destroy *everyone*, one soul at a time. Starting with this island Earth. This self-important rock in the ocean of infinity.'

'This microdot in the great book of the universe. This nullity which imagines that it has attained a level of civilization never before achieved.'

'We are going to obliterate it.'

'At least, that's the plan at the moment. It could change. We *could* strut the land as gods instead.'

'Or grant everyone one wish alone, with which to change the world.'

'Scatter the population of the planet to random destinations throughout space. Reveal a universe colder and vaster than they've ever imagined it!'

'Unleash some sort of monstrously tentacled extra-dimensional horror on London! But that might be too obvious.'

'But you – we're going to do what we always wanted to do. We can see how delicate your chemical structure is. We see it in infinite, fragile detail – the knife-edge on which you balance.'

'We're going to give you a shove and see what happens.'

'Now,' Gabriel and Tanith's voices blended together into one eerie echo. It howled in Sandra's head. And suddenly something focused in her mind, lean and aggressive, howling in the darkness.

The beast appeared on the black horizon. In a second, it was upon her.

Jane Page had a cold and systematic mind and she conducted her search in a cold and systematic way. Cold, systematic, frustrating. Every room she'd searched – every corridor, every floor – had been empty. Nothing but furniture and – occasionally – the dull, metronomic clicking of a clock. Her impatience began to get the better of her.

It was this house. It was too big and too empty. It was trying to impose its architectural bulk onto her identity. It was a cold place and it set her on edge. After so long searching in silence she longed for the sound of the human voice – something – *anything* – that would improve the atmosphere.

The two women who walked before her at gunpoint, clearing the way for her, were deathly silent. She didn't expect them to join the search with anything more than forced enthusiasm but she hoped they might say something. No matter how snide, how derogatory. It was getting to the point where she wanted to take a shot at them for no reason whatsoever.

Could she shoot them? In self-defence, yes – but could she shoot them on a whim, in cold blood? Probably not, it exceeded her brief. Besides, the blood was flowing like molten lava through her veins.

She prodded Bernice in the back with the barrel of her gun, to see what reaction she could provoke. She was almost disappointed when the woman just shuffled forward, saying nothing, not even bothering to look at her.

'That's kind of them,' said Gabriel.

'Together in one place,' Tanith added.

'One area.'

'On which we can focus.'

'What do you think?'

'Trauma, dark fears, the skeletons in their cupboards.'

'Sounds good.'

'Show them.'

And suddenly Professor Bernice Summerfield wasn't mute, brooding on her intimacy with death, the inevitability of her own oblivion. Suddenly she was somewhere else. Manywheres else. A myriad different places.

Mother's skin burning, peeling away, torchlight for the assault force, voice a siren screaming at an inhuman pitch, coward father turning ship and running like a cheetah from Dalek ships moaning and sobbing with terror as the sound of indiscriminate slaughter echoes behind him child at my feet bloody and bruised and close to death it just takes a little extra effort kill kill kill kill kill kill killkillkillkillkillkillkillkillkillkill kill bloody taste in her mouth tasting it loving it, seeping through to her brain mental orgasm like sex and betrayal and Judas each man kills the thing he loves the coward with a kiss so many people died in the transit tunnels because you let that creature inside you contemptible cowardly little things that meant nothing to you but must have made other people's lives hell you are a *bully* Summerfield.

Benny folded her arms, lips twitching into an unperturbed smile.

'I've seen this before, chaps,' she called to the absent couple she knew was listening. 'It's disappointing when you know how it ends. How about something new?'

Ace found herself elsewhere. A cold loveless elsewhere. Defiant wilderness. Vibrant jungle burned to nothing by repressive napalm. Dorothy fire-bombed her mind as she fire-bombed houses, burning away everything she saw as weak and girlish and, basically, like, not the sort of thing you need when a six-armed something whose name you can't remember is coming at you like it's hunting dinner (probably is too). She stripped away the baby stuff and there was nothing left. She'd tried to buck the system and ended up bucking herself.

(Something like that).

She'd been scared of ghosts, of fire, of fascists, of Doctors. She'd toughened mind, body and soul against them, took on the devil's methods as her own, right? So she'd shot a few things. Did it matter what they were, what they wanted? Did you kill men Ace, women Ace, children Ace, did you kill babies Dorothy?

Perhaps.

So she kicked back. Ace and no one else. There was no one leading *her*, no damn outside forces working on her – not any more. The funny thing was, she'd caught this fascist once, this real big Nazi who loved to hurt and kill and maim and it was like looking into a mirror. Just goes to show. She blew the Nazi away anyway because she could never stand glib endings.

Ace becomes baby Dorothy again, and Iceworld, Gabriel Chase, the Doctor, Benny and Daleks are things the future holds in store. Nevertheless, baby Dorothy's skin begins to smoulder and within seconds her body is a torch, burning away into nothing.

And Page?

Page believed in the greatest good for the greatest number, in the right of the strong to trample the weak to death, in right being might. Page believed in all these things and more, but she no longer believed in herself. Her name was forgotten, written on a long-lost piece of paper, floating away on the wind. At the heart of her slogans, her charters, her guns, her death camps, her job, there was nothing. A hard, icy block of nothing.

Jane Page believed in nothing, so Gabriel and Tanith showed her nothing in all its glory – a limitless arena. They showed her this, then they showed her herself in relation to it, how meaningless she was in comparison to it. They showed her that some things can be less than nothing.

The nameless woman clutched at two syllables, at 'Jane Page' because that was all she had left. Then she began to cry.

The interstitial light strobed violently, settling down as a swirling mist, tinged pink by leaping and writhing will-o'-the-wisp lights on the fringes of the interstix. The Doctor ignored it. He was becoming too accustomed to these changes of scenery.

'God, this is dull,' Winterdawn purred. 'Can you fix the chair?'

'It'll border on the makeshift.'

'Does it matter? It's not as if we're going anywhere.'

The Doctor smiled, but it didn't stave off the hollow growing inside him. Something was consuming his energy, his vibrance. His skin felt brittle as eggshell. So, for that matter, did his mind.

How long can I last here without going mad? How long can Winterdawn last? He looked up at the professor, sitting helplessly in the heart of the mist, sighing to himself and looking round in boredom. The madness that would consume him would be trivial. It would be nothing compared to the madness of a Time Lord. When *his* mind went it would unleash a storm across the surface of his brain. The Dark Design, the Time Lords called it, and went out of their way to hide the sufferers in institutions. The Doctor had known many insane Time Lords in his time, but no mad ones. Pretenders rather than kings.

How will I feel, when I am lost in the Dark Design? What will I think?

No. He didn't want to think about this. These were cold futures. They should not be dwelt on. He hurled himself into the task of repairing the wheelchair, relishing the concentration involved.

'Do you want to know,' Winterdawn asked, 'why I did this?'

'Yes,' the Doctor said, barely noticing the question.

183

'I want to destroy the world,' Winterdawn said calmly.

The Doctor's head bobbed up.

'Literally?' he asked cautiously, his fears softened by the droll smile Winterdawn was displaying. The professor shook his head in response.

'I want – wanted – to destroy society.' The Doctor listened patiently to that voice. Winterdawn didn't sound insane, and there was none of the deceptive clarity that might hide deeper madness.

'How would you ... destroy ... society?' the Doctor enquired cautiously.

'With technology. With *this*.' Winterdawn waved his arms round, gesturing at the void around them.

'I told you,' Winterdawn continued hurriedly, though he seemed more enthusiastic than obsessive, 'that interstitial travel would bring about revolution! It would be a revolution in culture, in thinking. Change people's minds and you change the world they live in. This is *real* freedom I'm offering them! An infinite universe, all within our reach, theirs to choose from. The whole superstructure of our existing societies would collapse.'

'You'd like that?' the Doctor asked thoughtfully.

'I would,' Winterdawn said. 'The old society is dying already but not fast enough. I want to see its *grave*, Doctor.'

He blinked, the fanaticism in his eyes softening. He turned slightly so that his face became shadowed and unreadable.

'When I was a student, in the sixties, I felt like a conservative in radical times. Oh, I've supported things like CND, Greenpeace, stuff like that. But they were the mainstream – radically respectable. I wanted to get the Americans out of Vietnam, I was on the Grosvenor Square march. But I wasn't *committed* – I just went along for the violence, the drinks, and the hope of getting a girl into bed.

'Well there wasn't any violence and there weren't any drinks. But I *did* get that girl into bed. Funny how things work out. I met a wonderful woman. And then I married her. Jenny was more of a firebrand than I was. She was at the heart of the stuff I dabbled in. She loved freedom . . . life . . .'

Winterdawn broke off. The Doctor sat silently, patiently. After a time, Winterdawn began again.

'What happened to the radicals?' he asked. 'Where did they go? Was there some intelligence that snatched them off the face of the planet? Feels like that. A decade after Grosvenor it seemed like it had dried up. There hasn't been anything since. Hundreds of movements, but nothing like the sixties. They didn't want to change anything, and they got respectable far too quickly. Youth culture's become a training ground for insurance salesmen! There's no challenge any more. No guts! No poetry! Just a stifling, steel-shelled *nothing*! We have a system that's worshipped like a new religion. It thinks it's secure. It's not.'

'There are worse societies,' the Doctor broke in. 'And better ones.'

'Ah well. It's not as if I'm in any state to do anything about it. Besides, it's killing itself. You've seen the future. Tell me.'

The Doctor frowned darkly.

'It ends, of course. Everything ends.'

'*When* does it end? *How* does it end?' Winterdawn's tone was suddenly aggressive and demanding. The Doctor felt pressured.

'If you had changed society,' the Doctor decided to defuse the question, 'surely the economic base of the old system would still be intact?'

'Yes, but not for long,' Winterdawn fielded the question hurriedly. 'It would be a dinosaur, quickly extinct.'

'Dinosaurs,' the Doctor whispered, 'are large, stupid and violent. The first years of your new society would be bloody, Winterdawn.'

Winterdawn leant forward, speaking with a low, wistful obsessiveness. He seemed to have forgotten his dreams of new societies, swapping them for a more personal moment.

'I can see her,' he said. 'Nineteen seventy. Walking in

the New Forest, arguing about the election result. It was nice, a lovely day. She was full of energy. A very intelligent woman, a wonderful person. Loved cats and logic problems. Fun while it lasted. What a bloody way to die.'

The Doctor felt that he should say something, but there was nothing there. A cold lump in his throat and a blank mind in his skull. Winterdawn's words reminded him of his age, of his past. It was not something he wished to remember. Concentrating his mind and energies, he leant forward, setting to work on the wheelchair once again.

There was a hand on her face, a hand so light it need not have been there. Fingertips tickled her skin. Someone was touching her – someone *scared*.

Page's eyes snapped open.

Bernice was crouched before her, hands pressing against Page's clothes and face. There was concern in her eyes. Page reciprocated with a pure glare, but she relaxed when she realized her fingers were still wrapped round the awkward shape of her gun.

'Are you feeling okay?' Benny was asking, voice stripped of any sense of malice or guile. 'You were screaming in C sharp . . .'

'Thanks, I'm fine,' Page responded kindly. It was an uncomfortable, almost forgotten feeling. She pressed her gun to Benny's throat. When she spoke, kindness had been replaced by weary cynicism.

'I'm sorry. You should have taken it when you had the chance.'

'There are worse things in this house,' Benny replied, sad but composed. She pulled back from the gun. Page didn't try to stop her. Ace stepped into sight, a harsh jagged shape in black and grey. Here was raw hatred. Once again Page felt something like remorse. She had to suppress it viciously. There were tear-stains on Ace's cheeks.

Page had seen terrible things. So, she assumed, had Ace.

'Thank Benny,' Ace said without passion. 'If it hadn't

been for her you'd've woken up with half that gun rammed up you.'

'Thanks Benny.' Page forced herself to stand, surprised at how little pain there was. She smiled broadly, checking the safety catch with a suitable amount of ceremony. 'Let's be off.'

Ace was shaking her head.

'I don't believe it. You're still after Winterdawn! After all *this* . . . You just don't care, do you?'

'I care,' Page whispered, 'enough to keep going.'

'What did they show you?'

Page let a blink play across her face, but Benny's question had opened a channel of fear inside her. A powerful, rushing current tore at her composure, threatening to drag her away. Her fingers tightened round the trigger of her gun – a rock, the last stable thing left to her.

I saw nothing.

'I saw myself,' Page said, forcing her finger from the trigger.

There was something in the air – uncomfortable and intangible like an electric current. Wedderburn could sense it, building up, forcing him out, crushing him. Something terrible was about to happen, a storm on the verge of breaking. And this house was at the heart of it.

It was affecting him, though he was far from the centre. He felt peripheral, as though the action was unfolding elsewhere. Terrible events were occurring under his nose, but he was left out. He had felt alone for the whole of the morning, and loneliness was turning to paranoia. There was a conspiracy to which he was not privy. Perhaps he was its target.

He had even begun to suspect that he had woken in the wrong house.

He gazed around the conservatory, sighing to himself. The plants, for all their comforts, were poor substitutes for humans.

His kettle was warming nicely on the portable hob but he began to suspect that it might have been a better idea to make the tea in the kitchen. He might have met someone. Found out how Jeremy and the Doctor had got on. Yet somehow he felt *safer* in the conservatory.

Tired of familiar surroundings, Wedderburn stuck his head round the door in the hope of catching someone. Against all odds, he did. Sandra was outside the door, her shoulder pressed hard against one wall. The blandness in her eyes worried Wedderburn. He watched her scratching obsessively at her forearm, listened to her harsh breathing and suspected she was sick.

'Sandra,' he called. The girl started, wheeling round to peer at him suspiciously. He'd startled her, obviously.

'Sorry,' he said, clapping his hands, watching her relax. A light whistle came from his side of the door.

'Kettle's boiling.' He flashed her a smile, wondering if she could see it. 'Enough for two, if you want a chat.'

Sandra said nothing, still regarding him suspiciously.

'Your choice,' he continued, slightly unnerved by her silence.

He popped back through the door and strode across the room to silence the frantic screeching of the kettle. He heard the door pushed fully open behind him. Smiling thoughtfully, he called,

'Take a seat, I won't be a minute.'

Page had hoped that she'd left the fear behind her. Something in the past, to be forgotten. She'd been wrong. It was following her. It clung to her.

She'd lost everything. Her name, her memories, her life. That was okay from a professional view. She didn't need her own life to help others lose theirs. She needed the experience, the skill, the practice. But that was *all* she had.

How had she become involved? She couldn't remember. Despite her love for the kill she was certain she wouldn't have become involved by choice. And before . . .? She must have been something. A normal person with friends, family, identity. She tried to remember, but there was nothing. Whoever she had been, she was gone. Jane Page was the best she could hope for.

She listened to Ace and Benny as they talked about their experiences. Gabriel and Tanith were to blame for everything, they said, though they weren't sure how. Page didn't understand. She'd never met this couple they were so eager to blame, but she could sense the frustration and the anger with which her companions invested those names.

Gabriel. Tanith.

A door rose before her. She made a threateningly metallic sound with her gun and the others drew up short.

'In there,' Page said. 'We haven't looked yet.'

There was no argument. Benny walked to the door first, reaching to pull it open then wavering, lowering her hand and pausing nervously at the threshold. The door remained solidly closed.

'What's wrong?' Page called.

'I can hear something. Someone talking,' Benny called back. 'I think there's someone in there already.'

'All the better.' Page smiled warmly. 'More targets. Shall we see?'

Benny pulled open the door. A black rectangle cut itself into the wall where the door had been, a silent portal into a silent room. Benny stepped through cautiously, the lightness of her back gradually absorbed into the gloom. Page rattled her gun and Ace followed. Page kept close behind her.

The room was wrapped in total night. There were no vague shapes on the edge of Page's vision, no light from any source, no sense of where they were. Page saw nothing in the dark, but she could hear. A voice in the darkness – a low, gritty tone that Page had to concentrate to catch. Each word seemed heavy as if speaking was a labour. Each word came slow and slurred, thick and accusatory. The owner of that voice hated not just Page, but everyone.

'You never gave us a chance.'

The lights came on.

Page assimilated her surroundings instantly. A small

189

room and a quiet one. The silence in the room was so thick it was almost tragic. It was the most depressing place that Page had ever seen. She'd been in torture cells with happier atmospheres. It was a nursery, filled with old toys and old memories, kept neatly in good order. Dust had built on everything – everything convinced Page that this was a place that had lost its purpose.

That was the room. The occupants were something different. A man and a woman dressed absurdly. Both were young, blonde and attractive. They were so perfect it was suspicious. Page found her gun wavering away from Ace and Benny and training on these new faces. They ignored it. They seemed calm and arrogant, condescension etched into their smiles. Page had the sudden feeling that she was confronting something worse than she'd ever met before.

Gabriel. Tanith.

They stood before a velvet curtain which stretched across the top of one wall – hiding a window or a mirror, Page guessed. It was a new addition.

'Welcome Ace, Bernice, Jane,' The woman spoke – Tanith, Page presumed.

'We are so glad that you could make it,' Gabriel added. 'This is a very special occasion for us.'

Page shot glances at her companions – she'd stopped thinking of them as hostages. She saw hostility and revulsion written large on both their faces, magnified by fear. Even Ace. Jane Page felt her knuckles itching, tightening.

Tanith was speaking:

'It may seem that our sole objective in life is to hurt people – specifically your good selves. It is. But that's not to say that we have no long-term plans.'

'You are about to see them unveiled.' Gabriel picked his words with relish. 'Them dry bones gonna walk around, O hear the word of the Lord.'

'We have the pleasure of introducing Jane to her fellow travellers.'

'And Ace and Bernice, to their victims.'

Page glanced at Ace and Benny and saw confusion.

'We present,' Tanith threw her arms wide, her voice growing louder and deeper and more strident; her voice was joined by Gabriel's to become a chorus, 'the damned!'

The curtains exploded, blasted aside by a storm of wind, light and noise. The nursery filled with sound and fury. Page was knocked back against a wall. As she fought to steady herself, her eyes flicked wildly round the room. She saw Gabriel and Tanith withdrawing through the door, too vague in the harsh light to be decent targets. She saw Ace sprawled on the floor, limbs flailing as she tried to climb to her feet. She saw Benny, better placed than Ace, anchored by a chest of drawers. The light flooded the room, blue-tinged, casting hideous black shadows that might have been faces. They rose through the room, speaking in tongues, deformed mouths howling rage and pain. There were words beneath the babble and the noise of the storm.

'We live.'

Two syllables beating again and again, lending rhythm and depth to the chaotic white noise. The voices were neutral, but punctuated by higher, accusatory shrieks, full of loathing for the women in the room.

'What choice were we given?' the shapes howled. 'From darkness to darkness with darkness between.'

Page tried to blank out the assault, staring upwards and shielding her eyes to see the heart of the storm. Behind the curtains. A window set high on the wall, jet black but radiating light.

Page pulled her gun up to level on that window. Screaming soundlessly into the storm, she let her finger squeeze. Fire burned from the barrel of the gun, spitting viciously at the window. Page scowled and swore and kept firing. Nothing was happening. *Nothing.* The window was as flat and unbroken as it had ever been, as if her bullets were evaporating.

She stopped, seeing Benny forcing herself to climb. She was balancing precariously on the chest of drawers. Weak though it looked, Page had no doubt it could support Benny's weight. And it was situated below the window. It swayed alarmingly as she balanced on its top, but Page could already see that it wouldn't fall. It settled down and Benny seemed to relax. One hand had slipped down the length of her body and was forcing a boot from her foot. Page watched with a growing feeling of expectancy. This was going to *work*!

Benny weighed the boot in one hand, a hand that swung pendulously with increasing force. With a swift, powerful action she thrust her arm up, smashing her shoe into the black glass.

Glass which failed to shatter.

The light imploded into Benny's body, becoming no more than a blue halo flickering round her shape. A brief, agonized scream formed on her mouth, sickeningly soundless in that storm of light and sound.

The light snapped off. The room reverted to normal.

The chest of drawers toppled over, smashing into the floor, shaking the boards, sending a shock up Page's spine. Benny was on the floor by the chest. She had fallen clear of it and was lying awkwardly on her back, her neck twisted out of its natural crook, her arms splayed wildly at painful angles. Her eyes were closed, her chest was still.

Page had grown too used to death to feel anything more than a flicker of sorrow. Even that surprised her.

Ace climbed to her feet, hawkish features softening into confusion. She stared vacantly at the body then switched her gaze on to Page, something pitifully hopeful in her face. Page shook her head. A deep, dark frown grew across Ace's features, then hardened. She stumbled across the room to crouch by the crumpled shape that had been Bernice Summerfield. With a façade of casualness, she reached for Benny's wrist, prodding it in a fruitless search for a pulse. When she moved again, she was agitated, her hands leaping to Benny's chest, to her neck, to her face, to her eyes. With each fresh move Ace's actions became shakier, less restrained. Page watched the woman disintegrate. It was difficult to maintain her detachment. She managed.

Ace pulled her hands away from the body and shot a

glance of utter hatred in Page's direction. It was an anger so thick and tangible Page nearly reeled. But it wasn't aimed at her. It was just anger, undirected and venomous, straight from the heart.

Ace turned back to the body, her shoulders rounding with renewed anger. Her arm swung down, the full force of her anger behind it, smashing a flat palm against the side of Benny's face. Flesh cracked against flesh. The dead head rolled aside. Ace looked up at Page again, her anger evaporating, tears guttering down her face. Page watched without passion.

'She's not really dead is she?' she asked. Page sensed the effort in that voice, the force keeping it calm and bland. Page nodded. She was dry and dead inside herself. She didn't know why. Ace turned away, her body twisting up into something painful.

Page loathed herself. She felt useless here. Her gun was hanging limply in a loose fist. She couldn't remember the last time she'd mourned for anyone she knew or loved.

'Get out of here,' Ace said suddenly.

Before she realized what she was doing, Page found herself at the door, turning the knob. She saw no reason to stop.

The passage outside the nursery was cold and dark and still. It was also full of insect. It was pink and grey-skinned, part fly, part locust, part beetle, unnaturally huge. Formidable when it came to teeth too. It had a maw that was a mix of twitching mandibles, wet jaw and chiselled teeth. Its eyes were multiple compounds – a maze of glazed honeycombs locking together without flaws. Each compound reflected a tiny human shape.

'Bloody hell!' Page exclaimed. It seemed appropriate.

The insect unleashed a howl composed of a hundred unique voices and lurched forward. It bore towards Page – an ominous shape looming towards her in the dark, shadows doubling its size.

Page watched fascinated as the bulk of the creature thrust towards her. She welcomed it, perhaps even worshipped it. She hadn't been surprised when it appeared.

Subconsciously she had been expecting something loathsome on the other side of the door. She bit her tongue until she could taste the blood; her eyes locked into those repellent compounds, willing the creature back. Here and now its appearance was perfect and meaningful. It was the ultimate confrontation between the pure human and the demon, the myth, to be cut away. Page despised mysticism but for an instant she felt a grudging respect for the power of romance. She would have to shoot it in a minute, or the climax would see myth triumphant. The human's head torn from her body and raised on a pole by her enemies. For the last few moments of the confrontation she remained still, savouring the moment.

Then she raised her gun until it was level with the hateful demon-eye, squeezing softly with her finger. The eye exploded. The demon shrieked.

It was a dull feeling. She didn't feel like a human avenger slaying the great beast, not any more. She was a woman with a gun making a mess of something else. The thrill of the kill wasn't there. One side of the insect's head was a nightmare, the shattered eye seeming to unbalance the whole symmetry of its body. In any other circumstances Page would have delighted in the visceral pleasure of it all.

The monster was howling and shrieking. It jerked and twisted in the passage, confined by its cramped surroundings. It twitched and flexed but was no longer moving towards her. It was scared, aware of its agony, too scared to keep going. Page felt something as she considered this, but it was too muted – too intellectual – to feel good.

She lined her gun against the other eye and shattered the compound into gory fragments. It was unnecessary and it didn't help.

Blinded, the creature began to move again. It wasn't running though, it was *charging*. Despite its pain, it was aware of Page, aware of how close she was, the role she played in the escalation of its agony. Wounded though it was, it was still powerful and vicious enough, Page had no doubt, to rip her head from her shoulders.

Blood burst in Page's mouth, flooding her nostrils, guttering down the back of her throat. Her heart began to pound under pressure. Something in her abdomen tightened. Page lowered the gun, pulled the trigger, didn't release it. The bullets riddled the creature's hide, marking it with deep, dense holes. Enough to slow it, not enough to stop its attack. Page fired and fired and fired and thrilled to the reaction she drew.

Ace appeared on the edge of her vision. There was a stone thing masquerading as her face. It stared at Page with cold eyes. Too distracting.

'Get out!' Page howled, having to scream over the constant rattle of gunfire. 'Get out of here!'

'But Benny's . . .'

'Leave her!' Page yelled, trying to keep a grip on her gun and her edge.

Ace tumbled past her suddenly, disappearing down the passage behind her. Page didn't turn – she couldn't, not now, *not now* – but she could feel the distance grow between them.

The insect blundered closer, the pain goading it on now.
five yards four closer three two closer closer
one yard
Page fired one final burst then kicked herself backwards, forcing herself to retreat. She turned and fled into the dark corridors.

The world began to swirl around her.

Gabriel and Tanith stood and watched the women from inside their minds.

Women running through passages on the uppermost storey of the house.

Gabriel and Tanith gave the world a tiny push. Small enough to change everything.

The laws of logic unbound themselves. The architecture of the house melted under the pressure of those minds. Corridors extended into places where there should be no corridors, passages linked with passages they should not, different floors blended together, landings grew to impossible lengths, rooms blossomed into the cracks between reality. Architecture distorted into a mess of arteries and veins of wood and dust and doors.

Now where are you going to end up?

A wall loomed in Ace's path, erupting from the floor like a blank tombstone. She kicked towards it, flattening herself against the wall, shaking, forcing herself to take heavy breaths and still the rapid throbbing of her heart. The texture of the wall was bristling cold against her cheek. Brick dust crumbled down her face, fragments slipping down the crack between her neck and her collar, scratching her shoulder. She didn't care. She didn't care.

There was blood on her cheek, mixing with the dust. When had she cut herself? She couldn't remember.

Didn't matter.

Benny was dead.

Ace found herself sobbing, working her grief out into a slab of brickwork. She smashed her knuckles into the wall pointlessly, perhaps enjoying the pain.

Pointless, everything was so bloody pointless.

She'd never felt like this before. Not when Julian died. Not when Mike died. Not when Sorin died. Not when Jan died.

So what did Benny have that they didn't?

Her fingers ground uselessly into loose mortar, crumbling it over her hands. She howled uselessly at the ceiling,

'Damn you Doctor! Why the hell are you never around when we really need you?! Benny's dead! Hear that! That's another! How many does that make?'

She scowled. Brick dust ground against the corner of her mouth, flecks scratching against clenched teeth.

'Bastard,' she muttered, hoping that whatever vantage point he had on reality, the Doctor could hear her.

A fluid, darting shape flitted across the line of her sight before vanishing into the darkness. She recognized it.

'Sandra!' she screamed after the receding shape. 'Wait!'

She kicked herself away from the wall and set off in pursuit.

* * *

Page had run from the nursery without really caring where she ended up. She had run until she found a door, and beyond the door she'd found sanctuary. Someone's bedroom. A temporary but cosy bolt-hole.

Secure position.

The door had no lock, but she was able to jam it shut. Check.

Check weapons.

She'd almost emptied the clip she'd been using. The result of her obsession with that monster Gabriel and Tanith had conjured up. Still, it didn't matter. There was still enough for one clean kill. Or three clean kills as she'd come to believe was now necessary. Check.

Freak out.

She flopped carelessly onto the bed and lay still, her face buried in the softness of a pillow. She wasn't trying to sleep – she doubted she could. All she needed to do was relax.

She rolled onto her back and stared at the ceiling, wondering how something so solid could seem so unreal.

She felt thirsty. She could live with that.

She felt angry and weary of anger. Sad too. She wished she knew how to react to that. She tried to find something she could latch onto inside herself, a reaction or an understanding. She saw blackness, a hole.

She wished someone would kiss her.

She wondered what she really thought. All her life she'd been telling herself that all she wanted was the best for people. Now she wasn't too sure that she believed it. It was as if all she'd been doing was working her way through the movements with none of the feeling.

She wanted to lie on the bed until she died.

There was a bullet hole in the ceiling.

Some colder part of her took control. Jane Page sat bolt upright, hands leaping to the barrel of her gun.

It was here that she'd first encountered the weirdos that infested this house. That Doctor, Truman, Cranleigh, Benny. All now dead, or mad. She'd held them all at gunpoint, wondering which one she could kill first.

She'd brought two guns to the house.

The wardrobe was the first place she thought of. She hurled it open. Her instinct drew her to the other gun, sitting squat on a plain carpet.

'Bittersweet,' Page whispered through her blissful smile. She spent a moment stroking the trigger, letting her finger become reaccustomed to the feel of the gun. It was as fine a feeling as she remembered.

Air rushed behind her. Suddenly she was spun around, down on one knee, arms projected from her body, gun an extension of her fingers. It aimed still and straight at the far wall.

The wall was growing. Bubbles expanded like boils on the wallpaper, ripe and taut, fit to burst. The bubbles merged into new shapes. Something was haemorrhaging itself into being out of that wall. Two distinct solid shapes, crude but familiar. They broke away from the wall, inflated bags of paper covered in a repetitive flower pattern.

Gabriel and Tanith stood before her. Mortar and brick dust churned in their eye sockets. They breezed towards Page, rustling as they moved.

Gabriel spoke first, solid lumps of brick spilling from his mouth. Page felt nauseous but refused to allow it to cloud her judgement.

'O dark, dark, dark, amid the blaze of noon,' Gabriel declaimed, 'irrevocably dark, total eclipse, without the hope of day!'

'Hiya Pagey,' Tanith intoned, spitting and speaking gravel. 'We've not been prop'ly introduced. Him's Gabs, me's Tan, y'know how it is?'

'Singing bitter songs of shattered flowers slice and slice and bloody and bloody staining white thighs and eyes quite mad how sad too bad and all things in totality my little blossom floating on the water in the land of murder where the shadows never lie.'

'One more time: We love you. We need you.'

'Come with us Pagey-girl,' Gabriel called. 'Like us

you are a shadow dancing on the edge of truth. Time to fall.'

Page made a hole in his head. The wallpaper man jerked backwards, dust fountaining from the crevice in his temple.

Page frowned. She'd aimed for an eye.

She put four more bullets into him, one in his shoulder, two in his chest, one in his groin.

She swung the gun round and took out Tanith's jaw, forehead, right thigh, womb, throat, finally making a crater in the heart of her left breast.

Page took no immediate pleasure from this. It wasn't as if they were real people. They were just parodies, grown out of the wall for the sheer kick of scaring her. Once they were killed, the wallpaper people lost their human shapes, becoming piles of dust and torn paper. There was no fun in inflicting pain on this kind of creature. The only real thrill was that which shook her body every time the pistol kicked.

Page surveyed her work with professional pride. Then she made for the door with a renewed sense of purpose. She knew what she was going to do and how she was going to do it.

It was nice to have things back to normal.

Ace didn't known where she was going, her attention was focused solely on Sandra, on little more than a fleeting glimpse of her back or a shoulder in the passageway ahead. Ace managed to keep her in sight. Just.

How could anyone run so fast?

She'd called to her a couple of times, weak shouts forced through breaks in her heavy, wheezing breath. She'd been running for so long, her head was feeling bloated and dizzy and there was a haze in front of her eyes. The exhaustion was going to kill her before anything else.

Sandra was there in front of her, a suddenly tall, suddenly imposing figure with soft, blank eyes. She was smiling, a kindly, motherly smile.

Ace grabbed the nearest wall and tried to steady herself.

'Shit!' she snapped, forcing herself to breath sensibly, forcing back the sick taste. 'Bloody *bloody* hell! Oh God, hard-boiled skull! How can you run so bloody fast?'

Sandra smiled in silence.

'Benny is dead.' Ace spat the words. They had a gristly taste which she wasn't yet used to. 'Benny is dead, we've got three psychos on the loose not to mention that bloody insect. Christ!' She clenched her arms against her stomach, half-falling to her knees as something seized painfully in her gut. The pain was long and dull and intense but it concentrated her mind, stopped her from crying.

'She's dead.' When she looked at Sandra again, her eyes were stark, filled with sadness. 'Travel a lot, you get close to the people you spend your time with, s'right? No one I've loved's been killed before.'

Sandra slipped an arm under Ace's shoulder. Slowly she levered Ace upright, gently but with a surprising strength. The pain still waged its war in Ace's intestines, but it was softer now. She rested against the other woman for support, letting herself be guided through the nearest door.

'I'll tell you what though,' Ace mumbled, wondering how much of the pain was her and how much of her was the pain. Sandra propped her up against a wall. 'A lot of people I've fancied've been killed. I can't remember half their faces now. I never hang around long enough to get to know anyone.'

There was a new burst of pain and she grimaced. The graze on her face was dribbling a steady stream of blood now, and Sandra had pressed something right against the wound.

'I wish I'd had the chance though.'

Sandra nodded, leaning closer to the wound. Her face disappeared from Ace's sight, becoming something dark on the edge of Ace's perception.

'Looks like a bomb's hit this place,' Ace announced, studying the room from over Sandra's shoulder. It wasn't an ill-judged statement. The room was a conservatory, filled from wall to wall with exotic plants and vegetation.

200

That explained the heat and the chlorophyll tang. Someone had gone out of their way to create a rainforest in this room, so Ace expected it would be more than a little chaotic. But it was also filled with the tools of civilization – and they were in a real mess. A desk had been overturned, books strewn everywhere – their pages stained dark red and torn to shreds. A gas hob had been smashed against the wall; beside it lay a twisted piece of kettle, water frothing from its crushed spout.

There was something warm and relaxing pressed against the wound on Ace's cheek. There was something thick with spikes expanding in her stomach. Between pleasure and pain, Ace found it difficult to concentrate.

'Hey,' she said, struck by a memory. 'This isn't the place with those plants that tried to eat Benny?'

She cast round the room, lighting on a patch of orchids, a few yards away from her. They were writhing and shaking, spitting long, thin tendrils from their crushed mouths. Ace reckoned this was what she was looking for. The orchids swept in wave patterns. Beautiful. They clustered round each other like a pack of hunting animals, swooping down on the corpse, sinking their tendrils greedily into its exposed flesh. The lines pulsed, redness seeping through in what was clearly a hungry transfusion.

Ace smiled.

The body was that of a man in his fifties, recently dead, Ace guessed. He was already pale from the blood drain, but there was some quality to his skin that suggested he had been heavily tanned in life. The plants hadn't killed him though. The marks on his face told Ace the whole story. He'd been attacked by something vicious. It had probably been a violent death. Ace had lived with death long enough to recognize the signs of death-agony. This man hadn't gone easily.

Ace smiled and closed her eyes.

After a couple of seconds, they were open again, staring.

She pushed Sandra away from her, shoving the woman so quickly that she stumbled backwards without putting up a fight. Ace stared at her face, repelled.

201

Sandra's eyes were blank and callous, dazed but sharp. There was blood on her lips and her teeth and her tongue. There had been something warm and wet against Ace's cheek, and she suddenly realized what it was.

'What have they done to you?' Ace asked blandly. Her well of emotion had already run itself dry, she couldn't make the effort. Exhaustion had got the better of her. All she wanted to do was curl up in a corner and cry. Hardly fighting talk; she'd had enough of that for one day.

Sandra leant forward, baring her teeth and hissing. Her eyes had become squints, sharp and venomous. There was nothing human in them.

'Look, don't give me this!' Ace told her, shaking her head in near-hysteria. 'I'm not going to fight you. Really, I'm too bloody tired!'

The animal Sandra tensed and leapt, smashing Ace into the wall. Sandra's face pressed against hers, a magnified mask of grotesque scowls, teeth and hateful eyes. Pain lanced through Ace's spine, across her shoulder-blades, bringing on a shocked surge of adrenalin. She shoved Sandra away from her and dived across the room, blundering through the undergrowth, crushing flowers under her boots. Her head was light and the world spun and shook around her. She lost track of where she was, of where she was going, of everything save the overriding need to get away.

Sandra howled with inhuman hunger. A dead weight crashed into Ace's back, sending her sprawling forward. Her knees cracked as she hit the floor, her body flattening itself across the corpse of the old man. Bulbous plant faces brushed against her face, sharp-tipped tendrils pinned themselves like razors into her face, one digging itself into the edge of her eye. There were claws in her shoulders, dragging her back. She crawled free of the orchids, smashing them aside. Sandra's grip remained firm.

The hands were at her throat, under her chin jerking upwards, trying to pull her head off. Ace could feel her spine curving backwards. There was enough force there to break her neck, enough pain to amply fill the seconds before that final bone-cracking wrench.

'Sandra!' Ace howled, opening her lips and gaining a mouthful of wet earth. 'Sandra! It's me! It's Ace! Sandra!'

Sandra growled by her ear, a guttural croaking sound issuing from the back of her throat, devoid of meaning, devoid of human sound. An elbow drove Ace's face into the earth, burying it in a cool haze of wet brown and green. Sandra was pressing her shoulders and neck down as if trying to drown her in the mud. Ace no longer had the energy or the inclination to rise.

Better if she died here. Now.

Sandra's teeth cut into the back of her neck. There wasn't any pain now, just the gradual sense of despair that had built up along with the mud on her face. Ace lay still and waited for the end.

'I think your chair's in something like working order,' said the Doctor.

'Fine. Where shall we go first?'

The Doctor raised the chair onto its wheels and watched it wobble slightly before righting itself. He felt no pride in the restoration. His eyes flicked down to stare at his hands. They were dark with grime from the dirtier parts of the wheel's anatomy. The layer on his hands conjured up images of the effort he'd put into repairing the chair. A pointless effort. It served to keep his mind off the situation – the last practical goal to be achieved in the empty plains of the interstix.

He'd been dreading this moment. The repairs were effected. There was nothing else to do but wait – and pray – for madness and death.

'All art is quite useless,' Winterdawn said, smiling without feeling.

The Doctor helped Winterdawn back into the chair then squatted on the pseudo-ground to watch the never-ending show.

Years passed. Perhaps they were seconds.

They watched together as the interstitial world turned

inside out, displaying patterns and colours and designs too complex to be conceived in the real universe. The Doctor smiled. At times he thought he could see people dancing in between those shapes, people and creatures from a thousand worlds and a million times. His eyes followed the tortuous geography, trying to find an end to it, certain that there was none.

He felt exactly like he had done as a child, sitting on a beach, tossing pink pebbles into a golden sea. A good feeling.

A shape moved in the very distance, on what the Doctor would have called the horizon, had such concepts applied outside of normal space. It was a speck, moving in a way that nothing else in interstitial reality had ever done. The Doctor couldn't define the difference. It was something he sensed.

It was a dreary sight, lacking the sparkle and the transience of the usual conjured images. Just the blot moving slowly, at the slowest crawl imaginable. As it moved it grew. It grew with proximity. The Doctor found he had the impression of a man trekking the incredible hot distances of a desert plain, forever walking towards the horizon.

After several days the shape was large enough to be made out as a man. Male humanoid at least. A man walking the interstitial planes, toiling grey paces in the direction of the Doctor. The man moved easily with long, measured strides. He wasn't hurrying.

'I've seen him before,' Winterdawn said quietly. His tone was bland, but the Doctor caught a hundred subtle inflexions. Hope, confusion, curiosity. Foremost was terror.

The Doctor nodded, turning back to scrutinize the man, contemplating his new knowledge, wondering what the figure's significance would be.

The man wore a long grey coat covering a grey shirt and grey trousers. On his head was perched a grey hat. His skin was thin and grey. There was no part of him that was not grey, save for the black glass of his spectacles.

The greyness lent him ambiguity. The Doctor studied the distant face, wondering whether this was a young man, or an old one. It was impossible to tell. He was neither. He was grey.

12

Notes from Underground

Time stopped inside Ace's skull. There was the taste, the stench, the warmth of mud against her face, frozen in a single moment. Her pain froze, Sandra's weight on her back froze. Both seemed cold, almost abstract. Ace lay half-buried in the conservatory wondering only why she wasn't dead.

Hands seized her shoulders roughly, pulling her upwards again. She shook weakly, a hopeless effort to free herself. There didn't seem any point in fighting, her body was riddled with weariness, aching with the sheer effort she'd gone through that day. She hated her weakness. Not much point, she'd be dead in a few moments. So close to the final end, she found herself harbouring a much more resigned attitude to life.

She turned her head, staring hopelessly into the face of death.

Jane Page smiled back at her.

'Oh, you are still with it then?' Page grinned, face like a scored potato. 'I was beginning to think I was the only one left.'

Energy kicked back into Ace's body. She pulled away from Page.

'Where's Sandra?' she asked coolly, trying not to match the assassin's stare. Page indicated a slumped shape lying in a damaged patch of fronds.

'Vicious little harpy isn't she?' Page said. 'You've not thanked me.'

'Is she dead?' Ace growled.

'No.' Page shook her head with dismissive sincerity. 'I was tempted.'

'Thanks.' It took an effort, but Ace managed to say it.

Page nodded, her features losing their sour sense of humour and becoming grim cold. She pulled something from the folds of her coat and pitched it in Ace's direction. Ace caught it in her cupped palms. It was metal. Familiar.

It was a pistol. An unfamiliar design. Ace guessed that it was an automatic repeater backed up by more than a fair force and capacity. Loaded with ... explosive bullets. Big league for a small firearm. A very heavy, very comfortable piece of weaponry. High kill-power. Very nice.

In the right hands.

'This,' she said flatly, 'does a lot of damage.'

'I like damage.' Page's voice was coarse. 'It's an art-form.'

Ace stepped forward and pressed the gun under Page's chin, forcing the woman's head upwards. Page made no attempt to move. Her face and eyes seemed to bloat, not with fear but with arrogance.

'That was a mistake,' Ace said.

'Possibly.' Page's voice was loose and easy, still seeming to sneer at her. 'You know how to use one of those? Which ends goes "bang"?'

'That's obvious. I've seen more action than you ever have.'

'Killed anyone?' Page was almost casual about it. There was a coolness in her manner which Ace found admirable. And callous.

'One or two.'

'I believe you,' Page said, her voice growing slightly more emotive. 'We're very similar, you and I. What I can see in your eyes ...'

'Shut up!' Ace spat. 'I only kill people who deserve it. I can name one now.'

'Only one? I can name two.'

Ace studied Page's face with new intensity. She kept the gun cradled in her hands, but no longer quite ready to kill.

'You're bloody good.' Page smiled, fixing Ace with a sharp stare, 'her voice becoming slow. 'I've changed my plan about Winterdawn. I'll catch some stick from Ten, but all I want to do is get out of this house with body and soul intact.

'Before I go, I have to kill Gabriel and Tanith.'

Ace said nothing.

'I can do it,' Page insisted. 'Go in with guns blazing and don't stop until they're scattered across the floor in bits. I can go alone. Or I could have help.'

'Me?' Ace asked, shrugging casually.

'So quick,' Page sighed. 'Everyone else is dead or mad. I'd lay odds those two are responsible. You've got the gun, the ability, the inclination and the desire to use it. Up to you.'

Ace stared at Page, then at the jagged shape in her hand, then back to Page. Her face was bland. Ace levelled the gun at it, wondering whether it would be worth it.

'I don't like you,' she said. 'Remember that.'

She lowered the gun and watched Page nod.

She felt as though she'd sold her soul.

A pentecost was babbling on the inside of Cranleigh's head. A thousand languages rattled from a thousand tongues across the landscape of his mind. They screamed their rage, anger and lonely emptiness, the hollowness left by the absolute destruction they had known. Worlds burned in meaningless holocausts. These were the voices of the survivors screaming for justice, or explanations.

Cranleigh might have sympathized, but Cranleigh was gone, buried deeper in his psyche than even the insubstantial legion could reach. They called to a husk Cranleigh, stripped of mind. The pentecost called to him, drawing him to its heart. Cranleigh's hollow body stumbled through twisted corridors to the nursery.

The husk stared with vacant eyes at its surroundings. The toys, the furniture, the chest of drawers, the body sprawled on the carpet. These were meaningless things on the edge of its perception. But there was something else.

Something that fascinated even the void Cranleigh had become, something that stimulated the last fragment of his mind. A black window, glowing with darkness. Cranleigh saw no reflection in its jet surface.

Unquestioning, Cranleigh leapt towards the window, driving his fist towards the glass. Contact came, brief and violent.

The sound of shattering glass reverberated along empty passages.

Sandra woke to the smell of mud and blood. The mud was on her face and hands and clothes, hardening into thick cakes. The blood was dry in her nostrils, on her teeth and flecked on her hands, black crusts gathered under her finger-nails. Both her sight and her memory were clear and sharp.

Wedderburn's body was a withered thing on the far side of the room. It seemed too fragile ever to have been human.

Shaking, Sandra climbed to her feet. What she had done seemed so unreal. She stared at her hands and remembered her blood-lust. She recalled the swiftness, the pleasure, the taste of the kill. Her body was dirty, covered in the stench of her actions. Her skin writhed. She began to scratch, finding she couldn't stop. She needed to purge herself of the scent of the kill.

The world tottered as she moved. This *was* real and this was *now*. She slumped against the door, barely reacting to the diffuse pain that shocked through her arm. She cupped her hands over her face and began to scream into the soiled darkness of her palms.

The gun was a weight in Ace's fist. The sweat building on her palms hadn't made the weapon easier to hold. She didn't feel happy, going coldly, without passion to kill. She thought she'd feel safer with a gun. Instead she felt inadequate. This wouldn't be a kill in the heat of battle, it would be her, alone with the gun, facing an unarmed enemy. The advantage was hers; she held all the aces. It didn't feel right. She steeled herself, working up the nerve to squeeze the trigger, working up a righteous hatred for her target. Not too difficult. She just thought of Benny. The rest was easy.

She stared at Page. The assassin was in her element now, deriving deep satisfaction from the moment. She would have no compunctions about slaughtering Gabriel and Tanith if Ace's nerve gave out. This was her show. She was making it work her way.

Tracking their targets hadn't proved difficult. Page guessed that they would have marked off some space in the house as their own, and Ace saw no fault in that reasoning. Despite – perhaps because – of the miscegenation of floors and passageways and rooms, they stumbled across Gabriel and Tanith's hideaway in minutes. The couple's voices caught in a passageway, echoing from another room.

They were together in that single room, a bedroom, Winterdawn's shrine to his wife. Through the gap in the door, Ace saw them moving, talking, kissing. She watched their activity with cold and hateful eyes. Benny was in the room with them, stretched on the bed. Gabriel and Tanith must have brought her there and the thought that they must have touched her to move her uncovered within Ace a deeper revulsion than she had felt before.

She glanced at Page, catching a glimpse of quiet confirmation in her colleague's eyes. Ace kicked the door wide open and tumbled into the room, into the midst of the enemy. The blood that surged through her body, the hatred she felt for this couple wiped away her guilt, fears and compunctions about killing in cold blood. So they were unarmed. It was better that way. There was a perverse pleasure to it.

She raised the pistol and pumped a bullet into Gabriel's chest. His shirt gained a scarlet-flower stain and he staggered backwards under the impact. Not quite dead, Gabriel released a low, jarring howl. Agony made sound. Ace ground her teeth into her lower lip and fired again. Each new shot knocked Gabriel further backwards in a perverse, jerking walk. He smashed into the wall. His lifeless shell of a body sunk to its knees, leaving long smears on the wallpaper behind him.

Tanith stepped forward. Ace spun round, training the pistol on her. Too late – Page was already by her side, arms swinging upwards in a perfect arc. The graceful motion of her limbs was accompanied by the monotonous music of the machine-gun. Tanith's body gained a clean line of red holes from thigh to neck. Pink stains blossomed across her suit.

Page let her gun fall. She grinned toothily.

'Lovely jubbly,' she announced.

Ace dropped her pistol. It hit the thick carpet with a near-silent *thud*.

'This,' Tanith patted her chest, '*burns*. We're grateful.'

A line of blood slipped from her lips down her chin.

Ace stared.

Jane Page loomed behind Tanith's shoulder. Ace registered the cocktail of confusion and determination picked out on Page's face. The assassin swung her arms, gun aimed at the back of Tanith's head.

The gun fired silently. Tanith's forehead exploded. Ace looked down, thoughtfully studying the butterfly patterns of blood that stained her combat jacket. And she felt nothing.

Tanith's lips assumed a rictus smile. Her teeth were ivory pillars flecked red.

'Jane!' she said slowly, mocking and deliberate. 'Are you selling your soul to a cold gun?'

Ace watched Page lower her gun, watched the incomprehension grow on her face, watched it blossom into rejection. She was shaking her head wildly, sharp eyes full of good-humoured madness. Ace watched and still felt nothing, as if this was an ancient piece of film – silent and unnatural. Page didn't seem real. Tanith didn't seem real. Ace didn't seem real. The reel spun, clicking through the projector. On the screen, Gabriel appeared behind Page and wrested the gun from her. Gabriel's body was a patchwork of bullet holes so that it seemed in danger of falling apart. Page's guns were designed to damage; they didn't do things by halves.

'Unimaginative.' Gabriel was shaking his head ruefully. 'We had hoped for something more original.' He broke into a hearty laugh.

He didn't seem real either.

Ace felt herself begin to shake. Tanith swung her head to one side, letting it loll like something dead. Her eyes and her mouth were alive with insanity. Slowly, aware that she had Ace's total attention, she dug her fingers into the wounds, twisting her hand to work it further into her body. She clenched her fist, her face wrenching into a contorted portrait of agony, hissing pain through gritted teeth. Ace tried to draw back, but Tanith's other arm leapt to grip her shoulder.

Tanith threw her head up, breaking into a scream of pain that endured for minutes, changing in neither pitch nor intensity. Ace kept her eyelids tight together for the duration of the screech, grateful she couldn't see her own expression, grateful that there was so little left in her stomach.

'The beauty of pain,' Gabriel was saying, his voice clear and concise above the scream. 'The ugliness of pain. Both lend us something unique. As the bullets cut us we were born anew, embodied in the experience.'

The screech stopped.

Ace opened her eyes.

Gabriel and Tanith stood before her, their bodies clean and repaired. Even their clothes were unbroken and unstained. The couple shared a smile – sweet, condescending curves quivering on their lips. Page lay slumped by one wall, shaking her head on the verge of tears. Beyond Page was the bed and on the bed lay the body of Benny Summerfield.

Ace felt the room grow arctic cold.

'What are you?'

'In the Dark Ages,' Gabriel said, as if he was a schoolteacher delivering a particularly dull lesson, 'Christians believed the suffering of the world was caused by the presence of Satan's evil in God's creation.'

Ace's eyes flicked from Gabriel to Tanith and back again.

'And what's this got to do with you?' she asked.

'We *are* the suffering.'

Ace opened her mouth to speak but was silenced by a gesture.

'Not in any religious sense,' Tanith said hastily, lowering her hand. 'We aren't responsible for *all* the ills of the universe. Not yet.'

'The cosmos is in agony. Its structure has been maimed.'

'We are the damage on this level of existence. We are the scream.'

'We are the cosmos, replicated in microcosm. We draw our power from the structure of reality, aligned to all things, all spaces.'

'We can do anything. We know everything. We are inextricably linked to the nature of now. Does that answer your question?'

Ace nodded, trying to appear knowledgeable, tough and grim. She wasn't fooling anyone, least of all herself.

'You're bloody mad!' Page snapped. Ace's eyes leapt across the room to the manically grinning face, the constantly shaking head. Ace could see that she hadn't believed. She hadn't seen their sincerity.

'There is no such *thing* as the cosmos!' Page declared. There was sincerity in her eyes too, but also something dangerous. 'There are individual humans and loyalties. There is *nothing* larger than human action!' She nodded, as if the act of nodding automatically confirmed the truth of her words. It confirmed only her instability.

Gabriel and Tanith were exchanging glances thick with humour.

'Nothing bigger than human action?' He sounded unusually reasonable.

'Nothing!' Page confirmed.

'Actions have consequences.'

'He that kills a breeding-sow,' Tanith chimed in, 'destroys all her offspring to the thousandth generation.'

'Bugger the consequences!' Page straightened up, shaking too freely to cut an impressive figure. 'They get in the way of freedom.'

'Freedom.' Tanith was humourless. 'Of course.'

'Don't you think your actions might have an effect? That you might influence the future?' Gabriel asked.

'The future sorts itself out,' Page asserted.

'Of course, but think. Every time you act, you negate all the potential futures in which you didn't.'

'Blink, and you erase a future in which you didn't,' Tanith suggested. 'Of course, bigger actions have bigger consequences, more futures erased. More potential lives burned away in a moment's thoughtlessness.'

'But there's chaos theory. The departed Professor Winterdawn was working on a holistic model of the universe. Every action affects everything else.'

'Blink,' said Tanith, 'and you kill millions who might have lived.'

'Crap,' Ace spat, barging back into the conversation. 'Okay, what we do affects the future, you can't avoid that. Doing nothing would have the same effect. You can't tell! You take the plunge and hope things work out.'

'You're right.' Gabriel spun round. 'That's wonderful, wonderful common sense. Now tell me, what happens if you're a time traveller and you wander into a time or place where by rights you should never have been. What effect do you think you'd have?'

'Time travel!' Page leered. 'You almost had me going for a moment.'

Ace opened her mouth to say something, but found nothing there.

'Oh please shut your mouth,' Tanith said disapprovingly. 'You look like a dead fish and you're dribbling on your jacket.'

'Just think, everything you'␣e done – or haven't done – since you appeared on Svartos. The smallest actions irrevocably altering futures of a hundred worlds on which you had no right to be. Millions of potential, real futures dislocated. You – every other time traveller – guilty of genocide to an unimaginable degree. How d'you like them apples?'

Tanith placed a friendly hand on Ace's shoulder, and adopted a sad, wide-eyed expression. Then, with exaggerated slowness, she winked. Ace stared back at her, old feelings of revulsion returning to her. That face was so close to her, so disgusting in its proximity.

'Those things in the nursery,' she began, tentatively. 'I thought they might be dead things. They're not, are they?'

'The dead have no reason to hate the living.' Gabriel clapped his hands in an extravagant mockery of delight. 'Besides, lurching zombies are *passé*. They aren't the undead, they're the unborn.'

Ace nodded, trying to turn away, but Gabriel's stare had her fixed.

'They may have been erased from destiny, but the possibility of them is still imprinted into the structure of the universe. We can sense them dimly, perhaps we even have a vague affinity with them.'

'Careful,' Tanith checked him. 'She'll think you're fond of something.'

Ace scowled.

'We can draw them from the structure, with our power we can remake them. The TARDIS came in handy. We set its computers to do all the leg-work, while we got on with something more interesting. Not only does it have the power required to calculate all the probabilities but it also kept the system tied up so you never got a chance to leave.'

'You brought the TARDIS here?' Ace blurted the question hurriedly, remembering the mystery that had seemed so important the previous evening. Gabriel shook his head.

'As far as we can tell, that was an enormous coincidence.'

'These things,' Ace asked. 'Why are they coming out of that window?'

Tanith laughed, pushing her face closer.

'For effect!' she announced. 'Why else?'

'Yeah.' Ace nodded, feeling shaky. 'Look, there's this insect . . .'

'One of them,' Tanith admitted. 'A dominant evolutionary life-form on Earth in one potential. You seemed bored searching those rooms, not finding anything remotely interesting. We introduced it to liven things up for you.'

'Thanks,' Ace muttered softly, half-closing her eyes and mulling over what Tanith had told her. Something had softened her sense of aggression and anger. She had a great deal to think about.

'I'll tell you what I think.' Page's voice cut through the careful silence of the bedroom. She slunk deliberately across the room, her body bursting with a desire for confrontation. Gabriel and Tanith wheeled round slowly to match her stare.

'You know what I think?' Page snapped.

'Very little,' Gabriel suggested. Page let it pass.

'I think you are talking meaningless, metaphysical shit. I don't know whether you're mad enough to believe it yourselves – I don't know how you got Ace to believe you. All you are is psychotic! You're as human as I am.'

'You shot us at point-blank range, yet we live. You may have noticed?'

'Tricks. Drugs, something hypnotic. There's nothing more. I know the truth. Ace!' she appealed to her former ally.

Ace shook her head, expecting to despise herself. But for that moment and no longer she felt good. She knew that she had more in common with Gabriel and Tanith than she ever would with the wretched, hateful woman she had been forced to ally herself to.

'Remember Page,' she snapped, 'I don't *like* you.'

Gabriel broke away from his partner, sweeping towards the angry figure.

'You know the truth.' His voice rang with terrible sincerity. 'Know this! Your world doesn't exist. You don't exist. You're another lost soul, a phantom from a potential reality destroyed by some clumsy time traveller. We pulled you into existence because we needed a wild card and you – because you wanted to make trouble for Winterdawn – were the perfect choice.'

Page stopped in her tracks, glaring at the oncoming figure,

'Crap! A figment of your imagination!'

'*You* are a figment of our imagination!'

'No!'

'You don't exist in this world. You know it's the truth.'

'Know . . . I mean, no . . . I mean . . .'

'Yes!' Gabriel snarled triumphantly.

'No,' Page mouthed, a hollow denial. She sank to her knees, fierce but hopeless anger blazing from her eyes. For a minute Ace thought that she was going to break down and cry. She didn't. Too proud. Gabriel floated closer, and as he moved his body unfolded like a cloak billowing in a gale. The folds of his body swept around her, enveloping her, swallowing her. Ace saw a final despairing scream play soundlessly on Page's mouth before she was engulfed.

Then she was gone. They were both gone.

Ace was alone with Tanith and the oblivious husk of Bernice.

Ace was weary. She let her body sink under its own weight. Everything that had happened in the house had led her here, now, to this moment. The big confrontation. And it was an anticlimax. She felt impotent – unable to do anything but watch and understand.

'Ace,' the Doctor's voice echoed, 'if you can force your heart and nerve and sinew to serve your form long after they are gone, and so hold on when there is nothing in you, except the will which says to them: "Hold on!", then you're the Ace I remember.'

'Yeah, thanks a bloody bunch Doctor,' she muttered.

She had a deal to make.

Look Mum, I've sold my soul twice in one day!

'Is Benny dead?' she asked, forcing herself despite the

weariness she felt, knowing what she wanted to say, what she was going to say.

'Her soul has been wrenched from her body.' Tanith shrugged.

'Is there any possibility ...' Ace proceeded slowly through the sentence making certain she used the most meaningful words possible. 'Any potential hope, that she could still be alive?'

'I know what you're saying.' Tanith smiled, not unkindly. 'I can't do that. There are only a few thousand potentials open to us. The chances of one of them being a Bernice Summerfield is remote to say the least. Besides, it wouldn't be your Benny. The woman you've known is gone.'

Ace nodded, raising a hand to her face to mask her disappointment.

Slowly, almost grudgingly, she began to cry.

'If it's any consolation, we didn't want her to die.'

'Does it matter? She's dead.'

'She'll fade in your mind. You won't forget her, but the pain will die.'

'I'm sorry, but that sounds bloody stupid.'

Tanith placed a palm against Ace's cheek. Ace pulled her head back to stare long and soft into her eyes.

'Think of it this way.' Tanith's voice was high and sweet. 'You've got me now.' Ace's eyes narrowed as she broke into a weary nod.

'I've got you now,' Ace agreed, dreamily whispering the electric phrase. Her hands leapt to lock round Tanith's neck, eyes alive with blood and fire.

'I've got you now, you bitch!' she snarled and tightened her grip.

Ace knew the pressure it took to kill quickly, the pressure it took to be certain of a killing, the pressure it took to snap a neck. All three became one pressure in her hands. She applied it, teeth gritted into a perverse grin.

Tanith's face burst open into a thick and hateful smile. Her eyes were black and burning. Ace's hatred was a furious storm, blind to everything, but she realized that the woman didn't even seem uncomfortable.

218

'You give me myself,' Tanith hissed, forcing the words through lack of breath. She broke into a stunted giggle.

Ace looked into Tanith's eyes and saw herself reflected there. A vicious animal, face contorted with hatred. She saw her own eyes – mere sockets, wet and dark. She saw Gabriel's hands locked round Benny's throat at breakfast. She saw doubt.

She relaxed, releasing the throttling grip. She could see the bruises she had made on Tanith's neck and discovered that she had lost the desire to tighten her grip.

'Can you imagine?' Tanith's black eyes shone, a hundred points of light reflected in their facets. 'Can you imagine what it is like to be dropped in at the deep end of existence, with intimate knowledge of everything yet not being a part of it?'

Ace shook her head grimly.

'Gabriel and I have no meaning. We are utterly point-less people. We are the notes from underground, chords, maybe whole tunes. Cognizant of every culture, of every identity, yet having none of our own. You little person, you're a programmed instrument, determined by influ-ences around you.'

Ace shook her head again.

'I'm not determined by anybody.'

'Oh yes, good little rebel. Even a reaction against a system is a product of that system. You're just so wrapped up in your own culture you don't realize it! Deep down, you're the biggest conformist of them all!'

'So what are you then?' Ace sneered.

'We had no influences, no culture. We were born cold into reality. Christ, it's difficult working on the level of one culture, addressing people as narrow and as limited as you. How can you possibly envisage the pain of using one rigid language? One grammar? One syntax? Just to get by? We have to make an identity for ourselves. Any-thing goes! Squeeze harder, it's good for me. I'm Tanith, Tanith the victim, Tanith the tortured. Don't care, doesn't really matter, any way the wind blows. Th-th-th-th-that's all folks!'

'You're sick.'

'I am, aren't I? But delicious with it. *Squeeze.*'

Ace shoved her away. She turned her back on her in disgust.

'What are you now?!' she yelled. 'Apart from insecure?'

'I'll be anything you want,' Tanith whispered, her voice a reedy exercise at Ace's back. 'I have to. Play games with me, my love. Anything will do. Tortured. Or *torturer.*'

A spasm of pain leapt up Ace's spine. She arched backwards, mouth twisting half into a gasp, half into a silent scream. She tried to claw at the source of the pain – deep in her agonized, curved back – but her arms remained paralysed, locked at her side.

'Sadist!' Tanith's voice rang clearly behind her.

Ace sank to her knees, a needle-sharp pain puncturing her skull and driving slowly into her brain.

'Dealer of pain!' Tanith declaimed.

Ace fell flat onto the floor and began to writhe. The pain was everywhere, encompassing all things, shrieking hideously through her body. She tried to howl, to cry out, but she couldn't bear to move her tongue.

Tanith's boot nudged her face gently.

'See what I have found, my darling.' The voice was high and distant and filled Ace with disgust. It wasn't an emotion strong enough to fight back the pain. 'Can you hear the sea?'

The grey man came to a standstill. He smiled, bowing slightly, removing his hat. The Doctor noted that there was a dark streak in his white hair. When he spoke, his voice was smooth and pleasant and as ageless as his face.

'Hello, Professor Winterdawn, Theta Sigma. I had hoped that this meeting need not take place, but nonetheless I am honoured to meet you.'

Theta Sigma.

The Doctor considered the grey man with colder eyes than before. Theta Sigma was a secret he kept well guarded. It was not his name but it identified him uniquely among the Time Lords. It should not have been spoken outside the Academy of Gallifrey, and the Doctor was certain that whatever the grey man might be, he was not a Time Lord.

'You know more,' he said, the coldness in his voice matching that in his hearts, 'than you should.'

'I have followed your movements for some time. I have noted your vendetta against the Dalek empire with considerable distaste.'

The Doctor frowned, leaping instantly to his own defence.

'The Daleks must be fought. They have no conception of morality.'

'Indeed.' The grey man clicked his tongue. 'At times the contest seems to be one to find which of you can display the least possible morality.'

The Doctor's next sentence was snapped and terse:

'The Daleks are irredeemably evil!'

'Nothing is irredeemably evil.' The grey man was shaking his head slowly. 'Especially not the Daleks. You should know, you've seen it.'

'There must be justice,' the Doctor insisted. 'And vengeance.'

'Nemesis?' the grey man asked suggestively.

'Yes, nemesis,' the Doctor agreed.

'Or guilt?' the grey man suggested darkly.

The Doctor seized up. He had to argue with the grey man, he knew that. He had to justify himself. But when he tried, he found there was nothing there, no justifications, not even explanations. He turned away, trying to hide his face.

'I'm sorry.' His accuser seemed upset by the effect of his barb. 'My remark was designed to wound. I can only apologize.'

The Doctor acknowledged the apology with a grim nod. But he still felt bitter and afraid and *small*. He wasn't fooled by physical shapes. The grey man was larger, more terrible, than he had imagined.

'I'm sorry,' Winterdawn said. 'All that went over my head.'

'We were discussing things of minor importance.'

'You said something about empires?' Winterdawn's eyebrows arched.

'Things of minor importance,' the grey man stressed. 'There are weightier matters to be considered. I am here ... against my better judgement. Normally I do not interfere. I try to encourage local solutions.'

Winterdawn smiled, a smile full of patience and lacking in humour.

'The problem is partly of my own creation, but mostly, Professor Winterdawn, the responsibility is yours.'

'Mine?' Winterdawn was genuinely startled by the remark.

'Your interference has unleashed a wave of destruction on the universe. I fear your actions have been negligent.' The grey man seemed to sense the confusion and fear growing on Winterdawn's face, and changed tack, 'No – I'm not here to censure you. No matter what else I may have become, my conscience is still my own. You acted in ignorance. No blame can be laid with you.'

The man in grey paused and Winterdawn took advantage of the situation to unleash a bellow mixing outrage, fear, confusion and anger.

'Blame for what?!'

The grey man spoke again, softer and slower:

'Your experiments with the metahedron. You do not understand the functions of the engine. Your manipulation resulted directly in the physical effects you desired, but there were ... other effects. The metahedron is a device for manipulating the structure of reality. When you used it, parts of the fabric of reality were affected.'

'Affected?' the Doctor asked, recognizing a euphemism when he heard one.

'Distorted.' The grey man stumbled through his words. 'Mutated. In some areas, totally destroyed. Much of it was of a trivial nature and was repaired by the natural functions of the cosmos. Other parts are beyond repair. I have no idea what the consequence of that will be. It will be many millenniums before their effects will be seen. And then . . .' He paused again. The Doctor saw that he was shaking.

'On the physical plane this damage has manifested itself as *sentience*. Wholly negative, destructive sentience. These sentiences have already, ah, killed or maimed a number of people.' A note of hysteria had crept into his previously calm voice. 'I . . . I heard a child die. Winterdawn, *they are loose in your house!*'

The silence that followed was brief.

'You knew!' Winterdawn howled. 'You knew and you didn't do anything! There's a bunch of bloody psychos in my house, and you're content to stand around and witter on about local-bloody-solutions! You bastard! If my daughter's hurt, I'll . . . Christ knows, I'll *haunt* you!'

The Doctor stepped forward trying to calm the screaming figure in the wheelchair. It seemed to work. The tirade ended, Winterdawn fell silent. But his eyes glowed with suppressed anger.

'I did my best,' the grey man said cautiously, his back to the pair of them. 'Local problems call for local solutions. There are . . . local agents.'

'Where were *they* then?' Winterdawn scowled. 'I didn't see them.'

The Doctor blinked. And understood. He faced the grey man.

'It was you.' he said simply.

'I have no affection for the Time Lords of Gallifrey, nor any mayfly-race that claims for itself the status of gods. But if flung into a chaotic situation, they are more than capable of stabilizing matters.'

The Doctor had nothing to say. He knew the power it required to disrupt the smooth functioning of a TARDIS.

'I plucked a TARDIS from the time streams at random,' the grey man confessed. 'I placed it in the house. I was certain a Time Lord would attend to matters without fuss. I underestimated the forces they would face. I continue to be surprised by the sheer magnitude of my stupidity.'

'That's easy for you to say,' the Doctor said smoothly.

'I was surprised it turned out to be you,' the grey man

223

continued. 'You would have brought new thinking to the situation. They side-tracked you.'

The Doctor nodded again, speaking with insistence:

'Yes. Now I'm side-tracked, and my companions are trapped in the same house as these destructive forces . . .'

The Doctor's voice snapped the grey man out of his lethargy.

'Yes, of course,' he said eagerly. 'You must go back. There is still time. There is always still time.'

' "There is always still-time, and there is always flowing-time," ' the Doctor replied, plucking the quote from memories of dusty books in the Academy library.

'I warn you things will have changed in your absence,' the man said.

'Are you still relying on "local solutions"?' Winterdawn spat.

'I cannot join you, if that's what you mean,' the grey man said. 'I have a prior engagement. The damage done extends far beyond the physical plane. I must attend to that. Now. Go.'

Darkness collapsed around them.

Jane Page's cell was bare. It was somewhere in the heart of Winterdawn's home. Page didn't know exactly where, nor did she care. She knew that she was something less than human, but she cared less. This knowledge was useless, sitting uneasily on the edge of her consciousness, acknowledged only because she hadn't the nerve to challenge the idea.

All Page cared about was herself. It was all she had left. She dwelt on the here, on the now, on the grey expanse around her.

She couldn't see it properly. Gabriel had stripped her of her gun, her coat, her freedom and her glasses. Her eyes were weak without them. She was a prisoner. Harsh ropes chafed at her wrists and ankles, binding her securely to a harsh metal chair. There was the cold – a light draught that cut through her body to stab at her bones.

New bones, she realized. No more than a day old.

Dark colours blurred before her. Gabriel.

'They burn Dante where you come from,' he said, casually terminating a long silence. 'Very apt. If you had read him you might understand why you must undergo this ordeal.' Dark blur held something towards her face, prodding it sharply into her cheeks.

'You will notice I have a number of instruments whose application will cause pain. To you. Possibly. I doubt that you feel pain. Your nervous system isn't developed enough. You are without a doubt not human. You will notice that however much you may scream, I will ignore you. You might be real, you might not be, but in the interests of individual freedom I would prefer to assume that you're not. After all I don't want my own prejudice to become outweighed by the possibility that I might be committing some vague ethical offence against a human's rights. Still, who wants to live when you're having fun? I don't care. Why do I bother justifying myself? You're not human, you don't deserve an explanation! Let's begin!'

'Praise be,' Page droned blandly. 'I haven't got all day.'

Something lodged itself into her throat – a huge, hard, solid shape with a metal taste and a mechanical curve. It stopped at the back of her throat. Page swallowed coolly, trying not to gag, well aware of what the shape was.

Between her teeth was the barrel of a gun, probably her own. Page went numb as she understood the danger. It was there – every time she breathed or swallowed she became aware of the icy lump of death in her throat.

'Come on Pagey, let's have a song.'

Page was silent, too scared to risk it.

'Sing,' Gabriel snapped.

Silence. The taste of the gun and the fear of death.

'Sing!' A hand smashed into the side of her face, matched by the force of Gabriel's yell. Taking the hint, she formed the words.

'Land of hope and glory,' the words were forced and unrecognizable, but they were coming, 'Mother of the free . . .'

'That's enough,' Gabriel insisted. 'That's quite enough.'

The thing was withdrawn from her mouth. Page relaxed, a little.

'Was it the singer or the song?' she asked.

'A bit of both. Tell me, have you ever tortured anyone?'

'I have. It's cruel to be kind.'

'You're a butcher, Jane Page.'

'That's what they said, while they still had tongues.'

'Did you enjoy it?'

'Yes,' Page lied without passion. 'Sometimes. I prefer the gun, the target. Torture prolongs the effect, makes me uneasy.'

'How does it feel to be on the other end?'

'Not good,' Page continued. 'Empty. Cold. Perhaps lonely.'

'Soon, we shall be together,' Gabriel said, his blade tickling the underside of Page's chin. 'Any tips? This is my first time. I'm a torture-virgin, I suppose.'

'Eyes are good. Nails and teeth if you have the equipment. Breasts, if it's a woman. Start with psychological torture, it gets them in a better state,' Page mused. 'On the whole it's a matter of technique.' She paused suspiciously. 'Why am I telling you this?'

'Because I want to hear. And I am very persuasive. Psychological torture,' Gabriel responded sympathetically. 'Possibly you think that if you're co-operative then I might change my mind.'

Page blinked, the longest blink she had ever known. It lasted for a fragment of a second. In that time she felt Gabriel tug away the topmost buttons of her blouse, felt the knife-point falling into the gap.

'Welcome,' Gabriel's voice sang loud and terrible in the darkness, 'to the outermost circle of Hell.'

Justin Cranleigh's body lay motionless on the floor of the nursery, a thing twisted and broken from a fall. Round his head was a halo of shattered glass. The window above him was punctured – a jagged hole punched into its surface. It was no longer black.

The voices were gone.

Tanith stood by the body, staring down and considering. Her mind was wrapped in chaos, a tumult of information absorbed into a structureless whole stretching into a void of static and white noise. Confusion screamed deranged songs on the inside of her head, too many to be learned properly.

After an hour's silent vigil, she was joined by Gabriel.

'It's over,' he said simply, smiling as he divulged the news.

'Today, the Shadowfell. Tomorrow, the world!' Tanith declared. The notes from underground broke into laughter, before kissing with all the pleasure and passion they could muster.

'Love and death!' Gabriel called.

'Love and death!' Tanith echoed. 'Long may they reign!'

Suddenly the real world came back into focus. There was stone floor beneath the Doctor's feet, electric light flooding his eyes, a tetrahedron by his shoes. The shock of being confronted with something real was almost too much for him. He placed a hand on Winterdawn's chair to steady himself.

He was in the cellar, the room from which he had left the universe years and seconds earlier.

The Doctor cast his eyes round the room cautiously. They fell on an object sitting abandoned in the corner, gathering dust. He picked it up, studying it sadly.

It was a mask, dirty and cracked. Two empty eyes stared up at him accusingly. A hollow grin sat poignantly on its brittle wooden lips.

'Truman,' the Doctor whispered. He felt an uncomfortable feeling of loss and sorrow.

The metal door of the cellar creaked suddenly. The Doctor tensed.

'Who's there?' he called cautiously, letting the mask fall, forgotten.

A dark shape burst through the door. It darted across the room, a flurry of awkward movements, flinging across the floor into the arms of Professor Winterdawn. The chair creaked ominously under the new weight.

'Dad!' the shape screeched. 'Thank God!'

The voice seemed to draw Winterdawn completely back to reality. The old sharpness entered his bleary, confused eyes.

'Sandra!' he exclaimed. 'I thought . . .' He never completed the sentence. He didn't need to.

'Dad. There are people here,' Sandra said, gasping for air and words. 'They got into the house. They killed Harry. They made *me* kill Moore.'

Sandra held up her hands so both Winterdawn and the Doctor could see the layer of blood built on her fingers.

'Gabriel and Tanith,' Sandra said. The hate and the fear with which she invested the names were difficult to ignore. 'They've made us do so many things,' she whispered.

'Sandra,' the Doctor asked slowly, 'Ace and Bernice, are they . . .?'

'I don't know.' Sandra turned. 'I tried to kill Ace, they made me. 'Sokay, she got away. Oh God.' Sandra's eyes burst with tears. She buried her head against Winterdawn's chest. The professor drew his daughter closer. A sour expression had grown on his face.

'I must find them,' the Doctor said simply, hurrying from the room.

On the far side of the door was a nightmare. The cellar passages were gone. In their place was a network of corridors from every floor of the house, woven together into a mockery of architecture. Tunnels swirled and shifted, forming new junctions, breaking older ones. The layout of the house spread out before him, labyrinthine and transient, a maze with liquid walls. The Doctor considered the new architecture carefully, not trying to map it nor follow its writhing contour.

He stepped into the heart of the storm.

Closing his eyes, he ran. The only possible direction. Forwards.

He stopped eventually, opening his eyes.

The house had reverted to an older, more formal structure. A staircase rose ahead of him, leading upwards towards an infinitely distant ceiling. The Doctor felt a shudder of *déjà vu*, but paid it little attention. The stairs seemed solid enough. The Doctor pounded upwards, taking long strides.

Two figures stood on the stairs, barring his way. A man and a woman dressed in eccentric clothes. They stared down at him with hateful eyes. The Doctor met their gaze with equal hostility.

He knew their names. *Knew*.

They were both beautiful from a humanoid point of view, perfect. The Doctor had never cared for perfection. 'Get out of my way,' he heard himself say.

Gabriel and Tanith moved aside, and the Doctor continued his journey. He didn't look back. He was afraid something terrible would happen if he tried.

The Doctor reached the top step gasping for breath. There was a pain under his ribs too, there had been one for most of the climb. He'd had the determination to ignore it on the way up. Now, at the summit, he felt it burning beneath his hearts, a burst of hot agony every couple of seconds. He let the pain cut him, waited for it to subside.

After a minute, he realized it wasn't going away, and pressed on regardless. A door flew open. He barged into the room beyond.

It was an ugly cubbyhole afflicted with a draught and a lingering smell of offal. In the centre of the room was a chair. Strapped securely into the chair was something that might once have been a woman. The Doctor recognized her, after a moment. The thing in the chair had once held him at gunpoint. Her head lay as far back as it could go, swaying slightly in the draught. A square of white cloth lay across her face, its shape moulding round her features. Two jagged pink stains had swelled and smeared on the surface of the cloth, discolouring it.

The head of the thing rolled to one side, falling to face the Doctor. The cloth slipped away. Carefully the Doctor retrieved it and tied it into a blindfold across Page's face.

229

He was trembling as he drew the knots tight. He remembered Ace and Bernice, and shuddered.

The lips of the thing twitched, formed tortured words.

'Who . . . is . . . that?' the thing said, each word an effort, a new pain.

'Me,' the Doctor said blandly. 'The Doctor,' he clarified.

'Heard . . . you were . . . dead,' Page continued.

'The report of my death was an exaggeration,' he replied coldly. Page forced herself to smile. The Doctor felt sick. He moved forward, tearing at the knots that tied Page's arms and legs to the chair. Despite her new freedom, she remained slumped in the chair.

'I . . . can't see,' she said, slightly puzzled. The Doctor bit his lip.

'No,' he said calmly.

He looked down and found that he was holding one of Page's hands clasped between his own. Her hands were small and cold and delicate and he felt more than one broken bone. He closed his palms and waited, in silence.

Quite how long he waited he was unable to remember. Perhaps an hour, perhaps longer. It seemed to slip by.

Eventually he released the woman's hand, letting it flop.

'I have to go,' he said.

'Don't,' Page slurred.

'I have to find Ace and Benny,' he insisted.

Page jiggled her head sharply as if it was too much of an effort to nod.

The Doctor strode away from what remained of Jane Page. He crossed to the door on the far side of the room. His fingers tightened round the handle reluctantly. On the one hand, there was the guilt of leaving Page to suffer. On the other, there was fear of finding something worse on the far side of the door.

He twisted the handle.

It was another bare room. A shape lay huddled in the far corner, a human shape wrapped into an embryo ball, knees tucked under its chin. Between the shape and the Doctor was a curtain of cobwebs. The Doctor ploughed through them, letting them fall to dust in his effort to reach the shape in the corner. Spiders chattered on the edge of his hearing. He ignored them, driving himself through older webs in his effort to reach the shape.

It was an Ace-shape. Her eyes opened to deliver a bleary stare.

'Benny,' she hissed.

'I'm going to find Benny now,' he said, trying to mask his worry and his relief. It didn't matter. Already she had slipped back into unconsciousness.

The Doctor straightened up. His eyes fell on another door.

The next room, he was surprised to discover, was the room in which he had first met Winterdawn – the unlived-in, dusty place which Winterdawn's wife had once used. There was a warmer feeling to it now, as if a great deal of activity and emotion had been crammed into this tiny space during his absence. November evening light was filtering through the window.

Professor Bernice Summerfield lay on what had once been Winterdawn's bed.

Cautiously the Doctor approached the bed. He reached for Bernice's pulse and found nothing. He checked her breathing but her chest was still and dead air hung around her mouth and nostrils. Her eyes were dull orbs. Her body was cold, stiff.

He looked upwards, bitter eyes turning to the ceiling.

'How did she die?' he asked. His tone was even and banal.

Silence answered him.

Professor Bernice Summerfield lay dead on what once had been Winterdawn's bed. The Doctor stood by the corpse, and closed his eyes, and waited.

13

Hark the Herald Angels Sing

Jane Page's body lived pain. Sometimes it was a knife slicing her nerves, a fire consuming her skin, steel driving through her marrow. The softest, most intense pain slobbered in her eye sockets.

Jane Page's mind lived pain. It danced round her soul with deceptive grace, striking delicate blows that paralysed her with agony. The instruments of mental pain were subtler. Old memories rose from her subconscious and into the hands of her torturer.

The memories were hollow. They were real, but the events they described were false. Page vividly recalled a life she had never lived. That torture was worse than anything Gabriel had done.

She remembered herself at school. A serious little girl studying the innocent faces of her classmates, watching for their weaknesses. A distant voice called her name. Her name. She tried to catch it but the voice was weak. The girl who was not yet Jane Page rose behind her desk, repeating a mantra drummed into her from birth.

Nation is strength. Dum-de-dum.

Blood is strength. Dum-de-dum.

Pain is strength. Dum-dum.

Nation is strength. That was the best joke Page had heard in years. Page's nation had never existed and never would beyond the confines of her mind. It was a worthless concept, save for the value *she* lent it. She stared through a girl's untouched eyes at the Union Flag on the class wall.

Blood is strength. That was better, Page had blood. It was young blood, less than a day old and borrowed at that, but it was blood. Her strength was there, running through her veins.

Pain is strength, Page thought, *so I am strong.*

Girls grow up. Page grew to understand the meaning behind the mantra, the logic of society. She *believed* it. That was odd. She stared at the faces of the self-seeking bastards around her and wondered why she alone was so pure in intent. She'd learned to distinguish the extent of liberty, the need for strength to expand to its full capabilities, the fine distinction between freedom and the baseless chaos of anarchy. She understood the need for the national symbol, the role that racial and cultural purity played in the definition of strength, the need to establish arch-realism to purge the individual of idiosyncratic morality. She had made herself strong, the Strongest Woman on Earth, on an Earth that didn't exist.

The pain led her to the core of her beliefs. The pain showed her how little she was, how *weak* she was. Page screamed and raged and denied it with all the energy she could muster. But it was true.

'I wish,' she said, wistfully, 'I was a girl again.'

She wanted to cry, but there were gaps where her eyes should have been. Her face remained dry.

She heard footsteps, dragging along the corridor outside the door. This would be how she would have to live from now on – by sound. She would have to learn the fine distinctions between sounds, the subtle shades of silence.

The door was opened and footsteps pulled into the room. Then the door was closed. The newcomer stopped moving, became a voice.

'There you are.' Page recognized it.

'Cranleigh?' she hissed.

'No,' came the reply in Cranleigh's voice.

'Then who are you?' she asked cautiously, afraid it might be Gabriel.

'Cranleigh is part of us,' Justin Cranleigh said. 'His mind was clean and new. We were dragged into its purity. We

233

made him one of us, both of him. It is no longer the glass that focuses us, it is Cranleigh himself.'

'I see,' Page spat, considering sourly. 'You're my fellow shades then? People without worlds? Might-have-beens?'

'We are. I am Qxeleq,' Cranleigh continued, his voice briefly becoming more relaxed and casual. 'I used to be a student, I must be going up in the hive, eh? *We* know you. You're a part of us. You belong with us.'

Page considered. The prospect was repulsive. It would be a descent into a crucible of impurity, losing herself in the heterogeneous mob.

'Join you?' she replied, coldly. 'That would be defeat. You're the weak. So weak you couldn't hang on to your own reality! It's survival of the fittest, remember, survival of the strong.'

'Where I come from, we call it survival of the luckiest,' Cranleigh-Qxeleq spoke. 'Being in the right place in the right time.'

Page purred. She pushed her body forward and shrieked into the darkness:

'I'm myself! Jane Page and no one else!' Her voice vanished with the sound. She couldn't see the *effects* of her words. Living by sounds wouldn't be enough. There would be no artistry to killing. She couldn't watch TV or see a sunset or a portrait. She could never read again. That struck hardest. Without eyes, without sight, without words.

She sank weakly into the chair in which she had been tortured.

'I am my own woman,' she insisted.

'So we gather.'

'I . . .' Page began.

'We can't have you arguing. You two should be all smiles and kisses and cuddles.'

Tanith's voice echoed through the shimmering black-ness of Page's world. She hadn't heard the woman enter. She assumed that Gabriel was with his sister, but the thought didn't move her. She felt nothing for him at all, not even hatred. Gabriel and Tanith were unpredictable, their actions pitched on such a higher level of thinking that attaching blame to them was unthinkable. She might as well rage against a storm, against the ocean, against the sky.

Gabriel coughed, disturbing her brood.

'Little Ms Page is an individual. She should be allowed to do her own thing. I'd prefer to talk with Cranleigh.'

'Yes?' Cranleigh replied suspiciously. Page sensed tension.

'The Doctor and Winterdawn have returned. They won't like us at all. Go. Be our eyes, our hands, our agent in the midst of their camp.'

Silence ensued, short and tense.

'You want us to work for you,' Cranleigh considered carefully.

'In a nutshell.'

'Why?'

'You *owe* us. We imagine you're keen on honouring debts.'

'No,' Cranleigh said sharply. Footsteps followed, out of the room.

'Well, what do you make of that?' Tanith said, faking offence.

'They've rejected us,' Gabriel continued, and Page felt certain that it was she who was being addressed. 'Our creations have cast us into the darkness. O tragedy, tragedy, all is tragedy.'

'They haven't the nerve to stand with you,' Page spat. 'They'd have to keep checking their shoulder-blades for unexpected protrusions.'

'We love our children. We would do nothing to harm them. Not much . . .'

Page felt someone's hands on her shoulders – gentle, smooth hands – it could have been either Gabriel or Tanith. She couldn't quite tell which. She felt something heavy drawn up onto her shoulders, sweeping round her like a cloak. She reached for it, her sore fingers finding thick, textured material wrapped over her forearms.

'What's this?' she asked cautiously.

235

'A little something,' it was Tanith's voice at her ear, 'to match the pretty pattern on your knickers.'

'A flag,' Gabriel snapped.

'The Union Jack,' Tanith intoned, lending the words a significance that thrilled Page. It also annoyed her.

'*Flag*! Union Flag! We're fifty miles inland!'

'No one's perfect,' Tanith purred. 'You'll be wanting a trident and a lion next.'

Page turned away from her, grinding her face up into a sour glare.

'Why?' she growled, not expecting a sensible answer.

'Do we need a reason?' Gabriel asked, closer this time. There was a casual arrogance in his voice that appealed to Page.

'Your only meaning is to have no meaning,' Page announced, more to clarify her own thoughts than to question the unseen pair.

'Exactly,' Tanith clapped her hands behind her. 'You don't approve.'

'Perhaps not.' Page adopted a twisted smile. She seized great bundles of the fabric hanging round her neck, drawing it tighter. She imagined her knuckles tensed and white. 'This is something different.'

'Well,' Gabriel said lazily. 'Better red, white and true blue than dead. My country, left or right.'

'And right is might, yes?' Page asked, imagining herself to be in the heart of a complex labyrinth of argument and counter-argument, a vocal maze where every syllable was laden with deep inflexions and meanings. This, as far as she was concerned, was the key question.

'Whatever you think, little girl,' Gabriel replied. It sounded like the key answer. Page nodded obsessively, feeling new forms of understanding blossoming in her mind.

'I think I want a gun,' she said simply. 'I have a job to do.'

One of the couple – she knew which – pressed the butt of her pistol into her fist. She weighed the gun, running the fingers of her other hand over its harsh shape. It was perfect. Untampered with and ready to fire. It would be simple enough to rake the room with bullets, smash Gabriel and Tanith's bodies beyond repair, but Page knew better. Gabriel and Tanith were ... ambivalent, but not her true enemy.

'I am the last of my race,' Page recognized the quiet obsession in her voice, an obsession that might hold nations together. 'This flag is meaningless. I must give it meaning. There must be a reckoning, a reassertion of strength and purity.'

'You're right of course.' Tanith sounded humbled. 'How could we have doubted you?'

'I am the Republic of Britain. I am the Flag,' Page continued solemnly. 'I am the Charter. I am the Executioner of State. I must seek out those who would seek to destroy me from within, the cancer on my body politic.'

'Attagirl,' Gabriel was encouraging. A true subject.

'I *am* Britannia!' Page declaimed, rising from her throne, wrapping her flag around her. She was determined to see justice done, her image and wealth restored and her enemies' thrones crushed beneath her size sevens. Gun in hand she swept from the room. Behind her Gabriel and Tanith broke into a rousing chorus of *Rule Britannia*. This was followed by a burst of what initially sounded like mocking laughter, but which she realized must be a round of applause and cheering, distorted by the acoustics of the house.

Jane Page, assassin and Englishwoman, had found a new resolve.

It was nice to have some sanity restored to her life.

The first thing Ace saw when she returned to the cellar was the tetrahedron in the centre of the room, still emitting its pale blue glow, though its gentle throb seemed to have become less regular. Maybe it was just reacting to the chaos it had helped create. Ace couldn't care less. She knelt down and scooped it up. She selected the most offensive expletive in her vocabulary and whispered it

237

into the light. It did not react, so she tossed it away without a second thought.

She looked round, seeing grey walls, seeing the sarcophagus against the wall, seeing Winterdawn. He was sitting in his chair, hugging his daughter to him, demonstrating an affection which couldn't be denied. Ace felt jealous for a moment, then dismissed the thought angrily. She hadn't needed affection. She had grown up in a loveless world and it had made her what she was – basically okay. Good for her.

She still suspected Winterdawn. Of what, she wasn't certain. Compared to Gabriel and Tanith, Winterdawn was almost likeable – but the suspicion lingered. This was a man capable of more than he seemed, Ace was certain. Perhaps the creation of Gabriel and Tanith hadn't been an accident. Perhaps he had planned it. The timing of his disappearance and the appearance of the couple seemed to fit together far too snugly to avoid suspicion.

He loved his daughter. Ace knew this and almost felt guilt. Almost.

She turned, seeing the Doctor loom in the doorway. He was a dark shape, like a solid shadow. There was something about his introspection that infected the whole of his environment, creating patches of shadow in the brightest of rooms. Patches of silence too – he hadn't said much since returning from the gap. He slunk into the room like bad news, squatting down on the floor with his back to a wall. Ace joined him. She rarely admitted fear but the Doctor's mood was scaring her shitless. She could handle him when he was ranting – silence wasn't something she could cope with. She lost track of what was going on inside his skull.

'Did you find anyone?' she asked tentatively. The Doctor replied with a curt shake of his head. His face was bloated, rank with despair.

'What about Benny? Did you bring her . . . her body?'

The Doctor inclined his head away. When he spoke his voice was a drone.

'I couldn't bear to touch her.'

238

Ace said nothing. She knew the darkness he felt.

'Ace, when – if -- this is finished, I'd like you to stay here. I don't want you travelling with me any more.'

Ace shook her head coldly. The Doctor continued insistently:

'The thing is, I'm thinking of returning home. It's time I settled down, high time. You wouldn't like Gallifrey.'

Ace scowled, trying not to feel too offended by this show of weakness.

'You're over-reacting. Lot of people you know've died. Lot of people out there still *need* you. They don't know it but they do.'

The Doctor closed his eyes and again inclined his head away from her.

'You know that if you – any of you – were in danger then I would tear out the cores of planets to help you. Believe me.' He made it sound like a demand. 'I can't go on. Benny's the *last*, she must be.'

'This isn't about Benny, is it?' Ace spat, keeping her voice restrained and whisper-low – it sounded dangerous that way. 'This is just another guilt trip. You're a total shit – understand that.'

The Doctor nodded thoughtfully.

'Of course I feel guilty,' he said wistfully. 'I'm bound to feel guilty.' An edge crept into his voice, lining his words with new sharpness. 'But I've spent the last couple of years of my life with Benny. And if you dare suggest that I haven't felt her death then our friendship is over. Now.'

Suits me, Ace heard herself say, but only in her head. She didn't like the way it sounded.

'No,' Ace said blandly. 'Sorry.'

She blinked and was about to move away, to leave him to his own thoughts, when he whispered something that held her in a tighter grasp than if he'd physically grabbed her.

'But there must be guilt.' The Doctor's voice was wistful again, as if remembering something. 'And vengeance, and retribution.'

Ace's head jerked back to stare at him.

'Gabriel and Tanith,' the Doctor continued. 'They must be stopped.'

'Stopped.'

'Annihilated. Destroyed. Killed. I don't sound like the Doctor, do I?'

Ace closed her eyes and thought: No, you sound exactly like the Doctor, as he used to sound.

'We'll do it now. It's safe to go back into the TARDIS, you can get your gun. I hate to say it but I think brute force is going to serve us better than anything else.'

Ace studied the Doctor's face in alarm, wondering how someone so infinitely clever could be so infinitely stupid.

'I've told you,' she snarled, pressing her face against his. 'I've tried that. It doesn't bloody work!'

The Doctor lowered his head, raising his hands to his eyes. Ace waited, wondering if he was crying beneath those fingers.

He lowered his hands and stared at her with cold, needy eyes.

'Ace. For pity's sake, I don't know what to do.'

'We have them up a gum tree, sis,' said Gabriel. 'They're stupid people.'

'Obviously,' Tanith agreed. 'Another diversion?'

'I think we should just kill them. They've lost their novelty value.'

'There's still some mileage in Ace and Sandra. We'll get nothing from the Doctor, but we've always known what a po-faced killjoy he is. The same goes for Winterdawn.'

'Sandra's our weak link then?'

'Absolutely. Kill a few birds with one stone.'

'Bloody big birds.'

'Now.'

It was the cry that alerted Ace. She turned, her immediate thought being that it was Winterdawn screaming. It wasn't. Winterdawn was choking, his daughter's hands locked round his throat – the only sounds he was making were

240

quiet agonized bursts of retching. No, the cry was coming from Sandra – an inhuman howl of blood-lust singing on her lips. Ace gaped for a moment, slow to react.

Winterdawn's knuckles were writhing, clawing at the arm-rests of his chair. His eyes were pleading and bulging. His daughter's vicious, animal face was reflected on his pupils. He didn't understand this, Ace could tell. He felt afraid and betrayed. She knew the feeling.

She sprang forward, dragging Sandra's hands from her father's throat. They gave, but she didn't have the strength to wrench the daughter away from the father. Suddenly the Doctor was at her side, firm hands clasping onto Sandra's forearms, trying to force her back.

'Must be a hormonal or chemical imbalance in her body,' the Doctor yelled, over Sandra's furious animal howls.

'Yeah?' Ace yelled, finding an elbow lodged painfully in her stomach. She bent backwards, but wasn't weakened enough to release her grip.

'They must be tapping into it, affecting the old brain, race memory centres. Goodbye to a million years of evolution!' The Doctor rattled off his words with the speed the situation demanded.

Sandra's face was suddenly pushed into Ace's. Ace could see the blood-raw eyes, the saliva building on her teeth and gums. She was leaning forward in a perverse mockery of a kiss, trying to get close enough to Ace's throat to bite. Ace delivered a blow to the oncoming face with the flat of her hand. She received a stinging pain on her palm for her trouble. Sandra writhed in their grasp. The strength coursing through her limbs was too powerful for them to hold for long, and Ace knew it.

'The wardrobe!' Ace heard herself gasping desperately. 'Lock her in!'

She saw the Doctor nod savagely.

It was an agonizing effort getting the spitting, hissing creature hauled across the room. It was even more of a strain shoving her into the sarcophagus, and keeping her there while they jammed the door shut. But they managed it. Ace flopped against the wardrobe door, counting her bites and bruises, scowling with exhaustion and, perhaps, with a little desperation. Benny was dead and this wasn't ever going to end.

'She'll calm down in a minute,' the Doctor gasped. 'Not much oxygen in there. The human body returns to its, er, default state to preserve the air.'

Ace nodded grimly, casting around the room.

Something was missing. The room was too empty. There was a hole.

She blinked, and realized.

'Winterdawn!'

The muscles in Winterdawn's hands and wrists were aching, his palms were raw. Both hands were tightened round the wheels of his chair, jerking it forward in awkward bursts. His palms ground and chafed against the wheel treads in an attempt to shuffle himself faster along the corridor. Rage outweighed discomfort.

He wasn't certain where he might find the monsters loose in his house. They were here somewhere, he would find them. And then he would kill them.

Sandra. They'd struck at him through his daughter.

Through my *daughter*!

Bastards.

His teeth ground together, fighting the pain in his hands, the ache spreading up his arms. His gums were bleeding. They always bled when he was in a vicious mood, or doing something exceptionally physical. Or both. The blood tasted watery in his mouth.

Gabriel and Tanith. He didn't know them, he'd never met them, but he'd created them. He had brought them into the world, however inadvertently, and he could destroy them. He remembered the ecstatic joy he'd felt over half his lifetime ago when he'd cradled Cassandra in his arms. There was no such joy now – simply loathing for the latest creatures he'd fathered. They were children. He could reach into the cots of the new-born. The slightest

242

pressure would shatter their necks. He would do that, he would, really he would.

Twisting forward, he screamed, forcing his words with all the pressure his lungs could manage,

'Whereareyou? Whereareyou? Where are you, *you bastards*?!'

'Wotcher,' said Gabriel and Tanith.

They were barely a yard from him. Impressive figures in extravagant clothes. Winterdawn barely registered the details, but he absorbed the impression of the whole with hateful relish. These were Gabriel and Tanith. There could be no doubt about that. There was no innocence on their faces, there was just sharp cunning, arrogant hatred and vicious hedonism. Their figures might have been specified from a catalogue. But their real shapes . . . they could have been a compound of everyone Winterdawn had loathed over the years, up to and including himself. They made his skin crawl on the inside.

'You wanted to kill us!' Gabriel stepped forward, his voice smooth and scornful, his eyes glowing with red fire. 'Kill *us*! And how would you have done that, old man? Run us over?'

Tanith laughed lightly. Winterdawn didn't laugh at all.

Gabriel was close enough to touch. His pupils were balls of red flame. He seemed to grow taller, towering over the chair now. Winterdawn realized that Gabriel's feet weren't touching the ground. He pulled his head up again in time to see a hand falling towards his chest – a hand bunched into a short, powerful fist – a hand that burned with a halo of scarlet flame.

Contact.

Winterdawn screamed. The blow had struck lightly against his shoulder, it probably hadn't even bruised him. But the touch – the touch *burned*. There was no buildup, no charging of intensity, no slow and tortuous ascent to the peaks of pain. The pain was simply there, shrieking through him, and he shrieked with it. Beneath him his chair creaked and shattered, collapsing underneath him. He fell backwards into a pile of twisted metal, metal which would never resemble a seat again. Not that it mattered. Winterdawn expected to die soon. Sometime in the next minute if the pain didn't let up. He lay flat on his back, trying to ignore the fear.

Gabriel leant forward like a priest preparing to take a final confession. He said nothing, his eyes reflected nothing. He raised his red hands and pressed them against Winterdawn's face, cutting off the light but doubling the pain.

Winterdawn spasmed, trying to ride the torment.

The hands were pulled away. The pain remained, a ghost pain haunting his limbs. He didn't dare move, he doubted that he could. He was too frightened to think of doing anything.

Tanith stood over him, legs parted, smiling lazily like a child on a summer day. Only the harsh blackness of her eyes robbed her of innocence.

'Don't think we've finished,' she said. 'It's just my turn, that's all.'

That's all.

She knelt beside him, reaching forward with hands that glowed orange. Winterdawn tried to pull himself away, tried to shout something – *anything* – but his tortured body betrayed him.

Tanith laid her hands on Winterdawn's face.

The pain returned in a new, different form. It had ceased to be pain, became a bland sensation that shook rather than stung Winterdawn's body. After a while it almost seemed pleasurable.

Tanith took her hands from his face and placed them on his knees.

'Do you know how many connections there are in a single human nerve?' she asked casually. Winterdawn heard himself replying, equally casually:

'Millions.'

Tanith nodded, and said nothing more. Her hands slipped between his knees and began to work up the inside of his legs, touching and stroking. Here was a new sensation, and one that Winterdawn hadn't expected. He stared thoughtfully at Tanith's face, at her precise, thoughtfully obsessed expression, and realized that for the first time since his wife died, he wanted to make love to a woman. To Tanith.

Tanith knelt beside him. Gabriel stood at her shoulder. Winterdawn looked between their faces, trying to make the connection.

'Get away from him, scum!'

Winterdawn frowned, realizing that neither Gabriel nor Tanith had spoken. The voice belonged to the Doctor's surviving companion and emanated from a distance, from the far end of the passage.

Tanith looked up from her work, then stepped away from Winterdawn.

'You're too late.' Gabriel was triumphant. 'You're far, far too late.'

Then both of Winterdawn's new-born children turned and walked away, the way they had come.

A shape appeared at Winterdawn's shoulder, falling to her knees beside him. Ace's face loomed in the corner of his eye.

'Sokay!' she hollered back down the passage presumably to the Doctor. Winterdawn felt like adding deafness to his list of pains. 'He's alive.'

'That's debatable,' Winterdawn muttered, but the woman didn't seem to hear him. The Doctor appeared in his line of vision, opposite Ace. His expression was concerned, but it was a deadened concern, as if he had lost his zest for life. Winterdawn frowned, realizing that his own zest for life had just returned.

'Do you have a spare chair we could get for you?' the Doctor asked. Winterdawn stared with sharp eyes into the hollows in the Doctor's face. Automatically he broke into a fit of infectious laughter.

'He's hysterical,' Winterdawn heard Ace mutter.

'Far from it,' he spat in the spaces between giggles.

He stretched out an arm, sweeping aside the fragments of metal and plastic, the pieces of the thing that had once been his chair, the cage that had bound him and frustrated him for five years. Five years he'd wanted to cast it aside like junk. Five years. Looking back was like trying to stare at the heart of an impenetrable black mist. His memories of the period were obscured by the hungry fog. For five years of his life he had hidden himself in the darkness alone and unloved.

'We'll carry you,' the Doctor said, his voice slow and slurred. The world had become soft and tired. Winterdawn smiled. It was like a dream. An old, old dream.

He raised his body on his elbows, forcing himself into a crouching position. From there he followed old, barely remembered movements, until he was once again standing on his feet. His legs shook after years of lifelessness, but they remained firm. The ground gradually stabilized under his feet. The Doctor and Ace stared stunned. Winterdawn allowed himself another smile at their expense.

'Now,' he asked, turning and trotting awkwardly back down the corridor to the cellar room, 'how is Sandra?'

14

The Painter of Modern Life

Bernice Summerfield woke to find ghost screams echoing in her ears, *her* screams. She had ghost memories of death, *her* death. They were wonderful thoughts to wake to.

She lay on her side, tucked cosily beneath the blankets of her deathbed. She was loath to move. Benny Summerfield was a pig when it came to rising in the morning, and she wasn't going to let her death stand in the way of old habits. She just wanted to lie in bed and rot.

She rolled onto her front, settling down to doze. Quarter of an hour later she raised her head blearily, forcing heavy eyelids open. She felt like risking a light headache in exchange for a few more minutes of oblivion, but decided against it. She shrugged the covers from her body and lay still, freezing in the chill air of the afterlife.

You'd think they'd leave the dead to rest in peace.

Death. She could only think about it dispassionately. She'd died. She was pretty certain of that. She'd felt her body shut itself down; no one could have survived the power streaming out of the window. She knew she was dead, she just didn't believe it. Death was somebody else's problem.

As a child, Benny had slept with death next to her skin. Then she'd grown up, reaching an age where it was chic to dwell on the grave. She dwelt on it and it terrified her. She assumed that everyone shared that terror, that all living creatures clung onto their lives with tight claws. You could measure other people's lifespans, but how could you measure your own? *C'est la vie, c'est la mort.*

She believed in the afterlife. That was something she'd considered odd – an atheist believing in life after death, even if only on broad, existential terms. It was the hope that kept her sane as an angsty teen. So here it was, laid before her. And the fear that purred in her ghost guts told her that it would have been much better if the door her death had opened led to oblivion.

This was not a good place. Not by a long chalk. Indeedy no.

She wondered if she could get pissed in the afterlife. Only, she suspected, if this was the *bad place*, and then simply for the sake of the massive hangover you'd receive afterwards.

She tipped herself over the edge of the bed and onto the floor. She landed awkwardly on her side, flagstones flattening her ribs. An ache spread along her side, the bruises writing themselves into her bones. But the shock had woken her completely, and she stood, clutching her tender shoulder, ready to confront the afterlife.

The afterlife was a gloomy chamber, heavy with the smell of smouldering wax. It was a massive, ancient place. The walls were built out of rough stone blocks. Similar blocks lay beneath her feet, worn down into a polished surface. The bulk of the chamber was empty. Benny's bed was an unwieldy item of black ironwork but it was a tiny fragment of furniture amidst a wasteland of blank stone. Shadows filled the emptiness, clinging to the walls like cobwebs. They growled and swam, their advance on the chamber held back by flickering candle-light. There were candles on stands, hanging from the ceiling or supported on wall brackets; a few sat unguarded on the floor, melting into ugly pools on the flagstones. These were *real* candles – fat, stubby, yellow. Their smoke was foul. Benny gagged as the smell swarmed into her senses.

The candle-light was warm yellow and Benny's skin was bathed in a sickly reflection of that light. Her whole body seemed so thin and weak. She was dressed in black, in a one-piece garment like a swimsuit, that hugged the shape of her body. Its surface rippled in response to tensing muscles, almost as if it was physically part of her. Handy for a quick get-away – though it had no *style* whatsoever.

She prowled round the chamber, tracing the walls beyond the shadows. The gloom stifled her senses, her eyesight lost its keenness. She stepped into one patch of shadows and almost knocked over a table.

Laid out neatly on the moon-shaped surface was a chessboard, readied for war. The pieces were squat caricatures carved from ebony and ivory. The hollow eyes of pawns and bishops and queens and rooks and knights stared at Benny from their positions. The kings had their eyes closed, blinding themselves. It was an impressive set. More immediately interesting was the bottle beside it.

Benny reached for the bottle, and checked the labels carefully. Two, both handwritten. The larger had an ornate border and was written in a strong, bold hand: *Lafite '28*. The smaller label was written in a light, more intimate hand and was stuck at an uneven angle.

To my oldest friend, on the occasion of our meeting in Munich, 23rd of April 1853.

Bernice raised the glass neck to her lips and took a swig – a mouthful of a half-way decent vintage. It was the only hopeful thing she'd so far found.

Further into the darkness she found an archway decorated by carvings of skulls, arranged so that each fleshless head seemed to gnaw at the scalp of that below. Benny passed by without closer inspection, grateful she no longer had a stomach. A thick curtain blocked the arch, composed of hundreds of separate strands of ivy strung from the stones above. Benny forced a gap between the heavy fronds.

The room brightened, the gloom was relieved slightly, but there was no blaze. Inside the chamber was still darkness, beyond was twilight.

Beyond the arch was a stone balcony – beyond the balcony, a panorama over a sprawling city extending to the horizon. The city was a bundle of soaring shafts – black, white, brick and grey rods thrusting skywards. Some were chimney stacks, pumping an unending cloud of black pollution into the sky. Others were towers, dirtied by the clouds billowing from the neighbouring flues. The air of the city was damp and filthy.

The city was a nightmare of industry. The chimneys erupted from ugly, angular buildings with grey roofs and tiny windows, walls discoloured by their own soot. The factories were cramped boxes packed together into industrial compounds, protected by high walls and barbed-wire fences. Benny had seen this on a hundred worlds – industry and exploitation dancing obscenely, cheek to cheek. The fences evoked memories of prison camps – and worse – the emaciated creatures concentrated within. Benny remembered them now. She wasn't certain whether the constant shriek of sirens was hailing a change of work-pattern or reporting another purge. She looked again at the smoke billowing across the city, wondering what it was that burned.

The city was steeped in symbols. Those buildings that were not industrial were bizarre, living images carved in stone. Architecture ran riot, as if the stones of the city were growing naturally. All the buildings climbed upwards, but not all climbed straight. Massive windows of stained-glass depicting incomprehensible scenes sat in the heart of their greying stones. Hewn into those walls were shapes and figures from a hundred cultures, nesting places for the ugliest gargoyles. This mess of architecture made a maze of the city, in which every street was an alley bounded by sheer walls ascending to infinity.

The city was decaying, rotting before her eyes. Buildings were crumbling or derelict. Some of the tallest shook uneasily. Those parts of the sky untouched by the damp smoke were dry with dust. This city was dying, falling apart as Benny watched. Yet it thrived on this decay, and even as the weeds or the urban entropy encroached on one building, more sprang up on the fringes, assembled haphazardly. The city was poisoning itself, revelling in its own self-destructive decadence.

Benny could see figures moving in the city – on raised

walkways, on ledges – but the shapes were vague, her glimpses fleeting. The population remained invisible.

The sky was grey. There was no sun. There was no moon. There were no stars. There were no clouds. The sky was bland and blank.

'I don't think I'm in Kansas any more,' Benny whispered before turning.

There was a shape waiting in the gloom behind her – distinct from the rest of the darkness.

'I want to know one thing. Is this the good place, or is it the bad place? I live in hope, but the landscape isn't reassuring.'

The shape seemed to consider. It replied in a pleasant voice of indeterminate age:

'Professor Summerfield, you will find that this place is neither good nor bad.' The shape stepped forward and became a man, dressed in a long coat and a broad-brimmed hat and dark glasses.

'I *know* you.' Benny's recognition blossomed.

'Our last meeting was rather brief and the conversation unstimulating. I'm quite glad it's you here. Of all the Doctor's party you strike me as the most personable.'

'Thanks,' Benny mumbled shyly like a teenage girl on a first date, her curiosity dampened by the man's quietly compulsive manner. 'It's, uh, Benny, by the way. "Professor Summerfield" is the name I want on my grave. I wonder if they remembered?'

'Benny.' The mellow voice pronounced it strangely. It was not used to addressing people in such intimate terms.

'A nice place you have here. Where did you find it?' Benny asked, her appetite for answers surging to the fore.

'This?' The man smiled, sadly, weakly. 'This is my creation. This is my prison, my home. This is Cathedral and it has stood for almost fifteen thousand million years.'

Benny frowned, indicating the chaotic nightmare beyond the ivy curtain.

'You're responsible for that?' Her voice was venomously critical.

'I am.' The man's face twisted into an injured frown. 'I

would not have built it this way given the choice. I am the messenger of Cathedral, I am its conscience and its soul. But I am not its architect.'

'But you *said* you created it,' Benny rounded on him.

The grey man smiled again. When he spoke, his voice was slow and sour.

'Between the conception, and the creation, falls the shadow. Other hands built this. I simply laid the foundations. Would you care for a game of chess?'

Bernice didn't reply.

'Benny?' the man prompted. After that there was only one answer she could possibly give.

'I thought,' Benny considered her position and found that she was almost disgusted, 'that everyone – *everyone* – had heard of Fool's Mate.'

'My opponents have been noble creatures,' the man said, with more humour than disappointment. 'They would not stoop to anything so underhanded.'

'Ah, you picked the wrong one this time,' Benny replied, feigning aggression. 'Dead or alive, I'm a devious bitch.'

The grey man nodded thoughtfully. His face was so bland, so dull, that Benny just had to laugh at the grotesque comic effect. She took another swig from the bottle.

'Dead?' The question and the smile were both innocent. Benny frowned, losing her sense of humour.

'I am,' she stated, half-questioning, half-reassuring herself.

'That depends on your interpretation,' the grey man sifted through his words carefully, 'of death.'

'How do you mean?' Benny's frown remained engrained onto her features.

'If you believe that when you die, your body ceases to function but your mind, your soul, your *ka*, is transposed to a new level of existence, well you are dead. This isn't a heaven – it isn't a particularly good imitation – but it does exist on a separate plane to your own. The explanations are not religious or supernatural, your circumstances are unique. I suspect your mind was guided here by the forces that are loose in Winterdawn's house.'

'Gabriel and Tanith?' Benny asked.

'For reasons of their own. I can't imagine what they might have in mind.' Benny took this as a 'yes'. She'd known the man for minutes but had already lost hope of getting a straight answer out of him.

'You remind me of the Doctor,' she said absently.

'Oh.'

Benny burst out laughing again. Her companion was quietly amused. When she had calmed down, she launched into the question she'd been saving up.

'So, what is this place?' she asked in a casual enough tone but with a cool undercurrent that demanded a serious answer. 'This Cathedral? A nice piece of real estate, yes, but I'd give it a clean before putting it on the market. Hot and cold running pollution, gargoyles optional. It's not real . . .'

The grey man raised a gentle hand. It silenced her.

'Cathedral is real. It is one of the most real places in the cosmos, but no, go on . . .'

Benny picked up the thread of her enquiry.

'What I want to know is, is it a parallel thingy, a virtual thingy or a computer thingy?'

For the first time since Bernice had met him, the grey man laughed. His lungs expelled short, half-hearted chortles. His face contorted uneasily, confirming Benny's suspicion that this was a man who indulged in the odd giggle every couple of centuries but otherwise stuck rigidly to rigor mortis lip-twitches to convey the apotheosis of good humour.

'Forgive me,' he said, coming to the end of his feeble chuckles and wrinkling his face in embarrassment. 'No, this is nothing like a computer. I'm no great technophile. I leave hardware to those amused by such things.'

He rose from his stool, pushing forward as he moved, and resting his knuckles on the table. Benny had the uncomfortable feeling of being in school, a teacher looming over her to unleash a tirade about the misdemeanours

253

of Summerfield. But the grey man's features were light. As light as they could be.

'Cathedral is a metacultural engine.'

Benny let her lips twitch in the manner of her host. He acknowledged this with a slight nod of the head.

I wish I could see his eyes, Benny thought. This one I can't read at all. Utterly inscrutable. Or so utterly transparent that I haven't noticed. *I wish I could see his eyes!*

'I know what an engine is,' she said slowly. 'I know what culture is. I even know what "meta" means – I looked it up once specially. But the combination of the words lacks that certain spark.'

The grey man nodded, head bobbing up and down happily.

'I'll tell you,' he said, and the happiness abdicated in favour of something darker, 'a story.'

'Fine. I'm sitting comfortably. I've all the time in the world.'

Benny spoke lightly, offhand. She regretted it. The grey man twisted away from her, losing his face in shadow. She had offended him, broken his precious darkness with something a little too light. Her face assumed sombre blandness, she listened and didn't speak again.

The grey man walked away from her. The story was delivered with his back to her. Surprisingly, Benny enjoyed it. The grey man's face was full of nuances, untranslatable, and his glasses were black disks covering his eyes and the meanings hidden there. Benny felt lost without decent body language to follow. His back was a different matter. She saw every twitch of his shoulder-blades, every contortion of his spine rippling across his coat and exaggerated by the odd lighting. There was much here that escaped her – but there was much she understood. She sensed the weight, the burden, the sorrow, the loneliness, the fragments of rage that underpinned his story. This was a friendless man unburdening his soul. Benny didn't mind that, she was a sucker for a decent sob story. But she also picked up something more, something that frightened her, something too vast to be visualized completely.

The power.

The grey man had told her he'd dragged the TARDIS from the time streams. She believed him.

Then there was the story.

'Fifteen thousand million years ago,' the grey man began, his shoulders arching, his head shrinking into his body, 'the cosmos formed during Event One. There was a hydrogen rush which defined the parameters of the material universe. The implications and resonances of Event One go beyond that simple explosion, but they don't concern us ... Suns formed. Systems formed. Life blossomed on a million planets. And when the first cells spawned in the first oceans on the first world, I was there, with my people, watching.

'Not all life survived. Not all children grow to adulthood. We watched, we mourned. But on other worlds, civilizations blossomed.

'The world in question is thirty thousand million light years from Earth. Should your race ever stray so far they will doubtless overlook it. But it was the first. It gave birth to humanoid life, and the culture they developed was similar to that on your world.

'Civilization means different things to different people. To some, it is the noblest of goals, to others a transgression of community and culture. I hold neither view. But at the time, I was ecstatic. My colleagues shared my feelings. This was a new experience. We wanted to see these creatures ascend to the stars that were their birthright, the common heritage of the people of the cosmos. Ten thousand years, we watched their development, the ups and downs, the striving to keep aflame their ideals in the dark ages that afflicted them. We shared their dreams.'

The grey man turned back to Benny. His face was bitter.

'They destroyed themselves.

'I don't suppose many see the effects of bacteriological war in close detail. I did. I spent years walking across the surface of the planet, through the cities and the countryside, past the doors with holy patterns stained upon their bark, past the black skeletons of neighbourhoods torched in vague efforts to keep back the death, past the bodies in the gutters, the bodies of the children. There were survivors, weeping in their shelters, but they didn't last. The world had become a tableau to the folly of its inhabitants – there was no decay, and the death-throes of every living creature were preserved as if frozen, until natural disaster scoured its surface. I walked across that world and despaired.

'The viral agents were genetically designed to destroy all life, even other bacteria. The virus sterilized the world. It became the dominant life form, ruling supreme. It consumed itself in the end, a form of race suicide echoing the suicide of the people who unleashed it. There was a madness manifest in the design of that virus.

'Them and us. Black and white. Good and evil, Professor Summerfield. Polarization and duality. Undiluted absolutes. Fine for chess but chess is a game, and these concepts had been applied to the real world.

'I call it madness. It was nothing of the kind. If it was madness I could have accepted it. It would have been a natural part of their mentality, its outcome unavoidable. But it was not. There were other agencies at work. Not alien forces, because no such things yet existed. I investigated and I found ... I ...

'I found the influence of my people, of *my* race. They had developed the madness because it suited their own purpose, it suited the rivalries and the tensions that divided them and to which I had not been a party. Their influence stretched through the cosmos, down to the universal structure itself. There is a structure – perhaps, it is difficult to explain – but it is a loose and pliable one. They had taken it and were making it rigid, imposing their own philosophies, their absolutes. They had taken the people of the first world to war. They had destroyed the oldest civilization for their own fathomless motives.

'I do not understand why. Perhaps they were jealous, perhaps they hate those who live the real life that has been denied to them. Perhaps they wish to be worshipped as if they were gods – they style themselves as such. I have never understood, perhaps I have not tried.

'I saw what would happen. I saw armies marching between the stars, I saw conquest, I saw blood, I saw vengeance, I saw hatred, I saw death unbound, death without end. I saw the soldiers charging to war believing beyond doubt that their gods were on their side; that all of "them" were duplicitous but all of "us" were pure of motive; that there is such a thing as a "just" war so long as you fight on the right side. I saw children murdered, women raped, men tortured in the name of "right". I saw dissidents oppressed, hounded and branded traitors. I saw the Daleks, Professor Summerfield, and more than the Daleks. I saw all the children of creation.

'I saw all this, and I knew, beyond doubt, that these things were inevitable.'

The grey man's shoulders sagged forward further than ever before. But then his back straightened, and he continued.

'I couldn't stop it. I had power, but in this new structure my colleagues had created I had no place. So I decided to create a place for myself. I constructed it in secret. It was a small village, beyond the physical plane. I named it Cathedral. It was the physical representation of an engine – a computer, if that helps you visualize it more easily – the machine code of a programme designed to alter the structure of reality. It would act on cultures, develop them, deepen them, awaken new trends, new thoughts, cut new paths away from the duality my colleagues had created. It would undermine, it would subvert, it would create challenges, place doubts in the minds of the faithful. It is free thought. A disease and a cure that I have spread through time and space. That is the purpose of Cathedral: Ambiguity and chaos! It makes the world a stranger place to live in.

'Its tasks were simple but its power needed to be enormous. I stripped myself of my energies, let them flow through the village. It tapped into the mathematical core of the universe, the Small Numbers on the edge of the quantum event horizon where the macro and the micro worlds become interchangeable. I will spare you the exact details.

'It was natural my plan should be discovered. The Cathedral metahedron was well hidden. It does not settle, it moves from world to world every eighty thousand years to elude discovery by those who would destroy it. I, on the other hand, was weakened without hope of recovery. I returned to our home well aware that I was courting destruction. I long to see it again, but I cannot approach it. To do so would not only guarantee my total destruction, but it would also reveal the location of Cathedral. I can never return.

'I was immediately placed on trial by my colleagues for my "blasphemy". They cast me out. I fell, and as I fell, I burned. I burned until I was dead.

'My Cathedral lived. But there were complications. I designed it to affect all the cultures of the cosmos, but I completely overlooked the likelihood that the cultures of the cosmos would affect Cathedral. They have. The village grew into a city. The trappings of a million societies are stamped upon it. You yourself are creating part of it now, perhaps your imagination has a touch of Gothic to it? It's difficult to move, some days, for the congestion of psycho-mythical avatars and emotional totems. In many ways, I enjoy it. I can fade into the crowd and experience the ambivalent pleasures that the city might offer. On other occasions, I feel like I have created a Pandemonium. The city creates its own rules and authority. There are times when I would like to be left alone away from them. More than any other citizen, that is a freedom available to me.' He turned back to Benny, brooding apprehension on his face. 'And there you have it.'

Benny had digested it all, but had not had time to mull it over. Parts of the story had appalled her, parts had intrigued her, parts had amused her and some parts had lost her completely. It was difficult to tell which part was which. She reckoned she had the gist.

'One point,' she said, feeling a surge of dry pedantry to her mouth. 'You said you died?'

'I said I died. I also said that I put my power into Cathedral. Both statements are true. I am my power. Where my power lives, I live. I told you that I was the soul of this place. I am its soul because my blood forms its foundations. I am its conscience because my blood remembers what I stood for and fights to keep those principles alive. I am the messenger of this place. That is my function. I am a machine code subroutine of Cathedral, incarnate in the image of a dead man, with a dead man's thoughts. I created this, and it creates me. There's a paradox for your Doctor.'

Benny felt something melancholy stab beneath her ribs. She looked down, finding her fingers locked round the black king's rook from the chessboard, skin absorbing the prickling texture. She turned the chess piece over and over in her hands, as if trying to transfer her sadness into it.

But it was only a lump of ebony, and Benny felt sadder than ever.

'Perhaps you would like to see the city.'

'I would love to see the city,' Benny droned, emptying her voice of all inflexions.

'Some parts of it are quite pleasant once you get to know them.'

'I really don't want to get to know them,' Benny said, looking up and finding his face close to hers. For a moment she lost herself, trying to find the eyes in that ambiguous visage. There was nothing, so she kept talking: 'Look, this is a nice place to visit – no, scratch that, it isn't a nice place to visit. I don't want to be here.'

'I don't want to be here, but I've put up with it for quite some time.'

'I have . . . I had . . . friends. In the real world. They'll miss me.'

'The war goes on,' said the grey man.

Benny looked at him sharply.

'Okey-doke, I'll see your bloody Cathedral,' she

259

snapped more with humour than venom. 'Like a school trip. Data sheets to be filled in afterwards and *please* don't be sick over the tour guides. Yes?'

'That is not something we have ever had complaints about.' The grey man turned on the charm. Benny rose, then looked down at herself.

'Could we change the clobber, perhaps?' she suggested. 'I'm sure I won't seem out of place but I prefer clothes that are a touch less obscene.'

'Of course,' the grey man nodded.

Benny felt nothing. When she looked down an instant later, she found her body occupying something strange. It was a flowing gown. Though jet black, Benny felt she could see shapes swimming on its surface, screaming silently, twisting into impossible shapes. She tried not to look. Elbow-length black gloves swathed her forearms; her feet balanced on thin heels. Her shoulders were bare and cold.

'I feel like the Bride of Frankenstein,' she mumbled.

'Forgive me. The Gothic imagination . . .'

'I've seen worse. Most of the time they were being worn by the three-headed things that inhabit tunnels and live only to add Benny-fricassee to their menus, but I have seen worse.' She patted the fabric of the dress reassuringly. It hummed as she stroked it, and she withdrew her hand hastily. 'Well, let's hit the town.'

Benny's room was situated high on a rotting tower called the Crucible. That was fine by Benny, if they wanted to give her the penthouse suite they could go right ahead, but it meant that the view from her balcony had given a deceptively calm impression of Cathedral's street life. On the ground she found the alleys of the city alive with crowds. It was reassuringly normal. Less comforting was the silence. There were no traders calling in the distance, no murmurings of the type traditionally employed for conversation in public areas, no bustle built from the echoes of the crowd. The people of Cathedral were silent.

'Charming,' Benny said weakly. 'I'm going to love it here.'

Most of the citizens were wrapped in robes and hoods – layers of worn, dirt-grey fabric burying their true shapes, heavy enough to grind down their shoulders. Their thin arms hung loosely out of the folds of their rags, wrapped in thick leather bandages. Benny doubted it was for warmth. Under their hoods were masks, decorated in harsh black and white patterns. There were holes in the masks but Benny never saw any eyes. Some of the shuffling, shambling citizens wore white sashes or collars, as if some attempt to impose a uniform had been made by a higher authority. Despite this each citizen was unique in appearance. The differences were subtle but powerful. Often the robes left misshapen limbs undisguised. Benny saw numbers printed on the masks – zeroes, ones or twos, nothing higher – or symbols: broken arrows, black squares, staring eyes, the yin-yang circle. Benny stared at the blank masks, wondering what – if anything – was being thought beneath them.

As soon as they had emerged from the Crucible, the grey man had been approached by a woman with parrot features and flowing hair. She was a good seven feet tall, dressed in the uniform of an Edwardian clerk. And her eyes, Benny saw, were bloody red orbs. The clerk leant forward to whisper in the grey man's ear. He nodded in response, his expression wiping itself clean. The clerk straightened up and hobbled away on cloven hooves. Benny stared, forgetting her manners. Her guide stood before her and focused her attention back on the here and now.

'I'm afraid our tour is postponed or augmented, depending on your point of view. I have been called before the Set.'

'Bloomsbury?' Benny asked mischievously, shaking her eyebrows.

'Mandelbrot,' the grey man confirmed dryly. 'They are the true masters here, the processors of chaos and order. The Mandelbrot Set blurs the distinction between them.'

Benny jerked her lips into a half-crook smile.

'They sound sweet. I'd like to meet them.'

'No. You wouldn't,' the grey man snapped, becoming angry for the first time since they had met. 'Still, they've granted you observer status. *That* is tantamount to a summoning.'

'My fame precedes me,' Benny joked, but something vital had left the conversation. The grey man talked about the Mandelbrot Set with resentment and barely concealed terror. Benny stroked her left shoulder, a shoulder that felt like a cold slab of meat.

The grey man was in no hurry to reach his masters. They strolled through the alleys of Cathedral at a leisurely pace, giving Benny time to take in some of the more interesting sights, and for the grey man to point out oddities of architecture, exotic figures, machinery and transport, monuments to commemorate events in the city's history (many seemed to have been erected at his insistence). The walls of the buildings were sheer cliffs around them, soaring into the black sky unburdened by the constraints of rational architecture. The buildings were too impressive for Benny, who felt trapped by them. *Oppressive* was the word.

The grey man walked beside her. His pace was uncertain, slipping from tiny, shuffled steps to sweeping strides. Benny kept a constant pace.

The alleyway widened and rose up between two buildings, becoming a plain walkway winding round the side of one massive structure. At the same time, it emptied of citizens. Benny and the man in grey ascended alone.

'This is the heart of the city,' the grey man explained, indicating the shaft, 'the Cruakh, court of the Mandelbrot Set.'

The antipathy in his voice was better disguised this time, but Benny still caught shards of it, buried in the subtlest inflexions.

The walkway extended on and up for what seemed like miles. Benny felt certain that her legs should be killing her by now – no pun intended – but she felt invigorated, ready for anything. Her whole body seemed much improved since her death, losing all the aggravating twinges that had afflicted her in life. But it wasn't really her body. It was the ghost of it.

Bernice Summerfield and the grey man reached the top and stood before the massive gateway that led into the heart of the Cruakh. Flanking it, dwarfed by it, were Gabriel and Tanith.

Benny might have been startled, if she had been alive and if Gabriel and Tanith had been startling people. But she was dead and Gabriel and Tanith were simply odd. The only thing she felt was curiosity.

They were dressed in the same type of leotard which Benny had woken in, and that made them look ridiculous, but kind of attractive – especially Gabriel, though Benny was embarrassed as soon as she thought of it. Their eyes were closed, their heads raised towards the sky, their hair streaming upwards, and that made them look serene.

She turned to the grey man. He was watching her expectantly.

'Should *they* be here?' she asked calmly.

'They were created in this place, though not deliberately,' the grey man replied. 'These are only embryonic images of them.'

'If Cathedral created them,' Bernice snapped, 'Cathedral should do something about them. They're not sociable people.'

'I imagine they are what this meeting will be about.'

The man in grey strode forward, crossing the flagstones to the gate with easy strides. Benny hurried after him, stumbling over the hem of her gown in her effort to catch him.

'What *are* they?' she demanded an answer.

The grey man swung round to face her.

'Gabriel and Tanith are an accident that has been waiting to happen since the time of my fall.' His voice was harsh. 'Their names are written in the history of the future. They have a significance beyond anything they suspect themselves.' He became terse and curt. 'Now, the Set awaits us.'

He turned on his heel and strode through the gateway into the Cruakh.

Benny snatched final glances of the pair standing guard on the gate. Their faces were so calm, as if they were sleeping. Benny hoped no passing prince would be stupid enough to kiss them.

'I wish you were that peaceful in the real world,' Benny told them harshly, before scurrying after the man. The sentinels offered no response.

Beyond the gate was a corridor, short and bleak. Benny caught up with the grey man at its lip, on the edge of a vaulted chamber, the domain of the Mandelbrot Set.

There were twenty-three Mandelbrot in total. Benny didn't bother counting them, the knowledge was there in her mind from the moment she entered their realm. They occupied different levels, sitting squat in niches and hollows carved into the wall that rose opposite the entrance. The wall was red, painted in blood, and where it was not red, it was ivory white. There were shapes, images, cut into the ivory wall, but Benny preferred not to dwell on them. She latched onto the Set itself.

At first, she mistook them for decorations, built into the walls. But they began to speak as she entered the chamber and the illusion was shattered. The Mandelbrot Set were heads, stone heads. They reminded Benny of the brooding statues of Easter Island, of the Karet'ah Tika on Plaemus Tau, ringing the ancient city of Tunq on Kristin's World, of a hundred different places she had visited or read about. It was a big galactic mystery, it suggested a common cultural inheritance across Earth's sector of the galaxy. There had been hundreds of experts researching this field by the time Benny was born; Oxford University's Cultural Studies Sub-Department of Easter Island Heads had grown so large it had its own car park.

The Mandelbrot Set spoke in a chorus. Twenty-three stone voices, rich and resonant, echoing across the courtyard.

'Greetings, grey-walker.'

Benny shot a surprised glance at the grey man and was surprised to find him shifting with uneasy embarrassment.

'Pretentious courtesy,' he muttered.

'Oh,' Benny mouthed, turning back to face the Set.

'Hi,' she said.

'Observer status requires only that you appear, Summerfield,' a Mandelbrot addressed her in tones so polite they could only be a threat. 'Your participation is not compulsory.'

In short: belt up, or find yourself in the foundations of the Cathedral bypass. Ah-ha!

'I am here,' the grey man announced, making it sound like a guilty secret.

'You were summoned. We have considered the existence of these Gabriel and Tanith. We are decided that they are no longer conducive to our programme. Their presence accelerates generation of entropy, draws forth the time of levelling and the end of all things. We now predict this several metacenturies earlier than expected.'

'I know,' the grey man mumbled so that only Benny heard.

'We are decided that your methods in removing this particular threat to the programme also undermine the smooth functioning of the programme!' another Mandelbrot chimed in. 'Entropic decay circuits have kicked in on three of the major arcana. Many of the minor arcana flood already. Such events would have happened not had you acted promptly.'

'If I had acted promptly, without due care, then I would have attracted attention to myself,' the grey man protested. 'Then where would your programme be?'

'Then there are these effects on the personal level. Considerable is the death-toll and rising.'

The grey man's teeth began to grind impatiently.

'That is underhanded. You see these deaths in terms of statistics. I see them as they really are. That makes me even more determined not to burst in on Gabriel and Tanith and blow them away like something from a power fantasy. Violent solutions have never been my forte. They only make things worse.'

'This is your opinion,' three or four Mandelbrots sang as one.

'That is the principle on which the whole of Cathedral is built!'

'These are destabilizing agents . . .'

'*We* are a destabilizing agent!'

' . . . generating entropy!'

'*We* generate entropy!'

'But our cause is just. These Gabriel and Tanith do it – colloquially – for the hell of it.'

'You will never understand.' Benny heard the grey man, but she doubted that the Mandelbrot Set had. His head was lowered like a man defeated.

I am its conscience, he had told her, *I am its soul*.

'We are decided,' the Mandelbrot Set roared in unison, sounding like a gaggle of schoolchildren screaming abuse at things they couldn't comprehend. 'You will return to plane physical. You will seek out these Gabriel and Tanith. These will be destroyed. This is what you will do.'

'And Bernice?'

'Summerfield remains.'

The grey man hummed thoughtfully.

'Go,' Mandelbrot voices echoed off the walls.

The grey man moved close to Benny, taking her unresisting hands.

'I could hardly refuse,' he said. His voice was wistful. He almost sounded happy.

'That was a threat,' Benny hissed angrily. 'They were threatening me!'

The grey man nodded, but stared to the side of her, as if distracted by his own thoughts.

'I fear this may not be easy for you,' he said. 'But it removes the element of certainty from the threat. I'd like to thank you before I go. If you had not been here I would never have chosen as I did.'

And with those words he pulled her into a tight embrace. It was too brief, but while it lasted Benny felt

266

like a baby again, held securely and with love in the arms of her father. She didn't flinch at the intimacy.

The grey man said nothing further to her. He simply smiled and flowed from the arena of the Mandelbrot Set, back into the black corridor and beyond that, into the material world.

Benny didn't watch him. Her attention was fixed on the ranks of the Mandelbrot Set. She was smiling, and she wondered why. And even as she wondered, her smile cracked and she burst into tears.

15

Götterdämmerung

The sky was a churning sea, dark and ominous. Subtle pastel shades coloured the clouds, lining the darkness for fleeting moments before being swallowed by the overall greyness. The clouds swirled. The grey man watched patterns form and dissolve. He felt no cold, but shivered.

This was ominous weather.

No – he quickly dismissed the thought as superstition. The weather was the weather, no matter how bleak. It simply set the tone. The grey man considered this wearily before starting the journey to the house. He was in no hurry. He did not relish this moment. His path led either to death or compromise – he wasn't certain which would be worse.

The earth was silent, as if life had been extinguished in his absence. This, the grey man mused among a jumble of pessimistic thoughts, is a world holding its breath.

As he reached the bottom of the hill, he saw Gabriel and Tanith already there, dark shapes invisible against their context. He halted beside them, breaking the fragile silence with a sigh.

'I don't want to fight you,' he said, perhaps apologetically.

Tanith turned her head towards him, and it seemed to the grey man like the slowest action he had seen in his lifetime.

'We know,' she replied.

'Nice weather for it,' Gabriel remarked, folding his arms

against the cold. 'We could rustle up some thunder and lightning if you want.'

The grey man shook his head, forcing a smile onto his lips.

'That would be needlessly Wagnerian.'

He found himself warming to the atmosphere here. Here was a cheery vein of nihilism which appealed to him. In better circumstances he might get along well with this couple.

'But appropriate,' Gabriel continued languidly – there were three people here and none of them were in a hurry. 'Götterdämmerung.'

'Twilight of the Gods,' the grey man said, almost to himself.

'Or Dawn of the Gods. It depends,' Tanith was as listless as her partner, 'on the translation.'

'Tell me again,' the grey man caught the prevailing mood with a bland monotone, tempered by a wry smile, 'which of us here rank as gods?'

Tanith giggled. Gabriel shrugged.

'There's no point to this,' Gabriel said softly.

'Does there have to be?'

'Yeah.' Tanith grinned. 'You've come to display your moral superiority to us by beating us into bloody pulps.'

'You are threatening the structure of things,' the grey man said, realizing how unnatural this must sound from his lips, 'eroding the balance of time and space. With regret, I must put an end to you.'

Gabriel snorted. The grey man blushed and pulled his head away, deeply aware of his hypocrisy.

There was nothing more to be said. The grey man turned his back on his enemy – he supposed he should call them that – and climbed back up to the top of the hill.

'And when they were up,' he said to himself, 'they were up.'

He turned to take up a vigil over the house. It was a stark shape beneath him, black as death, devoid of light. Only its outline hinted at the monstrous majesty of the

269

architecture. It was a solid black anchor against the turbulent sky. Gabriel and Tanith had made it derelict, uninhabitable – a place tainted with their pure negativity. The grey man tried to harden his heart for the fight, but found it difficult.

His wait did not last. Barely a minute had passed before they appeared. They were levitating, rising smoothly upwards to hang in the air above him. Their outlines were jagged shapes cut into the sides of clouds. The grey man breathed heavily before stepping off the hillside to join them in the sky. A gulf of air separated them, physically empty but filled with crackling anticipation. Three inhuman things in human shapes wheeled slowly round the sky. The man sensed that Gabriel and Tanith were waiting for him to make his move, that he would have to strike first. It occurred to him that this was how their minds worked, by *reacting* to others. He let the thought go.

Time slipped.

The grey man hung in the sky. Orange light danced on the canopy of clouds. A sickly-sweet perfume filled the air. Accompanying the smell was the sound. A low howl that spread out across the land and silenced the world.

Time and memory were brief patterns cutting in and out of darkness in a random manner. There was nothing stable, no references. Memories had been plucked from his mind and stretched wafer-thin over wide frames. Each became a world in itself – perhaps this was memory in its purest state.

Gabriel and Tanith. At some point they must have re-engineered the state of his mind or the flow of time. A dangerous ruse but an effective one, requiring more imagination than he would have granted them. They deserved his respect if nothing else.

The grey man perused each disjointed memory in turn, seeking some clue that might define his present condition.

He extends an arm. Hand open, flat, fingers splayed. Cold

fire streaming from his shaking fingertips. No light, no sound, no effects. Pain and fire striking at Gabriel, absorbed by mental shields.

Stretched to slowness, split-second action seeps over an hour.

Counterstrike: Tanith: ostentatious, pretentious, hedonistic. She loves effect, the urge to play with fire. Her attack is a light-show. She weaves a spiral web of energy from the sky. The grey man cannot dodge its complexity. Even as he clicks his tongue to disapprove of her display, it snares him.

Pain: fire crackles through nerveways.

Energies are exchanged, blink-of-an-eye bursts of sound and fury. Without subtlety, without imagination, without irony. The grey man hears snatches of intermittent, internal conversation carried on the wind.

Gabriel: dark, brooding, stylish. Seeing the world from behind a veil of shadows. A lover of many things (though never for more than a minute).

Tanith: thoughts on a string. A love for beautiful, shiny things. Dicewoman, precious and vain, dancing in the light, lover of pain.

They hate him.

End-game: up until now the grey man has been playing with this couple. He grows weary.

Memories: his city, his Cathedral. Professor Summerfield. The crude faces of the Mandelbrot Set. A friend he would never see again. The first world, the world on which he learned despair.

He steps into the path of the attack.

Power surge, ripping through mind and body. The grey man hurls back his head and screams. The scream is silent but it echoes. It rolls through the sky, reverberating across the surface of this world and a thousand others. Children shiver in fear of imaginary horrors, believers make the relevant symbolic gestures against evil, sleepers thrash in fits of night terror, the animals and the demented and the poets howl out their inner rage.

Something old and powerful is dying.

In the eye of pain, the grey man is rational. His body smoulders and explodes. Tongues of flame – insubstantial streams of colour and heat – lick hungrily at his limbs and torso. His hair burns, his skin sizzles, his clothes grow black in the inferno. Despite the pain he feels calm. He knows he is dying, that the destruction extends far beyond his body, that the energy network that lingers after the death of his physical shell is tearing itself apart. He is dying. His soul is dying. It is the final death.

He hangs still in the air, consumed by fire. His memories break up. He discards them one by one, losing himself.

He is afraid.

Time slips.

The grey man died. The burning corpse slipped from the sky, plunging towards the ground far below. By the time it impacted against the cold earth it was a blackened thing, burned beyond recognition.

Gabriel stepped out of the sky warily, wandering up to the dead, hot shell and watching curiously. Tanith appeared beside him. She found the manic light of triumph playing in his eyes.

'God is dead! God remains dead! And *we* have killed him!'

Tanith shrugged wearily, unable to share his enthusiasm.

'No big deal,' she muttered. 'I thought it was anticlimactic.'

With no spirit left to hold it together, the corpse was beginning to decay into dust. There was little left to burn. Tanith felt something like sadness.

'It was fun while it lasted,' she mused.

Her brother's voice hummed by her ear.

'I believe it's time to make our move. The encore.'

Tanith nodded, smiling.

'This will have driven the Set into a tizzy.' She bared

her teeth in a zealous smile. 'I do so believe in striking while the iron's hot.'

They left what remained of the grey man's corpse and trudged back towards the house.

'We should burn this place,' Gabriel said. 'Kill everyone, destroy the house and set sail for the real world.'

Tanith was in broad agreement. 'It's become tiresome. The people here aren't fun any more. They've lost their novelty value. What happened to the really interesting ones?'

'We killed them.'

'Yes . . .'

They reached the front door, opening it with a tiresome mental command. Standing on the threshold was Professor Jeremy Winterdawn, an arm pressed against the door frame to steady himself.

Gabriel and Tanith exchanged glances. This had not been anticipated.

'Good evening,' the Professor said languidly. 'We've not been introduced properly but I think you're the sort of people I could do business with.' He paused to clear his throat. 'Can I offer you a deal?'

16

Blood Circuit

The Cruakh of Cathedral was a place of dust and silence. Tragedy hung in the air, infusing the place with an understanding of its loss. A silent whisper descended on the city, drowning the alleys and the towers and the factories. Cathedral heard the rumours of death.

The Set knew. The grey Mandelbrot faces were still stone slabs. A frightened silence sapped their arrogance.

Bernice Summerfield knew. She knew because she was now as much a part of the city as the Set. Her anger was reserved for the Mandelbrot Set. Benny stared up at them, seeing cancerous grey stains spread across the wall. They had sent the grey man to die in a war which he did not want and could not win. Benny herself had been the lever with which they forced him to act. She felt used. The grey man's body lay at her feet, there was grey blood on her hands. She was upset. And angry.

She turned, prepared to march out of the Cruakh, but found the exit blocked by citizens dressed in elaborate robes decorated with stark death's-head shapes. Their masks were blank metal.

One of the Mandelbrot heads rumbled uneasily, as if clearing its throat. When it spoke, its voice was light, without the normal self-assurance.

'He dies,' it said, slurring through a ghastly parody of a memorial address. 'These Gabriel and Tanith have killed him. Evident it is that Cathedral may not stand up to these. We are confounded. Where is our course?'

Another Mandelbrot spoke, its voice retaining some

arrogance. This was the first time Benny had heard one Mandelbrot address another. It was like listening to a schizophrenic arguing with themself.

'He stepped into the bounds of death. His soul was willingly spent. To spite *us*! His care for the programme is sham! He destabilizes our efforts. He seeks the ruin of Cathedral! He betrays *us*!' The Mandelbrot voice screamed into higher pitches of hysteria. A third head took over.

'Courses of action should be deciding upon of an immediacy,' it droned. 'Otherwise Cathedral gives way to entropy. Survival of the programme is imperative.'

'Close ranks! Close ranks!' warbled a smaller face on the edge of the ranks of the Set. The others inclined their fixed faces towards it and strained to nod.

'We must conserve. Seal Cathedral 'gainst the outer realities. We must be *fasces*. Bound rods become, axe-strike when threatened.'

At this the entire Set screamed its agreement and Benny felt a ghost headache twinging inside her reconstituted skull. Then she felt heavy hands falling on her shoulders and locking her forearms.

'Take this one,' a Mandelbrot called. 'Her existence threatens the city. She is outsider, alien. Worse, she conspires with the traitor-builder. For her, execution!'

Benny's mouth opened, but there was a rag-gloved hand clasped over her face and her yells were blocked. Thrashing ineffectually, Benny felt herself being borne away, dragged outside by the citizens. The harsh voices of the Mandelbrot Set squawked behind her, echoing across the soulless city.

'Protect and survive! Protect and survive!'

Benny was dead and Ace felt angry. At first it had been a sentimental, irrational anger that left her screaming inside. That had changed. Numb disbelief had given way to a sad, pragmatic acceptance of the reality of her friend's death. Her anger became cold and callous – geared to rage, to revenge. She stopped thinking about who she could blame for Benny's death. She began to consider her actions.

Ace's anger focused on Gabriel and Tanith, and the best ways to kill them.

Open aggression was out. She'd tried it – it didn't work. She needed a more imaginative approach. Ruthlessly logical, she decided that her efforts would be best served by bringing the survivors of TARDIS and household together for a brainstorming session. Even if no one else could come up with anything, the Doctor would have some scheme up his sleeve.

Shit. Cliché.

The Doctor wasn't interested.

That was great, that was just bloody great.

Ace had never seen him so disinterested. He squatted in the cellar, withdrawn into contemplation. He answered questions with a unintelligibly low murmur. Ace guessed he was wallowing in self-examination and angst and similar psychoanalytical crap. Ace had gone through patches of depression in the past, but she'd been a kid and she'd grown out of it. Watching a grown man endure the same was embarrassing.

No, she was being cruel. Benny's death had got right to the core of him. Ace didn't like it, but she understood. She just wished he'd snap out of it and *do* something. But then the Doctor had never been very practical. She'd seen his moods before but nothing quite as dense and disturbing as this. Here was a Time Lord on the verge of neurosis, Ace decided, and she felt bitter.

Who else?

Sandra was no use. The last time Ace saw her she was a panicking whirlwind figure, disappearing from the cellar in an unco-ordinated rush. Ace heard her later, sobbing behind the security of a locked bedroom door. Just like a little girl. Ace realized she was judging too harshly. Her frustration was taking over.

Cranleigh: too far gone to help.

Ace had no idea where Gabriel had taken Page but Ace doubted that she would think of anything constructive. She was locked into a cycle of vicious, unthinking aggression. Ace was a big fan of aggression but she knew when to give it a rest. She was beginning to think she was the only one left without severe emotional problems, or with the balls to deal with a practical problem in a practical way.

There was Winterdawn. She didn't like him, but he was in better spirits than most others in this house. She believed the Doctor had a quiet respect for his intelligence and expertise. She'd find Winterdawn. If nothing else, he might be able to draw the Doctor back into the game.

Winterdawn had disappeared into the labyrinthine house the moment he'd reacclimatized himself to the sensation of walking. Briefly Ace wondered why Gabriel and Tanith had restored movement to him but she didn't dwell on it. She doubted they had any good reason; it'd probably seemed like a good idea at the time. It made Winterdawn happy, and happiness was rare. He'd probably disappeared off for a good long walk through the house, regaining his feel for its floors and stairways. Good for him, Ace thought. Winterdawn had a lot of energy. She could use that.

The passages were empty. Silent too. They were dead, Ace realized as she prowled in search of her quarry. Gabriel and Tanith had torn its heart out. It was no longer a fit place to live. No way was Winterdawn staying here once this was over.

She didn't like him, but he didn't deserve this.

Winterdawn's voice carried through the stillness, indistinct but audible. Ace caught the sound on the air and crouched, eagerly searching for its source. This was just like hunting, like tracking. Ace felt a little better.

Winterdawn was talking earnestly in low tones. He was in one of the better furnished rooms at the front of the house. Once she had a voice to follow, Ace found it quickly. She reached the door, reached for the handle.

Let her hand fall.

She held back. No particular reason. Just instinct and lingering suspicion. And a question.

Who is he talking to?

'That's not mine. I,' (a long, indistinct passage), '... tetrahedron. I don't know anything about a tardis ... what ...?'

Ace could feel her heart – a steady thump beneath her ribs. She could hear her breathing – her lungs were like wheezing engines inhaling and expelling whole atmospheres in one go. It was an irrational thought, but she was certain Winterdawn could hear.

This was stupid. She was just scared.

'You can have the tetrahedron and my promise that we won't harm you.'

'That's not much. We could have all that and leave you with nothing.'

Tanith's voice.

Ace's eyes narrowed. She'd been right, she'd been right all along. A tide of anger welled inside her. She rode it with vicious enthusiasm.

It was nice to have someone easy to kill.

'So what d'you want?' Winterdawn growled.

'Oh, we don't want anything,' Gabriel replied smoothly. 'Your way is more interesting.'

'And it touches us inside deep down,' Tanith purred, 'to know that in our short time in this cosmos we'll have done something truly good.' There was far too much charm, far too much sincerity in that voice.

'You mean you will ...?' Winterdawn's tone was almost incredulous. Ace wasn't impressed.

'My dear fellow, yes!' Gabriel enthused. 'We have a small matter to deal with first.'

'How long?' Winterdawn asked cautiously.

'Half an hour. Perhaps less,' Tanith estimated. 'Your acquiescence over the tetrahedron was most generous. It will bring matters to a swifter conclusion than we expected.'

'And then ...?'

'Then, Professor. *Then.*'

Winterdawn coughed and Ace could picture him shuffling uneasily in the room beyond the door. It was a particularly vivid picture given that the last time she'd seen him he'd barely been able to stand.

'This is ... far more important to me than you can understand. More important than *this*. Thank you.'

'Don't thank us now.'

'We'll be off then.'

Silence. Ace strained to listen.

'Where are you going?' Winterdawn asked, suspicion trembling on his lips. Ace frowned, pondering on the precise nature of their deal. It didn't deflect her rage. The moment Winterdawn was alone, she would be there.

He'd never walk again.

'Nowhere!'

'Goodbye Professor.'

Silence.

Sick of the silence, Ace pushed herself into the room, determined to make a dramatic entrance. She screwed up. Neither of her feet ended up where they were supposed to be. Ace tried to compensate, swayed uneasily then toppled forward. In an act of treachery, the floor slipped from beneath her, came up and hit her in the face. Suddenly there was the hairy taste of carpet in her mouth and a textured bruise running down one side of her face. She groaned, not so much with the pain as with shame.

Awkwardly, she looked up and saw Gabriel and Tanith standing over her, their lowered faces fixed into gloating smiles and their arms raised towards heaven.

And suddenly Ace could no longer hear the thump of her heart and she was terrified that the beat had stopped for good.

'If you can meet with triumph and disaster, and treat those two impostors just the same,' the Doctor murmured, 'Then yours is the Earth, and everything that's in it. And – which is more – you'll be a man, my son.' He smiled sourly. He rubbed his face with the flat of his palm, detesting the worn, ugly texture of his flesh.

He had left the cellar for no good reason and was wandering the house for no good purpose. He was up to no good. No good could come of it. In his left hand he held a cracked and abandoned object – a mask that grinned incessantly despite the absence of any face behind it. In his right hand was a pyramidal object that glowed with blue light. Its edges were almost razor sharp.

He was thinking about what he should do.

A door opened ahead of him, becoming a room.

Lying before him on a bed was the corpse of Bernice Summerfield.

He would have to arrange her burial. That would be an experience. He'd never buried friends before. They had so many interesting ways of dying, they rarely left corpses behind. Reduced to dust, incinerated in antimatter explosions ... No evidence. No corpse discipline. This time was different.

'What am I going to do?' he asked, sitting by the body.

'I don't know.' Benny was beside him, radiating sympathy. 'There's that place in Norfolk. You know the vicar ...'

'Yes,' the Doctor nodded. 'Reverend Trelaw. I could ask him, but it would have to be done in secret, otherwise the Church would start asking awkward questions.'

Benny smiled and sat beside him.

'I'm going to have to stop Gabriel and Tanith,' the Doctor mused, wondering if the dead could offer suggestions.

The dead? She looked healthy enough.

'You'd need a weapon of some variety,' Benny told him. The Doctor frowned, wondering why he had never noticed the Scots tinge to her accent before. He let it pass.

'What sort of weapon? Ace says nothing works. Gabriel and Tanith are the universe. How do you kill the universe?'

'With a weapon that can kill universes,' Benny said brightly.

'I'll ask Winterdawn. He's bound to have one stashed away somewhere.'

Benny laughed. It was pleasant, but it seemed to lack

something. A vital, animating spark. Her smile. It wasn't Benny's. It was a smile he had only seen in mirrors.

'Bernice,' he said slowly. 'Do you think, perhaps, that it might be better, if I ... died? Would that be a good way out?'

'That would be shameful and cowardly and wasteful,' Benny told him in strict tones. 'It's not good for anyone to die, Doctor.'

'Not even Gabriel and Tanith?'

'Not even them. You might have to kill them. But you respect life, in all its forms. Bloody little hypocrite.'

The Doctor smiled wearily.

'Then I need a weapon,' he said.

Gabriel and Tanith didn't move. They had even stopped breathing. They smiled, but serenely, vacuously. Their eyes were closed.

They didn't move.

Ace gave Gabriel a shove. He swayed unsteadily, then righted himself. Ace allowed herself a callous smile. She placed a finger-nail against Tanith's chin and made a small scratch. The woman didn't stir.

'They're like statues.' Winterdawn was at her side and for a moment she forgot her antipathy. 'They've just been standing there.'

Statues. Right.

Gabriel and Tanith were gone. They'd put themselves into a trance, or let their minds wander. They'd left their bodies as monuments to themselves. Ace stared from one to the other, wondering what she could do. She remembered seeing these bodies broken by gunfire. There was no sign of that now – these bodies were whole and unblemished. And, without their guiding minds to repair them, they were vulnerable.

There was a fireplace set in one wall, ready for cold winter's nights. The hearth was empty and cold, devoid even of ashes. Ace stared at the implements gathered around it. She reached for the poker. Quite heavy, nice swing. Could do a lot of damage if applied in the right manner.

'Angels in marble,' she told Winterdawn, winking at him.

She raised her arm, ready to bring the poker down to make contact against Tanith's neck. She held her arm high just for a second, enjoying the heaviness, the sense of satisfaction, the potency of the moment. She held her arm high for a second too long. Winterdawn stepped forward and snapped a hand around her wrist. He was stronger than Ace would have expected. The swing would not come, the moment was lost.

'No, please . . .' Winterdawn sounded reasonable but pleading. Ace was disgusted, frustrated. She caught him with a curious, aggressive gaze. Ever since she'd first laid eyes on him, she realized, she had really, really wanted to beat him into a whimpering mess.

'Bastard,' she spat. 'You sold us out.'

'You don't understand,' Winterdawn mouthed. Ace stared at him, seeing not a betrayer but a worthless old man. She saw him withering in her gaze, his brittle body sinking into itself. *Worthless.* She dismissed him unthinkingly and turned back to the two still figures. They were still, defenceless. Beautiful, frozen angels in a beautiful, frozen tableau. They were the real enemy.

And it was beautiful.

Ace's eyes were painfully raw, ready for bitter tears. She raised the poker, weighing it eagerly in her palm. She was enjoying this too much. This was a locked moment, filled with energy and aggression that begged to be freed. This was a moment of *potential*. She would remain calm. She would smash them, without feeling, definitely without relish, because it had to be done. She would try not to enjoy it. She owed that to Benny.

But it was still beautiful.

'It is our considered opinion that violence solves nothing.'

The potential was spent, exhausted before its time. Ace's body sagged in disappointment, the poker slipping from her hands and hitting the floor with a crash. The howl that perched on her lips, ready to sing, vanished in a slipstream silence. Someone spoke and the magic went away. She scooped up the poker and thrust it at Gabriel's shoulder, striking it at an awkward angle. A juddering pain drove up Ace's wrist. Ace snarled bitterly. She could still smash the statues of flesh and bone before her, but the thrill of destruction was gone. She'd lost the poetry.

She blamed Justin Cranleigh. He was framed in the doorway, arms folded and face smoothed into an expression of sympathetic melancholia. There was as much sadness in his eyes as there had been in his voice. Madness too, Ace reckoned, but a *coherent* madness. Ace didn't dwell on the miracle of his recovery. She was too angry to focus on anything other than the immediate.

'What did you say?' she hissed, raising the poker. It was supposed to look threatening but Ace's hand was shaking and the poker shook with it. It ruined the effect. Ace felt her self-confidence crumbling.

Cranleigh was calm and composed and everything that Ace wasn't. She hated that. *Hated.*

'Violence solves nothing,' Cranleigh said softly, trying not to match Ace's glare. His eyes were focused on a patch of the carpet beside the door frame. There were shadows round his eyes. Ace saw this and felt nothing.

'So, what're you going to do about it?'

'Nothing. Nothing.' Cranleigh jiggled his head and a light smile came to his lips. 'I just think you should think things through.'

'I've thought things through and I'm going to kill them,' Ace spat. 'I'm going to smash every bloody bone in their bodies! Now shut up and let me get on with it.'

Cranleigh nodded. Ace grunted, satisfied, and hefted the poker.

'It won't work though.'

'What?' Ace snapped.

'You won't kill them. They're *statues*. Flesh statues with bones and nerves and blood, built to house spirits. Smash the bodies and the spirits grow new shapes. You're working off your aggression on inanimate objects.'

'You're so smart.' Ace decided to call his bluff. 'Tell me where their spirits have got to.'

Cranleigh shook his head wearily.

'We don't know. They're communicating with us from a great distance. They want us to defend their bodies in the absence of spirit. If you attack they want me to intercede on their behalf.'

Ace blinked.

'We refuse. We don't do that. We've known the darkness, the shadows. We know what is pointless and what is not. We know.'

A brief pause, punctuated by a moan from Winterdawn.

'Oh,' Cranleigh said, the sadness on his face growing. 'They ... are unbinding the DNA of our host. Cranleigh will dissolve. When it is gone he will be dead. But our minds will be annihilated. There is no hope for us.'

'Who's we?' Ace purred.

'The many minds. The might-have-beens. We've been brought together in this vessel. It's an incredible experience. So many different ways of thinking, so many cultures. We're getting along well. A little acid-head anarchist commune in JC's skull.' Cranleigh paused. 'We can't last. Not without a body.'

'You're a sad, sick man,' Ace growled. 'You need help.' She turned away from the madman and swung the poker against the side of Tanith's torso. There was a satisfying crunch of harsh metal against soft flesh.

But Cranleigh was whispering another gobbet of madness in her ear.

'I think you should know,' he purred, 'there are others of us Gabriel and Tanith could call on, more amenable to their cause. More destructive too. In fact, we suggest you hit the floor – now!'

Then there were hands shoving her shoulders. Ace overbalanced and, once again, the floor leapt up to attack her and the sore texture of the carpet bruised her exposed hands and face. Moments later a chunk of plaster exploded out of the wall beside her. A bullet lodged in the fabric of the house. It was followed into the room by Jane Page. Wrapped around her clothes was a ragged, dirty towel, hanging limp from her shoulders like a loose cape. Her eyes were covered by a white handkerchief stained a distinct red.

'Behold, the woman!' Page declaimed. The grandiose arrogance in her voice was new to Ace. It was an arrogance that had lost all claim on sanity. 'We are amused. We declare holidays from the tedious condition of life. Step forth Ace that we might knight her in a manner befitting.'

Silently, Ace sat up. She was wary, but she sensed little danger. Page had checked out for lunch and she wasn't coming back. What remained of her was so grotesque it was entertaining.

'It may seem to you, Ace, that I have departed for that realm where madness rules as queen,' Page purred, fingering the trigger of her gun. Her old sardonic sanity had returned to her voice but Ace wasn't worried. It was an act, no more. 'While I might seem strange at times, you'll be glad to hear that not only have I retained skill, speed and sharpness, but I have been transfigured with new vision!

'I have no eyes but I can see!

'I see clearer than before. And I will find you. I am invested with divine vision. I am the monarch of assassins, and my power derives from God.'

'You don't believe in God,' Ace sneered.

And suddenly there was the barrel of a gun pressed against her temple but by that time it was too late to make right her mistake.

'That was stupid.' It might have been the old, saner Page. Mad or not, she pulled the trigger.

Winterdawn's body smashed into her side and knocked her gun arm wild.

Ace found herself breathing and was surprised. She decided to let surprise give way in favour of survival.

285

She pounced up and pitched herself through the door, narrowly beating Cranleigh in the flight from the room.

Gunshots exploded behind her. She felt nothing. There was a passageway before her, stretching in two directions. Winterdawn was at one end, disappearing round a corner into the dark confines of his house. Justin Cranleigh pushed past her and fled down the other passage.

A bullet drilled into the wall beside her and Ace took a snap decision, hurling herself into one corridor and running and running and running until she was lost in a maze of delirious architecture. This time though, the maze was built by little more than her own perception, and a terrible fear of joining Benny in the arms of death.

Bernice Summerfield had lived alongside death for most of her lifetime. She'd faced it many times and lived to compare experiences. There were no good ways to die, but many bad ones. The very worst she could think of was death by hanging. It was the last thing she wanted to experience.

So now the citizens of Cathedral were going to hang her.

She was taken to Golgotha, the place of execution. She went directly to Golgotha. She did *not* pass go. She did *not* collect two hundred pounds. She was taken there by the city militia, tall citizens in heavy black robes and no faces beyond their cold steel masks. The masks were blemished by grooves and pock-marks but there were no holes in the blank wholeness of metal.

Benny was taken to the place of execution aboard a vehicle that the grey man had pointed out to her during a more pleasant moment – a war machine constructed to fight back the Great Snake that had breached the city walls millions of years earlier. It was a bloated, overgrown mess of engineering; every gear, every piston, every cog, every working part was exposed and fluid. The machinery growled and throbbed and churned and pumped and seethed. Clouds of soot erupted from the chimneys at the machine's rear. At least ten robed citizens sweated as they shovelled tonnes of coal into the engine, attempting to satiate its ceaseless hunger. At the aft stood the helmsciti-zen, arms strapped to the wheel, waiting for the chance to steer the beast. Where the helmscitizen was patient, the machine screamed with mechanical expectation. Once Benny was safe aboard, a signal was given – a harsh peal of a bell – and the machine roared with joyous life. It lurched forward under a black pall, ploughing through the streets towards Golgotha.

It was to be a public occasion, one of the militia said: half Cathedral would be there. There was a sense of enthusiasm and expectation in the streets, driving out the uncertainty left by the death of the city's soul. Benny caught a snatch of the atmosphere and cheered up for a moment. At other times she brooded. She understood exactly what was going to happen, but harsh reality of death hadn't stamped itself into her heart.

There were airships floating over the city skyline. They gathered like a swarm of black, bloated insects over Golgotha Square, hovering in anticipation of the revels. Cradles of all sizes hung from the bodies of the airships, but the largest and best decorated were reserved for the watching stone heads of the Mandelbrot Set. Even they couldn't resist the allure.

Vultures.

As the machine growled closer towards Golgotha, one of Benny's guards bound her wrists together behind her back. She didn't resist. She had caught futility. There was no escape from the city, save for the path she was offered. A second guard held a flower to her face. A glorious, healthy red rose – its stem covered in fine thorns. The guard pushed the stem into Benny's mouth and told her, in curious, cracked tones, to bite on it.

She bit. She tasted chlorophyll.

'Keep it clenched between your teeth,' said the guard. 'Eventually it falls of its own accord.'

Benny shivered.

Golgotha Square was a vast openness, a plain of grey slabs at a point where major roads intersected. In the centre was a gallows, beckoning. A crowd gathered round it, waiting for someone to die. They stood shoulder to shoulder in still and formal ranks. There was no real enthusiasm there, only what the city itself had instilled in them.

Benny was dragged to the gallows while the crowd watched with rapturous silence. Benny saw masks and robes around her – time became muted and fluid and the world washed around her. Fleeting impressions, so unreal. She saw the steel faces of her guards; the black-wrapped outline of the executioner, two fat hands fondling the lever that would open the door to oblivion; the chessboard-patterned mask of the officiating dignitary – a stooped creature, bent to half its height, standing only with the help of an obsidian rod.

There was a rose in her mouth; there was a flimsy trapdoor beneath her feet; there was a noose around her neck. Finally Bernice Summerfield knew what was happening and she began to panic. It was a quiet panic, she trembled in silence. She wanted to say something, but there was a rose between her teeth, and when it fell it would be too late.

She still liked to think of Cathedral as a computer. The grey man wouldn't have liked it, but she suspected that he simply had a habitual dislike for technology. No, Cathedral was a computer network. Everything she perceived was distorted images of the matrix of data surrounding her. She was corrupt data that would be erased painlessly. She had died once, she could die again. It was a good analogy.

No, it was a stupid analogy. This wasn't a computer. This was real and she was going to die.

She stared across the panorama of meaningless masks and featureless faces. She wondered if they knew what was really happening now, how significant it was. Trembling, she wondered how much longer she had. The anticipation was killing her. In a minute she was going to cry, and she wanted to be dead before she started.

The dignitary shuffled forward, still resting on its rod.

The staff was a long shaft, tipped with a sharp metal point that squealed against the wooden floor as its owner moved. The sound set Benny's teeth on edge. She almost laughed at herself for dwelling on something so petty.

'Citizens of Cathedral,' the hunchback announced. 'A funny thing happened to me on the way here!'

The crowd was unresponsive. Unperturbed, the dignitary continued:

'A very peculiar thing indeed happened. There are rumours in the night, rumours that we are all lost on a tiny ship floundering in the storm of all oceans.' Now the ancient voice seemed to echo, each deeper than the last. The response from the crowd remained underwhelming.

'I'm sorry,' the voice of the citizen continued to drone, perhaps a little smoother, a little sadder than before, 'I never said I loved you, I just want your money. I'm reminded of a similar occasion, on the eleventh of September, seventeen seventy two, at Aix in France, when the Marquis De Sade was executed in effigy because they hadn't caught him yet . . .'

'They're not in the mood for it,' Benny called lightly through her clenched teeth, 'but you're not very funny, and it's not you they've come to see.' Benny felt cheated. Even on the occasion of her death, she felt like she was on the periphery of the action.

The dignitary straightened up, raising its cane towards the crowd. The rod was held horizontally, clenched in a firm fist that extended from the citizen's body on the end of a rigid arm.

'All the world's a stage,' the figure whispered, so that only Benny could hear.

Then the dignitary's arm was flung back, curving in a smooth, violent arc. Its hand was empty, palm flat and fingers splayed. The crowd's silence became deeper, gaining a dangerous quality. The staff impaled the executioner; its sharp steel point erupted from his back. Blood bubbled from the wound, dribbling lazily down the death-robes. The executioner fell over, probably more from surprise than from death.

Benny's guards kicked forward. Knives erupted in their hands. The dignitary seemed unconcerned. The crowd buzzed expectantly, their blood-lust well satisfied. The guards fell upon the murderer and the light blazed off the angles of their knives.

An anonymous citizen mounted the platform so quickly, in the midst of such turmoil, that its entrance almost went unnoticed. Benny saw it first. She was the first to see the machine-gun cradled in its arms. Fire blazed from the barrel, accompanied by the spit of bullets. Two short bursts. The militia fell. Blood flowed freely on the wooden floor of the gallows.

The armed citizen turned to the crowd and, with a burst of gunfire into the sky, created a wave of panic. Its comrade had already snatched up one of the fallen knives and was scurrying across the stage towards Bernice.

The dignitary tore the noose from Benny's neck, then slashed the cord binding her hands together. Benny found herself breathing again. The rose slipped from her teeth.

'What's your name?'

'Bernice Summerfield,' Benny replied wearily. Her eyelids flickered heavily, a sudden exhaustion gnawing at her heart.

'Middle name?'

She was too tired to speak.

Surprise.

A hood was thrown back and a mask stripped away.

Tanith smiled, producing a second machine-gun from her robes.

'Welcome to Golgotha! Can you use one of these?'

She didn't wait for an answer, preferring to shove it straight into Benny's waiting arms. Benny stared down at the gun, wondering numbly what it was and what she was supposed to do with it.

And then she woke up. And she understood what she was holding and how she might use it. With cold deliberation she raised the gun so that it aimed directly into Tanith's face.

'What are you doing?' she hummed in a voice thick

with lingering suspicion and potent aggression. Tanith reacted with a rich, wet smile.

'Tanith! Benny!' Tanith's co-conspirator called. It was now wearing both the voice and the face of Gabriel. Startled back into a practical frame of mind, Benny lowered the gun and inclined her head to see the object of Gabriel's concern.

Golgotha was covered in shadow. A thick, fat, cigar-shaped shadow cast by the largest of the dirigibles hanging over the execution square. Three stone-featured Mandelbrot stared over the side at the insurrection.

'Surrender! Surrender!' squawked all three Mandelbrot heads together, though not quite in unison. Their voices overlapped each other, turning the chant into a chorus of chaos, noise and discord. Below them, the Cathedral militia were strutting warily across Golgotha towards the stage. Each was armed, radiating an air of caution.

Benny's eyes flicked from Tanith to Gabriel and back again. Gabriel's face was depressed and revealed nothing. Tanith was still smiling. One of her hands was hidden in the shadow curves of her robes. Benny looked closer and saw a small black globe cupped in the palm of the invisible hand. A fuse was strung from the globe's surface – a long, thin cord whose end flickered with fire. Benny looked into Tanith's eyes and saw the same fire there.

'Come now,' she whispered. 'We're good sports.'

In one single, smooth motion, she pulled the globe out of the lining of her clothes and pitched it into space.

It flew through the air, the fuse burning low. Gabriel and Tanith had already thrown themselves flat onto the floor. Benny joined them but not before seeing the globe land perfectly at the feet of the leading citizen.

She was already on the floor with her head held low when the globe exploded. She didn't see the explosion, fortunately. The flash would have burned her eyes dry. She felt the winds dragging at her, fruitlessly trying to tear her from the safety of the gallows. She heard the screams of the militia as the winds caught them, sucking them into the heart of the brief, angry firestorm.

The screams didn't disturb her. They weren't human screams. They were only imitations. Cathedral wasn't real, nor were its citizens.

They just sounded real.

The screams didn't disturb her until she thought about them.

When the screaming stopped she looked up and saw that a large area of Golgotha's flagstone floor had turned death-black. There were no bodies. Only the citizen who stood closest to the globe remained, as a white shadow burned into the heart of the black.

Other citizens had been distant enough to escape the nukeflash. Some carried small arms and skidded across the blackened square, firing at the gallows. Bullets and chunks of wood exploded round Benny and she threw herself to the ground again.

'Shoot them down!' screamed the Mandelbrot. 'Wade in gore!'

Gabriel and Tanith threw themselves from the gallows platform, leaping joyfully across the square, howling as they returned fire with enthusiasm to equal that of their enemy. Certain in the knowledge of their survival, they charged berserk to the battle. The ground that had been stained black became stained red.

Benny kept her head held low. She didn't want to kill anyone, but she had the disquieting feeling that she had started this massacre, the events leading to it. The vicious glee her allies brought to the slaughter sickened her. They revelled in the tide of blood.

But Cathedral was not a real place and the only real person who had ever lived here was dead.

She reached for her gun, finding its weight and the feel of its cold skin unpleasant. She raised her head, wondering where to begin.

'Summerfield!'

The Mandelbrot voice was close and spiteful. It rekindled the anger Benny had felt in the Cruakh chamber. She hated that voice. For the first time since taking up the gun, she had the urge to use it. The Mandelbrot

292

airship was lower now, the passenger cradle level with the gallows stage. Less than three yards gap separated Benny from the closest head.

She leapt to her feet, her caution smothered by a thrilling, aggressive anger. The air between her and the airship was empty and she kicked herself through it. A citizen of the militia was waiting for her, a vicious, short-bladed knife in its hand. Its mask was blank.

Benny shot it. Once. Twice. Three times. Benny fired until the knife fell from its hand and the body collapsed on the deck. Her nerves and her mind were numb. It wasn't real. It was only a game.

Benny felt nothing.

When the crew member's body was twitching on the ground and dead beyond doubt, she turned to train her gun on the helpless stone faces of the Mandelbrot Set.

'Take this airship to Cuba!' she demanded.

'You will die for this!' one of the heads declaimed and Benny killed herself laughing. Then she saw the body on the deck.

Silence reigned locally – both Benny and the Mandelbrot Set could hear the gunfire from the square, but as the moment stretched longer, the sounds became less frequent. Then total silence asserted itself.

It ended less than a minute later when Gabriel and Tanith climbed aboard, bloody and victorious.

'Permission to come aboard?' Gabriel called. Benny nodded, suppressing a smile.

'This is piracy!' roared a stone head but no one, least of all Benny, dignified it with attention. The Set grew aloof, saying nothing more to the boarders. The pirates themselves were too busy at the controls of the airship to say much. The flight began in silence.

Golgotha Square fell away until it was a small grey dot in the vastness of the city. Cathedral was no less ugly, seen from above, but now the ugliness was revealed as a magnificent, sprawling design. The towers of the city were like grasping hands, reaching up to drag them down from the sky, but it was too late. The airship rose high into the clouds over the city, beyond the height of the tallest towers. It was so high now, the crew could see the stars through the grey smear clouds.

The city was on fire. Whole areas of the city burned, flames licking as high as the Cruakh itself. The stench of the burning wafted into the atmosphere. Benny caught the stench and began to gag.

'They're burning the myths,' Tanith said solemnly, no trace of humour in her voice. 'They're purging the city of the cultures that flourished in its streets, the creatures nurtured by Cathedral's soul.'

'They?' Benny asked.

'The Mandelbrot Set,' Gabriel intoned. Both he and his sister spoke in sadder voices than Benny had ever heard them use before. 'You've known us a while, Bernice, you might think we don't care about anything.'

'You don't,' Benny said bluntly, recalling exactly who her allies were and what they had done.

'Perhaps not, but we can mourn.'

'After this, the Set will turn on the functions of the city, the citizens. They need to make things nice and homogeneous. The only things they will allow to live are the other Mandelbrot. Then they will fight among themselves until one remains, where a city once stood, crowning itself Monarch of All Time and Space.'

That was terrible. One thing among many.

'But not now!' Gabriel announced with considerably more enthusiasm than before. There was a vicious smile on his lips, and Tanith's too. Brother and sister locked arms and began to dance around the deck whooping and howling and laughing in the eye of the storm.

'Cathedral dies,' one of the Mandelbrot voices intoned, too low for any but Benny to hear. 'Your insurrection destabilizes structure. The entropy we control consumes us now. You have killed the city.'

And as Benny watched, a star fell from the sky, landing on the city and exploding in a spectacular display of light and fire. Others followed its path to the ground. Gabriel and Tanith were laughing. And Benny felt nothing.

It wasn't real.

The Doctor dropped the tetrahedron. Its surface was burning his palm.

Benny was falling. The wind lashed her, tearing her hair, her face, her clothes. She plunged through a funnel of rushing air, hearing the voices of Gabriel and Tanith merged as one. The words were memories. She had heard them before, on the airship, just before she had jumped overboard.

'This was the point. The whole point.

'We can't touch the city because we are its children and we do not yet share its power.

'So we needed to introduce an independent mind into Cathedral, when the city was in its most critical state. The smallest disturbance could wreck this place. An independent mind could do that.

'Sucker!

'We have an appointment with Sandra Winterdawn now, but that's okay. *We* can leave. There's no way out for you.

'You'll stay here and die with it.

'Die!

'You killed it for us. We used you so easily.

'Because, you see, we are tied to this place. We want its corpse. Then we will be free.

'What's the matter? Why aren't you *laughing*?'

At that point Bernice Summerfield jumped overboard. As she fell, she heard Gabriel and Tanith speaking again. And again. And again.

The ground accelerated towards her and she was fully conscious when it hit her.

The sky was a bleak grey, the colour of tears. The grass was the colour of stone. The food had the texture and taste of excrement. They were three; Winterdawn and his daughter, and one other who was not there and appeared as a shadow. Winterdawn hugged himself, loving this dream. Sandra was a statue with a robot voice that broke the cosy reminiscence. Winterdawn loved her.

Her questions were awkward. Questions like: *where's mummy?* Like: *why can't I see?* Like: *what came first, the chicken or the egg?*

They springboarded into existence out of nowhere simultaneously, Winterdawn told his daughter seriously. *We call this the Free Lunch theory.*

Winterdawn opened his eyes and lost his memory.

He was in his daughter's bedroom.

In the middle of the room were the two people he recognized as Gabriel and Tanith. They were smiling at him, vicious little smiles that stabbed at Winterdawn like hot needles.

Their clothes were red-wet, butchers' aprons.

'Sandra,' Winterdawn said. Not his voice, too distant.

'You can thank us now,' Gabriel said, happily.

'Her eyes . . .' Winterdawn continued in his quiet, wistful little voice.

'Over there.' Gabriel gestured and Winterdawn did not look to see where he pointed.

'I'll kill you for this,' he said calmly, though there was a note of bitterness creeping in. 'Kill you, you bastards. Kill you, kill you dead.'

'You're too late!'

'We've won!'

'Here comes the night!'

They left the room and Winterdawn made no move to stop them.

There were scraps of Sandra's clothing lying on the floor.

Why can't I see, Daddy?

Pain lurched up his leg, momentary, agonizing. Weakened, he sank to his knees. The strength in his legs was leaking away. He fell against the floor, and his immediate thoughts were concerned with how soft and wet it felt.

He was in his daughter's bedroom. Without thinking he began to cry.

296

Where can I find a weapon that can kill universes?

The Doctor stared at his feet, at the object pulsing with a light which no longer burned as bright as it had done.

'A weapon that can kill universes,' the Doctor said. His voice was dry and his face plastered with a grim smile.

Cautiously he touched the tetrahedron. His hands blistered under an intense, but not intolerable heat. The light began to flicker and spit.

'Ha.'

He squatted on the floor by the crackling pyramid, easing himself into a familiar cross-legged position, as if in meditation. His hands pressed against separate flats of the pyramid, the light and heat tanning his palms.

For a minute, he sat in silence, trying to empty his mind. The pyramid offered no response, its blue light seeming like a lighter shade of black. The Doctor's cheeks bristled red to match his hands.

'Aummm,' he intoned, trying to shake off his embarrassment.

And the tetrahedron replied:
doctorwheretheHELLHAVEYOUBEEN?!

None of this is real.

Benny lay still in the rubble of Cathedral, her arms and gun pinned under her, her face smothered in concrete dust, imitating the corpse she had expected she would become.

She looked up and saw a city in ruins. She had landed, intact and without pain, in the heart of a quad that resembled Golgotha in architecture if not in scale. The quad was strewn with damage, both structural and human.

Shattered buildings rose from its edges like rotten teeth from dead gums. Cathedral had been corrupt but solid. Now the corruption had eaten into the solidity, into the core. Benny looked up and saw a fragile corpse of a city.

Jagged cracks opened in the floor of the quad. Black plants sprouted from the stone, like tongues, pushing into the corpse for one final meal.

Benny pulled herself clear of the rubble which had so

improbably cushioned her fall, and began to strut around the square like the last barbarian in a ruined Rome. She had killed the city, driven the knife into its stone heart, and now she was lost. Aimless.

A meteorite fell out of the sky, onto the place where Benny had fallen. It didn't survive the fall. It smashed apart on impact. Benny stared at the curious stone shape that now topped the pile of rubble. Even crushed into itself, it was familiar.

Another meteorite smashed into tiny stone pieces. It was better preserved than the first, and Benny recognized it with a wry smile.

It was raining Mandelbrot heads. Gabriel and Tanith must be throwing them off the airship. Benny shot a glance upwards and threw herself aside in time to avoid being crushed by the third of the briefly airborne heads. It splintered anonymously beside her.

Benny smiled serenely. She was enjoying herself, mutedly. She was alone at the end of the world, she would die happy and fulfilled. Mystified, she considered, but happy and fulfilled nonetheless.

Then a voice intruded on her peace.

Aummm.

Benny threw her head back and screamed into the cracked sky:

'Doctor! *Where the hell have you been?!*'

Benny?

'I'm here!' Benny howled, waving her arms around to little effect.

You're not dead.

'Oh, I'm dead, I just haven't stopped talking yet. You know me, I don't let these little details get in my way. Where are you?'

Winterdawn's room. The Doctor's voice was smooth and wooden. Benny never noticed the emotion in his voice until it had gone. *With your body.*

'Good, you can get me back into it. You've got the tetrahedron?'

Yes . . .

'Listen,' Benny called, flattening her voice to match the Doctor's. 'I'm in a city called Cathedral. The tetrahedron is the extension of the city into real space. The city can manipulate reality, but I killed it. This was careless of me, I admit, but it's done now. It's dying. So, for pity's sake, *get me out of here!*'

A pause. Benny ground her teeth in frustration.

How do I know that you're not an illusion, a hallucination, a trick of Gabriel and Tanith's?

'Heavens, I'll be dead in a minute and the man's still concerned with proof. Have you ever considered tax inspection as a career choice . . .? Oh, bloody hell Doctor!' Benny snapped. 'Can't you just . . .?'

'Summerfield!'

The growl cut her short. The growl of a Mandelbrot voice, laced with aggression. She hadn't heard that streak of violence before.

'Summerfield!' growled the last of the stone heads. It was moving under its own steam, lurching across the quad, ploughing through stone. Its face was stone-set, of course.

'Summerfield!' A voice boomed from the unmoving mouth. 'I am the last, sole ruler of this place, King of Kings. The cosmos is mine. Bow!'

Benny swore at him.

'Purged,' the King rambled. 'Purged them all. You too.'

The head surged forward and Benny caught sight of its malevolence. She was going to die here, murdered in the ruins of the dead city by its deranged ruler. That was not the way she wanted to go, indeedy no. She raised her gun and fired, blowing chips of stone from the implacable face. The damage was slight. The head kept coming while Benny emptied her gun. Disgusted, she hurled the gun at the Mandelbrot face. The stone jaws of the King closed around it.

Crunch.

Benny had left it too late to run. The Mandelbrot mouth was a black hole bounded by stone. It closed around her.

'Doctorrrr!'

Crunch.

Crunch.

None of this is real.

The tetrahedron screamed with light and fire. Trapped within, Benny screamed. The Doctor's flesh burned and he screamed. The scream became a storm of noise. The walls blistered into static. The bed opened up and swallowed Benny's corpse. Howling, the Doctor grasped the tetrahedron as if to throttle it. And it spoke to him.

It was not Benny's voice. It was a calm, plain voice – a grey voice.

This is only a foretaste of what is to come.

The Doctor screamed. The grey voice spoke, whispering its instruction.

Run Doctor, run, run, run! You can escape. You can be free.

I don't want to run. I must stay and fight.

Run.

Irrationally, he ran. The storm followed. It swirled round the tetrahedron and the tetrahedron remained clutched in his hands. The voice urged him on, faster, deeper, into the house. He fought it. This was cowardice, this was retreat, this was abandoning friends and allies, this was defeat . . .

No. This is your last chance.

Somehow he clung to that thought. He hoped it might mean something. Mostly he ran. He ran and he ran and he ran and he didn't stop running until the tall block rose before him, sturdy and unmoving in the reality storm.

POLICE. PUBLIC CALL. BOX.

Ace bounced from wall to wall, clutching each new surface, drawing strength from their solidity. She no longer had any goal in mind, no aims, no motives. She kept moving, she kept surviving, she kept her mind off reality. Her constructive, logical thinking had given way to desperate defeatism. She knew when she was beaten. She knew when the enemy was bigger, better, faster, cleverer, wittier and even sodding sexier than her. She knew a lost cause when she saw it and she saw one all round her.

'We've lost!' she yelled at each new wall. 'We are the dead!'

Yeah. She didn't care. It couldn't last. They'd get her eventually.

She giggled, realizing she was getting paranoid, had always been paranoid to a small degree. She stroked the nearest wall, finding its wooden strength reassuring.

Then she saw the wall was dissolving. A shapeless rust was eating its fabric, a rust of reality. She looked down and saw a similar rust chewing at the carpet. The rust hummed and hissed like static.

Not fair! How could she fight an enemy who could steal the boards from under her feet? She couldn't. She considered panicking.

The floor became sparse. She kicked herself across the growing void and through the nearest door.

It was Winterdawn's room. Reality-rust ate the walls, but slowly.

Her eyes fell on the bed. There was a rust-shape where Benny's body should have been.

Winterdawn was standing in the middle of the room, staring at her coolly. In one hand he hefted a poker – the very same item, she guessed, that she had almost used to smash the bodies of Gabriel and Tanith, his allies, his friends. She stared back at him, determined to wear down his gaze.

He lost interest in her, his eyes flicking at random across the room. He prowled, pacing to the window. It hadn't been opened in five years. Winterdawn opened it now. He opened it with the poker, driving it clean through each pane. A shower of light glass shards glowed in the night, catching the light before the rust caught them.

Winterdawn seemed satisfied with the destruction, though not satiated. Silently, without fuss, he wrenched at the curtains, tearing the material and breaking the runner. He tore and tore at the fabric until it was a bundle of rags. The destruction spread. Winterdawn smashed ornaments and knocked down furniture – kicking and beating until the weaker items were reduced to firewood. He wrenched paintings and photographs from the walls and dashed their glass façades to pieces on the floor before driving his feet onto each, obliterating art with stamped shoe-prints. He tore pages from books, hurling them across the room until the carpet was obscured beneath a layer of paper snow, the words of Nabokov, Spinrad, Heller, Peake and a hundred others.

Ace watched silently, enthralled by the competent violence.

The final act of destruction was the simplest. Winterdawn tore the sheets from the bed, hurling them into the corners before setting to work on the mattress. The surface battered and broke, stuffing and springs bursting spontaneously from the tears. Pleased with the effect, the destroyer flung the poker away and turned, arms held wide apart like an actor declaiming.

No. Actors fake their feelings. The pain on Winterdawn's face was real.

'Now!' he announced in grand, declamatory tones. 'They've taken everything!'

His booming voice died away, consumed by silence. Winterdawn scanned Ace's face, looking for a reply. After a moment, he seemed to understand that none was forthcoming. He spoke quietly this time, muting his voice as if to hide the truth it contained.

'My daughter is dead,' he began. 'I wanted her to see. They promised.'

Ace stepped forward, taking Winterdawn's hands.

'They lie,' Ace whispered.

'I know,' Winterdawn replied. His voice and eyes were obscured by pain.

'You were stupid.'

'I was.'

'We'll destroy them.'

Winterdawn laughed creepily. Made Ace feel stupid. He sank to his knees and Ace became aware that there was little holding him up. She glanced around her. The rust was spreading, as if fascinated by the destruction. Soon the floor on which she and Winterdawn stood would be an island.

She sank to her knees beside the Professor, clasping her hands against his. It was strange that they should be together, at the end.

'Professor Winterdawn,' she said. 'Jeremy. I'm sorry.'

He stared at her, confusion in his eyes.

'What for?'

Ace almost cried.

They huddled together. And the rust ate them, as it ate the world.

You're too late, they said,
  We've won, they said,
    Here comes the night.

17

The Waste Land

Awareness. Seeping. Gradual.

Thump (Sound) *thump* (Regular) *thump* (Familiar) *thump* (Close) *thump* (Heart. Beat) *thump thump*.

   Thump.

There was air in her lungs, strength in her muscles and spirit in her flesh.

   And then she woke up.

Ace sat upright, eyes snatching at her surroundings. The bedroom had survived. There was no sign of the reality-rust, no damage save that inflicted by Winterdawn. Mundane light filtered through the window, making the room ordinary. Ace was suspicious. She had seen this place eaten. The hiss of hungry static chewing the walls lingered with her. So too did the buzz that had crept along her flesh when she too had been consumed. Her instincts whispered of the *wrongness* of the room around her.

   Winterdawn lay beside her, unconscious. He was alive, and peaceful enough. Ace decided it would be best to let him sleep. She rose, stumbling to the door and pushing through. Then she locked still, her instincts chattering dangerously as she stared at the new world unfolded around her.

   She stood on a concrete expanse beneath a cloud-choked sky. Ranks of chimneys thrust around her, coughing thin streams of black smoke into the alien air. The air shivered around her as if her presence offended it. There was the smell of dust and burning in her nostrils and an unhealthy watery taste in her mouth.

'Shit,' she said, concise and appropriate.

The plane was finite. It had an edge, distantly. Spurred by her curiosity and irritated by her ignorance, Ace made for the edge. As she moved she felt she recognized fragments of the world around her. Nothing tangible, just a sense of familiarity. She glanced down and found her feet planted on a carpet of vaguely familiar pattern – it had lined the passageway beyond the bedroom. Neutrally she registered it before running on. She began to pick up on more details. She recognized decorations, ornaments, scraps of wallpaper from Winterdawn's house. Some seemed to have been abandoned haphazardly across the concrete plane. A pot-plant decorated a niche in a wall. Regency wallpaper was plastered on a brick chimney-stack. Another passage was glimpsed through a small, grime-covered window. Ace noted them all and ran.

She clattered up a corrugated iron slope and was suddenly at the edge.

She was on a roof, the roof of a factory. It was at the heart of a neatly regimented industrial complex of functional block buildings. Ace squinted, gazing into the distance, seeing towers and spires and shafts rising on the edge of the complex. They pushed awkwardly into the sky, helped or hindered by architecture which was impractical, unorthodox and grotesque. Ace's eyes were met by a shock of urban styles, none conducive to sanity. She tried to follow the outline across the horizon but her head began to ache with the effort.

Some of the distant towers burned. Others seemed shattered, abandoned. Ace itched, feeling the laziness of the city, the absence of activity or motion. That was bad. Cities were supposed to breathe. Cities were supposed to bustle. A city without movement was a city without life.

A distant tower creaked unsteadily on its foundations, toppled and collapsed. The factory rumbled sympathetically as the tower struck the ground. Ace teetered on the edge of the roof, grabbing at a nearby gargoyle to steady herself. The gargoyle fixed her with a scowl.

The clouds above her seemed to shake, and a gap opened in them. Fire flickered in the gap. The sky was alive with light and motion and frantic, colourful frenzy, hidden behind the smoke. Colours weaved together, clashing and struggling incessantly. Ace grinned, enjoying what she saw, realizing she was in no danger. She was moved by the sight. She treasured that feeling. It was rare.

'It's beautiful,' a voice came from behind her. She turned languidly. The voice did not threaten or invite danger. If anything it was wistful.

It belonged to a ghost. It was man-shaped but transient. It crackled and spat and faded between existence, sometimes solid, sometimes transparent, sometimes absent entirely. It was colourless. It was grey.

The shape wore a hat, a coat, a shirt, trousers. All grey. All swam in and out of reality with it.

'They are a sign,' the shape pronounced. 'There are powers so old they have forgotten what impotence is like. They are afraid.'

'Yeah?' Ace said, feeling too relaxed to add more.

'The old certainties are suspended,' the shape said. 'The cosmos rests on them. Good and evil, light and darkness, time and space. White and black are dead. Now there is only grey!'

'You sound happy,' Ace told it. She found its earnest tone curiously convincing. 'So what's going down? I mean, I went to sleep, and when I woke up . . .' She left her history unfinished.

The grey shape flickered. Its voice grew melancholy.

'There is no longer a house. Now it is part of Cathedral, this city. The city dies, its structure burned away, its soul living only as a shadow. It must feed on the material world for strength and unity. So it overwrites the cosmos, absorbing the world slowly.'

Ace felt a flicker of irritation.

'And what if the world doesn't want to be absorbed?' she murmured, as aggressively polite as she could manage.

'There will be a succession before any true damage occurs. The city is dormant. Maybe it will die. Maybe it will rise anew. Who can say? It will be interesting finding out.'

'You're keen on the sound of your voice, aren't you?' Ace tried a little open hostility. 'Who the hell are you?'

The shape flared, became almost solid. Its eyelids fell open. Ace clenched her teeth and turned away, too late to disguise the horror she felt.

'*I*? I am a shadow,' it crowed, though its voice lost none of its calm. 'And if I lived I might be a friend. Remember that. And this: the people you travel with both live, somewhere in this city. I wish you well . . .'

The shape crackled one final time and vanished.

Ace shook, trying to absorb the implications of what the shape had said, hoping it was true. That was almost beyond doubt. The shadow told no lies, she was certain. He'd been long-winded, but she didn't doubt his integrity.

She smiled and turned and stared out across the cityscape, searching its buldings and its streets with keen eyes.

She saw a wide road and, on a whim, she let her sight trail along it until it opened into a vast, rubble-covered square. In the centre of the square was a wooden stage that had been smashed apart by falling masonry. That wasn't interesting. Her attention focused on the police box that sat on a pile of rubble beside it.

She grinned again, a happy child. The square was close. If she could just get off this roof she could be there in no time. She skirted along the edge of the roof, searching for a way down. As she ran she called out with enthusiasm and energy.

'Doctor! Hey, Doctor! She's alive! Benny's alive!'

Her voice bounced off the factory walls, echoing in the canyons between buildings. If the Doctor could hear her he made no reply. She didn't care. She shouted at the stones, at the city. She didn't care who could hear. Just for once she was really, really happy to be alive.

Winterdawn woke, remembering everything. The haze was

307

gone from his mind, light touched his eyes, the tiredness was lifted from him. Only in his legs did he feel pain. Only in his legs and in his heart.

Sandra was still dead. He had walked again, briefly, and now that sensation was gone forever. He'd sold his soul, his daughter's life, everything, for false hope. Wedderburn was dead. He understood now, for the first time he realized what it meant. It upset him gradually. There had been too much death and suffering packed into the past few days. Tragedy had lost its potency, becoming only sad and spiteful.

This couldn't get much worse.

He opened his eyes and found a monster standing across him.

He closed his eyes and whimpered.

'Please, Professor,' the monster spoke softly. He knew its voice.

He opened his eyes and looked again, closer. It wasn't human. It might have looked human once. It even had a vaguely human shape and was wearing the remains of human clothes. It was a human body that had begun to decay. Flesh, bones, nerves, muscles, organs – all had lost their rigid structure and were flowing. The once-human creature had become semi-fluid – rolling and rippling outside of its original form. It left a trail of wet, sticky flesh in its path. It was falling apart. It was Justin Cranleigh.

'They've taken him apart,' the thing spoke rapidly in tongues. 'There's nothing left to hold him together. There's only us.'

Winterdawn's stomach lurched. He coughed blood.

Cranleigh was like a cancer. His whole body was a loathsome cancer cell. Articulate and in pain. Horrible.

'Justin,' Winterdawn said quietly. The creature nodded, setting his flesh writhing in a manner Winterdawn would never forget.

'We are Cranleigh and Truman and many others. Gabriel and Tanith brought us to life, and now they kill us.'

'Fearful symmetry,' Winterdawn considered, beginning

to lose his horror of the Cranleigh-creature and finding pity.

'More fearful maybe, than you imagine.'

Winterdawn frowned, trying to understand.

He tried to stand, an automatic action. He managed to lift himself partly with his elbows, but this was too great an effort and he collapsed wearily onto his back.

'What have they done?' he whispered, half-rhetorically.

'They have destroyed your house.'

The answer was unexpected. He almost leapt to his feet in surprise.

'What did you say?'

'We'll show you.' The creature leant forward and enveloped him with its ample flesh. Thin, tight limbs grew out of the bulk of Cranleigh's flesh, clinging to his back and shoulders, raising him slowly and painfully upright. Cranleigh held him in a curious parody embrace. Parts of Winterdawn felt repulsed by the sensation, others oddly comforted. Whatever Cranleigh had become there was a part of him that he could like and admire.

How often had Cranleigh held Sandra like this, he wondered? He had seen them walk hand in hand to Sandra's bedroom on more than one occasion, and had been touched by the close love between them. He had overheard them making love once, and had felt only a long, unsettled ambivalence.

Only after Cranleigh's madness had set in had Winterdawn learned how cruel he could be, how vicious, how possessive. He stared into the eyes of the monster and wondered whether he was looking at an improvement.

The creature who had been Justin Cranleigh carried the professor gently to the shattered window. Winterdawn stared out and saw a world changed beyond recognition. He stared, too numb to cry, too dull to feel anything.

'I've seen enough,' he said eventually. 'Thank you.'

Cranleigh lowered him into an armchair. He sank into it, grateful for its familiarity and its soft surface. Cranleigh hovered over him, perhaps waiting for a lead.

'Who am I talking to?' he asked.

'At present, our name is Qxeleq. One of us. I was a student once.'

'Ah.' The professor's eyes shone. 'So was I. Would you like to talk?'

The Doctor sat on a mound of rubble and hummed softly to himself. He regarded the new world around him with a curious eye, wondering what he could make of it. The TARDIS, its surface mottled and bleached with white dust, sat on a distant mound. It was the last link with the world the Doctor remembered. Dormant though it was, the TARDIS had sheltered the Doctor from the effects of the storm. It remained a rock – steady in an ocean of change where all else would be washed away.

The Doctor had clung to it desperately, fearing – perhaps knowing – that sooner or later the storm would smash him away from the security of the rock. But not yet. Winterdawn's house had gone. The Doctor had emerged from the TARDIS once the storm had abated and found himself here, in this city.

The city disturbed him. The TARDIS had been put down among desolation, on a vast black-scarred stone square, amid collapsed and gutted buildings and collapsed and gutted corpses. He had paced around the square slowly, the dry dust crunching beneath his feet. The city smelt of a summer day, of dead flowers. Its air tasted of dryness and lemon. Its sky was hidden by a blanket of smoke. Its buildings were hollow towers, soaring upwards, trapped in earthbound stones. There was no noise but the sound of his footfalls, no breeze, no life. Even the bodies only appeared to be dead. On close inspection he found that they had never been alive. They were bodies of flaking dust. That the city was dead disturbed him. That the city was desolate disturbed him. That there was nothing in the city but despair disturbed him.

He had climbed to the top of the nearest mound and sat down to think. Behind him was the TARDIS, before him a pond of stagnant water that had seeped up through a crack in the ground. His reflection was dark and melancholy on the water, obscured by a reef of scum. There was something regular and bulky pressed inside his jacket.

Benny had spoken about a city – a city that was inside the tetrahedron, or maybe *was* the tetrahedron. This city, he guessed. Benny had been alive there, might still be alive now, somewhere. He hoped so, though his surroundings did not encourage hope.

'Happy, happy!' came the voices of Gabriel and Tanith, striking the walls of the surrounding buildings, making them shake slightly. 'Joy, joy!'

The Doctor reacted sharply, tumbling down the mound and pressing close against its surface.

Gabriel and Tanith had wandered into the far end of the square. The Doctor kept low, peering at them with keen eyes. He watched them leaping across the square, arms and eyes and mouths constantly meeting and parting. They were evidently in a good mood. The Doctor's hearts sank.

'Look,' Tanith cried, pointing. 'There's the TARDIS!' There was innocence in her voice – but not enough to hide the malice. The Doctor crouched down further, watching carefully as brother and sister bounded across the square to the police box. He saw their movements become less open, more cautious. They prowled round the TARDIS, taking short and cramped paces, pressing hands to the door and faces against the windows, circling it again and again as if it had become the centre of their universe.

The Doctor crouched still, wondering how much of what he saw was genuine.

Gabriel's palms pressed against the door of the TARDIS, stroking the paintwork with care and reverence.

'Box of delights,' he exclaimed. 'Chariot of the gods.'

'D'you think he's in there?' Tanith asked. Her knuckles tapped lightly against the police box shell. The noise made was loud and hollow and unnatural. 'Yoo-hoo, Doctor! Are you in there? Are you hiding from us?'

'No need to be frightened,' Gabriel joined in. 'It's only us.'

Tanith kicked the TARDIS door. It creaked under the impact and the Doctor winced, but it held fast.

'We can't touch you,' Tanith called. 'Not there, in your hole, outside the real universe. Now you can stay the boring old sod that you've practised long and hard to be, or you can be a pal and let us in for the party.'

There was a moment of silence. The Doctor squinted, disturbed to see them wearing manic, inane grins.

'Then there's something else,' Gabriel hissed, low voice bouncing across the square, tumbling against the distant walls. '*This* is useless. From your time rotor to your fault locater – plastic, metal and dead machines! Time and space don't exist any more! We abolished them. Or are abolishing, or will. Throw your preconceptions in the air and guess where they'll come down!'

'So, there's us,' Tanith added sweetly. 'Only us. There is here, and now, and us. Pretty damn soon us will *own* here and now. We'll make a toy of the universe, we'll make it spin and dance and giggle and break apart. We'll make a kaleidoscope of the world. Everything will mean anything and nothing will mean anything. You and your pretensions will be meaningless. Get out of your bloody shell and go with the flow!'

'Otherwise we might turn you into a deck-chair, or a wing and a prayer. And you wouldn't like that at all!'

'And Ace will make a gorgeous snack. We'll swallow her down, bones 'n' all. Or we'll flay her and turn her pelt into a colourful umbrella. And there's Benny too! Lovely in body and soul. We haven't thought about what we'll do with her.'

'We can do *anything*. We go *anywhere*. We can be *anyone*!'

The Doctor watched unfeeling as the couple locked hands and began to prance around the TARDIS, chanting. Their voices became a deranged howl, escalating towards a misshapen crescendo.

'Anything! Anything! Anything goes! Anything! Anything! Anything goes! Anything! Anything! *Anything goes*!'

They stopped, suddenly, sharply, staring at each other's faces. The silence between them was thick and obvious. The Doctor tensed involuntarily.

'He's not in there is he?' Gabriel murmured. The Doctor caught the words on dead air.

'He's over there,' Tanith waved an arm towards the Doctor's hiding place. 'He's behind the mound, by the pool, listening to us. He thinks he's learned something. Silly man.'

The Doctor decided that now was as good a time as any to break cover. He rose, so that Gabriel and Tanith could see him. They stared at him as though he were something small but incomprehensible, alien to their experience. He hoped that was genuine; it gave him something to hope for.

'Come and talk,' Tanith said. She seemed lucid and sober. The Doctor shook his head, edging slowly towards the edge of the square. His arm was still pinned inside his jacket, clutching tight at the bulk hidden there. He moved jerkily across the square, followed by Gabriel and Tanith's eyes. Their stares were full of ill-natured humour, as if he had stopped being strange and had become an obscure joke. His face stung red, with something like humiliation.

It was there on Gabriel and Tanith's faces. A message for him.

You've been defeated, at last.

A gap opened up between buildings beside him. He dived into it, into narrow cobbled streets that wound close and tight into the city. Here it was silent and less deadly. Gabriel and Tanith were not following him but their voices were, howling and shrieking their triumph at him, bombarding him with shame. So he ran.

He *had* learned something, he was certain. He had learned that – unless he had been witness to an elaborate act – Gabriel and Tanith *could* make mistakes, that they didn't know everything. He hadn't been defeated.

Not yet.

He clutched the shape under his jacket and ran on.

* * *

Bernice Summerfield woke in the heart of a dead square under a dead sky. She recognized it slowly. This was Cathedral, her afterlife. She was surprised that it was still here. Then she stared around at the buildings which rose like tombstones, and smelled the air that tasted of embalming fluid, and felt a surface like hardening flesh beneath her back. This was an ex-city. It had popped its clogs, gone to meet its maker.

He was dead too.

She wasn't though, and that delighted her.

She tried to move her legs to lift herself upright. Her legs didn't respond. She stared along her body and saw why. Both hung limply from the half-closed mouth of a stone Mandelbrot head. She closed her eyes, hoping that when she opened them again the scene might have changed. It hadn't.

It might have been worse. Chewed though they were, her legs were still attached to her body. She took comfort from this small mercy.

'My God . . .' she moaned softly, stroking her temples. 'That must have been some party. What was I drinking?'

She pulled her legs from the Mandelbrot's dormant mouth and waggled them in the air thoughtfully. Her left leg stung with pins and needles but otherwise they seemed undamaged. The last of the Mandelbrot must have tried to swallow her. It had probably choked on her.

'I'll never be cruel to a jellybaby again,' she vowed solemnly. She kicked at a stone cheek with a flailing foot before setting herself upright. 'So, you're one of the type who goes for the legs first. That's a sign of psychosis. It's what the Doctor does.'

The head remained dark and dormant. Its mouth and eyes were dark hollows in the stone, not quite vacant. Benny peered closer and saw shapes seething in the darkness, in the cavities. Wedderburn's orchids. She recalled them without much fondness or hatred. They seemed like something from the distant past.

'*Les fleurs du mal,*' she whispered to the orchids, 'but

you're not bad at all. You're just misunderstood.' The nearest of the orchid heads rose and spat at her.

'Ah,' she said, losing interest. She patted a stone temple.

'I'll tell you this,' she told the head in conspiratorial tones, 'you were a dreadful bureaucrat but you could make a career out of being a rock garden.'

The head said nothing. Benny pulled a face at it and turned away.

She almost wished she hadn't. A dead Mandelbrot was amusingly grotesque at least. A dead Cathedral was bleak. The streets had cracked. The façades of the buildings had cracked. The towers had toppled and some still burned like a funeral pyre in the distance. Benny no longer sensed rot in the city – save the clean corruption of death. She had killed everything. Or maybe the grey man had, by sacrificing himself. Or Gabriel and Tanith, by setting the whole thing up. Or . . .

This was stupid. Who was going to argue about the responsibility for the murder of a pile of stones constructed in a vaguely logical pattern? She couldn't imagine the case getting to court.

The grey man suddenly seemed to be at her side. *There is more to a city*, he seemed to whisper, *than its stones.*

Benny spun round in shock. There was no one there. Her heart began to beat again.

Winterdawn's bed was jammed into a crack in the street. A wardrobe Benny vaguely recognized lay broken open on its side nearby, spilling its contents. There was a lampshade, and a painting and an unopened bottle of wine. Benny recognized all from Winterdawn's house.

She didn't think about it. She went for the bottle, holding it out for the Mandelbrot head's inspection.

'You wouldn't have a corkscrew on your person, would you?' she asked.

It gave no answer, but Benny had expected disappointment.

She looked down at herself and a thought flitted across her mind.

These are my clothes. My real clothes, from the

315

TARDIS, not the grey man's idea of fashion. This is genuine, one hundred per cent Benny-clobber.

The second thought came slower, more tentatively. This was okay, it meant a lot more to her.

This is my body. I'm not dead. This is my real body, the one with the aches and the pains, the one I've hung on to since birth. My soul and body have been smashed into each other. I'm back. I'm back and arms and legs and head and everything!

'I'm alive,' she told the head jubilantly. The plants within trembled ominously. 'I'm real. I am some body. And you're just a head. You ain't got no body, my friend. I shouldn't joke I know, but do you get anything other than hats for your birthday? I could quite fancy you in a straw boater.'

'Summerfield,' the head slurred. Benny slipped back in alarm, the bottle falling from her loosened grip and shattering on the paving stones. She stared at it wistfully.

'Now that's not fair,' she pronounced. She stared at the broken glass and the pool of wine slaking the pavement. She felt suddenly sour. 'Like life,' she added.

'We cannot move,' the head rumbled on, voice churning uneasily. 'Exhausted is Cathedral, moribund and immobile. As it dies, so die we.'

Benny said nothing.

'Carry us, Summerfield,' the head pleaded. 'To the Cruakh, to the seat of our power. If we might be restored then the city might grow phoenix-like. Become great again. Return to the programme. World saving and doubt spreading.'

'*Carry* you?' Benny spat the suggestion. '*Please*, I'm a delicate organism not a wheelbarrow! Besides, you don't deserve it.'

The head rumbled, apparently frustrated. The plants in its eyes and mouth gibbered and thrashed.

'Not for *us*, Summerfield. For the programme, for the grey-builder. Antipathy there may be between us, but also agreement on the programme.'

'Listen,' Benny said coldly, her voice and body tightening. 'If you wanted me to respect you or your programme then there are some ground rules you should've stuck to from the start. For example, you should not have gone round chanting, "Death to Summerfield!" It's bad for my soul.'

The head howled. Benny turned away in disgust.

A short, familiar figure tumbled round a distant corner. His clothes were stained with dust and water-dirt. Despite his dishevelment, his body was bristling with energy or exhaustion. One hand was pushed into the folds of his jacket, clinging compulsively to a bulky shape concealed there. He froze as he saw Benny, staring dolefully and shaking.

'Benny,' he called, slightly suspicious. 'Is that you?'

'Oh yes,' Benny replied sweetly. 'This is a genuine Summerfield, quite rare and worth a bit on the open market.'

The Doctor nodded abruptly, seeming relieved. He said nothing more but seemed to have accepted her as genuine. For her part Benny hadn't the slightest doubt that this could be anyone other than the Doctor. Gabriel and Tanith were capable of many things, but she doubted they could fake *him*. She smiled wistfully, studying his face from across the Cathedral street. She saw much on the Doctor's face – a cocktail of nuances. It was difficult, as always, to tell what he was thinking. His eyes seemed wide and tired. She fixed on them intently, trying to seem calm.

They stepped into each other, hugging briefly. It was a weary reunion, untouched by speech or humour. Cathedral wasn't designed for gentle camaraderie. Benny was comforted by the embrace. She was alive, the Doctor was alive, they were together and just maybe things were going to be okay. And just maybe, the Doctor felt the same.

They swapped experiences slowly, stumbling over every word because every word might mean something important. As the Doctor spoke Benny found herself studying his face, finding new lines and worn patches. His eyes lacked their usual sparkle, grace and humour. There was

317

a relentless quality in their place. Benny felt herself reflected in those eyes.

The Doctor came to his conclusion.

'Winterdawn's home was being eaten, great chunks being cut out of reality. The tetrahedron was at the heart of it . . . maybe it was hungry? I ran to the TARDIS where the hunger couldn't reach, so I was safe.'

'The tetrahedron and Cathedral are the same,' Benny interrupted cautiously, as the Doctor paused. 'Bit of a knotty concept to get your head round but . . . um, I can see odd bits of the house here and there, particularly here. It looks to me like the city has swallowed the house and everything in it. That's what I call an appetite.'

The Doctor was nodding.

'That's what I thought,' he agreed. 'Have you tried asking your friend?'

He indicated the last of the Mandelbrot Set whom Benny had introduced with good grace at an appropriate point in her story. The Doctor had greeted it with a ferocious smile. The head had matched with stone silence. Only now did it speak. It recognized that it had their attention – its hard arrogance was returning. It still grated in Benny's ears.

'True,' it said. 'To survive collapse, Cathedral chews into the world, tasting and taking what it finds. This house was close. From this Cathedral takes new structure until the old is restored. This TARDIS – being outside of space and time – was inedible. Now to the Cruakh carry us, so that . . .'

'Belt up, there's a good head,' Benny suggested. She turned back to the Doctor and found him grinning.

'Have I said something funny?'

'Yes,' the Doctor responded innocently. 'You said the city and the tetrahedron are one and the same. But I took the tetrahedron with me. I took it into the TARDIS where it couldn't be eaten.' He made a baffling smile.

Benny blinked. There was something meaningful here but it eluded her.

318

'Do you know what I've done?' the Doctor asked. Benny plumped for honesty and shook her head.

'I've created a paradox.'

He pulled his arm out of his jacket. Sat on his palm, sizzling with a new, yellow light, was the tetrahedron.

'Cities within cities,' Benny heard herself say, her eyes caught by the pyramid glare. 'So how does it help us?'

The Doctor smiled again. His broadest smile in a long time.

'It gives us leverage,' he said.

A woman was dreaming in the darkness.

She was mad. The voices told her that. Gabriel and Tanith spoke to her, whispering the truth. She was a queen, wrapped in the one true flag. (*She was an assassin, ruling over a mind in madness, wrapped in a dirty rag*). She was ruler of the red, white and blue land of Do-as-you're-told, of subjects who loved and cherished her and would fight to protect her and to glory her. She would lead them willingly to war. Nations would fall before her advance. Then when the atlas became too small, she would lead them into space. Imperial Earth! Her dream, the dream of empire. (*That's right. A dream of empire. That's all it ever was. A* dream.)

'Assassin,' said the voices. 'Crazy Jane.'

Here sir, ready and waiting and willing for the number from Five, the ticket from Ten, the Voices, the real power, they who must be obeyed. I am here, hear, only obeying orders.

The people want blood. Blood is a part of them, has always been a part of them, it runs in their veins. What's a death camp but an efficient Roman circus? Blood is strength, nation is strength, pain is strength. Liberty is absolute, hierarchy is truth, anarchy is chaos. Blood, mind, soil!

First, before I do this sir, there is one thing I must know.

'Ask. We know everything.'

(*They do, they really* do *know everything.*)

My name. I must know my real name.

'Your name is Jane Page! Sally Carpenter! Elisabeth Pinner! Christine Dennison! Penny Holmes! Stephanie Lister!'

Page was a little girl again. *Want* my real name! Want! Want! Want!

So they gave her a name.

I knew it, Page sang, I knew it all along.

'So kill.'

Page took up her gun.

Cathedral's day passed into night and the sky turned rust-red. The surviving towers of the city glowed dim white, failing to dispel the new depth of darkness. A few flames still flickered on the horizon, but there was little left to burn. Benny hugged herself, not against the chill but against the night. It was a slow night, corpse-cold. It was the last night of the city. Benny snuggled up against the immobile Mandelbrot head. Its stone exterior smouldered with dying warmth. It was better than nothing.

The tetrahedron lay on the ground nearby, crackling with intense, cold light. The Doctor sat squat before it, hands dancing against its blazing surface, eyes closed and face calm in meditation, trying to change the world. So, Benny mused, he was sticking to what he knew best.

He hadn't moved for hours. He didn't seem to feel the cold, or the tiredness, or the oppression, or the hunger that Benny did. She was beginning to recall her time as a ghost with fondness. Little things like that hadn't seemed important when she hadn't a body to worry about.

'Om,' she said, forcing her numb lips into a smile.

'Humour is not appreciated,' the Mandelbrot head rumbled. Benny grimaced but deep down she knew it was right. It wasn't the right time for jokes, or warmth. The cold would kill both.

Besides, she was worried about Ace.

She hugged her stone head and waited.

Finally the Doctor spoke.

'Dark,' he murmured, his voice flute-soft. His face was

set and solemn, caught stark in the glare from the tetra-hedron. 'Kneel to worship piled relics. Heart and soul become stone, dead, dust. But there's nobody there.'

'Tell me something I don't know,' Benny purred without humour.

'The old system is dead.' The Doctor was smiling faintly. 'A skeleton remains, ragged corpse framework. It's enough. If anything wants to rebuild control here . . . It's enough.'

'This is as we have said,' the Mandelbrot began.

'You keep out of this,' Benny warned it graciously. She turned to the Doctor, a question forming on her lips. 'What about Ace? Is she here?'

'Yes. She's . . . faint. Fading. I can't fix on her properly. There's something else. Something much stronger than us, swamping us.'

Gabriel and Tanith, Benny considered. They were bound to be out in the city somewhere, loitering with intent. They seemed vague and ambiguous in her memory, as if they were something she had once dreamed. Ace, on the other hand, was stark and vivid but Benny could barely remember the last time she'd seen her, or the last words she had spoken. They'd parted too abruptly.

The Doctor let out a quick gasp. Benny looked up wildly, torn from her thoughts.

'It's *not*!' he pronounced. 'It's not Gabriel or Tanith. It's much *bigger*. A multiplicity of selves and souls. Many and one. It's beautiful. I don't think I've ever seen any-thing quite so . . . oh!'

The Doctor howled and leapt back from the tetra-hedron. Concerned, Benny rushed forward to steady him. In the light of the tetrahedron his face was blanched. She imagined she caught a glimpse of fear, of revulsion, of apprehension, of admiration, almost of love. And guilt. Intense, fascinating guilt. Something inside her jarred.

'What did you see?' she asked. She expected his reply to come slowly and weak. Instead his voice was strong and forceful. Almost too strident for the Doctor. She guessed he was trying to hide something. There was a dangerous quality to this lucidity.

Par for the course, she supposed.

'Patterns,' he said calmly. 'The pattern underlying everything. It's like a kaleidoscope. You and I, Ace and Truman, Gabriel and Tanith, Page and Winterdawn, and ... and Cranleigh. Enough, maybe ... I never thought murder could seem so beautiful.'

'Doctor!' Benny squawked, wondering if some spring had finally snapped in the workings of his mind.

'I'm sorry. I saw something that disturbed me,' the Doctor apologized. His words came tumbling now, like stream-water splashing down a hillside. 'And that's rare. I saw a connection, clear and bold in my mind. It had always been there and I was too stupid to see it. *Gabriel* and *Tanith*! I know them now.'

'Well that's nice,' Benny judged. 'There's also this small question of stopping them ...'

The Doctor placed a soft, warm hand on her shoulder. He was smiling benevolently. Benny wasn't fooled for an instant.

'I think we can be afford to be obvious.'

'You stopped being obvious a long time ago ...' Benny hummed wearily.

'Gabriel and Tanith have destroyed Cathedral,' the Doctor continued. 'But its structure remains intact. I think they're waiting to seize that, to step into the places occupied by the Mandelbrot Set. Imagine what they could do then. No, there's a simpler question: imagine what they couldn't do. They'll take the universe apart. Nothing will *mean* anything. And I like things to have meanings.'

That sounded simple enough.

'So, we field our own candidate for the job?' Benny suggested. The Doctor nodded. Benny let her eyebrows dance questioningly.

'What we need,' the Doctor explained, 'is someone experienced, someone with a thorough understanding of the way this city works, someone with a head for the

heights of power, someone utterly ruthless and determined, someone with a noble countenance.'

'Who's the lucky candidate then?' Benny asked, feeling
revitalized enough to try some dishonest sarcasm.

The Doctor smiled like the devil. He patted the immobile Mandelbrot head on its prominent nose. Benny
regarded it with disgust.

'Finally, you agree. Finally, you accept,' the head twit-
tered with renewed arrogance.

'Doctor...!' Benny began, bristling with anger and
resentment. She'd told the Doctor what the Mandelbrot
Set had done, how they'd run the city, how they'd sent
the grey man to die for them and then torn themselves
apart in the ensuing panic. Hadn't he listened?

'I'm not saying it's a perfect solution,' the Doctor
shushed her. He continued, and the distaste in Benny's
mouth was matched in his voice: 'With our candidate here
installed in power, I imagine Cathedral will declare total
war on Gabriel and Tanith and they'll destroy each other
in the minimum time with the maximum effort. That's the
way these things tend to work out.'

The head roared, its mouth swinging open and closed
in rapid succession, crushing the flowers too slow to react.

'Conflict swift and vivid! Victorious we will be! Gabriel
and Tanith will be crushed from their lives! *Our eyes have
seen the glory*!'

Its face was unmoving but Benny seemed to see it
glowing with proud energy. She made her own face flat
and contemptuous in response.

'I know how you feel,' the Doctor whispered reassuringly. 'But it's better this than Gabriel and Tanith.'

Benny stared at the jubilant head and wondered if that
was right.

'Carry us!' the head crowed. 'Carry us to our Cruakh,
to our throne. Carry us, King of Kings! Carry us! Carry
us!'

Benny took a weary step forward. The Doctor seized
her by the shoulders and flung her aside. She landed hard
against her side on a pile of rubble, the Doctor's modest

bulk crashing down beside her. Her head spun round wildly, in time to see the stone head, last of the Mandelbrot Set, King of Kings, vanishing in a fireball. Its voice soared with the flames, then died. A shower of pebbles fell across the square, one glancing sharply off of Benny's scalp.

A few scattered stones remained to mark its passing.

Jane Page stood on top of a mound of debris on the edge of the square. An old towel was draped reverently round her shoulders. A handkerchief covered her face – stigmata blossoming on the fabric over her eyes. Slung on her shoulder was a rocket-launcher, its tube daubed with Cathedral symbols. Benny guessed that it had been abandoned by the city militia during the fighting.

'Death to all kings!' Page shouted, voice reverberating off the distant buildings. She hurled the weapon aside and pulled a gun from within the folds of her jacket. It was more compact than the rocket-launcher but Benny found it no more reassuring.

'History is bunk,' Page declaimed. 'Burn everything! No one gets out of here alive!' She descended from her mound and began to pace towards them.

'It's a time for new learning,' she announced stridently. 'Practical learning, of what is real and what is myth. There's no time for abstraction, and no place for professors or doctors.'

Benny began to move aside cautiously. The Doctor placed a restraining hand on her shoulder. She rounded on him, whispering harshly.

'Doctor, she's blinder and madder than a bat that thinks it's Napoleon. I'm getting out of here before she starts shooting.'

'No,' the Doctor said calmly. 'We're responsible for her.'

Benny frowned.

'Don't think I don't know where you are,' Page called. She was moving closer, pacing towards them with even strides. 'I can't see you, but I know. They taught me how to use my hands and ears. They . . .' she trailed off. When she began again her voice was laced with sadness and quiet thought. 'It's funny. I have to kill you and I thought you were both already dead.'

'You don't have to kill us,' the Doctor said sweetly. 'Unless you believe Gabriel and Tanith.'

'That's right,' Benny added. Page was close to her, almost in touching distance. 'You've more in common with us than them, surely.'

'Oh yes,' Page said. Her voice had become weary and wistful. She slipped forward and placed a hand against Bernice's face. It was warm and smooth, fingers trembling, memorizing the details of the face. Benny didn't flinch, surprising herself. 'I'll tell you. I don't want to kill anyone. I never did. None of us did, none of us who really believed.'

'You don't want to kill people?' Page's hand still played across Benny's face but she felt secure enough to manage a few cheery words. 'I imagine that's a drawback in your line of work.'

'Please,' Page murmured. 'No, we wanted to build a better world. But the people are shackled by their false beliefs. Even Marx recognized that. You know, the flower on the chains?'

'Not personally.'

'We realized that we would have to destroy the idea that there is anything special or unique inside people. We had to kill their souls. Maybe there's a clean way to do that, an easy way to suppress all the rubbish. That was our dream.'

'A dream to some . . .' the Doctor said, distantly.

Page smiled. Her teeth seemed as lonely as ice.

'We had to do it somehow!' She blurted the words. 'There's only one really effective way of killing someone's soul.'

Her lips trembled into a wistful smile. Her other hand rose to meet Benny's face, her gun lodged tight in her small fingers. Benny was suddenly and sharply afraid. Her eyes focused into the barrel.

'You don't know how happy this makes me feel,' Page said softly.

The Doctor appeared by Page's side. Benny saw his shape as a blur in the corner of her eyes but paid him little attention. Her world had grown tight. The Doctor, on its edge, seemed less important than death.

In a smooth, casual motion he seized Page by the shoulders and tipped her over. There was a gunshot, distantly. Reality – what was left of it – slipped back before Benny's eyes.

Page was on the ground, stunned. The Doctor crouched beside her, his hands pressed against his knee, blood seeping between his fingers. The pain on his face was vivid.

'Jesus!' Benny pronounced, darting forward. The Doctor waved her back.

'A graze,' he insisted in a heavy voice. 'We have to go, she'll be coming round soon.'

Benny ignored his frantic gestures and stepped closer, slipping a hand round his shoulders and helping him to his feet.

'We're lost, aren't we?' she murmured, glancing at his wounded knee and seeing that his diagnosis was accurate. 'Everything's falling apart.'

The Doctor shook his head grimly. With Benny's help he began a slow hobble towards the edge of the square.

'We try another approach,' he suggested. 'There's a better solution, one more final. It's not one I'm keen on.'

'Why not?'

'Because I'm scared of the truth,' he said. He glanced over his shoulder and turned back, speaking more urgently. 'We have to find Cranleigh. And quickly, she's starting to come round.'

By the time Ace reached the ground her exhilaration had given way to a heavy sense of foreboding. On the roof she had been close to the sky, she could see across the city and felt free. Once her feet touched the earth, she had become shackled. The city was tight around her. She no longer had any way of gauging where she was or where she was going. The streets and alleys were endless and meandering, the buildings close and distracting. She slipped through the city, trying to keep track of herself in her mind, trying to move ever closer to the square where she had seen the TARDIS.

The city came in short bursts around her. She caught fragments of architecture, of signs and symbols, of shapes in the distance, but no movement, no sound. There was diversity here but it was sterile. She lost interest in what the city had to offer, preferring to concentrate on her own ends. The variety gradually become numb. Even the occasional bonfires of corpses slowly lost their morbid sting. She tried to ignore them, finding it disturbingly easy.

She turned a corner. A figure, robed and masked, loomed before her, covering her with a revolver. She tumbled aside instinctively before relaxing. The figure was as dead as anything in the city. He was held upright by a rope tied to a lamp-post and strung round his neck. The gun swayed as his arm swayed as his body swayed on its makeshift gallows.

'Oh Christ,' Ace pronounced, frustration welling inside her. It was not the bodies or the death that disturbed her, it was the tragedy, the injustice. This city had risen up and slaughtered itself. There was no telling why. The only expression she saw was death.

'What did you do?' she asked the corpse, as she prised the gun from his stiff fingers. It was an old-fashioned military revolver. She checked the chambers. Six bullets. Shrugging off the sensation of distaste, she pushed the gun into her belt and moved on, leaving the corpse swaying pendulously.

After that nothing seemed to touch her. The city flowed by. She ignored it and it ignored her.

It opened into a square. The TARDIS sat on the far side. Ace stopped, regarding it without emotion. She had spent so long searching for it and it hardly seemed worth the effort. The Doctor wasn't here. Benny wasn't here. She was beginning to doubt that they were alive at all.

Still, here was the TARDIS. It was better than nothing. She moved across the square towards it, trotting round the chasms, avoiding the bodies and bounding over the rubble.

She stopped, listening. From nearby, she caught sounds. The crash of water, screams of delight and excitement. Innocent sounds. She turned towards them, half-suspicious, half-fascinated, searching for their source.

She climbed a mound of rubble and found herself overlooking an expanse of water. It was almost a lake, settled in a depression that had opened in the square. The water was an unhealthy shade, choked with black plants.

Gabriel and Tanith were paddling in the stagnant pool, jumping and kicking and splashing to make ripples and waves. They had their backs turned to her, seemingly preoccupied with their fun. They laughed frequently – long and healthy giggles and squeals of happiness. Ace watched them with a bitter eye, waiting for the moment to break. Her hand hovered around her gun.

Gabriel and Tanith were dressed as if this was the seaside. Their clothes were strewn casually along the shore, swapped for brief and colourful swimwear. Ace cast round, half-expecting to see deck-chairs, beach-balls, wind-breaks and ice-cream-wielding tourists bursting out of nowhere to fill the desolation. The city remained drab and bleak and for a moment Ace found herself preferring it that way. She turned back to Gabriel and Tanith, wondering whether their incongruous behaviour and clothes were just another obscure weapon they were using against her.

They were displaying themselves, Ace realized. Their beachwear was incongruous because it *meant* nothing to them. It wasn't part of their style, simply something they happened to be wearing. They were showing off their bodies – their wonderful, custom-built, desirable bodies – flesh sculptures built from corpses. Gabriel was so sexy it hurt to watch him, Tanith had a body worth killing for (*she* had *killed for it*). Ace felt them pull at her emotions, jerking them to their whims and desires. She felt her body grow tight, hating them for manipulating her so casually, hating herself for enjoying the manipulation so much.

Her palm pressed against her gun, learning its shape.

'You two have got *severe* body fascism!' Ace howled at them.

They turned. They stared at her. Ace bit into her lower lip, feeling her body loosen and shake. They had snared her and she was lost.

'Only perfect people,' Gabriel said blandly, 'should do perfect things.'

'Of course,' Tanith added. 'Perfection comes in infinite packages. But we like this brand best.'

They turned to each other, pulled their bodies together, became one body, and kissed. Ace watched all the gory details, sneering.

'You're sick,' she called when the scene became unbearable. Tanith broke the kiss, broke the embrace.

'If you've not got anything constructive to say then kindly go and boil your head and let other people get on with their lives.'

Gabriel shushed her, pressing a forefinger to his sister's lips. It lingered there and Ace felt her insides churn with disgust, and perhaps a little frustration. She trotted down the slope to the shore, cautious of getting too close but anxious not to lose her grip. Her hand still danced round her gun, wondering how it might be put to most constructive use.

'We could make you perfect,' Gabriel said suddenly. Ace looked up, realizing he was addressing her.

'You're too late,' she said grinning. 'I beat you to it. I *made* me perfect. I made myself Ace!' She quite liked that one.

Gabriel and Tanith wore patronizing smiles. They began to wade towards the shore, water glistening off their unblemished flesh and finely set muscles, the grim light catching their eyes and smiles. Tanith shook her head slowly and a fan of loose droplets opened around her. Ace squeezed her forearms defensively, wondering why this seemed so familiar.

Gabriel and Tanith met her at the water's edge. They seemed vividly real and colourful now, larger than life, dominating the drab square. Ace could smell tight damp skin and feel the close warmth of their bodies. They were overpowering her with their selves.

'We are going to make a new world,' they said together in a single, melodious tone, 'a world of fragments and bridges, of infinite experience and eternal delight. It will be our world and you can share it with us.'

'You can have a palace,' Tanith whispered seductively, 'a shining pearl of a building with turrets and spires and flags and everything. To keep you company we will fill its halls and passages with an army composed entirely of stereotypes, or amusingly anthropomorphic furniture, or anyone you desire.'

Ace shuddered, not so much at the nature of the vision, but the allure with which Tanith spelt it out.

'What about the Doctor,' she asked, clinging to reality, 'and Benny?'

'A room of your own, Benny next door and Doctor makes three? Don't be so obvious. They're squalid people. They won't want to be perfect!'

They took her arms. Confused, she didn't resist. She allowed them to lead her into the heart of the pool. The water lapped round her waist, clinging to her clothes and staining them grey. Her legs grew sodden, heavy, uncomfortable. She didn't let it concern her, keeping her attention fixed on Gabriel and Tanith.

Tanith stood behind her, hands clasping at her forearms in a manner that was either friendly and reassuring, or designed to restrain her should she make a break for it. Possibly both. Gabriel stood in front of her, hands pressed against her thighs, warm eyes smiling down on her from what seemed like an impossibly distant height. Ace felt small in his shadow, crushed between their two bodies.

Their hands were warm and wet. That was the most disturbing part.

'We will show you something,' Gabriel hummed. 'If you are ever lonely we will take you out on a dry, baked plain. We will walk for hours and chat about our feelings and memories, and we will come to a great overhanging rock.

And we will take you into the shade of that rock, where we can be together for hours or days or weeks or years, forever. Doesn't that sound like perfection, peace, freedom?

'There's a price,' he warned. 'Perfection costs.'

'It's not much though,' Tanith reassured her. 'Only a little thing.'

'Yeah? What?'

Gabriel and Tanith smiled. They spoke in unison.

'We want you to *like* us.'

Ace considered. Gabriel's face loomed over her, smiling benevolently, warm and caring, framed against the sky. At that moment it could have been the face of God smiling down on creation from a crack in an impenetrable cloud. His hands were tight at her hips and his promise seemed strange and attractive in Ace's ears.

She grinned viciously and spat into Gabriel's eye.

'That's a no,' she added.

Gabriel and Tanith howled and tipped her up into the water.

She felt herself fall, the hard impact of her body with the pool's surface, the sudden dragging, the dirt-water clinging to the exposed skin of her face and her hands. Dreamlike, unreal sensations. It was only when she was fully submerged and her eyes began to flood with wet greyness that she realized what had happened. It came in a short self-conscious burst. It was happening now, not in some distant memory. It was happening to her.

This wasn't an unfamiliar experience. The water was still and brackish and she was cautious not to swallow, but she didn't panic. She shoved at the ground with her feet, kicking herself up. Her head burst back above the surface and she caught her breath.

Gabriel and Tanith grabbed her by the shoulders and pushed her back under. Again there was the shock of coldness and dampness and water flooding into her ears, deafening the world. Gabriel and Tanith's voices reached her ears, muffled. Their hands still pressed down against her shoulders. One pushed her neck down, holding her head under the surface. She thrashed with her arms and legs, flailing at random. She kicked herself upwards. The couple's grip remained firm.

How much air did she have? Enough to last a couple of minutes. It depended on how long Gabriel and Tanith planned to keep her there.

After a couple of minutes their hands remained clutched round her. Ace's world had become dizzy and came in short bursts between blackness. She would have panicked but her lungs were empty and her energy at a low ebb and Gabriel and Tanith weren't letting go.

Two thoughts came quickly. *Don't swallow the water* and *Don't pass out*.

She let her mouth open and fill. The world slipped away.

18

The World, the Flesh and the Devil

I am a quantum physicist. I deny what I see.

Winterdawn sat with his back to the window, unprepared to move. With his legs limp and useless he was incapable of rising from his chair, but he was also stilled by fear. He didn't want to turn and catch a glimpse of the place which had eaten his home.

He distracted himself by reading. There was a book within reach, a miraculous survivor of the bibliocide he had wreaked on the room. C. Moore Wedderburn's *The Trail of the Black Orchid: A botanical and zoological guide to the journeys of George Cranleigh*, inspired by the author's own expeditions. Winterdawn had never bothered to read beyond the subtitle before, and now he regarded with some guilt his feeble pretence that he had. Wedderburn was dead now, and the dead deserved a little honesty.

As he read, he wondered if there was any family connection between Justin and Wedderburn's historical anti-hero. He doubted that Justin would ever admit to it.

Sandra had tried to write a novel once, before the inconsistency of her sight defeated her. He'd read scraps of it without her knowledge and had been a little shocked to find it full of elaborately deployed sexual descriptions. Sandra had never finished it. Maybe if he'd been more supportive she would have. Then maybe her death wouldn't have been so total. Even Wedderburn's dead words – dead criticisms of a dead man – were a snatch at immortality.

333

Winterdawn no longer feared death, though he sensed it was close. He welcomed it cautiously, wanting to be forgotten.

The door opened. He looked up, expecting to see Cranleigh returned from his exploration. He was wrong. It was a woman dressed in black. Her face was concealed behind a blood-stained blindfold and she fondled a stubby, ugly pistol carefully. Winterdawn didn't know her at all. The woman's head shook randomly as if feeling the shape of the room from behind her mask.

'I'm looking for the Doctor and Summerfield,' she said coolly.

'Who are you?' Winterdawn croaked. 'What are you doing in my house?'

The woman turned towards him, alerted by the sound of his voice.

'My name is . . . No, *no*, call me Jane Pain. Page. I am an instrument of justice. A killer, assassin, alive. Your house? You're . . . Winterdawn?'

Winterdawn couldn't bring himself to reply. The woman's lips curled.

'Winterdawn,' she gasped. 'At last.'

She danced forward and lashed out, her blow bouncing against the side of his head. Winterdawn reeled, pain singing inside his skull. The woman wrenched him from his chair, dashing him to the floor. Wedderburn's book fell to one side, abandoned, unfinished. The woman slipped onto one knee, raising her gun so that Winterdawn could see into the barrel. He felt and understood nothing. This didn't seem real, it couldn't *be* real.

'Am I aiming at you?' the woman asked. Winterdawn nodded slowly, waiting for the end – almost excited by the prospect. He kept nodding, before realization dawned and he broke into a stupid, final giggle.

'Jane Page?'

It was one voice and a thousand. Each was slurred. The voices came from multiple mouths on a proliferation of heads that sprouted on the surface of Justin Cranleigh's body. He no longer resembled anything human. His flesh was viscous and shifting, creeping like liquid, never still. He lingered in the doorway, skin seething and melting and moulding into new forms.

'We're dying!' The creature's heads grew twisted from its neck, easing towards the woman.

'Good,' Page said coldly, quietly. 'You deserve it.'

'Perhaps.' Mouths rippled and burst from interlocked faces. 'But who are you to say that? You just love being able to dictate who lives and who dies.' Cranleigh oozed closer. Page half-turned, inching her gun round to train on the closest of the unstable faces.

Winterdawn was so close, it was so clear. He had a perfect view of Page's tightening, closing finger. He heard the shot echo. He saw the foremost of Cranleigh's heads collapse into itself.

'Don't bother.' Another of Cranleigh's faces blossomed out of the demolished head. 'His nervous system's gone. You owe for the flesh. Join us.'

Page fired again. Again. Again. Wounds opened in the fluid surface of the shape. Again.

The gun fell silent. The disgust that shook on Page's lips became fear. Cranleigh's shadow fell over her. New inflexions rose up on the surface of his skin, flowing around Page, smothering and absorbing her.

There was no sound. No screaming. No thrashing. Winterdawn watched, unable to help himself. It was fascinating. It was beautiful. When Cranleigh pulled away, Page was gone. Her coat hung across the front of the flesh-form, and there was a long red smear on the carpet.

And it seemed to Winterdawn that Cranleigh was larger than before.

Mouths opened on the surface of his skin, howling in one voice:

'Unclean!'

Page's voice.

Winterdawn coughed violently, forcing sickness from his mouth. Thick dollops of blood came with it, hitting the floor in Rorschach patterns. Winterdawn stared at the mess he had made, trying to make sense of it. It didn't seem to fit the world. There were no answers – just fragments of death and bile scattered without meaning, without hope of interpretation, without hope of redemption. He felt *useless*.

Someone was beside him, hugging him gently, raising him back into his chair. For a moment he thought it was Jenny or Sandra, and for that moment they lived in his mind. When he looked, he found it was the Doctor's friend, Bernice. He recalled that she was supposed to be dead, and felt a little melancholy reassurance.

'We saw what happened,' she said quietly. Winterdawn saw the Doctor over her shoulder. 'Cranleigh's going to have trouble. Page isn't a good mixer. I expect she was the sort of girl who cried at her own birthday parties.'

Winterdawn tried a weak smile. It hurt.

'The Doctor seems to think he can stop Gabriel and Tanith,' Bernice continued blithely. 'He's the patron saint of lost causes.'

'Good luck to him,' Winterdawn whispered. 'How can I help?'

'Don't worry about it.' Bernice shook her head and smiled again. 'We don't need your help. You can be safe. You don't have to do anything.'

Winterdawn had been patronized too frequently to take offence, but there was something about this calm dismissal that *irritated* him. Bernice was smiling at him and telling him he was useless. He was an old man with no legs who had to be bundled into a corner out of harm's way. He resented that. Her smile, her words confirmed everything that Winterdawn felt he knew. But his body was weak and battered and he was in no position to resist. He resented that too. He sank back wearily.

'It's you we need,' the Doctor was saying, addressing the untamed and daring mass that had been Cranleigh. 'All of you. I need a favour.'

'What do you want?' the multiple voices sang.

'I want you to die for my sins.'

* * *

336

A siren blared across Cathedral. It filled the air with ugly noise, with sterile muzak, the last discord of the city.

The Doctor and Benny heard it. Benny's teeth shook in accompaniment to the howl. The Doctor's expression became dangerous.

Gabriel and Tanith heard it and grinned like wolves. They dried themselves with their thoughts and dressed for the occasion. They prepared props: a knife taken from Bernice, a gun from Ace, a half-conscious body lying on the water's edge.

Ace half-heard it in her drowned delirium. She dreamed of Gabriel and Tanith and the world they would make for her. The siren added a welcome sour note. Ace grumbled and moved closer to wakefulness. Soon Gabriel and Tanith would kick her awake, but she had this moment to herself.

Cathedral heard, and understood, and waited.

The Cruakh had collapsed as the city died. What had been the highest tower in Cathedral had sunk into itself, caving inwards and downwards until it was no more than a stump, rotten inside. The siren hummed off its walls. Benny recalled the endless walk she'd taken to the top of the tower with the grey man. This looked much less daunting and – now she had legs to worry about – much easier exercise. It was the shaking that worried her.

'Don't worry,' the Doctor said blithely. 'It will collapse, but not until it's finished. When it collapses it will be the end.'

'So,' Benny grinned, 'we're going to bring the house down, are we? I'm sorry, I couldn't resist that . . .'

'We'd be worse off without your sense of humour, Benny,' the Doctor replied obliquely. Benny frowned, wondering frantically if she'd missed his sarcasm, wondering until she itched with paranoia.

'They're coming,' the Doctor said abruptly.

There was movement in the gloom. Shining white shapes moving.

'Please,' the Doctor said quietly, 'whatever they do, be calm. I wouldn't ask if it wasn't important.'

337

Benny nodded responsibly.

The shining shapes stepped from the darkness and became solid – Gabriel and Tanith dressed in suits so immaculately white they glowed. Their hands and their faces, so vibrantly fleshy, were drab by contrast. Their movements were translated into flickering white light. They were never still, as if stillness could trap them.

Ace walked before them, her hair matted and damp, her expression sullen and single-minded. Gabriel held a knife at her throat – the same knife, Benny realized as they moved closer, that Cranleigh had once used to threaten her. Tanith had a revolver, swinging from the back of Ace's head to the Doctor, to Benny, and back to Ace.

They were props. Gabriel and Tanith didn't need guns and knives. This flaunting of weapons was derisive, a facetious gesture of strength.

Ace looked aggressive but defeated. There were bruises on her cheek. Benny struggled to keep her anger in control.

'Is this it?' Gabriel pronounced. 'The whole gang together?'

'Isn't it great!' Tanith enthused. 'The greatest show ever performed!'

'It starts tonight! Near you, everywhere!'

'This one will run and run, forever!'

'The Cabaret Physical!' they screamed together, voices chiming and swaying against the single monotone of the city siren.

'Feel free to join us.' Tanith offered them a grin wide enough to swallow the city. Benny's eyes flicked coldly from her face, to Gabriel's, to Ace's sharp features. Beside her the Doctor trembled and stepped forward. Benny felt her legs move, she slipped in alongside them.

'We're glad you could make it,' Gabriel told them. The Doctor smiled sickeningly. Benny flattened the feeling in her stomach and said nothing.

'Are you all right Ace?' the Doctor asked slowly, self-consciously.

'She's fine. We had to pump her stomach out but she's right as rain now, and really looking forward to the fun.'

The Doctor ignored Gabriel and Tanith, cocking his head towards Ace.

'I'm alive,' she replied. Benny sensed suppressed danger in her voice.

They moved. Ace went first, the knife at her throat, the gun at her back, the Doctor and Benny flanking her. Gabriel and Tanith followed, suits gleaming like beacons in the night. Together they climbed the Cruakh tower. It was not as easy on the feet as Benny had hoped. This time the company was less polite, though hardly less interesting.

The Cruakh chamber was changed. The darkness lent it a greater dignity and obscured the more disturbing decorations. Better yet, none of the Mandelbrot Set remained. Benny had been afraid that some might have hidden while the others destroyed themselves, but she realized that none would have had the imagination. Their absence was pleasing to eye and ear. What had seemed gaudy the first time around now seemed austere.

But not pleasant, she realized, biting her tongue.

Someone, somehow, had erected a seat in the chamber, in the shadows. It was a minimal metal frame with a plastic back and seat. Axles stuck out of either side, seeming small and forlorn without wheels attached. Instead the throne had been raised on a pile of bricks. A few Gothic ornaments aspired vainly to disguise its true shape.

'That's it,' Tanith said without reverence. 'It's a symbol, important when you know what it means, what's attached to it.'

'It means Cathedral, it means everything,' Gabriel added. 'And it's ours to take. The only catch is who's going to have to sit on whose lap.'

'It's not yours by right,' the Doctor suggested, mutedly.

'It's not anyone's,' Gabriel continued smoothly. 'There is no right.'

'All power, by definition, is abuse,' Tanith added. 'And abuse is something we're very happy with.'

She was smiling, her face broken by a triumphant grin that was almost innocent and almost content. Gabriel wore a similar smile. Benny stared from face to face expecting them to say something, to act, to effect their triumph. They didn't, they stood immobile, watching their throne. Only after a long, lazy silence did Benny begin to feel that something was wrong.

The Doctor was gripping her arm, squeezing quite tight. His breathing became loud and grating. She glanced at him, seeing his attention fixed on the chair. She turned, not certain of what to expect.

Professor Winterdawn was sitting on the throne, his face obscure in the shadows.

'Jeremy,' the Doctor said softly, moving forward.

'Quiet,' Winterdawn snapped. The Doctor froze.

'It's funny,' Winterdawn continued, his voice wavering between hard certainty and fear. 'I never liked this chair. I always used to think it trapped me. I never imagined that anyone could see it as a symbol of power. Funny.'

'Excuse me,' Gabriel purred. 'You wouldn't mind moving . . .'

'I can't move,' Winterdawn retorted. 'It was never the chair that was the problem. It was my legs. They were dead. End of story. I wanted to change the world. I can sit here and change anything I like. *Anything*.

'But I'm not going to. You want to take the world apart. You want to throw away everything, tear down the icons and the temples and install nothing in their places!'

His hands came together, clapping slowly, loudly, deliberately.

'Bravo! I wanted my children to take after me, and you have learned. But you'll get this chair over my dead body, because your new world sounds so very much like the old one. You're spiteful, you're ignorant, you act for your own gratification and *then* . . .! Then you try and tell me that your leadership is going to be *different* from anything before.

'I love my children. I loved my daughter and you killed her,' he said simply, finally. 'You killed her.'

340

Tears began to burn down his cheeks, but he made no sound. Benny flinched, trying very hard to keep calm, trying very hard not to turn on Gabriel and Tanith and scream with hate. Winterdawn's words had touched her, teaching her a new level of frustration.

'Yes,' Gabriel replied languidly. 'We killed her. We enjoyed it. The rending of flesh, the spilling of blood, the screaming and the despair. She wanted to live, we disapproved.'

'But,' Tanith took up the theme, 'amidst the horror and the gore, the true instant of elegance was that moment when she *knew* she would die. She pleaded. She offered us so much. We were tempted . . . but we had to experience the ecstasy of murder.'

'And it is *ecstasy*!' Gabriel declaimed, hurling his arms wide, almost slicing off Ace's ear with his knife (Ace took it without comment). 'Transfiguration! Ascension! *Rapture*! Of the five people you see before you there isn't one who can honestly say that they don't know that to be true.'

'Actually . . .' Benny protested. She was interrupted by Tanith.

'Four out of five,' she said smoothly. 'Bernice prefers alcohol and orgasms. She doesn't know what she's missing.'

'Why did you kill Sandra?' Winterdawn said. Benny followed his voice closely, hoping it stood for something saner and kinder than Gabriel and Tanith.

'That's exactly what she wanted to know. And you know what? We couldn't remember then either.'

He laughed stupidly. Tanith joined in.

'You don't think what you do means anything,' Winterdawn purred. 'You're *stupid* people, so I'm going to give you something, something for you to keep and remember.'

'A present?' Gabriel asked, with little enthusiasm. 'Goody.'

'I'll show you.' Winterdawn's mouth made itself a slight smile, ominous, humourless. He stood up. He steadied himself, swaying slightly but displaying little difficulty.

That came when he spoke, when his voice forced itself in thin bursts between hard breaths.

'Anything ... you can do ... I ... can do ... better!'

Pain slipped up his face, fixing his mouth, his eyes, his brow. He gasped. He fell forward onto the cold floor. He lay still.

Benny dropped onto her knees beside him. She reached for his pulse. It throbbed quickly at his wrist, then deadened into stillness.

'He's dead,' she said. 'His heart's stopped.'

She saw the Doctor hide his face behind his hands. She saw Ace turn brusquely on the couple beside her.

'You killed him!' Ace said, her tone accusing but bereft of anger.

'No.' Tanith shook her head. 'He managed that all by himself.'

The silence lingered. The stillness lingered. Death stifled the chamber, emptying it of even the grimmest humour. Something sullen and depressed had entered the faces and bodies of the assembled company. Even Gabriel and Tanith seemed unprepared to move and spoil the effect. Benny stayed crouched beside Winterdawn's body, staring at the dead man's face. His expression conveyed a sense of satisfaction. Or rigor mortis.

It was the Doctor who moved first, who spoke first. Smoothly he disturbed Death, making sacrilege seem easy. He strolled to stand by Benny, looking down on Winterdawn's corpse. Benny glanced upwards and saw bitterness in his eyes.

'He should have stayed where he was,' he said softly. 'He would have been safe. He didn't have to do this.'

Benny shrugged.

'Maybe he did,' she suggested. The Doctor frowned, and offered her a hand. She rose without his help. His hand, outstretched and empty, was small in the darkness. Benny felt guilty for ignoring it.

The Doctor stepped away, approaching the throne that Winterdawn had vacated. He grasped the arm-rests, stroking and squeezing the fabric as if trying to push his fingers

342

through to the brittle metal frame beneath. He pulled away abruptly, turning with equal sharpness and sinking into a squat beside the chair. His fingers formed an accusative point, stabbing at Gabriel and Tanith.

'*Who* are you?' he said, his voice cold and loud. Gabriel and Tanith shuffled. They seemed more embarrassed than afraid.

'We're us,' they said together. 'We're free. We're wonderful.'

'You want to sit here?' The Doctor indicated the chair curtly.

'Oh bloody hell!' Tanith moaned. 'Haven't you been paying attention?'

'Is that a yes?' The Doctor's face was flat but his eyes were alive and fiery. His pupils were sky-dark, sparkling with cruelty.

'Yes,' Gabriel insisted languidly. The Doctor's disgust wasn't touching them, Benny thought. Maybe it was boring them.

'Nothing can stop you?' The Doctor smiled mischievously. If anything his lightness disturbed Benny more than his anger.

'Nothing,' they retorted proudly.

'If I asked you,' the Doctor spoke again, his voice coming in slow chunks, 'would you relinquish your claim on this throne?'

Their heads shook deliberately. The Doctor smiled slightly and sprang to his feet.

'You're not free,' he said, his sprightly energy returning. 'If you can't say no, you're not free.' Gabriel and Tanith blinked, perhaps confused. Bernice allowed herself a smile at their expense. She looked down at Winterdawn's dead face. His lips were twisted and his skin was turning cold-grey, so that he seemed to be wearing a ghoulish smile, as if even death couldn't prevent him from following events.

Gabriel and Tanith pushed past her, trampling over the corpse to reach the Doctor.

'There's a wound in your knee,' Tanith said.

'It bursts,' Gabriel continued. 'It bleeds. It bubbles.'

343

The Doctor sank, clutching his leg, and Benny felt a stab of sympathetic pain. Gabriel kicked at him. A portion of darkness flowed round his leg and held it tight. A flicker disturbed Gabriel's perfect features, half-surprise, half-irritation.

The darkness grew. It gained form, structure, colour, texture. It became flesh. It became human. It became Cranleigh. It became almost-Cranleigh. He was naked and Benny could see the way his skin seethed and rippled. He had gained height – his body seeming stretched and elongated but far too *full* to appear thin. There was too much flesh to fit into Cranleigh. It was in danger of over-flowing, of spilling out of his frame. When he spoke, it was a babble of voices. Benny recognized every one. They had killed her once.

'Please don't kick the Doctor,' they said. 'He means well.'

'We took your shape,' Tanith squeaked in protest. 'That's not fair! We took your structure!'

Cranleigh nodded, a grotesque smile growing on his sharpened features.

'We are the essence. We can make our form. We are whole, we learned.'

As if proof of this, Cranleigh's flesh swelled and burst. His body spilled into a profusion of new shapes – some human, some not. New bodies coming so fast they could hardly be seen, and it became impossible to tell where one shape ended and another began.

'Justin Cranleigh.' The Doctor had straightened up. Pain lingered in his voice, accompanied by wistful melancholy. 'I offer you a chance to nullify your selves, they who might have been, but weren't. Through Cathedral, through this chair, you could erase from the cosmos that core of pain which gave rise to your existences. I offer you peace. Sit here, and die. It's your choice.'

Cranleigh's flesh-form dance froze. The woman who might have been Jane Page stood by the chair, her naked body tapering as Cranleigh's had done. Her body rippled as though her essence was trying to break free from the body that constrained her. Her torso expanded and contracted in short, sudden bursts. She had eyes again, though these were balls of gristle.

'Page liked being alive,' she said in many voices. 'We all did.'

She shoved past Gabriel and Tanith and lowered herself onto the throne. Only then did her body harden into a single, permanent shape. Page's body seemed tiny between the arms of the chair. Her skin was pallid – colour seeping from it. Her smile was a corpse-grin, shared with Winterdawn.

Benny crept forward. Ace fell in at her side. The Doctor watched calmly, his face betraying no feeling. Gabriel and Tanith shuffled uneasily. Page's chest rose and fell, though this rhythm grew slow. A pentecost of chuckles fell from her mouth – each weak and breathless, together they drowned out the city's siren.

'What's she got to laugh about?' Ace pondered. 'She's dying.'

'*They're* dying,' Gabriel interrupted. 'They're killing themselves.'

'We'd done so much for them too.'

'They're healing the pain that made them,' the Doctor said simply. 'I have a confession.'

Bernice looked up, intrigued. Ace too turned. Gabriel and Tanith kept their heads lowered.

'Gabriel and Tanith were born of pain. Cosmic pain,' the Doctor said abruptly. He was forcing the words, as if they hurt him in a far deeper way than the graze on his leg. Benny recalled things he had said about guilt, about responsibility, about truth, and about fear.

He'd seen a pattern in Cathedral. He had refused to tell her about it.

The Doctor spoke slowly, because he was afraid of what he said, because it was true.

'It was Winterdawn's experiments with Cathedral that gave the pain a form of expression, sentience, as Gabriel and Tanith.'

They bowed graciously. The Doctor continued, his tone sour.

'Winterdawn took on guilt for you. He didn't deserve that, because he didn't create you, not even accidentally. If you're the wounds of the cosmos you pre-existed Winterdawn by a long, long time. I'm a Time Lord. When I looked into the tetrahedron and saw the patterns that created you I perceived more than a creature of any other race might.

'I travel in time. The mere fact of that is enough to erase hundreds of futures. Wherever I go I leave footprints, my testament. *There's* your pain – the scream of infinite futures erased from the cosmos. And through Cathedral, through Winterdawn, that scream gained life. Gabriel and Tanith.

'You were never Winterdawn's children were you? You were mine. Mine, and many others. You're my guilt, my responsibility, so I'm stopping you. Now.'

Something clicked in Benny's mind. She grinned wildly.

'Ah!' she exclaimed. 'So Cranleigh . . .'

'. . . is easing the pain,' the Doctor finished for her. His face was stern. He was not glaring at her though, but at Gabriel and Tanith who matched his stare with perverse smiles.

'When it dies,' he growled, 'it will take your identities, or at least your power. And that's justice. Come on – Ace, Benny. We're leaving.'

Ace's mouth opened, forming an aggressive shape with thin, wide lips and sharp teeth. The Doctor raised a finger to his lips, silencing her.

'They're finished. We can leave them. Let's go.'

Ace's face bristled with fury. Benny understood, but she felt nothing similar. Only aching, muted disappointment. Maybe the Doctor was right, maybe it was over. It didn't feel that way. She glanced at Gabriel and Tanith. They held themselves in slumped and wretched poses, but when they grinned back at her she saw little defeat in their attitude. Quite the opposite, in fact.

'Ah Doctor, there's no justice,' Tanith said graciously.

She reached into her gleaming white jacket and, with a theatrical flourish, removed the tetrahedron. It burned with a weak light, though its surface had become a corrupt black. 'You left this in the street. Litter bug.'

The Doctor frowned. Benny caught his unease.

'Dear me, you really don't listen, do you?' Gabriel's voice was sickly and smooth with triumph. He waved dismissively at the throne, at the shape that had been Page shimmering in its seat. 'All this is symbolism. It isn't real! Cranleigh's sitting there, he's got the structure of this place. But we never wanted that.'

'We want the power that's locked into the structure, the power that can tickle the universe.'

'We'll smash the frame, leech out the power and drink it all up ourselves. It comes to the same thing. And you come to a sticky end. Sorry.'

'I knew it wasn't over,' Ace muttered darkly. She leapt at them. Gabriel threw his body into her path, wrapping his arm smoothly round her neck. The knife blade shone in the tetrahedron-light, playing against her throat. She froze, her anger slipping again into motionless patience.

The light winked and died. The tetrahedron crumbled, becoming dust in Tanith's hand. She tipped it to one side, letting the dust slip to the floor. The beings in the throne seized tight and became dark and intangible.

Gabriel and Tanith smiled, teeth shining.

The throne sank into itself, metal framework jarring and intertwining.

The Cruakh juddered and shook. Benny's stomach rose and fell disconcertingly, her eyesight swayed and her feet gave way beneath her. A steady arm clamped round her waist, holding her tight until the floor grew firm. She muttered her thanks distantly.

She looked up and saw four faces staring at her. Tanith was pointing. Gabriel's arms were locked round Ace but he managed to aim a startled expression at her. No – not at *her*. Beside her. She half-turned to see.

The man at her side wore a long coat, a hat, dark glasses. He was in all respects grey, but it was a strange,

347

vivid shade – a grey composed of rainbow colours, a dense variety of tones, infinite hues.

'Excuse me. You're dead,' said Benny.

'We killed you,' Gabriel elaborated.

'No, you killed *me*,' said the man of many colours, the grey man.

Tanith threw her arms in the air, an assumed gesture of despair.

'Get out! This is our game and *you can't play*!'

The grey man paced towards her, a smile on his thin lips.

'You would have deconstructed the cosmos. That would've been ... interesting, but not to my taste. You can't divorce the art from the beliefs of its architects.

'We have met before and we have not. I love such obscurities.' He smiled broadly. Benny smiled too – no one else did. 'When I created the Cathedral for the Congregation of All Peoples, I put much of my power into it. And then I died. Cathedral survived and since it contained my essence, part of it became me. And then you killed me, and I was left without form, as energy infusing the city-structure. But you destroyed that too, because you thought it would be neutral, because you thought you could use it, because you didn't think that it might have an identity, or priorities of its own. Because ...

'You,' the grey man said, 'were wrong.'

Tanith looked at her brother and he looked back at her.

'Oh shit. Yeah,' she said. 'We never thought of that. Shit.'

Benny surveyed the gathering before her. The Doctor stood on the fringe of the chamber, his face calm and thoughtful as if he was sifting his way through the grey man's words to find the meaning. The light in his eyes was neither triumphant nor defeated. Tanith prowled warily round the grey man. *He* seemed relaxed, his shoulders slumped and his expression confident. Gabriel looked uncertain, introspective. He still held Ace tight in his grasp. For her part she remained inscrutable. Typical Ace.

Winterdawn was dead. He lay at the grey man's feet.

'Excuse me, please,' Benny chipped in, hearing her voice brimming not so much with confusion as with enthusiasm.

'Bernice, I'm glad to see you safe.' The man turned to her graciously. 'I apologize for the behaviour of the Mandelbrot Set after my death. I was in a poor position to help.'

'I cried,' Bernice mumbled, wondering whether she should feel betrayed and then wondering why she didn't. 'No, I'm sorry. I, er, is this over?'

'Oh yes.' The grey man nodded, removed his hat and bowed slightly. 'Gabriel and Tanith no longer feed from the world's pain. There is no other source forthcoming. They live now by force of will.'

'Like everyone else,' Tanith's voice was husky, horrified.

'There are some who'd envy you,' the Doctor told them. Tanith scowled and waved her revolver at him. Benny could see how crudely and desperately she moved.

'This hasn't changed anything,' Gabriel announced.

The grey man shook his head smartly.

'Oh it has. Now you face the world on its own terms.'

'Hey! Yeah.' Ace was smiling broadly, wickedly. 'Awright.'

She wrenched hard on Gabriel's arm, letting her head drop and her teeth sink into his hand. He gasped. The knife handle was clasped in his hand, but now there was a second, smaller hand clawing at it.

'Ace! No!' the Doctor was yelling, his voice bursting out like a wall of meaningless sound. He sprang forward. Tanith too was whirling, her gun spinning to find a target, her eyes darting like a frightened animal's. Benny felt a sudden sickness, a sudden panic. She saw the knife slip out of Gabriel's grip and slide into's Ace's. She saw the blade zig-zag before Gabriel's face.

There was a scream that seemed to emanate from everywhere, blending with the distant siren note. Gabriel's hands leapt to his face.

Ace weighed the knife in one bloody hand. Its blade was scarlet.

Three stabs in quick succession. Chest. Stomach. Groin. Spots of blood leapt into the air. Gabriel howled and his voice was desperately human.

Tanith's gun hand came up. There was a burst of sound and fire.

Ace threw the knife without blinking, then flinched, then clutched her shoulder, then balanced herself, then pursed her lips.

The knife touched Tanith's hand as it flew. The revolver leapt from her fingers, though there seemed to be little blood or pain. Tanith stared at her hand, then at the gun on the floor, then at Ace's determinedly satisfied expression. A thought ruffled her face. She turned and sprang for the exit, barrelling past the grey man at high speed.

Ace leapt, pouncing on the fallen revolver. She sprinted after Tanith.

'Ace.' The Doctor offered a quiet warning. Ace stopped in the door and looked back, her face expressing indifference. She slipped out of the Cruakh and away.

Gabriel stumbled, falling against Benny. His white suit and his white skin were turning a damp, sick pink and his fingers left a sticky red trail on Benny's face and chest. She closed her eyes and swallowed and waited until she felt his body sink to its knees, to the floor, to its death.

Dear Diary, You know I'm not the screaming, vomiting and fainting type but please bear with me in these testing times . . .

She started to laugh, which puzzled her because she had seen the crude tears across Gabriel's dead face and it hadn't been funny at all.

Someone took her by the hands and gently led her away. She opened her eyes and saw the Doctor, his face grim but sympathetic. The grey man was out of her sight, maybe tending to the corpse. She didn't want to think about it.

'Are you going after Ace?' she asked.

The Doctor's features seemed older and more pained than she remembered. He pressed a hand under his eyes, stroking his face. He was tired too.

'Yes,' he said wearily. 'She'll kill Tanith. If I tried to stop her, I'd fail, so I won't try.'

'That doesn't sound like you,' Benny told him, but she smiled in sympathy. He was still holding her hands and his skin was warm.

'I'm weak,' the Doctor said, and he smiled to prove it.

The grey man slipped unobtrusively into Benny's view, blending into his surroundings as if he had always been there. And, she realized, in a way he had. His forehead was furrowed and his lips pursed.

'Gabriel had a jewel, set in a ring,' he said. 'Now it's gone. How strange. Still, since I delight in loose ends I should be happy . . .'

'Gabriel and Tanith? Are they dead?' Benny asked.

'Dead in all the senses you would understand,' the grey man said. 'The pain that gave rise to them endures. It cannot end, so long as there is time travel. But so long as there is no Cathedral that pain cannot be expressed.' He sighed. 'It is an ending, though not a satisfactory one.

'Doctor, I was impressed by your solution. You perceived patterns which I did not. I may command time, yet it binds me and you are free. I brought you here because I believed Time Lords had the insight I lacked, a clarity of vision beyond me. But I suspect yours surpasses even that of your fellows.'

The Doctor snorted. He released Benny's hands and she felt instantly isolated.

'I have friends,' he said in a ground, dangerous voice, 'who in the past few days have been tortured and intimidated. I met a man whose home has been invaded, despoiled, destroyed. He's dead, his family is dead. And the people who did this are also dead. I'm not happy with what I've done. Everything you've said is . . . *perverse!*'

'Ah,' the grey man said. 'I'm sorry.'

'Sorry.' The Doctor's eyes were shadowed, turned away from the man's. 'Oh yes. I don't like being used. Not by you, not in your metaphysical war. I don't care what you do now, I'm going to find Ace.'

He turned and walked to the exit. Benny hung back, casting wistful glances between the two men. There was a tension between them, pushing them apart. Benny tasted the air – it was sharp and foul and upsetting. But she was too tired to raise much emotion over it.

'Doctor,' the grey man called. The Doctor stopped, turned back.

'I've . . . never been dishonest Doctor. I'd be happy if our paths never cross again,' the man said softly. He nodded to Bernice and frowned. 'Benny maybe, I'd count you as a friend, and remember you fondly . . . But it may be that my metaphysical war will force us together, as allies, as enemies, as something other.'

'I don't . . .' the Doctor blustered. The man silenced him with a smile.

'I have never deceived you, but you have allowed yourself to be deceived, in the past. Be careful Doctor, please. When you return to the TARDIS you will find it restored.' The Doctor turned brusquely, slipping through the door. The grey man called after him:

'And Doctor, thank you.'

The Doctor was gone. Benny glanced after him, then turned to the man. He squatted on the floor looking wretched and lonely.

'You two shouldn't be fighting, you know.'

'That is what I've been saying for a very long time,' the man said. He laughed gently. It was a beautiful sound, as cool as the first drops of rain to fall, as fresh as spring flowers, as young and as light as life. When the grey man had spoken, or laughed before, it had been false or forced. Not this time. Benny slipped to her knees beside him.

'What will you do now?' she whispered conspiratorially.

'I'll leave,' he said. 'The cosmos is large. I shall walk and watch, and help where I can. There are people out there who would destroy me, but so many more I would like to meet . . . Perhaps I have more in common with the

Doctor than I imagined.' He shuddered. Benny placed a hand on his shoulder.

'You can count me,' she said, 'as a friend.'

'Thank you.' The grey man looked away, distracted. 'Cathedral will collapse soon. Winterdawn's house will be expelled back into physical space, and there will be nothing left here but dust. Dust was all it ever was. I must remain and mourn its passing, alone.'

'You won't try and build another one?'

'Frankly Benny, you must be joking.'

'Haven't you heard? I'm a funny girl.'

She looked round, seeing the bodies of Gabriel and Winterdawn lain across the cold floor of the Cruakh.

'Most of the time,' she added.

The siren-song of the Cathedral had dried away. The ground, the stone, the buildings were empty and silent. They grew vague, blurred round the edges, transparent in the distance. The city blazed as their substance drained – a glow harsher than day, harsher than the sun. But it grew dim, passing into blackness, into death. Ace paced through the shining streets, knowing that she walked in a corpse-city.

She didn't think about it. She was single-minded. She was determined.

She imagined that Cathedral was the sort of city in which you only had to look to find something. No need for maps, no need for guides, no need for policemen on the corner – she doubted the geography was stable enough to be rigidly defined. In this city you walked until you found the building you wanted, the street you wanted, the person you wanted.

She'd dreamed about places like this, as a child.

She walked until she found Tanith, crouched in an alley-way. Her suit glowed like the wall around her. She hid in the light, almost invisible. Ace saw her, Ace had been *looking*.

Ace raised her revolver. There were five bullets in their chambers. The sixth had impacted badly on the shoulder of Ace's jacket. The jacket had absorbed most of the smash, as it was designed to – but Tanith had been lucky. The bullet had torn the jacket fabric and broken Ace's skin. The pain, the blood running down her arm, the gun-shape in her fist all helped concentrate her mind.

'Tanith,' she called. The name reverberated against the city walls.

Tanith. Tanith. Tanith. Tanith.

Tanith looked up. There were dark patches under her eyes, vivid against the whiteness of her flesh and the buildings round her. She squealed, dived out of her hiding place, into the alley.

Ace made four slight gestures with her forefinger.

There were four explosions, echoing against the city walls, howling.

Four wounds opened on Tanith's back.

She stumbled, pitched forward, smashed into the ground.

Ace moved towards her, feeling nothing and thinking nothing. Her body trembled as she moved, perhaps with exhilaration, perhaps with fear. The alley walls soared about her, seeming to shake in time with her. The stone floor was like rubber beneath her feet.

Tanith was alive. She lay face down, moaning and stirring, her hands pushing at the ground as if trying to lift herself. Ace could see she lacked the strength even to crawl. She was alive, but she would die here.

Tanith looked round, looked up at Ace with wide, piti-ful, desperate eyes. Ace met her gaze with a thoughtless stare. She knelt beside her and placed the barrel of the gun against Tanith's exposed, smooth temple.

One bullet.

Ace squeezed.

There was a minute when she saw nothing, heard nothing, felt nothing. At the end of the minute she rose and stepped back to look at what she had made. It was clumsy. It was messy. It was the sort of thing Page would have liked. Ace didn't like it, and was grateful for that. She let the gun fall from her fingers.

She didn't bother with regrets. Tanith was dead and her head was spread across the pavement. There was no way of changing that. Ace had squeezed and the squeeze was irrevocable.

She walked away. Behind her the alley grew dark and lost its shape.

Ace walked. She was looking for nothing in particular and the dying streets rolled past, allowing her to wander.

She came to a courtyard, to a plain fountain that still ran with clear, clean water. She paced up to it, pushing her hands into the stream and finding the water cool and lively. In Cathedral these qualities were rare.

She took off her jacket and let the thin stream play across her damaged shoulder. The water stung her wound and the thin trickle turned pink. She shook and splashed the water onto the bruises Gabriel and Tanith had made on her arm, on her chest, on her face. Her hands slipped into the water and she began to wash Gabriel's blood from them.

'Feeling guilty?' asked the Doctor. He had appeared from nowhere beside her. 'Lady Macbeth syndrome,' he said, rubbing his hands together. Ace shook her head without feeling. She realized that the water and the air had become cold, too much like death against her skin. She pulled her jacket back on.

'I was thinking about something Gabriel and Tanith offered me,' she said. 'I don't think they were lying, not that time. But I said no.' She shrugged. 'I killed Tanith. It was easy. It didn't feel any good. We've not *done* good, have we?'

The Doctor smiled sadly and offered no reply. They found themselves hugging briefly, bitterly, without knowing why.

They walked back to Golgotha together. Benny was there, waiting for them, waving to them. As they grew closer the wave became a point – a finger aimed towards the sky.

'Look,' she called. They turned. They looked. Behind them great cracks were forming in the dead black sky.

The cracks intersected, making fragments, making jagged chunks. One fell from its place, disappearing at the horizon, leaving a cold blankness behind. Another piece fell, another, and another. A vicious wind screamed in the distance, toppling buildings.

'The sky!' Ace whooped, out of a sense of childish glee. 'The sky is falling!'

'Someone should go and tell the king,' Benny murmured beside her.

'I think he already knows,' the Doctor replied. 'And he's abdicated.'

They walked together to the TARDIS.

The grey man, the man of many colours, stood in the Cruakh, singing to his city. His song had no words, no tune, no rhythm, no sound. The song was the trembling of his throat, the tiny movements of his lips.

Hear me stones of the city. I remove your burden from you. Become mere stones again, become dust. Go in peace.

Cathedral was gone. He smiled ruefully.

He raised his head and turned to the old world he had inherited, to the Earth and beyond, to the cosmos.

He slipped into it, onto soil, onto a path winding through a wood. It was a lonely path, as good as any other. The grey man tasted the air and found it fine. He stepped into the crisp November night, following the forest track, following his whims, beneath a sky full of stars.

Already published:

TIMEWYRM: GENESYS
John Peel
The Doctor and Ace are drawn to Ancient Mesopotamia in search of an evil sentience that has tumbled from the stars – the dreaded Timewyrm of ancient Gallifreyan legend.

ISBN 0 426 20355 0

TIMEWYRM: EXODUS
Terrance Dicks
Pursuit of the Timewyrm brings the Doctor and Ace to the Festival of Britain. But the London they find is strangely subdued, and patrolling the streets are the uniformed thugs of the Britischer Freikorps.

ISBN 0 426 20357 7

TIMEWYRM: APOCALYPSE
Nigel Robinson
Kirith seems an ideal planet – a world of peace and plenty, ruled by the kindly hand of the Great Matriarch. But it's here that the end of the universe – of everything – will be precipitated. Only the Doctor can stop the tragedy.

ISBN 0 426 20359 3

TIMEWYRM: REVELATION
Paul Cornell
Ace has died of oxygen starvation on the moon, having thought the place to be Norfolk. 'I do believe that's unique,' says the afterlife's receptionist.

ISBN 0 426 20360 7

CAT'S CRADLE: TIME'S CRUCIBLE
Marc Platt
The TARDIS is invaded by an alien presence and is then destroyed. The Doctor disappears. Ace, lost and alone, finds herself in a bizarre city where nothing is to be trusted – even time itself.

ISBN 0 426 20365 8

CAT'S CRADLE: WARHEAD
Andrew Cartmel

The place is Earth. The time is the near future – all too near. As environmental destruction reaches the point of no return, multinational corporations scheme to buy immortality in a poisoned world. If Earth is to survive, somebody has to stop them.

ISBN 0 426 20367 4

CAT'S CRADLE: WITCH MARK
Andrew Hunt

A small village in Wales is visited by creatures of myth. Nearby, a coach crashes on the M40, killing all its passengers. Police can find no record of their existence. The Doctor and Ace arrive, searching for a cure for the TARDIS, and uncover a gateway to another world.

ISBN 0 426 20368 2

NIGHTSHADE
Mark Gatiss

When the Doctor brings Ace to the village of Crook Marsham in 1968, he seems unwilling to recognize that something sinister is going on. But the villagers are being killed, one by one, and everyone's past is coming back to haunt them – including the Doctor's.

ISBN 0 426 20376 3

LOVE AND WAR
Paul Cornell

Heaven: a planet rich in history where the Doctor comes to meet a new friend, and betray an old one; a place where people come to die, but where the dead don't always rest in peace. On Heaven, the Doctor finally loses Ace, but finds archaeologist Bernice Summerfield, a new companion whose destiny is inextricably linked with his.

ISBN 0 426 20385 2

TRANSIT
Ben Aaronovitch

It's the ultimate mass transit system, binding the planets of the solar system together. But something is living in the network, chewing its way to the very heart of the system and leaving a trail of death and mutation behind. Once again, the Doctor is all that stands between humanity and its own mistakes.

ISBN 0 426 20384 4

THE HIGHEST SCIENCE
Gareth Roberts

The Highest Science – a technology so dangerous it destroyed its creators. Many people have searched for it, but now Sheldukher, the most wanted criminal in the galaxy, believes he has found it. The Doctor and Bernice must battle to stop him on a planet where chance and coincidence have become far too powerful.

ISBN 0 426 20377 1

THE PIT
Neil Penswick

One of the Seven Planets is a nameless giant, quarantined against all intruders. But when the TARDIS materializes, it becomes clear that the planet is far from empty – and the Doctor begins to realize that the planet hides a terrible secret from the Time Lords' past.

ISBN 0 426 20378 X

DECEIT
Peter Darvill-Evans

Ace – three years older, wiser and tougher – is back. She is part of a group of Irregular Auxiliaries on an expedition to the planet Arcadia. They think they are hunting Daleks, but the Doctor knows better. He knows that the paradise planet hides a being far more powerful than the Daleks – and much more dangerous.

ISBN 0 426 20362 3

LUCIFER RISING
Jim Mortimore & Andy Lane

Reunited, the Doctor, Ace and Bernice travel to Lucifer, the site of a scientific expedition that they know will shortly cease to exist. Discovering why involves them in sabotage, murder and the resurrection of eons-old alien powers. Are there Angels on Lucifer? And what does it all have to do with Ace?

ISBN 0 426 20338 7

WHITE DARKNESS
David McIntee

The TARDIS crew, hoping for a rest, come to Haiti in 1915. But they find that the island is far from peaceful: revolution is brewing in the city; the dead are walking from the cemeteries; and, far underground, the ancient rulers of the galaxy are stirring in their sleep.

ISBN 0 426 20395 X

SHADOWMIND
Christopher Bulis

On the colony world of Arden, something dangerous is growing stronger. Something that steals minds and memories. Something that can reach out to another planet, Tairgire, where the newest exhibit in the sculpture park is a blue box surmounted by a flashing light.

ISBN 0 426 20394 1

BIRTHRIGHT
Nigel Robinson

Stranded in Edwardian London with a dying TARDIS, Bernice investigates a series of grisly murders. In the far future, Ace leads a group of guerrillas against their insect-like, alien oppressors. Why has the Doctor left them, just when they need him most?

ISBN 0 426 20393 3

ICEBERG
David Banks

In 2006, an ecological disaster threatens the Earth; only the FLIPback team, working in an Antarctic base, can avert the catastrophe. But hidden beneath the ice, sinister forces have gathered to sabotage humanity's last hope. The Cybermen have returned and the Doctor must face them alone.

ISBN 0 426 20392 5

BLOOD HEAT
Jim Mortimore

The TARDIS is attacked by an alien force; Bernice is flung into the Vortex; and the Doctor and Ace crash-land on Earth. There they find dinosaurs roaming the derelict London streets, and Brigadier Lethbridge-Stewart leading the remnants of UNIT in a desperate fight against the Silurians, who have taken over and changed his world.

ISBN 0 426 20399 2

THE DIMENSION RIDERS
Daniel Blythe

A holiday in Oxford is cut short when the Doctor is summoned to Space Station Q4, where ghostly soldiers from the future watch from the shadows among the dead. Soon, the Doctor is trapped in the past, Ace is accused of treason and Bernice is uncovering deceit among the college cloisters.

ISBN 0 426 20397 6

THE LEFT-HANDED HUMMINGBIRD
Kate Orman
Someone has been playing with time. The Doctor, Ace and Bernice must travel to the Aztec Empire in 1487, to London in the Swinging Sixties and to the sinking of the *Titanic* as they attempt to rectify the temporal faults – and survive the attacks of the living god Huitzilin.

ISBN 0 426 20404 2

CONUNDRUM
Steve Lyons
A killer is stalking the streets of the village of Arandale. The victims are found each day, drained of blood. Someone has interfered with the Doctor's past again, and he's landed in a place he knows he once destroyed, from which it seems there can be no escape.

ISBN 0 426 20408 5

NO FUTURE
Paul Cornell
At last the Doctor comes face-to-face with the enemy who has been threatening him, leading him on a chase that has brought the TARDIS to London in 1976. There he finds that reality has been subtly changed and the country he once knew is rapidly descending into anarchy as an alien invasion force prepares to land . . .

ISBN 0 426 20409 3

TRAGEDY DAY
Gareth Roberts
When the TARDIS crew arrive on Olleril, they soon realize that all is not well. Assassins arrive to carry out a killing that may endanger the entire universe. A being known as the Supreme One tests horrific weapons. And a secret order of monks observes the growing chaos.

ISBN 0 426 20410 7

LEGACY
Gary Russell
The Doctor returns to Peladon, on the trail of a master criminal. Ace pursues intergalactic mercenaries who have stolen the galaxy's most evil artifact, while Bernice strikes up a dangerous friendship with a Martian Ice Lord. The players are making the final moves in a devious and lethal plan – but for once it isn't the Doctor's.

ISBN 0 426 20412 3

THEATRE OF WAR
Justin Richards

Menaxus is a barren world on the front line of an interstellar war, home to a ruined theatre which hides sinister secrets. When the TARDIS crew land on the planet, they find themselves trapped in a deadly reenactment of an ancient theatrical tragedy.

ISBN 0 426 20414 X

ALL-CONSUMING FIRE
Andy Lane

The secret library of St John the Beheaded has been robbed. The thief has taken forbidden books which tell of gateways to other worlds. Only one team can be trusted to solve the crime: Sherlock Holmes, Doctor Watson – and a mysterious stranger who claims he travels in time and space.

ISBN 0 426 20415 8

BLOOD HARVEST
Terrance Dicks

While the Doctor and Ace are selling illegal booze in a town full of murderous gangsters, Bernice has been abandoned on a vampire-infested planet outside normal space. This story sets in motion events which are continued in *Goth Opera*, the first in a new series of Missing Adventures.

ISBN 0 426 20417 4

STRANGE ENGLAND
Simon Messingham

In the idyllic gardens of a Victorian country house, the TARDIS crew discover a young girl whose body has been possessed by a beautiful but lethal insect. And they find that the rural paradise is turning into a world of nightmare ruled by the sinister Quack.

ISBN 0 426 20419 0

FIRST FRONTIER
David A. McIntee

When Bernice asks to see the dawn of the space age, the Doctor takes the TARDIS to Cold War America, which is facing a threat far more deadly than Communist Russia. The militaristic Tzun Confederacy have made Earth their next target for conquest – and the aliens have already landed.

ISBN 0 426 20421 2

ST ANTHONY's FIRE
Mark Gatiss

The TARDIS crew visit Betrushia, a planet in terrible turmoil. A vicious, genocidal war is raging between the lizard-like natives. With time running out, the Doctor must save the people of Betrushia from their own legacy before St Anthony's fire consumes them all.

ISBN 0 426 20423 9